Abou

Velvet Carter is not ju[...]
but the name of one [...]
'exotica.' She's a prol[...]
with her words. Velve[...]
knows how to make your heart race with her tantalising
stories. Her novels have been translated into German
and released in London to critical acclaim. Velvet uses
the world as her muse, travelling the globe for
provocative inspiration.

Michelle Douglas has been writing for Mills & Boon
since 2007, and believes she has the best job in the
world. She's a sucker for happy endings, heroines who
have a secret stash of chocolate, and heroes who know
how to laugh. She lives in Newcastle Australia with her
own romantic hero, a house full of dust and books, and
an eclectic collection of sixties and seventies vinyl. She
loves to hear from readers and can be contacted via her
website michelle-douglas.com

Rosanna Battigelli loved reading Mills & Boon
romance novels as a teenager and dreamed of writing
them one day. Rosanna is the author of a Gold IPPY
Award winning historical novel, *La Brigantessa*; a
fiction collection, *Pigeon Soup & Other Stories* (a 2021
Finalist, American BookFest Best Book Awards); and
two children's books. Rosanna is thrilled that her early
dream has come true, with five Mills & Boon romances
published so far.

Passion in Paradise

Passion in Paradise:
Caribbean Escapes

VELVET CARTER

MICHELLE DOUGLAS

ROSANNA BATTIGELLI

MILLS & BOON

BLISSFULLY YOURS

VELVET CARTER

To those who found bliss when they least expected,
and to those who are still joyfully looking!

Chapter 1

Ayana awoke to a gentle breeze flowing through the screened French doors of her parents' Jamaican hillside home. The delicious smell of ackee and saltfish tickled her nose as she stirred underneath the white cotton sheet. She yawned wide and stretched her long limbs before climbing out of bed. Today was her last full day in Negril and she planned to make the most of her time before heading back to her hectic New York life.

She showered and dressed in cutoff blue jean shorts, a T-shirt and flip-flops. Ana—as she was known in Jamaica—pulled her long raven hair into a ponytail before trotting down the small back staircase that led to the kitchen.

"Hmm, something sure smells good," Ana said to her mother, who was laboring over the stove.

"I made ya favorite—ackee and saltfish, callaloo

and johnnycakes," her mother answered in a thick Jamaican accent.

Ayana looked at the plate of food that her mother had dished up. "Ma, I can't eat all of that." Having lived in New York for more than ten years, Ayana had adjusted her eating habits and now ate mostly salads, fish and very few carbs.

"Ya too skinny, gurl. Gotta fatten ya up." Mrs. Tosh was a traditional Jamaican mother who believed in eating heartily at every meal.

"I'm not skinny, Ma. I still have plenty of thighs and a butt," she said, looking over her shoulder at her full rear end.

"Yeah, ya are. Don't argue wit me, gurl. Sit down and eat."

Ayana didn't say another word. There was no use in debating. Her domineering mother always got the last word, so Ayana sat at the wooden kitchen table and ate every morsel. She then polished off her mega breakfast with a cup of Jamaican Blue Mountain coffee. She had to admit that eating some of her favorite childhood dishes felt good and satisfying.

"Ma, do you wanna go with me over to New Beginnings?" New Beginnings was a local women's and children's shelter that Ayana helped support with generous donations of her time and money.

"Me got no time to go to the shelter today. Got too much housework to do," she said, taking Ayana's plate and rinsing it off.

"Ma, I bought you a dishwasher so you wouldn't have to stand there and hand wash every dish. Where is the dishwasher, anyway?"

"Why ya waste ya money?"

Ayana just shook her head. She never stopped trying to spoil her parents, but they were simple people and didn't want the modern gifts she bought. "I don't consider buying my parents gifts a waste of money. Ma, you and Dad struggled for so long. Now that I'm in a position to make your lives a little easier, that's what I'm going to do." Ayana had her own stubborn streak, a trait she'd inherited from her mother.

"Go on, gurl." Her mother waved her away and continued washing dishes.

Ayana kissed her mother goodbye, went to the living room, grabbed her sunglasses and keys off the parson's table near the front door and left. She hopped on her canary-yellow Vespa and took off down the winding road. The lush hillside, dotted with hibiscus and white bougainvillea, whizzed by. Ayana loved jetting around Negril on her scooter. She had driven one ever since she was a teenager. The open air was refreshing and helped to clear her mind. This was where she'd fled to two years ago after her nasty, well-publicized divorce. Ayana thought back to that time.

"If you walk out on me, you're not getting one red cent!" Those were the last words her ex-husband, millionaire Benjamin Lewis, the founder and CEO of BL Industries, had said as Ayana left their sprawling Long Island mansion. The estate was set on three manicured acres, complete with a pool, tennis court and guest house.

Although Benjamin ran one of the world's leading electronic manufacturing companies, making millions in the process, he was a tightwad. After three years of marriage, Ayana had become sick and tired of adhering to his strict budget. He had given her a weekly allowance of two hundred dollars, much less than she had made when she was his secretary. He only increased her allowance when he wanted her to buy expensive outfits for their black-tie affairs. Benjamin loved parading her around. To him she had been nothing more than a trophy wife.

Ayana had become tired of being treated like one of his prized possessions. She couldn't take any more of his selfish ways and filed for divorce, citing cruel and unusual punishment. While the proceedings wore on, Ayana had spent her days in a tiny studio apartment on the Lower East Side, sparsely furnished with a futon, throw rug and nine-inch television.

A few days after she'd moved there, the phone rang, startling her out of her sleep. She'd reached for the cell and pressed Talk. "Hello?"

"You are still asleep? It's eleven-thirty," Reese, Ayana's best friend, had said.

"What's up?"

"You need to get out of that apartment. It's a beautiful sunny day, so let's go to lunch at that new restaurant in the Village."

"I don't have money to waste on lunch. All my cash is going toward attorney fees."

"What happened to all that jewelry Ben gave you?"

"I have a few pieces here. But the rest is in my safe-deposit box. Why do you ask?"

"You need money, right?"

"Of course I need money. You of all people know how stingy Ben was," Ayana had said, sounding irritated.

"Instead of sounding like a wounded victim, you should sell some of that ice."

"I'm not selling my jewelry. That's the one thing Ben did right. He may have been a frugal SOB as far as giving me cash, but he didn't hesitate giving Tiffany, Cartier and Harry Winston his plastic. He loved telling his business associates how much he spent on my jewelry. It was like a competition to see which man could spend the most on their wives."

"Girl, you have a fortune sitting in the bank collecting dust."

"Like I said before—I'm not selling anything. I like my jewelry."

"Have you ever heard of paste?"

"No. What's paste?"

"Basically, paste is leaded glass made to look like diamonds and colored stones. I know a place where you can take your jewelry, have it copied and then sell the originals." Reese had once worked in the Diamond District as a sales clerk, and she still had connections on Forty-Seventh Street.

"I don't know, Reese. This jewelry is the only thing of value I have left. If I sell it, then what?"

"You'll be able to pay your bills and not have to wait for the divorce settlement to get some much-needed cash."

Ayana had digested her friend's words. Reese made perfect sense. Ayana thought about the five-carat diamond engagement ring, set in platinum and sitting in the safe-deposit box. The ring that she had once treasured and wore with pride had little meaning now that her marriage was over. "I guess you do have a good point."

"I have an excellent point. Besides, you'll still have the same jewelry designs to wear—they just won't be the real thing. This jeweler is so good that no one will be able to tell the difference."

"Okay. I could actually sell my wedding set and a few other pieces. That should hold me over until the divorce is final."

That afternoon, Ayana had gone to the bank and taken her five-carat engagement ring, diamond-encrusted wedding band and sapphire necklace out of the safe-deposit box, then met Reese at the jeweler's shop on Forty-Seventh Street. A week later, she'd picked up the pastes and couldn't believe how authentic the pieces looked. She'd sold the originals, making enough money to sustain herself for the duration of the proceedings.

"Ana! Ana!" yelled the children from the shelter when they saw the yellow scooter pull into the yard.

New Beginnings was near and dear to Ayana's heart. The small, privately run shelter relied on donations from generous patrons, and Ayana was at the top of that list. She didn't have any children of her own and considered the kids at the shelter her babies.

"Hey, guys! What's happening?" Ayana hopped off the scooter, gathered as many children into her arms as she could hold and gave them all a huge hug.

"Now, now, chilrin, leave Ms. Lewis be. Go now and do yo work," Marigold, the shelter's administrator, said as she came into the yard waving her hands and shooing the children away.

"Did you get the shipment yet?"

"All dose big boxes come, and me didn't know what to do wit all dose clothes." She smiled. "We thank ya."

"You're welcome. It was no problem. All I did was

collect clothes from friends of mine who were purging their closets."

"Ya do more than send clothes. Ya send checks too, and dey help keep dis place going."

Ayana looked a bit embarrassed; she didn't like when Marigold praised her for helping. The shelter needed assistance, and she was just glad that she was now in a position to help.

"And dat stuff you send look brand-new. Some of dem tings still had da tags on 'em."

"Yeah, I know. I only select clothes that are gently worn, if not new. Did you see the note attached to that blue dress? It's for you."

"I saw it, but dat dress is too fancy fo me."

"It's only a sundress."

"Yeah, a sundress by Ralph, uh…uh…"

"Lauren. Ralph Lauren."

"Where me gonna wear some designer dress to? After me husband die, I don't go out much."

"Well, you never know what life has in store. Maybe you'll get invited to a party or asked out on a date. It's always good to have a go-to dress in your closet."

"I no want no date. James was de love of me life and after he die, a piece of me died too."

"Marigold, you're still a good-looking woman, and I'm sure James wouldn't want you to be alone for the rest of your life." Ayana sympathized with her friend but always tried to be encouraging.

"James did tell me not to pine away for him for too long," she said with a sorrowful look in her eyes.

"See what I mean. James wouldn't want you spending every night home alone."

"Okay, okay, me keep Mista Lauren. Ya wanna come

in fo some lunch? Me make kingfish stew and coco bread."

"No, thanks. I already ate. I have to go back home and pack. I just came by to see if you got the clothes and to see you and the kids."

"We hate to see ya go." Marigold gave Ayana a warm hug.

"I hate to go, but duty calls."

The truth was, Ayana wasn't looking forward to returning to New York, but her hiatus was over. The reality show that she starred in was resuming filming in a few days. She had spent two glorious months in Jamaica, eating her mother's home cooking, taking long walks on the beach and meditating at her favorite place high in the Blue Mountains. The serenity and beauty of the island, and being surrounded by people who loved her, had rejuvenated her soul. Now Ayana was ready to resume her hot-blooded persona and tackle another season of *Divorced Divas.*

Chapter 2

"We'll be starting our descent in the New York area shortly, so please return to your seats and fasten your seat belts."

Ayana heard the flight attendant's announcement through the lavatory door. She looked in the mirror and was satisfied with her transformation. Gone was the girlish ponytail, replaced by a long, flowing, platinum-blond lace-front wig. She'd traded in her island uniform of cutoff blue jean shorts, sleeveless T-shirt and flip-flops for a sexy black-and-white Tom Ford pencil skirt that hugged her full hips. The matching chiffon blouse with blouson sleeves was secured around her slim waist with a wide black leather belt dotted with silver studs. Black-and-white layered necklaces and a pair of five-inch strappy platforms completed the high-maintenance look. She applied a double coat of ruby-red lipstick to her perfectly made-up face to add a pop of color. Ayana gathered her belongings and put them back in her Prada tote. She exited the lavatory and returned to her seat in first class.

"Would you like anything else before we land?" asked the attendant.

"I'll have a glass of champagne. Actually, make it two."

After the attendant brought the drinks, Ayana drank the two flutes of bubbly and readied herself for any photographers or reporters who might be waiting for her once she deplaned. *Divorced Divas* led in the ratings due to Ayana's prima-donna persona. The gossip rags were always trying to get dirt on Saturday Knight—Ayana's name on the show—and stalked her on a regular basis. The latest story going around town was that Ayana was the reason Erick Kastell—her love interest on the show—had fled the country.

"Welcome to New York, and thanks for flying with us today. You are now free to use your cell phones," the pilot announced once they'd landed.

As the plane taxied to the gate, Ayana called Reese. "Hey, girl, we just landed. Where are you?"

"In the car, waiting outside of baggage claim."

"Okay. See you in a few."

Once the doors opened, Ayana put on a pair of oversize shades, retrieved her carry-on from the overhead bin and strutted down the pedway, into the terminal and out the door.

"Saturday! Saturday Knight! Look this way!" a photographer yelled, snapping pictures as she strolled past.

"Saturday, is it true you're the reason Moses Michaels left his girlfriend, Lisa?" a reporter shouted.

"Have you read Lisa's tweets? She's calling you a home wrecker," another reporter blurted out.

Ayana didn't even glance in their direction, though that didn't stop them from blurting out questions.

"Is it true that you and Moses Michaels are dating?" another reporter shouted.

Moses Michaels was the hot single moderator of the reality-show circuit. He and Saturday had gone out a few times, but it had not lasted.

She kept walking, looking straight ahead as if they weren't there. She saw Reese's black Benz and concentrated on making it to the car without acknowledging the annoying paparazzi and reporters.

"Hey, girl, welcome home." Reese turned to kiss Ayana on the cheek. "Well, it isn't such a good welcome with the media stalking you and accusing you of breaking up Moses and his girlfriend," Reese said as Ayana settled into the car.

"Their claims are totally untrue. Moses had broken up with his girlfriend before we'd started to date. Anyway, Moses and I are now just friends. The lies remind me of my nasty divorce," she said, remembering the highly publicized proceedings.

During the divorce trial, reporters and photographers had lined the steps of the courthouse, begging for interviews and snapping pictures. Salacious details of their marriage had made interesting headlines. Ayana had been embarrassed to read about their rather unorthodox love life.

Benjamin had leaked photos of Ayana dressed as a dominatrix, beating him with a whip. He'd accused her of dominating him against his will. It had incensed her. The entire bondage and sadomasochism idea had been his. Benjamin had bought her the black latex cat-suit, platform boots and whip, and he'd even made her watch an instructional DVD to teach her the nuances of BDSM. Ayana had resisted at first, but Benjamin had insisted. He'd said it was the ultimate thrill to have her beat him. But he'd backpedaled in court, playing the victim. He'd even produced pictures of bruises on his back.

In addition to the accusations of sexual abuse, Benjamin had accused Ayana of spousal abandonment, saying that she spent months in Jamaica. On the stand, Ayana did admit to visiting her parents. However, it was Benjamin who'd insisted that she extend her stay, saying that since they didn't have children, there was no need for her to rush back home to New York.

His team of highly paid attorneys had earned every dime of their retainer, working overtime to paint a negative picture of Ayana. Her attorney had presented her case, stating to the court that Benjamin willingly withheld funds from her, making her practically lead a destitute life, except for the times when they were out together. Her case was weak in comparison to Benjamin's. And as the weeks had dragged on, Ayana became worn out. With her funds dwindling and her emotional state deteriorating, Ayana had agreed to settle. Initially, she had been seeking half of the money he'd made while they were together but then realized that Benjamin was willing to fight dirty in order to keep from paying Ayana her share. To put an end to the spectacle and move on with her life, she'd settled for a fraction of the estate, signed the divorce papers and never looked back.

Although the proceedings had been emotionally draining, one good thing had come out of the ordeal—a job.

Little did Ayana know that tracking her divorce proceedings was show creator Ed Levine, who had struck gold with his string of reality TV shows. He had been looking to staff *Divorced Divas,* his latest undertaking about divorced women of millionaires seeking a second chance at love. He had seen Ayana on the news and in the papers and had become taken with her. Ayana was tall, attractive, stylish and well-spoken—all the ingredients of a television star. He'd contacted her attorney and set up a meeting.

However, Ayana had had no interest in exposing her life on camera. Being in the media during the divorce was enough, so she'd turned down the meeting. Ayana's post-divorce plan was to reenter corporate America. The only problem was her limited experience. Her last job had been as Benjamin's administrative assistant. She'd dusted off her résumé, made calls and tried to set up interviews to no avail. Her skill set wasn't the problem; being the former Mrs. Benjamin Lewis was. Apparently, he had put the word out and blacklisted her.

In need of an income, Ayana had asked her attorney to contact the producers. Their initial meeting had gone well, except for one glitch. Ed had wanted Ayana to play the role of the good girl, but he had filled that role after she had turned him down. The only slot left to fill was that of the "diva." Ayana had been reluctant but was in dire straits and needed money badly, so she'd accepted the role along with the stage name. A year later, Saturday Knight was a household name. Luckily, the show wasn't broadcasted in Jamaica. Ayana couldn't stand the thought of her family knowing that she degraded herself on camera for a living. She hated her job but was determined to make it work. Ayana read about reality stars branding themselves, launching clothing, perfume and cosmetics lines and even going on to co-star in prime-time network series and movies. Some of them were making millions, and that was exactly what she planned to do.

"So are you well rested and ready for another season of *Divorced Divas?*" Reese asked as they drove along the FDR.

"I am rested, but the thought of another unnecessary catfight makes my stomach churn."

"Girl, what's up with that? Why do people love to see grown women acting like teenagers, fighting and yelling at each other?"

Ayana hunched her shoulders. "Wish I knew. Seems the more controversy on the show, the higher the ratings."

"Does the creator of the show even know your true personality? You're the nicest person anyone could ever meet."

"Yeah, he knows, but for Ed, it's all about ratings."

"Then have a meeting and ask him to change your role so that the viewers can see who you really are."

"Last season, a director made some show suggestions and he was fired."

"I thought reality television was all about depicting people in their true form."

"Reese, the *reality* is that reality television is a money-making machine. The creators of these shows will go to any length to ensure ratings, even if they have to fudge the truth and stage scenes."

"What an oxymoron."

"That's an understatement. After losing nearly everything in the divorce, my focus is on building a solid financial future so that I won't have to rely on a man ever again."

"You may not need a man for money, but what about for sex?"

"Girl, sex is the furthest thing from my mind."

"When was the last time you had any?"

"Any what?"

"Stop playing. You know what I mean."

"I haven't had sex in months."

"I couldn't go a week without Joey."

"Well, consider yourself one of the lucky ones. You and Joey have a happy, healthy relationship." Reese and her husband, Joey, had met in the Diamond District.

"Yes, we do, but it didn't happen overnight. In the beginning Joey traveled to South Africa a lot on business, and the distance was hard on our relationship. It's taken years for us to get to a good place. One day you'll find your Mr. Right. What about Moses Michaels? You two went out a few times. Maybe he's the one. He sure is one good-looking man."

"No, he's not *the one* for me. I can't handle the ladies'-man type. The problem is he's *too* good-looking. Women throw themselves at him all the time, and he loves the attention. He told me in no uncertain terms that he was only interested in sex—not a relationship."

"He said that?" Reese asked, astounded.

"Yep, he sure did."

"Well…maybe you should have at least tried him on for size. He looks like he'd be a good lover."

Ayana lightly pushed Reese on the shoulder. "Ohhh, I can't believe you're saying that!"

"Why?" She smiled sheepishly.

"Because you are happily married to Joey, that's why."

"I'm married, not dead, and you would have to be dead not to notice Moses Michaels."

"Guess you have a point, and I was soooo tempted to take him up on his offer. I just didn't want to become another one of his many conquests."

"I understand that, but did you at least kiss the man?"

"Yes, we kissed."

"So was he a good kisser?"

"Aren't you the nosy one?"

"Well…curious minds want to know."

"Yes, he's a great kisser. Are you satisfied? Now can we change the subject, please?"

"Okay, okay. Forget about the players of the world. Plenty of men out there want a committed relationship. What about that guy from Switzerland who was on the show?"

"You mean Erick?"

"Yes, that's him. From the episodes I watched, you two appeared to have mad chemistry."

"We did. The producers sent us on several romantic dates and we were getting along really well until he had to go back to Switzerland and take care of some issues regarding his work papers to stay in the U.S."

"That's too bad. Don't worry. You'll find Mr. Right," Reese reiterated.

"I'm not worried, and I'm not waiting either." Ayana looked out the window for a moment, digesting her friend's words. She didn't want to admit it, since she had talked so much about getting her financial house in order, but she silently hoped for a true love of her own.

"Oh, I forgot to tell you that Joey and I are going to South Africa and then we're heading over to Antwerp, Belgium, for a diamond-buying trip. After our business is done, we're taking a holiday in Capri. We'll be gone for at least a month. I'll call you when we get back."

"That sounds like a fun trip."

"It should be. I can't wait."

Listening to Reese expound about her overseas trip with her husband, Ayana couldn't help but be a little jealous. The thought of spending time away with the man you loved was not in Ayana's near future and that reality saddened her.

Chapter 3

"Man, have you heard from Jaclene?"

"No, not since I moved back."

Brandon Gilliam was at home talking on the phone with his best friend, Jon. Brandon had recently moved back to New York from California. Luckily, he had sublet his apartment in Tribeca and was able to make a smooth transition without having to search for months for a place to live.

"What happened between you guys? I thought you were in love."

"I thought so too. Jaclene, the wannabe starlet, was into me when she thought I was going to be a Hollywood director and cast her in a movie. When I wasn't able to land a major gig, she wasted no time dumping me. Last I heard, she was involved with some studio executive."

Brandon prided himself on his stellar career. Over

the course of ten years at a major television network in New York, he had earned five Emmys for outstanding directing of a newsmagazine show. Brandon's dream was to parlay his television skills into directing movies. Feeling that he'd done his time at the station, he'd quit, packed up his awards and moved to Hollywood. But breaking into the movie business wasn't as easy as he had envisioned. The only thing he had to show after being on the West Coast for a year was a failed relationship with a starlet and a list of contacts who would no longer accept his calls. Frustrated and tired of the endless sunshine, as well as the fake people, he'd moved back to New York as soon as his sublease agreement was over.

"Don't worry. When you become a famous director, your casting couch will have a waiting list of women begging to have sex with you."

Brandon chuckled. "Man, I'm not interested in women who want to use me to advance their career."

"Hey, as long as I'm using them back, I don't have a problem with it. Use my body, just don't abuse it." Jon laughed.

"I guess we differ in that way. I want a woman who loves me for me and not for what I can offer professionally."

"Oh, listen to you sounding like a soap opera. You were always the soft-hearted one of the group." Jon and Brandon had grown up together in Queens. They, along with three other boys, were a tight-knit bunch. Jon and Brandon were now the only two guys still single with no kids.

"Soft, my ass."

"Don't try to sound hard now. Remember that time

when we were sixteen and fine-ass Lisa McCoy came crying to you because her boyfriend left her?"

"Yeah, I remember. What about it?"

"She wanted to have sex with you to make her ex jealous. Instead of taking the panties, you talked to her on the phone all night. Now, if that ain't soft, I don't know what is."

"I didn't want to take advantage of her situation. She was clearly upset over being dumped and needed a friend."

"See, that's what I'm talking about. Even at sixteen you had a conscience."

"All men aren't dogs like you, my brother." Brandon was always a one-woman man. He had never dated multiple women at the same time, like most of his friends had.

"I prefer the term *ladies' man.*"

"Whatever, Mr. Ladies' Man. Enough of memory lane. I gotta get off the phone. I have an early call in the morning."

"That's right—you start your new gig tomorrow."

After moving back to New York, Brandon had landed a job right away. However, the position wasn't on another newsmagazine show. He was the new director of *Divorced Divas.* Though he wasn't thrilled about directing a cheesy reality show, after being out of work for a year and exhausting his savings, he had to take what he could get and that was the only show hiring.

"Unfortunately," Brandon said, sounding disgusted.

"Why do you say that?"

"Don't get me wrong. I'm grateful to be among the working class again, but directing a bunch of catty women isn't what I call good television. I can't believe this reality genre is still going strong."

"Personally, I love reality TV—the cattier the better. Seeing them chicks fling their boobs and fake hair is a turn-on. Those chicks on *Divorced Divas* are all fine, especially that Saturday Knight. I'd love to get that beautiful body of hers into my bed and show her a few tricks."

"I'll bet you would."

"You gotta hook a brother up."

"I don't think so."

"Come on, Brandon. I'm serious. Hook me up."

"I know you're serious, but I'm not there to make friends or play matchmaker. I've seen clips of the show and those chicks are cutthroat, *especially* Saturday Knight. She's the worst of them all. If I didn't need the money, I would've turned down the job. The last thing I want to do is spend my day directing a train wreck."

"Don't worry. With your smooth-as-butter nature, I'm sure you'll calm them down when they get out of hand."

"See, that's where you're wrong. I'm not going on set tomorrow playing mediator or trying to talk sense into those wildcats. I'm leaving Mr. Nice Guy at home. Tomorrow, I'm Mr. Hard Nose. I refuse to let those chicks run all over me. They'll never see my, as you say, 'soft' side."

"I can't believe you pick now to be a hard-ass, when I need you to score a number or two from the divas."

"The only thing I plan to score are high ratings while I'm working on the show, and, hopefully, once my contract is over after this season, there'll be an opening back in news." Brandon had had his agent negotiate a one-season deal in the hopes of him returning to a reputable newsmagazine show like *60 Minutes*. He wanted to work on a television show that he could be proud of.

He laughed inwardly. He hadn't even started the new job, yet he was already planning his exit strategy. Thankfully *Divorced Divas* only ran half a season, so he wouldn't be subjected to the lunacy that was reality television for too long.

Chapter 4

Ayana was getting her hair and makeup done in the dressing room she used while taping the show. She looked at her reflection in the huge mirror and barely recognized herself. Her face had three layers of makeup—foundation, powder and blush. Her naturally long eyelashes were glued with two sets of extended lashes, giving her eyes a dramatic look, and her lips were painted a bright glossy orange. Covering Ayana's real hair was a platinum-blond wig with natural curls that cascaded midway down her back.

"You're all set," the makeup artist said, giving Ayana's face one last swipe of the sable brush.

"Thanks, Denise."

Ayana rose from her chair and walked to the rack of clothing the wardrobe stylist had selected for the day. She looked at the first outfit and shook her head in disgust. "Do they really expect me to wear this?" she muttered to herself.

As she stood there looking at the neon orange micro-mini shorts and matching midriff top, Ed Levine, the creator of the show, walked in.

"Hey, Saturday, are you ready for another great season?" Ed waved his chiffon scarf in the air. He was full of enthusiasm and wore a wide grin that spread across his face. Ed had every reason to be happy: *Divorced Divas* was now the number one reality show in the country.

"Ed, why do I have to wear this whorish-looking getup?" she said, cutting right to the point and ignoring his question.

"Saturday…"

"Can you please call me Ayana when we're off set?"

He folded his arms and said, "Ayana, when I approached you about doing the show, I pulled no punches. I told you that the nice-girl role was already taken and you were being hired to play the bad, malicious girl."

"Bad girl, not slut. Look at this trash," she said, pulling the orange two-piece violently off the rack.

"Why do we have to go through this every season? Last season you complained about the hair and makeup, so we toned it down. Now you're complaining about the clothes. You should be used to the Saturday Knight persona by now."

It was Ed himself who had created the outlandish character in the first place. Years ago, before becoming a successful show creator, he'd worked as a female impersonator under the name Saturday Knight. He'd worn heavy makeup, flashy clothes, towering heels and waist-length wigs. When he'd conceived *Divorced*

Divas, he'd jumped at the chance to see his alter ego come to life on camera.

"I'll never get used to dressing like a slut and acting like a wild banshee."

"I could always release you from your contract if you're tired of playing the role. I have a list of divorced wives of millionaires waiting in the wings to take your place. Give me the word, and I'll tear up your contract and you can walk away, free and clear, before the season starts. No hard feelings. But once we start production, you'll have to honor your contract and stay for the duration of this season."

Ayana plopped down on the sofa, tossing the outfit to the side, and exhaled. She wasn't in a position to quit. She hadn't amassed enough money to secure her financial future, nor had she made inroads into the licensing business so that she could brand herself. As much as Ayana hated the charade, she hated being poor more. She wasn't going to leave the show until all of her ducks were lined up. She was determined to make the most out of being on the show, even if that meant portraying herself as a loudmouthed troublemaker. "No, Ed, I don't want to be released from my contract, but can we come to a compromise?"

"And what might that be?"

"Let me choose my clothes. The stylist isn't quite getting my look right."

"I guess you can do that. Just don't come on set in anything conservative."

"Thanks. I won't," she said with a broad smile spreading across her face.

"Don't get too happy. I came in here to tell you about the new director."

"What about him?"

"We didn't tell him that Saturday Knight is a fake persona. He doesn't know your real name is Ayana Lewis, and I want to keep it that way."

"Why is that?"

"We want to maintain a sense of reality, and the less he knows about your real personality, the better he can direct you as a wildcat."

"So you're telling me that he doesn't realize my role on the show is an act?"

"No, he doesn't. As you know, the rest of the cast doesn't know either. Remember the confidentiality clause in your contract binding you to keep quiet about your true identity."

"Of course I remember."

"So you'll keep up the act?"

"Yes, but I refuse to be tacky."

"Deal. On another note, I've been introducing the new director to the cast individually before we start shooting. He's meeting with Trista now and will be in to meet you shortly."

"No problem."

As they were talking, in walked the new director. Ayana looked at the handsome man and nearly gasped. He was tall—well over six feet—with broad shoulders and an athlete's build. His head was shaven, giving off a slight glisten. His eyes were warm, the color of chestnuts, and his skin looked as if it had been dipped in milk chocolate. The white cotton shirt he wore seemed to glow against his dark skin. He was handsome in a rugged urban-cowboy-type way. In fact, he was exactly her type. If they were in another setting, she could envision the two of them sitting down and having a friendly chat over a cup of coffee. However, she had a job to do and wasn't going to let his good looks distract her.

"Brandon, perfect timing," Ed said, turning toward the door. "Let me introduce you to Saturday Knight, the show's hot-blooded diva."

Ayana took a step backward and went into character. She sucked her lips, put her hand on her hip and rolled her eyes in his direction.

"Hello." Brandon extended his hand.

Ayana looked down at his hand. "Whatever."

"Ed, I'll be on set," Brandon said, turning his back to Ayana, ignoring her rude behavior and directing his comment to the creator of the show.

"Okay, sounds good." ·

Brandon walked out without giving her a second look. Once he was gone, Ed closed the door. "Nice work. You did a damn good job of showing him how nasty you can be."

"That was nothing. Wait until I get in front of the camera. Then I'm going to really cut up."

"Perfect. That's what I want to hear. *Divorced Divas* is leading in the ratings and I want to keep it that way."

"Don't worry, Ed. You can count on me to do my part."

"See you on set, Ayana."

When Ed left the room, Ayana closed the door and walked back to the clothing rack. As she was looking for another outfit, she thought about how rude she had been to the new director and began feeling guilty. He didn't deserve to be disregarded, but as long as she was under contract, she wasn't going to do anything to jeopardize her future.

Ayana changed into a pair of white skinny jeans and

a sheer black blouse with a deep V-neck that showcased
her ample cleavage. She completed the casual outfit
with a pair of four-inch cork platforms. The shoes added
to her height, making her a towering figure of six feet.

Ayana left the dressing room, and as she walked
down the long hallway, she took a series of deep breaths.
With each step, she dreaded the beginning of another
season of lies. To make her job tolerable, Ayana tried to
find something to focus on. Last season, she'd concentrated on the shelter in Jamaica. The thought of helping the women and children in her homeland had gotten
her through the catfights, backstabbing and blind dates
gone awry. This season, she hadn't picked a focal point,
until meeting the director. Although she had treated
him like dirt on the bottom of her designer shoes, she
found him extremely sexy and attractive. Even if she
couldn't have him personally, she could at least fantasize about his muscular body being pressed against
hers. That thought alone would sustain her for at least
a few episodes.

Chapter 5

I must admit, Jon was right. Saturday Knight is one pretty woman. Her body is made by Frederick's of Hollywood, but her attitude is made by Freddy Krueger. Her ugly interior totally cancels out her gorgeous exterior, Brandon thought as he walked down the hallway toward the set. The first scene of the day was being shot in a sprawling Central Park West penthouse that the show leased for taping. Brandon was the first on set. He sat in his director's chair and waited for the ladies—Trista, the Good Girl; Petra, the Russian; Brooke, the Flirt; and Saturday, the Bad Girl—to arrive.

The beginning of the day's show centered on Saturday's blind-date follow-up. Last season had ended with her being set up with three seriously wealthy men. Now the audience would find out if she picked one of the three. If not, her search for love would continue.

Trista was the first to enter the room. She had once been married to a strict CFO of a finance company. He detested tardiness and was always the first to arrive and the first to leave. His mantra was that time was money, so he waited on no one. His punctuality had rubbed off on Trista. They would still be married if he hadn't gotten caught embezzling millions from the company. After he was sent to prison for ten years, Trista instituted his mantra and didn't waste any time filing for divorce. She wasn't going to waste ten whole years waiting around for him.

Brandon looked at the petite redhead with a pixie haircut. She was soft-spoken and had a girlish quality. She looked more befitted for a family with two kids and a dog than a cutthroat reality show. But for contrast, Ed had Trista going on dates with rocker types who wore leather, torn jeans and tattoos—the opposite of her sweet personality.

As Brandon was reading over the show notes one last time, he heard footsteps and commotion coming down the hall in the form of two loud voices.

"I'ma do you a favor, and let you have first pickings over the men that I turn down."

"I no want you damn leftover!" a voice with a Russian accent bellowed.

"If I didn't give you my throwbacks, you wouldn't have any dates at all."

Brandon turned toward the entry of the living room as the two women marched in. *I should have known it was Saturday arguing with someone.*

"No true. I have entee man I want," Petra responded.

Petra Kazakova was a Russian immigrant and former model who'd married the head of a cosmetics conglomerate. The two had divorced when he was caught wearing lipstick in a compromising situation with his business partner. Petra's dates for the show ran the gamut from European millionaires looking for trophy wives to taxi drivers. The broken English spoken by Petra and her dates often had to be accompanied by subtitles, which Ed loved because he thought it made his show unique.

"You should want some English lessons. It's not *entee*.... The word is *any*. And you also need to learn to pluralize your words," Saturday spouted.

"And you need lesson on how to be nice person."

"Nice ain't never got me nowhere. I prefer to tell it straight with no chaser. I can't help it if you can't take the truth."

"I take truth. You bully. How is that for truth?"

Saturday walked close to Petra and got in her face. "I got your bully."

Ed watched their exchange from the sideline, where he sat along with the executive producer, Steve. While Ed looked on in admiration at the way Saturday was performing, Steve watched in disgust.

"That Saturday is some piece of work. She should give poor Petra a break," Steve whispered to Ed.

"She's perfect just the way she is. Everyone on the show can't be Mary Poppins, or the show would be a bore," Ed said, coming to Saturday's defense.

"Well, I guess you're right. But at least she could wait until the director says 'action' before giving Petra hell."

"I'm sure this is her way of warming up before we start taping," Ed said.

Saturday continued to go at Petra, insulting her broken English and pointing her finger in Petra's face.

"Hey, you two, save the bickering for the camera," Brandon said, breaking up the spat. He had seen enough.

Petra stomped over to the huge picture window, folded her arms and muttered under her breath.

"What is all this chatter going on? I could hear you two all the way in my room, *and* the door was shut. This is not a barroom brawl. We're in an elegant penthouse and should act accordingly," Brooke said in a chastising voice as she entered the room.

Brooke Windsor had once had it all. Born with a platinum spoon in her pretty mouth and raised on the Upper East Side, her great-grandparents were blue bloods who'd made their fortune in the railroad industry. Rumors had it that she and her ex-husband were first cousins, which wasn't unusual for people of their stature. What was unusual was for a family with old money to lose their fortune within a generation. And that was exactly what Brooke's husband did when he invested all of their money with a shifty investment adviser who swindled them in a Ponzi scheme. Distraught over losing his family's fortune, her husband fled to Europe, leaving his wife to fend for herself. With no marketable skills, Brooke jumped at the chance to star on *Divorced Divas.* The only problem was that Brooke had an air of superiority and thought she was better than the other divas. Also, in her quest to find her next meal ticket, Brooke flirted with just about any man with earning potential. Brooke, who had grown up with the best of everything, had now lost everything. She still had her family's name, but that didn't keep her in designer clothes or pay for lavish vacations. Ed thrust Brooke in the world of athletes when choosing her dates, setting her up with basketball players, football players, hockey players and the like. Most of the guys had no problem being seen on camera with the beautiful Brooke. And she had no problem dating these men earning seven-figure salaries.

"Don't worry about how loud we are. Worry about finding another cousin to marry," Saturday shot back.

Brooke rolled her eyes, swung her long blond hair and whipped her slim body around, giving Saturday her back.

"Girls, girls, save all the backbiting for the camera," Brandon repeated.

Saturday started in again. "First of all, we're not girls. Second…"

"Second, I'm the director and this is now my show, so when I say save it, I mean save it," Brandon interrupted her. "I assume everyone has read the show notes for the day, so let's get started. Saturday, I want you sitting on the sofa next to Trista. You two are discussing Saturday's latest blind date. When the bell rings, Saturday, I want you to answer the door."

"Wait a minute—isn't the maid supposed to answer the door?" Brooke interrupted.

Brandon shot her a look. He turned back to Saturday and continued. "Like I said, when the bell rings, answer the door. Got it? Good."

Saturday went over and sat beside Trista. Brooke and Petra were seated in the background at a table set for high tea.

Once everyone was in position, Brandon yelled, "Action!"

The set lights came on, and the cameras began rolling. Saturday and Trista starting chatting as if they were best friends. Saturday recalled her past dates, a mix of businessmen, athletes, rockers and Europeans. Ed wanted her dating base to span the range so Saturday could swoop in at any given time and steal a cast member's date, bringing high drama to the show.

"That guy Anthony you went to dinner with seems nice. Are you excited to see him again?" Trista asked.

"He's the one who should be excited."

"And why is that?"

"Hello, have we met? Look at me." Saturday stood up and twirled around. "Who wouldn't want to see me again?"

Damn, that chick has no shame, Brandon thought, sitting in his director's chair and staring at Saturday.

As they were talking, the bell rang. Saturday strutted over to the door, paused and opened it. Standing before her was a portly Italian man who looked as if he had eaten too many meatballs. He was dressed in a navy business suit, wore rectangle glasses and carried a black briefcase. He looked like a public defender heading to court instead of someone standing on the set of a reality show.

"Hey there, how are ya? You're looking fine as ever," he said nervously.

"Hello, Anthony," Saturday answered drily.

"Cut!"

"What? Why'd you yell cut?" Saturday asked. "We just got started."

"I want you to show some enthusiasm. Act like you're happy to see him. Take two. Action."

Saturday leaned in and gave the man a hug with a friendly pat on the back. Obviously there was no chemistry between them. She towered over him and they looked mismatched, like complete opposites.

"Cut!"

"What now?" Saturday rolled her eyes and put her hand on her hip.

"When I said show some enthusiasm I meant give him a hello kiss. Take three. Action."

Saturday leaned down and gave him a quick peck on the lips.

"Cut! Cut!" Brandon was getting frustrated. He walked over and got in Saturday's face. "What's wrong with you? Why did you kiss him like he's your brother?"

"I didn't kiss him like a brother."

"You sure didn't kiss him with any passion."

"That's because I don't feel any passion toward him," she said as if the man weren't even standing there.

"Look, the viewers want to see chemistry. Not some lukewarm peck on the lips. Now try it again." Brandon went back to his director's chair and yelled, "Take four! Action!" Saturday kissed Anthony again, and again Brandon cut the scene.

"What the hell do you want?" she hissed, rolling her eyes.

Brandon got up, went over to Saturday, took her firmly by the shoulders and gave her a long juicy kiss. He could feel himself responding to her; his crotch was getting heated with every passing second. "That's what I want," he said, releasing her before he had a full-blown erection.

Saturday was speechless. "Got it," she said once she recovered from the surprise kiss.

When Brandon returned to the director's chair and yelled "action" again, he didn't have any more problems. She kissed Anthony as if he were her long-lost lover. As Brandon watched the scene play out, he could still feel the warmth of her lips against his. Her lips were soft and he could envision kissing and making love to her all night. His mind momentarily drifted into a fantasy where their naked bodies were intertwined in a heated embrace and their tongues were doing a sensuous, synchronized dance. Brandon shook his head, trying to rid himself of the image. He was there to work, not fantasize. Besides, divas were not his type, and Saturday was beyond your typical diva. After being dumped by an actress, he wanted nothing more to do with the entertainment types. He wanted a down-to-earth woman with traditional family values, and Saturday Knight certainly didn't fit that description.

Chapter 6

The first day of taping had been long and drawn out. By the time Ayana returned home, she was exhausted. After showering and putting on her favorite pink Hello Kitty pajamas, she climbed into bed. She then pulled the comforter up to her chin and shut her eyes. An hour later, she was still wide-awake, sleep eluding her. Ayana tossed and turned, switching from her left side to the right, in an effort to get comfortable, but it wasn't working. Ayana sat up and attacked the pillows, punching them with her fist, trying to soften them. Satisfied that she had loosened the down feathers sufficiently, she laid her head back on the creased pillows. The moment she closed her eyes, visions of Brandon appeared. Ayana could see him walking toward her with a sexy strut. Her body's memory could still feel his strong hands taking hold of her shoulders, pressing her against his body and giving her a sensuous kiss.

His lips touching hers had been a welcome surprise. The last thing Ayana expected was to be lip-locking with the new director. She could tell from the way he introduced his lips to hers—purposeful, yet gentle—that he was an experienced lover. He had turned her on with only one brief kiss, and now her body craved more of his touch.

Ayana bolted straight up. "Get that man out of your mind," she said quietly, underneath her breath, in the darkened room. She inhaled several times, fast at first and then slowly in a Zen-like effort to calm herself. As Ayana was going through the breathing exercises, her cell phone rang. She froze, and her heart started beating fast. Her mind instantly flashed to Brandon. *I wonder if that's him calling?* A phone list with all the cast and crew's home and cell numbers had been passed out before rehearsals began, so it wasn't unlikely that he could be calling.

She turned over, looked at the nightstand and saw her cell glowing in the dark. As Ayana reached for the phone she glanced down and was disappointed to see Reese's name on the screen. Ayana didn't really feel like talking. She wanted to focus on going to sleep, but she knew if she didn't answer, Reese would only call back in a few minutes. Reese didn't leave messages; she was a repeat caller, and she hit Redial until she got an answer.

"Hey," Ayana said without an ounce of enthusiasm in her voice.

"Are you asleep already? It's only nine o'clock," Reese said, full of energy.

"No, not really. I'm just lying here."

"What's wrong? You sound agitated."

"Nothing."

"Come on, now. I know you better than that. Something must have happened on the shoot today if you can't sleep." Reese and Ayana had known each other since high school, and they were adept at reading each other, much like an old married couple.

"Well, something out of the ordinary did happen, but it was no big deal." Ayana was reluctant to tell Reese what had happened because she didn't want her friend blowing the incident out of proportion, trying to make a love connection like she had done so many times in the past.

"Do tell. I like hearing about the action on the set. It's like watching the show before it airs. Did you get into another catfight with Petra? Or did Brooke piss you off with her hoity-toity attitude?" Reese knew the antics of each cast member as if she were part of the show.

"No, it had nothing to do with either of them. It's the new director. He kissed me today."

"What! Are you kidding? Why did he kiss you?"

"He was demonstrating how I should've kissed one of my dates," Ayana said, as if kissing the director was an everyday occurrence.

"Why do you sound so matter-of-fact about it? Was he a bad kisser?"

Ayana closed her eyes, reminiscing. "On the contrary— the kiss was awesome. I can't stop thinking about him," she said, unable to hide her feelings any longer.

"Girl, you sound like you have a crush on him!"

"You see, this is why I didn't want to say anything. I knew you were going to blow the whole thing up. I'm not in high school, and I don't have a crush. I was just surprised at his bold demonstration, that's all." Ayana had said enough and didn't want to fully admit how much the kiss had affected her, so much so that Brandon and his lips were on repeat in her mind, playing over and over.

"Yeah, right."

"I'm serious. I don't have time to get involved with anybody, let alone someone I work with. I'm concentrating all of my energy on the next phase of my life. I don't plan to be on *Divorced Divas* forever. My focus is on branding myself, not on romance," she said, redirecting the conversation.

"That's a good speech, but what's wrong with having a relationship and working on your career at the same time? I'm working on my gemology certification and taking care of my husband at the same time."

"Well, that might work for you, but for me romance is often a distraction. Remember when I started working for Benjamin? My plan was to climb the corporate ladder at BL Industries. Instead, I ended up dating and then marrying the boss. Look how that turned out. I don't plan on making the same mistake twice. I'm not getting any younger, and I need to secure my financial future while I can."

"My point exactly. You're not getting younger and you need to find a man so you won't grow old alone. Don't get me wrong—I understand your financial concerns, but love is important too. Money won't hug you around the waist at night and keep you warm."

Ayana sighed. She was tired and ready to end the conversation. She had heard Reese's speech on finding true romance more than she could count on two hands. "Love will just have to wait. Look, Reese, I need to get to sleep. I have an early day tomorrow."

"Okay, but maybe you need to give that director a second look. He might be the *one*."

Ayana sighed into the phone.

"I'm not preaching. I only want you to be happy like Joey and me."

"Everybody isn't as lucky as you guys. Maybe finding a soul mate isn't in the cards for me."

"I don't believe that, and I'm sure you don't either."

"Having a significant other would be the icing on the cake, but at this point in my life, I'm not going to hold my breath for my soul mate to come along. I'll just take the cake and forget about the icing."

"All I'm saying is just don't close yourself off to an opportunity that presents itself. You never know when love will come knocking."

"I hear you, Reese. I hate to cut our conversation short, but I really have to get to sleep. Talk to you later."

"Okay, good night."

After Ayana ended the call and put the phone back on the nightstand, she thought about Reese's advice. Although she had made a point of saying that true love wasn't in her future, Reese was right about finding someone to grow old with. Ayana didn't want to be alone the rest of her life, but for now, her search would have to wait.

Chapter 7

Barneys New York, the swanky department store on Madison Avenue, was the site of the day's shoot. The cast was scheduled to come in and comb through the designer racks in search of outfits for their upcoming dates. Viewers loved seeing the ladies buy five-thousand-dollar shoes without blinking an eyelash and adding their names to the waitlist for designer purses that cost as much as a small house in some cities. The producers were adamant about portraying the ritzy world of glitz and glamour, and Barneys, with its multiple floors of designer swag, was the perfect venue.

Brandon was scheduled for a brief meeting with Ed before the cast arrived to discuss blocking for the shoot. The lighting and audio teams had already set up and were waiting patiently for the show to begin. Ed had arrived ahead of Brandon. He was dressed in teal-blue skinny jeans, a yellow silk camp shirt, a pair of pink platform sneakers, a monogrammed Louis Vuitton messenger bag strapped across his chest and his signature chiffon scarf—this one in multicolored shades of teal, yellow and pink. He strutted through the store looking like a designer-clad peacock.

"Hey, Ed, how's it going?" Brandon said, entering the cordoned-off shoe section the store had reserved for the shoot.

"Other than a little heartburn, I'm good. Guess I shouldn't have had a second helping of lasagna and tiramisu last night." His protruding belly was indication of his love for fattening Italian food.

"Why don't you send the PA to Duane Reade to pick up some Pepto?"

"Good idea." Ed took his cell phone out of his messenger bag. "Hey, Gabby, can you run to the drugstore and buy a large bottle of Pepto-Bismol? Thanks."

"Where do you want the first scene to start?" Brandon asked as Ed completed the call.

Ed crossed the room and stood next to a display of designer pumps. "Here is fine. I want the girls to ogle over these beauties."

"No problem." Brandon picked up a shoe to inspect it. "Are they serious with these prices?" he asked, holding a red, leather-bottomed pump.

"Those are Louboutins. What do you expect?"

"Lou Who?"

"Christian Louboutin. Don't tell me you've never heard of him. Everyone is familiar with his signature red bottoms," Saturday said in a snarky tone as she walked up behind him.

Brandon put the shoe back on the display. "Not everyone is as consumed with material possessions as you ladies seem to be," he said, looking her dead in the eyes.

For a few moments they stood face-to-face without saying a word. Brandon could feel himself being drawn to her. His eyes scanned her body up and down. She wore a slinky, red, ankle-length dress that fitted her curvaceous body like a second skin. Saturday oozed sensuality, and there was no doubt that he was attracted to her. Brandon shook off the feeling. Although Saturday was beautiful, her personality was offensive and he couldn't imagine spending his life with such an abrasive woman.

"Whatever." Saturday twisted her lips, flipped her long wig and turned her back to him. "So, Ed, what's wrong with you? You look pale as a ghost. Are you okay?"

"I'm fine, just a little heartburn. Let me sit down until Gabby gets here with the medicine." He sat in one of the cushy chairs and continued talking. "Now, about today's shoot, Saturday. I want you and Petra to really go at it. Get in her face and don't back down until the director says 'cut.'"

"I don't have a problem with that, but you need to tell Petra this is your idea. I'm tired of her thinking that I'm always picking on her."

"I'll have a chat with her when she gets here."

As they were talking, Gabby, the production assistant, came in with the pharmacy bag. "Here you go, Ed."

"Thanks." He took the medicine out of the bag, opened the bottle and tilted it up to his mouth, guzzling the pink liquid as if it were a refreshing beverage.

"What is that you drink?" Petra asked as she entered the shoe section.

"The word isn't *you,* it's *you're,* and it's *drinking,* not *drink,*" Saturday said, ribbing Petra on her broken English.

"I so tired of you teasing about way I talk."

Saturday started laughing. "You just can't get your tenses right. Ed, why don't you get Petra a speech coach?"

"I no need coach. I need you to shut up and leave me alone." Petra crossed her arms tightly across her chest.

Ed stood up. "Petra, can I speak to you for a minute?"

While Ed and Petra talked near the edge of the room, Brooke and Trista entered the set. Neither woman acknowledged Saturday, but they did glance at her as she sat in a nearby chair holding an iPad in her hands.

"So, Brandon, what's your story?" Brooke asked, coming closer to him.

"Excuse me?" Brandon asked, taking a step back.

She flipped her golden-blond tresses. "I mean, are you married? Have a girlfriend? Have a boyfriend? What's your status?" Brooke spoke as if he were required to answer her questions.

"First of all, we're not friends and my personal life is none of your business, and second, we are all here to do a job, so I suggest you read over today's notes before we start shooting."

She moved closer to him, smiled and put her hand on his arm. "Oh, sweetie, I was just trying to make conversation."

Brandon stepped back, allowing her hand to drop from his arm. "My personal life isn't up for general conversation," he said sternly.

Saturday glanced up and smiled, obviously pleased that he had put the snooty flirt in her place.

Brooke huffed, flipped her hair again and strutted

away, her charms totally lost on the director. Trista then sat down next to Saturday. "Good morning. How are you?"

"I'm good," Saturday said without glancing up.

Trista looked over at Saturday's iPad. "What are you doing? Playing a game?"

Saturday flipped the gadget over. "I don't like people looking over my shoulder. It's irritating," she said, putting the tablet in her purse and standing up.

"Okay, ladies, let's get started," Ed announced after his brief meeting with Petra. "Saturday, I want you and Petra over here near the Louboutins, gushing over the shoes and then arguing about who's going to buy the last pair of silver pumps. Saturday, after about five minutes of verbal sparring, I want you to throw the shoe at Petra, but be careful not to hit her—just make it look deliberate."

"Why she throw at me? Why I not throw at her?"

"She'll throw the first shoe, and then you can throw the next one. I want you guys to have a shoe fight."

This show is such a joke. I can't wait to get out of here, Brandon thought as he stood there listening to the creator's stage directions.

"Why not let the action flow organically?" Brandon knew the former director had been fired for being too opinionated. He had been committed to keeping quiet, doing his job, completing the contract and hightailing it back to a major network, but this staging was ridiculous and he couldn't hold his tongue any longer.

"I know you're the director, but this is my show, and to keep the ratings high, I want to ensure there's plenty of drama," Ed responded.

"Don't you think there's enough drama between the

ladies without you orchestrating it? Isn't this supposed to be reality television?" Brandon countered.

"What's with all the questions? When you came on board, you knew what type of show you were going to be working on," Ed replied, slightly raising his voice.

"Of course I knew what I was signing up for. However, I don't think forced conflicts are the way to go."

Saturday watched the exchange in silence. Outwardly she showed no emotion, but inside she was doing somersaults. Brandon was expressing exactly how she felt. Saturday found herself being drawn to him as he stood his ground against Ed.

"Look, Brandon, this discussion is over. I don't feel like arguing with you. Just shoot the scene like I requested." Ed inhaled deeply and plopped down in a chair.

Brandon backed down. He couldn't afford to lose this job. If the creator of the show wanted a train wreck, then that was exactly what he would direct. "Ladies, we're going to start shooting in five. Saturday and Petra, I'm going to need you two over here by these Louboutins. Brooke and Trista, you guys aren't in the frame yet. I want you off camera. Walk in once the shoes start flying. Understood?"

"I want to throw first shoe," Petra said.

"Sorry, hon, that's not going to happen. Ed said that I'm throwing the first shoe," Saturday said with her hand on her hip.

"Why you throw first? I throw you."

"You're not throwing me. You're throwing a shoe." Petra huffed. "You know how I mean."

"It's *what I meant*."

"Ladies, again I'm going to tell you to save it for

the camera." Brandon interrupted their ongoing spat. "Okay, places, please. Cue lights and sound."

The shoe salon brightened up and everyone—actors, cameramen, soundmen—took their respective places. Saturday and Petra positioned themselves near the designer shoes. Brooke and Trista waited on the sidelines until their turn to enter.

"Take one. Action!" Brandon announced.

"What are you wearing tonight for your date?" Saturday asked Petra.

Petra picked up a silver metallic platform shoe off the display and held it in her right hand. "Platinum mini-dress and this shoe. It perfect together."

Saturday walked up and snatched the shoe out of Petra's hand. "Actually, it goes perfectly with my fuchsia-and-silver pantsuit. I'm going to buy them."

Petra snatched the shoe back. "No! Mine!"

"How dare you take something out of my hand!"

"You take from me first," Petra said, holding on tightly to the shoe.

Saturday stepped closer and tried to take the shoe back, but Petra had a firm grip and she couldn't pry it out of Petra's hand. "Give me the shoe!"

"No! Mine!" Petra held the shoe to her chest.

"Cut!" Ed yelled, getting up and walking onto the set. "I said I wanted a shoe fight, not a tug-of-war. Petra, hand me the shoe so I can demonstrate what I'm talking about." Ed raised the shoe in the air and hurled it across the room with such force that he fell forward, landing on the carpet.

After a few seconds, Ed was still on the floor. He hadn't made any attempt to get up.

"Hey, man, are you okay?" Brandon asked. When Ed

didn't move or speak, Brandon came over and knelt beside him. He shook him softly. "Ed, Ed, are you okay?" Still no answer.

Saturday knelt next to Brandon, reached down and felt Ed's pulse, but there was no rhythmic beating. She immediately started doing CPR, pressing on his chest and blowing air into his mouth.

"Somebody call nine-one-one!" Brandon yelled.

The cast and crew looked on as Saturday repeated the CPR routine over and over until the paramedics arrived. They quickly checked Ed's vitals. He now had a faint pulse, thanks to Saturday's emergency CPR. They placed an oxygen mask around his nose and mouth, loaded him on a gurney and rolled him out of the store and into a waiting ambulance.

Brandon grabbed Saturday and they quickly hopped into an approaching taxi and followed the ambulance as it wove in and out of traffic. They rode to the hospital in silence, each with pensive looks on their faces. The shoot had begun with an orchestrated frivolous scene, but it had ended with a real life-and-death drama.

Chapter 8

The bright rays of the midday Caribbean sun kissed Ayana's brown skin as she lounged on the sandy Negril beach in a snow-white two-piece swimsuit. She looked up from the romance novel she was reading and stared off into the calm turquoise waters. Looking out into the ocean, Ayana took a moment to reflect on the recent events that had shifted her life momentarily.

The past week had been a traumatic whirlwind. It all began with Ed's unexpected heart attack. He barely escaped death that day on the shoot when he collapsed. His condition was critical, rendering him bedridden, hooked up to intravenous drips and monitors in the intensive-care unit. Steve, the executive producer, had told the cast and crew that because Ed was the visionary for the show, he had no other choice but to halt production until Ed made a full recovery. And, based on the cardiologist's grim prognosis, that wouldn't be anytime soon.

During the same week, Ayana's father had had a mild stroke. Her mother's tone had been cool and calm when she called to tell her the news. She had told Ayana that everything was under control and that she didn't need to rush home. But with the show on hold indefinitely, Ayana booked a flight to Jamaica and was at her father's bedside two days later. Luckily, his stoke hadn't caused any major paralysis. He was back to his old self, piddling around in the garden, in less than two weeks. Although her father was back to normal, Ayana was sticking around to monitor his condition. She wasn't taking any chances.

With her father's health under control, she used her time on the island like a holiday. After dealing with fake confrontations and staged fights, and acting like an out-of-control hyena, Ayana welcomed the downtime.

The more she gazed at the aqua-blue waters, the more inviting they seemed. Growing up on an island and spending her summers at the beach, she was an avid swimmer. She stood up, took off the oversize, floppy straw hat, tossed it on her towel and padded through the warm sand toward the ocean. She then dipped her toes in the water and splashed around a bit before wading in farther. This secluded spot along Seven Mile Beach was off the beaten track where tourists didn't tread.

Ayana slowly waded in until the water was waist high. The ocean was so warm that it felt like bathwater. She cupped her hands, taking in the salt water and splashing it on her face. Gone was the heavy makeup, long, flowing wig, false eyelashes and ugly personality. Ayana dipped down into the clear waters, submerging her entire body. She held her breath and said a silent prayer of gratitude. Even though she hated her job, she was grateful for the opportunity to make a living and not have to

rely on a man for her financial security. She was also
grateful for her father's speedy recovery and for the CPR
efforts that had saved Ed's life. When she reemerged,
she felt renewed, as if she had been through a much-
needed baptism. Ayana lay on the water, arched her back
and floated. She felt free and closed her eyes, savoring
the feeling of being carried away by the gentle waves.
Her body drifted effortlessly, and her mind was clear
of any negative thoughts. With her head tilted back and
ears partially submerged, she could hear only muffled
sounds. Ayana felt as if she were in a safe cocoon and
continued floating without a care.

The tranquillity of her solitude came to an abrupt
halt when she heard the roar of a motor. Before she
knew it, she was flipped over and submerged by a series of violent waves. Her eyes popped open underwa-
ter, and she kicked her legs quickly until she was back
on the surface.

"Oh my God, are you all right?" asked a handsome
man straddling a bright orange Jet Ski. "I'm so sorry,
but I didn't see you. What are you doing floating all the
way out here by yourself?"

Ayana glanced around the vast body of water and
didn't see the beach. She had drifted out farther than
anticipated. "I hadn't planned on floating this far. Guess
the waves carried me away," she said, treading water.

He reached out his hand to her. "Get on. I'll take you
back to shore."

She brushed her hair out of her face, rubbed the salt
water out of her eyes and looked up into his face. She
couldn't believe her eyes. Behind a pair of dark aviator
shades was Brandon. "Uh…sure." She took hold of his
hand, climbed out of the water and settled on the back

of the Jet Ski. Ayana wrapped her arms around his bare chest and held on tight as he sped off.

"Where are you staying?" he yelled.

With the Jet Ski creating a cascade of waves and the roar of the motor, she could barely hear him. "What'd you say?"

"I said, where are you staying?" he repeated more loudly.

"Just keep straight," she responded, finally hearing him.

He doesn't know it's me. Ayana held him a little tighter, enjoying the anonymity of the moment. She thought back on his unexpected kiss and smiled. She could see the beach coming closer and closer and wondered what Brandon would say once he learned who was hitching a ride with him. It was no secret they bumped heads on the set and that Saturday gave him a hard time whenever she could. Her heart began beating faster and faster in anticipation of the reveal. *Might as well enjoy the moment.* As the Jet Ski cut through the water, she took in the sights. She spotted a bright yellow banana boat filled with tourists. A catamaran was heading farther out into the ocean, probably taking people snorkeling. Waves crashed against the Jet Ski, and the spray of water in her face was refreshing. Being a native of the island, Ayana had never bothered renting a Jet Ski; that was something tourists did. This was her first time on one and she found the ride exhilarating.

"Is this it?" he yelled, approaching the sand.

"Yeah."

Brandon turned off the engine and slid the Jet Ski into the shore with the precision of a race-car driver. He hopped off first and then helped her.

"Thanks for the ride," Ayana said, keeping her head down. She was enjoying his kindness and wasn't ready to be outed.

"No problem," he said, secretly admiring her toned, bikini-clad body from behind his shades. She was au naturel and beautiful—wet hair and all. The more he stared, the more familiar she seemed. He took off the dark glasses to get a better look. "Saturday?"

Ayana hung her head even farther, trying to bury her chin in her chest. Realizing there was no use attempting to hide her identity, she inhaled deeply, exhaled and said, "Yes, it's me."

He stood there seemingly in shock. "What are *you* doing here?"

"I grew up in the area. I'm here visiting my parents."

"Wow! *You're* Jamaican?"

"Yes, I am. Why are you saying it like that?"

"Most Jamaican women I know are sweethearts, but…"

"Stop right there. You really don't know me like you think you do."

"I know enough."

Ayana knew the impression she made on Brandon as Saturday Knight wasn't a positive one, and that was putting it mildly. Standing there in front of him stripped of that persona, she was embarrassed about the way she portrayed herself on the show and how badly she had treated him. She looked into his eyes and could see judgment. She wanted to tell him the real reason for the fake persona, but what was the use? His impression of her had already been sealed in his mind. She couldn't take his critical stares any longer; she had to get out of there. She reached down, grabbed her hat, plopped it on her head and put her beach towel and novel in her tote. "'Bye, Brandon," she called behind her as she walked away as quickly as the sand would allow.

Brandon stood there in shock and watched her scurry away. He was speechless. The last person he'd expected to see was *the* diva of *Divorced Divas*. He also couldn't believe that Saturday was a beach person, floating in the water and actually getting her hair wet. Nor in his wildest dreams did he think that she was Jamaican. She seemed to have been born and bred on Madison Avenue among the multitude of designer boutiques. He watched as she disappeared over the cliff, and then he returned to his Jet Ski. Riding back to his hotel, he wondered if he would bump into Saturday again. She had thrown him a curveball, and now he was intrigued and wanted to know more.

Chapter 9

It had been two days since Brandon scooped Saturday out of the ocean. He still couldn't believe how different she looked without the heavy makeup, wig and designer clothes. With the water splashing against her face, he didn't recognize her as she recovered from being flipped over by the waves created from his Jet Ski. She had a vulnerable quality as she stood in front of him on the beach clad only in her bikini. He had quickly dismissed that thought and reminded himself that she was the same person who demeaned the cast members on a regular basis. Be that as it may, Brandon couldn't help but wonder where she was staying. She had fled so fast that he didn't get a chance to ask where her parents lived—not that it mattered because he wasn't planning on visiting. Seeing her in New York on the set was more than enough.

The reason for Brandon's trip to Jamaica was two-fold. He was there to unwind after the untimely hiatus from the show and to check on his sister-in-law. His brother, James, had married a Jamaican woman, and they'd had one of the best relationships that Brandon had ever seen. Even after ten years of marriage, they were still inseparable. The vows "till death do we part" fitted them. They were together until the day James died of cancer two years ago. Before he'd passed away, James made Brandon promise to look in on his wife from time to time. Marigold was such a sweetheart that Brandon didn't have a problem flying to Jamaica whenever he had the chance.

"Marigold, I don't know how you do it," Brandon said. He was having lunch in the industrial-sized kitchen of the shelter that his sister-in-law ran.

"Whatcha mean, mon?"

"I mean, dealing with all these kids on a daily basis is so much work."

"T'is no problem a'tall. Most of dem mommas is here wit dem. And da ones wit no momma are da sweetest, so I don't mind givin' dem extra attention." Marigold ran a private shelter for women and children. She and James had never had any children, so she treated every child at the shelter as if they were her own.

"No, Marigold, you're the sweetest. Not many women would give of themselves like you do." Brandon thought back to the cast of *Divorced Divas*. They were some of the most selfish women he had ever seen.

"Go on now wit dat," she said, getting up from the table and waving her hand. "You want more goat stew?"

"No, I'm full, but I will have another glass of your famous pink lemonade."

"Comin' right up." Marigold took his bowl, put it in the sink, then went to the double-door refrigerator and took out the pitcher of homemade lemonade.

"Is that my favorite drink?"

Brandon's back was to the door, so he turned around to see who had come into the kitchen. His mouth flew open as he stared at Saturday coming toward Marigold. She was looking directly at his sister-in-law and didn't see him sitting at the long communal table. Being unnoticed gave him the opportunity to check her out before she spotted him. She wore a simple yellow cotton sundress with matching yellow flip-flops. Her hair was pulled back in a ponytail, and again her face was makeup free. Her toned-down look gave her an innocent quality, which he found very attractive. He sat there in silence and watched their exchange.

"Oh, me Lord!" Marigold gave Saturday a big bear hug, released her and asked, "Whatcha doin' here, chile?" Her voice was full of excitement.

"My dad had a mild stroke so I came to check on him."

"Oh, no! He okay?"

"Yes, thank God. It wasn't major and my mom got him to the hospital quickly, which is so critical when someone has a stroke. He doesn't have any paralysis. He's even back planting in the yard. I keep telling him to take it easy, but he won't listen. You know how stubborn most men are."

"Yeah, me do." Marigold poured two glasses of lemonade and handed one to Saturday. "Come, chile, let me introduce ya to me brother-in-law." Marigold walked over to the table with Ayana following behind.

When Marigold stepped to the side to make the introductions, Ayana instantly began to perspire. One, she hadn't expected to see Brandon. Two, he was related to her friend, and three, she wondered if he would unknowingly divulge her secret. No one on the island knew she worked on a reality television show, and for obvious reasons she wanted to keep it that way.

"Ayana, this here is Brandon, me late husband's brother," Marigold said, handing Brandon his glass of lemonade.

"Nice to meet you," she said quickly before he had a chance to say that they already knew each other. Based on the look registered on his face—mouth agape and eyes slightly bulged—he was just as shocked as she.

"Ayana, huh?"

"Yes, but we call her Ana 'round here. She a gem. Without she pitchin' in and helpin', we wouldn't have enough clothes and shoes for da women and chilrin. Ya know most residents come here wit only da clothes on dey backs. She ships boxes and boxes of stuff on a regular basis. And she even send checks, which we need so much." Marigold gave Ayana another hug. "Me couldn't get along witout she."

"Is that right?" Brandon remarked in a shocked tone.

"Yep, dat's right. I'm surprised ya don't know her since ya both live in Manhattan."

Saturday—Ayana—and Brandon glanced at each other. She quickly spoke first before he could respond. "New York isn't like a small village where everyone knows each other." She evaded Marigold's comment with a generalized response, probably because she didn't want to outright lie to her friend, but she wasn't prepared to tell her the truth either.

Before Marigold was able to ask any questions or

make any more comments, her assistant came into the kitchen. "Excuse me, Marigold, but ya have a phone call in da office."

"Me be right back."

When Marigold was gone, Ayana exhaled. She smoothed down the front of her dress and then ran her hand over her hair. She seemed to be a ball of nerves and didn't know what to say or do.

"So, Marigold is your sister-in-law? Small world," she said, sitting across the table from him. Ayana took a long sip of lemonade and exhaled.

"Yep."

He'd answered with an edge to his voice, still viewing her as the troublemaker on the show.

"Brandon, I'm sure you have a ton of questions."

"Yep, I sure do."

"First of all, my real name is Ayana Lewis. Saturday Knight is a name that Ed created."

"Did he create your wicked personality too?"

She cast her eyes down in shame, stared in her lap for a few moments, then looked in his eyes and said, "As a matter of fact, he did."

"And you're okay with demeaning yourself? If what you're telling me is true, I would have told him to take a hike, as any other person with decency would."

"I wish I could have, but I wasn't in the position financially to turn down the job. I was recently divorced and my bank account was running on fumes."

Brandon hadn't expected her to be so open. He'd automatically assumed, based on her Saturday Knight persona, that she would get defensive and come up with a ton of lies. Upon hearing the truth, his resolve began to soften. He more than understood her financial situation. He had been in the same predicament after moving to Los Angeles trying to become a Hollywood director, exhausting his savings in the process. "Why didn't you ask him to cast you as the good girl of the show?"

"I did, but that role was already taken. When Ed initially approached me, he wanted me to play Trista's role, but I turned him down. I had no interest in acting on a reality show. To be honest, I think the entire reality genre has become one big joke." Her eyes were welling up. She looked down in her lap and said softly, "And now, unfortunately, I'm the headliner."

Brandon studied her face and could see she was on the verge of tears. He reached across the table and patted her hand. "Don't cry. It's not that bad," he offered, surprising himself.

Ayana seemed to try to fight back the tears, but they fell anyway. She sniffled and wiped her face with the back of her hand. Brandon gave her a napkin and she blew her nose. "I'm sorry for being such a crybaby," she said with a slight smile, trying to lighten the mood.

"No problem. I've been where you are, so I completely understand. Actually, the reason I'm working on the show is because I also exhausted all my savings."

Ayana stared at him inquisitively.

"I quit my job with a major network, moved to L.A. and tried to break into the movie business. I pounded the pavement for a year with no luck. My living expenses, as well as trying to schmooze and network in La-La Land, devoured my savings quickly. When I moved back to New York, the only show hiring was *Divorced Divas*. I had no choice but to take the job. I already have my agent contacting the networks so I can get back to 'real'—" he put his fingers in the air and made quotation marks "—television, once my contract is over."

"I have an exit strategy myself. I don't plan on being a *Diva* forever. Acting the way I do on the set is so out of my comfort zone. You have no idea how bad I feel every time I insult Petra. The poor girl doesn't deserve my constant brutal tongue-lashings."

Brandon was both pleased and surprised to hear her confess. His judgment of her had been all wrong. "So what should I call you?"

"Ayana or Ana. My family and friends here don't know about the show or my fake Saturday Knight persona, and I'd like to keep it that way. My parents would have a fit if they knew I degraded myself for money. If they had known about my financial hardship after the divorce settlement ran out, they would have tried to scrape up and send me whatever money they could. I think grown children should provide financial support to their elderly parents, not the other way around."

"I totally agree."

The more they talked, the more Brandon admired her. Not only did she do good deeds for the shelter, but she also took care of her parents. She was exactly the type of woman he could see having a future with. "Don't worry. Your secret is safe with me."

"Thanks. I'm relieved that you now know the truth. I saw the way you looked at me on the set every time I acted out."

"Honestly, I couldn't stand you. I'm glad you told me the truth. I must confess you are a really good actress. The way you portray Saturday Knight, no one would ever guess that isn't the real you."

"It's really hard to pull off, but for now I have no choice."

"Have you ever thought about acting as a career?"

"You mean in the movies?"

"Yes, or television. You're acting anyway, so you might as well put your talent to good use."

Ayana was silent for a moment, digesting his words. "You know, I never thought about it that way, but you're absolutely right. I portray a character on the set every day, and the audience thinks that's the real me. Thanks for the idea. I will definitely look into it."

"What ya two over dere gabbin' about?" Marigold asked, coming back into the kitchen.

"Nothing much. Just getting to know each other," Brandon said, smiling at Ayana.

"So, are ya goin' to da dance tonight?"

"What dance?" Ayana and Brandon asked in unison.

"Da Reggae Fest down at da pier. Dey gonna have a live band, plenty of food and barrels of rum punch."

"Sounds like fun. Ayana, would you like to go?"

Her eyes perked up. "Sure," she answered with a huge smile, exposing her pearly bright teeth.

"Where are you staying? I can pick you up."

She gave him her parents' address. "Do you know how to get there?"

"Yes. I'm familiar with the island. I've been here enough times. Marigold, what time does it start?"

"Eight o'clock."

"How about I pick you up at seven-thirty?"

Marigold looked at her brother-in-law and then back at Ayana, watching their conversation. She smiled.

"Sounds good. Let me dash. I have a few errands to run. Marigold, I'll talk to you later."

"Okay, me love."

Brandon watched her leave and couldn't believe the sudden change of events. He had totally misjudged the woman he knew as Saturday Knight. Now he couldn't wait to get to know Ayana Lewis.

Chapter 10

A cover band was wailing "Buffalo Soldier" when Brandon and Ayana walked into the open-air concert. The crowd was thick with both islanders and tourists, shoulder to shoulder, grooving to the music and drinking rum punch, Guinness Stout or Red Stripe beers. The smell of jerk chicken permeated the balmy night air. The mood of the crowd was happy and carefree, conducive to dancing the night away.

"I'm so glad Marigold told us about this. I haven't been to a Reggae Fest in a while," Ayana said over the music. Cameramen had been present at her last date, observing her every move. Being there with Brandon on a real date was a welcome change of pace.

"Me either."

"Is Marigold coming out tonight?" Ayana asked.

"She had planned on being here, but a mother and

her two children came to the shelter as Marigold was leaving and she wanted to make sure they settled in comfortably."

"I'm not surprised. I know how dedicated Marigold is to the shelter."

"She's amazing. My brother was a lucky man to find such a good woman." Brandon looked into Ayana's eyes, paused for a moment and then said, "Some people are just meant to be together."

Listening to his words and peering back into his eyes, Ayana could feel herself being drawn to him and subconsciously took a step closer. "Do you believe in fate?"

"Never really thought about it much until now, but life has a way of throwing you a curveball when you least expect it."

"That's true." Brandon was the last person on earth that Ayana thought she'd be spending time with. The possibility of them getting even closer was now ever present in her mind. She tried to shrug it off. They were just beginning to get to know each other and she didn't want to push the envelope. In an effort to dismiss her growing desire, she looked around, spotted the food vendors and changed the subject. "Do you want something to eat?"

"No, thanks. I had dinner earlier. Are you hungry?"

"No. My mother cooked a small feast and made me eat before I left. She thinks I'm too thin."

"That's sweet. I wish my mother was still alive to fuss over me. She died five years ago from lung cancer, which was weird because she never smoked a day in her life."

"I'm sorry to hear that. I'm also sorry about the loss of your brother. He was such a nice guy."

"Thanks." He didn't want to dwell on the matter, so he quickly switched the subject. "How about a drink?"

"A stout would be great."

"Guinness?

"Yep."

"Wow, I would've never imagined you as a dark-beer drinker."

"And why is that?" she asked, putting her hand on her hip.

"Remember, I've only seen you on the set all dolled up, and you look like a girl who only drinks dainty pink cocktails that are served in chilled martini glasses."

"Well, looks are deceiving."

Brandon raised his eyebrow. "They surely are." He took Ayana's hand and led the way through the throng of people toward the drink stand. Once there, he ordered two cold beers.

"To new friendships," she said, tapping her bottle to his.

"I'll drink to that."

"Yo, Ana!" a voice behind them yelled.

She turned around and saw her friend Cedella cutting through the crowd. Cedella and Ayana had grown up together and remained close even after Ayana had moved to the States years ago. The two friends hugged, happy to see each other.

"Me moms told me ya were here," Cedella said. As she spoke she checked Brandon out from head to toe. Cedella was a serial flirt with no shame in her game. "And who is dis fine bro'her? Is dis yo man?"

Ayana looked over at Brandon and had to admit that

he looked sexy in his baby-blue polo shirt that comple-
mented his milk-chocolate skin, straight-leg jeans that
hugged his muscular thighs and a pair of sandals. She
loved men who were confident enough to show their
feet. *I wish he were my man,* she thought. "No, he's just
a friend from New York."

"Ya two look good together. Ya should be a couple.
If ya don't want him, maybe me'll have a chance," she
said as if Brandon weren't standing there.

"CeDe, you still haven't learned to keep your thoughts
to yourself."

"Ya know me'll never change," she said, laughing.
"So, ya gonna introduce me or what?"

"Brandon, this is my friend Cedella. We were next-
door neighbors growing up."

"Nice to meet you, Cedella."

"Call me CeDe," she said, making googly eyes at
him. "So ya married, Brandon?"

"No, I'm not. CeDe, would you like a drink?" he
asked.

She raised a plastic cup filled with a ruby-colored
liquid. "No, thanks. Me already have a rum punch. Me
meeting some friends up front near da stage. Ya wanna
join us? We have a good spot."

"No, thanks. We're good," Ayana said before Brandon could answer. She and Brandon had melted the ice-
berg between them, and she wanted to continue their
getting-to-know-you session without CeDe interrupting or trying to hit on him.

"Suit yourself. Be sure to call me before ya leave
town," Cedella said as she gave Ayana a hug goodbye,
then disappeared back into the crowd.

"Tell me something—why don't you talk with an accent?"

"Me can talk wit da Jamaican accent if me want to," she said in a sassy tone. "When me interviewed for da show, Ed didn't want me to use me accent. Me worked wit a vocal coach to perfect me U.S. accent. So whacha tink of me talk now, mon?"

Brandon started to blush. "Your accent is sassy. It suits you."

The band was now singing "No Woman, No Cry." Ayana turned the beer up to her mouth, drained the bottle and tossed it into the garbage can. Brandon followed suit.

"Com on, mon. Let's dance," she said.

They walked hand in hand through the masses and joined the concertgoers dancing to the music. Brandon wrapped his arms around Ayana's waist and gently held her close.

The old-school reggae was soothing, transporting Ayana to a state of total awareness. She could feel her body molding into his as they swayed to the beat. Ayana closed her eyes and rested her head against his broad chest. She was so accustomed to being on the defensive that it felt good to let her guard down. Being in his arms felt comfortable, as if they were a couple that had been together for years instead of coworkers getting to know each other.

When the song ended, the band switched gears to an up-tempo beat, but Ayana and Brandon continued clinging to each other, seemingly in their own world, oblivious to the change. Brandon spun her around so that her backside was to him. He grabbed her hips and moved them to match his steps. Ayana looked over her shoulder, surprised that he was adept at a traditional reggae dance.

"I see you've got skills," she said, turning to face him.

"You haven't seen nuthin', mon," Brandon responded, using his own Jamaican accent.

They began doing a sensuous butterfly dance, spreading their legs in and out with their hands on their hips. Ayana hiked up her skirt, exposing her long legs. She bent her knees and squatted low near the ground. Brandon kept pace with her, placing his legs against hers. Together their waving limbs resembled a butterfly in heat. One song blended into another as they continued their hedonistic moves.

Brandon put his hands on his knees, easing his long, lean body lower and lower. Their legs were now intertwined, moving in sync. Brandon then wrapped one hand around her waist, pulling her close. He put his other hand on her exposed thigh, rubbing her smooth brown skin. Sweat was pouring off their bodies, dampening their clothes. The cotton gauze material of her top stuck to Ayana's skin, accentuating her breasts. Brandon licked his lips as he stared at her sexy body. He wiped beads of perspiration off his brow.

The combination of the humidity and the heat emanating from within was igniting a passion for Brandon that she was finding hard to resist. The feel of his hands on her body was driving Ayana crazy inside. One hand was clinching her waist, while his other hand was moving slowly up her thigh, getting closer and closer to her forbidden fruit. She was wet with perspiration and desire. Ayana was craving him sexually, but she didn't dare make the first move. She firmly believed that if a man wanted you, nothing could hold him back. And then, as if he were reading her thoughts, he leaned down and whispered in her ear.

"Come on. Let's get out of here." Brandon took Ayana's hand and led her off the dance floor.

No words were spoken as they wove through the crowd toward the exit. The intensity of the moment spoke volumes. Their sensuous dance moves were a prelude for a much-anticipated night of passion.

Chapter 11

Longing and lust filled the beach bungalow where Brandon had taken Ayana. She hadn't objected when he took her by the hand and led her out of the concert to his rented Fiat. When they reached the bungalow, Brandon didn't turn on any lights. Moonlight bathed the small cottage, creating a romantic glow. He closed the door and pulled her to him. They stood face-to-face, looking deeply into each other's eyes without saying a word. He took her face in his hands and rubbed her smooth cheeks. He leaned down and touched his lips to hers. The soft kiss slowly intensified, turning passionate, their tongues dancing harmoniously together, hungry for one another.

Brandon released her face, slipped his hands underneath her top and gently touched her nipples through her mesh bra. He rubbed the surface of the material, teasing her with each touch. Ayana covered his hands with hers and guided him toward the front snap closure of the bra. He took the hint, unsnapped the bra, unleashed her ample breasts and gently touched her erect nipples. He held her breasts in his hands and sensuously massaged them until he heard her moan.

"Hmm, that feels so good."

"That's just the beginning," he whispered and then licked the inside of her ear.

She gasped.

Brandon abandoned her breasts momentarily and unhooked her skirt, allowing it to slip to the floor. He roamed the soft surface of her skin, looking for delicious treasures. He moved his hand down her taut stomach and fingered the edge of her panties. Brandon was a patient man and didn't plan on rushing their first time together. He was going to savor every moment. He inched his hand into her panties. He could feel coarse hairs as he rubbed her neat bush, moving his fingers one at a time, and applied a little pressure with his index finger directly above her clit.

She gasped.

He leaned down and scooped Ayana up into his arms and carried her across the living room and into the bedroom. The room had floor-to-ceiling windows that looked out over the ocean. The windows were open and a soft breeze blew through the sheer curtains into the room. He laid her on top of the crisp white sheets, took off her wedge-heeled sandals, reached up and slid off her black lace panties. Brandon stood at the edge of the bed and admired her curvaceous body. She was well proportioned. Thick in all the right places—thighs, hips and butt. He licked his lips.

"Like what you see?"

He nodded. "Yes."

Brandon didn't take his eyes off her as he unbuckled his belt, unbuttoned his pants and slipped off his shirt, exposing his muscular chest.

Ayana's eyes were glued to him. Standing there bare-chested, with his jeans hanging off his hips, he looked like a sexy male model.

"Like what you see?" he asked, tossing the question back at her.

"So far, so good." She reached out and tugged at his belt.

He stepped back.

"Come here," she said, crooking her finger.

"Let's not rush. Do you have to get back home?"

"No."

"Good. We have all night, then."

Brandon kicked off his sandals and slowly stepped out of his jeans, one leg at a time. He stood in his boxer briefs with his legs slightly apart. She could see his broad shoulders and firm pecs by the moonlight.

Ayana bit her bottom lip as she gazed up at his sculpted body. The sight of him made her squirm with desire. She wanted him to devour her. She wanted to take her time as much as he did, but the anticipation of lovemaking was getting to be too much to bear. Ayana reached for him again. This time he didn't step back. She touched the imprint of his mound of manhood, which was nice and firm.

"Take them off," she said in a low, seductive tone as she tugged at the band of his briefs.

Brandon peeled off his underwear in slow motion. First, he fingered the elastic waistband suggestively and then eased the boxer briefs past his pubic area and down over his semierect penis.

She gasped.

He took hold of himself and began stroking the shaft of his penis, going all the way to the tip and back, causing his penis to grow with each stroke.

Ayana watched intently and could feel herself getting moister and moister. She put her hand between her legs, found her clit and started pleasuring herself too.

Watching her masturbate brought Brandon's penis to a fully erect state. His body was now aching for her, but he wasn't going to rush the moment. "Here, let me do that," he said, kneeling on the bed.

She spread her legs wider. "Be my guest."

He placed his massive hands on her knees and trailed his tongue from the inside of her right thigh, circling around to her left thigh, and back again, stopping at her exposed clit. He tasted her erogenous zone with the tip of his tongue before wrapping his lips around her clit. He alternated between sucking softly and firmly.

Ayana closed her eyes, grabbed the sheets with both fists and arched her back in ecstasy. "Ohhh, don't stop."

Brandon increased the pace, saliva dripping from his chin as he made love to her clit. He was a selfless lover and always wanted to please his partner first. But her oral climax was just the beginning. He reached for his jeans and retrieved a condom from his pocket, tore the foil package and rolled it onto his manhood. Brandon wedged himself between her legs and eased the tip of his penis into her ready vagina.

She gasped.

Ayana was wet and tight—a perfect combination. He wrapped her up in his arms and worked his rod, inch by inch, into her deep canal. The muscles of her vagina gripped his dick, causing him to pump faster, flexing his butt with each move. She held on to him with both hands and they rode the motion of lovemaking, pumping, pushing and panting. This was the first of many explosive climaxes.

After recovering, they changed positions. Now Ayana was on top, positioning herself near his manhood. She rolled the used condom off and replaced it with her mouth. She leaned down, wrapped her lips around his substantial manhood and went to work sucking in a rapid motion. She stopped and trailed her tongue up and down the sides of his shaft before using her tongue to tease the tip of his penis. She could taste his essence. Ayana covered him with her mouth again, and again went to work sucking and licking his penis as if it were a delicious chocolate-covered banana.

Brandon could feel himself coming. He moved her to the side, retrieved a fresh condom and rolled it on. "Get back on top."

Ayana did as instructed. This time, she squatted down over his erection and didn't stop until he was all the way inside. With her knees pressed close to his sides, she bounced up and down on his penis, crying out in ecstasy with each decadent move.

"You feel so good inside of me."

He held tightly on to her waist, thrusting upward, matching her moves with his own. "Being inside of you feels so right." He then flipped her over in one smooth motion. Now he was on top. Sweat dripped off Brandon's forehead as he increased his pace. The swiftness of his moves knocked the headboard back and forth against the wall. The noise of the bed coupled with their moans created the soundtrack of their first night together.

"Are you coming yet?" he panted.

"Almost."

Brandon reached underneath Ayana, grabbed her butt cheeks and pressed them toward his crotch, bringing her closer to him. He was on the verge of climax but wanted to ensure she was on the same page. "Tell me when you're ready."

"Okay, just don't stop."

He slowed down long enough to move his hands down her legs, grab her ankles and hold them high in the air, positioning himself deep inside of her V.

She gasped.

He ramped up the pace again and again. They each gave some more until their bodies gave in to yet another scrumptious, addictive climax.

Chapter 12

Ayana began to stir underneath the crisp white sheets as the sound of waves washing against the sand brought her out of a restful sleep. With her eyes still closed, she took a deep breath, inhaling the fresh ocean air. She stretched her arms, touching the bed and pillow next to her, but all she felt was the coolness of the sheet. She expected Brandon to be lying there. She opened her eyes to look for him, but he was nowhere in sight. The small bedroom was empty. She glanced at the night-stand, looking for a note from him, but there wasn't one.

Ayana's heart started to beat faster, in a mild panic. *Did he just leave without saying anything?* After sharing an intense night of lovemaking, staying up until the sun rose, she assumed that he would be cuddled up next to her, exhausted and enjoying the aftermath. The thought of him abandoning her didn't sit well. *Maybe I was wrong about our connection. Maybe it was just sex for him. And now that he got what he wanted, he has no further interest in me.* The inner dialogue was making her madder by the second. She began to feel used. The beautiful aftermath of lovemaking quickly evaporated.

"I'll be damned if I just lie here like an idiot and wait for him to show up," she said aloud. Ayana ripped the sheet from around her body, threw her legs over the side of the bed and stood. She looked on the floor for her clothes, but found only her lace panties. She then remembered that their foreplay had begun in the living room, where he had disrobed her. She put on the underwear and marched toward the door, her breasts bouncing with each purposeful step.

"Hey, pretty lady, where are you off to?" Brandon asked, entering the room.

Ayana took one look at him and saw he was holding a breakfast tray complete with a bud vase with a single yellow rose. "Uh, I was looking for my clothes." Admitting what she'd really thought was too embarrassing. Besides, it would make her seem paranoid.

"I folded them and put them over there," he said, motioning his head toward an armchair.

Now Ayana really felt silly. Not only had he brought her breakfast, but he had also picked her clothes off the floor and folded them. "Thanks," she said, walking over to the chair, picking up her top and slipping it on.

"You were sleeping so peacefully that I didn't want to wake you. I'm an early riser. It doesn't matter what time I go to bed, I'm always up between six and six-thirty. As a kid, my mom would wake us up an hour before school so that we could do our morning chores. Guess the habit of waking up early never wore off."

"What were your morning chores?"

"We had to make our beds and feed and walk the dog. Before getting ready for school."

"I always wanted a dog growing up, but my mother was allergic to them. What type of dog did you have?"

"A Siberian husky."

"Oh, a snow dog. I love huskies. The first one I ever saw was on television. As you can imagine, that type of dog is rare around here."

"Yeah, who ever heard of a husky living on an island?" He chuckled. "So, are you hungry?"

"Starving. What do we have?" she asked, peering at the tray.

"Cod fish, ackee, callaloo, johnnycakes and Blue Mountain coffee, of course."

She raised her eyebrow, amazed at his culinary talents. "You cooked all that?"

Brandon started smiling. "Well…no, I didn't. Marigold did."

"Marigold!"

"Yes, this bungalow is on her property. She and my brother bought this place years ago. They used to rent out the bungalow during the high-tourist months. After my brother died, she decided that she didn't want to be bothered dealing with renters, so she just leaves it empty for when I come to town. She lives in the main house."

Ayana was half listening as he spoke. She had something else on her mind. "You told Marigold about last night?" Ayana was totally embarrassed. Although she was a grown woman who could do as she pleased, she didn't want her friend thinking that she slept with men on the first date.

"Don't worry. She thinks it's all for me. She knows

I'm a big eater. Marigold makes me breakfast every day before she leaves for the shelter. She's gone to work already and didn't ask any questions before she left. Our secret is safe." He put the tray on the bed and sat down. "Come on. Let's eat before it gets cold."

Ayana sat next to him, took a fork and dug in. She loved her native cuisine and didn't edit her eating habits when she was home. "So what's on your agenda today?" she asked, in between bites.

"I thought we'd tool around the island. You could show me some of your favorite places—that is, if you're not busy."

It had been years since a man wanted to spend quality time with her and it felt good. "No, I'm not busy. I need to call home first and let my mother know I'm all right."

"That's sweet."

"What?"

"Letting your mother know you're okay, so she won't worry. I can't believe that brassy Saturday Knight has to call home like a teenager with a curfew."

"I really should have called her last night but…" She blushed just thinking about their heated lovemaking session. "I was preoccupied."

"That's an understatement."

Ayana went into the living room, where her purse was, took out her cell phone and made the call.

Brandon could hear her telling her mother a little white lie.

"Hey, Mom. I just wanted to let you know that I stayed at CeDe's last night. Hope you didn't worry too much. We're going to hang out today. I'll be home later. Okay. 'Bye."

When she came back into the room, Brandon said, "I didn't mean to eavesdrop, but didn't your mom see me pick you up last night?"

"No, she wasn't at home. She and my father had gone over to my uncle's for dinner. I don't like lying to her, but my parents are old-fashioned. I would want them to meet you and spend some time with you before I announced that I'm sleeping over at your place."

Brandon looked stunned.

She noticed the strange look on his face. "Don't panic. I'm not saying I want to introduce you to my parents. I'm just saying I'm not going to announce that I slept with a man they don't know. You might find this hard to believe, but they still look at me like I'm their little girl."

"I understand." He picked up his fork and began eating.

Suddenly there was an awkward silence between them. Ayana sipped her coffee and stared out at the ocean. After a few moments, she was the first to speak.

"Actually, I'm going to take a rain check on today. I really need to get back home and check on my dad."

"Oh, okay," he said, sounding a bit disappointed.

"Look, Brandon, I think we might have moved a little too fast. Last night was great, but let's not pretend we're a couple. We don't have to spend the day together. I'm sure you have other things to do," she said, sounding more like Saturday Knight than Ayana. Though she had been looking forward to spending more time with him, she didn't want him to feel obligated. The look on his face when she'd mentioned her parents being old-fashioned and wanting to meet her potential suitor told her that Brandon was uncomfortable with that idea. And she had to admit it was too soon to make any formal introductions, if he even met them at all.

"Aren't you going to finish eating before you leave?" he asked, looking at her half-eaten food.

Ayana had lost her appetite. "No, I'm full. I'm going to get ready to go so I can get out of your way."

"You don't have to rush off. There's no hurry."

She stood up. "I really need to get going." Ayana didn't have anything to rush home to, but she wanted to get out of there and fast. She had given the impression that he *had* to meet her parents, which wasn't true. Ayana was now feeling like one of those needy chicks who force-fed their families to a man on the first date. She was anything but needy, and she wanted to redeem herself. Fleeing the scene would send the message that she wasn't trying to latch on to him.

"I'll drive you back."

"You don't have to do that. I'll call CeDe. My mother will be full of questions if she sees you, and I'm not ready to introduce you," Ayana replied, reiterating her point.

"Ayana, I don't have a problem driving you home, but if you insist…"

"I do. What's the address here?"

He gave her the address, and she walked back into the living room and called her friend.

Then she showered and dressed in less than ten minutes. When she reentered the bedroom, Brandon was standing at the window looking out at the ocean. "I'm leaving now. Thanks for a nice evening."

He turned around. "Come here."

When she got within reaching distance, he pulled her close and covered her in a huge hug. "Can I call you?"

"Don't feel obligated."

"I don't feel obligated. I want to see you again."

Ayana stood still within his embrace. She was confused. One minute they were sharing a tender moment, and the next there was an underlying tension. In New York, Ayana was a brazen city girl, but in her hometown she was a traditional country girl. Blurring the lines had caused friction between them, and now she felt the need to pull back. "Brandon, I'm going to be busy for the next few days."

"Uh, okay."

Standing face-to-face, neither said a word. What had started off as a great morning and a potentially better day had soured into a misunderstanding, with neither really to blame. The sound of a blaring horn broke the silence.

"That's CeDe. See you around," she said and left without a kiss goodbye.

When she was gone, Brandon sat on the edge of the bed. "Damn, what happened?" he said out loud. His plans for the day had quickly fizzled out. Brandon was enjoying Ayana; she was completely different from Saturday Knight. He had been looking forward to getting to know her better but hadn't expected her to drop the parent bomb. Maybe she was right about them moving too fast.

Chapter 13

"Why ya so quiet?" Cedella asked Ayana as they drove along with the windows rolled down and the morning breeze flowing through the compact car.

Ayana didn't answer right away. She was still reeling from the unnecessary exchange with Brandon. She wanted to stay, but the tension between them had made her feel uncomfortable. "I'm not quiet."

"Ya no say more dan two words since ya been in da car. Wat's up? I see ya still have on da clothes from last night, so I guess ya spend da night wit ya boyfriend." CeDe always said exactly what was on her mind.

"Brandon's not my boyfriend," Ayana snapped.

"But ya did spend da night wit him? No?" she said, cutting her eyes at Ayana.

"Yes, I did. So what? We are both consenting adults."

"Since ya got some, ya should be beamin'. Why ya

sounding so mad? What him do? Tell ya to leave once da sheets cooled off?"

"Absolutely not!" Ayana exhaled hard and put her arms across her chest. "If I'd known you'd quiz me all the way to my house, I would have called a taxi. That way I wouldn't have to play twenty questions with you," she said, totally annoyed.

"Calm down. I'm just asking. We used to be able to talk 'bout anyting. Why ya actin' so defensive?"

Ayana looked out the window at the lush landscape and thought about what had transpired with Brandon. Maybe she'd blown the whole thing out of proportion. Maybe she needed another opinion on what had just happened. "I'm sorry for snapping at you. Last night was wonderful, but this morning, when I mentioned how old-fashioned my parents are and said that they like to meet the guys I go out with, his whole attitude changed."

"Oh, me word, chile! Ya know better than ta mention anyting about family ta men, especially in da beginnin'. Dey tink we tryin' ta trap dem in a relationship, or worse…marriage."

Ayana sighed. "You're right. Well, it's not like I straight-out said for him to come and meet my parents."

"Don't matter. Menfolk don't tink like we do."

"True."

"I could tell by da way ya was looking at him last night dat ya really like the man. Dat's why me back off. Oderwise me would've been in him bed last night."

Ayana chuckled. "CeDe, you're too much. But you're right—I do really like him. I haven't been into a guy this much in a long time." Ayana saw no sense in denying the obvious.

"So whatcha gonna do about it, mon?"

"What do you mean?"

"I mean, ya gonna let a little misunderstanding get in da way of ya seeing him again?"

"Well, he did say he wanted to get together, but I told him I was busy."

"Chile, ya need to get unbusy. Dat's one fine man, and if ya don't stake ya claim, dhen some o'her woman will."

Ayana thought about what her friend was saying and knew she was right. Brandon was a catch and probably wouldn't be on the market for long. "I don't want to call him and seem desperate."

CeDe pondered the situation for a few seconds and then said, "Iggy is giving a beach party tonight and everybody's talkin' about it. Maybe he'll be dhere. Dat way ya can see him witout callin' for a date. And if him don't show up, at least ya can get your flirt on. Maybe ya meet someone else. Da party will be filled wit plenty of hot guys."

Iggy was a local event promoter and was known for his legendary beach parties, where the mandatory dress code was some form of beachwear. The women usually wore bikini tops with shorts, swimsuits underneath cover-ups or just swimsuits. Men came in various types of trunks, from traditional boxers, to Speedos, to G-string trunks that showcased their packages. The party was all-inclusive with conch, escovitch and curry goat served, along with plenty of rum punch, dark-and-stormy cocktails and Red Stripe. Live bands and deejays jammed until the break of dawn.

"That's a great idea. I'll definitely go." Ayana's mood

lightened. She didn't like the way she and Brandon had left things and wanted a do-over.

"Ya want me to pick ya up?" CeDe asked once they reached Ayana's parents' house.

"No, I'll drive. Thanks for the ride! See you later."

"Hey, Ma!" Ayana yelled as she entered her quaint childhood home.

"Whatcha doin' home? I thought you and CeDe were spendin' da day t'gether," her mother said, coming into the living room holding a freshly caught kingfish.

"We're going out tonight instead."

"I know CeDe's glad to have ya home. Ya two were thick as thieves growin' up."

"Yeah, we were. CeDe is still the same outspoken person she was when we were little. She says things most people only think."

The truth was, Ayana modeled some of Saturday Knight's characteristics after Cedella. The straight-talking tell-it-like-it-is persona that she displayed on the show was her version of CeDe, coupled with Ed's well-crafted brazen character.

"Yes, that's Cedella a'right. Ya hungry? I'm making kingfish stew."

"No, Ma. I'll be in my room."

Upstairs, her bedroom was still decorated in varying shades of pink and lavender, complete with twin beds and posters of boy bands from back in the day. Ayana rushed into the room and went straight to the closet. She combed through the racks looking for the perfect out-fit. Brandon had seen her as two polar opposites—the tempestuous star of *Divorced Divas* and the dutiful Ja-maican daughter. Tonight she planned on showing him a hybrid of the two—the sultry, au naturel temptress. After an hour of trying on various outfits, Ayana finally made a decision. Then she climbed into bed. She was exhausted from the night before; she and Brandon had done very little sleeping.

After her nap, Ayana showered and dressed for the evening in a pair of white short-shorts that looked more like panties than shorts and a string bikini top underneath a white T-shirt. She was excited at the possibility of seeing Brandon and was eager to get to the party. She told her parents that she would probably stay the night at CeDe's. Ayana wanted to cover all bases in case she ran into Brandon and they spent the night together again. She didn't want a replay of earlier.

When she reached the beach, the sun was setting, creating a beautiful kaleidoscope of oranges, reds and yellows. Ayana parked in the packed parking lot, got out and made her way to the equally packed beach. The party was filled with scandalously clad bodies gyrating barefoot on the sand to a steel band jamming to a reggae beat. Ayana stood on the raised concrete sidewalk and looked over the sea of red, green and yellow knit caps bobbing up and down to the music, trying to spot Brandon, but she didn't see him. She took off her sandals, put them in her tote bag and made her way onto the sand to get a closer look.

"Hey, Mama, ya lookin' mighty fine tonight. Let's dance," said a buffed, bare-chested man with dreadlocks.

"Uh, sure, why not?" She didn't really want to dance with him, but she did want to get in the middle of the crowd without drawing attention to herself.

He took her hand and they wove their way to the

middle of the dance area, where sweaty bodies were working to the beat. A woman wearing a thong bikini was clapping her butt cheeks to the music. Her dance partner had his phone in the air, taping her. After the song ended, Ayana told Mr. Dreadlocks thanks and left the dance area.

She moseyed through the party, casually searching for Brandon and Cedella, but she didn't run into either of them. She went to the grass-hut bar, ordered a stout and waited, hoping that he would show up. Two beers later, and still no Brandon. She left the bar and moved on. Across from the bar, a wet T-shirt contest was getting under way.

The emcee was on a raised platform with the microphone in his hand and asking for contestants. Several women in the crowd hopped onstage, eager to show their goods. Out of the corner of her eye, Ayana thought she saw Brandon. She slowly turned to her left, and there he was, standing in the crowd. But he didn't see her.

Let me show him what I'm working with, she said to herself. Ayana took a deep breath, swallowed her inhibitions, bolted through the crowd and leaped onstage. She set her purse to the side and joined the other women.

"Okay, ladies, are ya ready?" the emcee asked.

In unison they all said, "Yes!"

Ayana tied a knot in her T-shirt, exposing her taut belly and making her skimpy outfit even more revealing.

"Me gonna need the first tree ladies front and center." When the women stepped forward, the emcee continued. "Where's da Hose Mon?"

A bare-chested man wearing a Speedo appeared at the front of the stage holding a green water hose.

"Ya ready?"

The crowd yelled, "Ya, mon!"

"Okay, Hose Mon, hose dem down."

The man holding the hose turned on the water and sprayed the first three contestants. The women screamed when the ice-cold water hit their bodies. The water assault lasted only a few seconds, but it was long enough to thoroughly drench them.

"Dat's good." The emcee signaled the Hose Man to turn off the water. "Now, ladies, strut yo stuff."

The women went into action, smoothing down their T-shirts and pressing the wet material, showcasing their breasts. The first contestant had a small chest and didn't elicit much response from the crowd. The second woman had on a swimsuit underneath her T-shirt, so nothing was exposed. The third contestant had fake boobs that jutted out from underneath her T-shirt like parking cones. The crowd had a mixed response.

"Lade Numbar Tree, step to da side. Da rest of ya can leave da stage," the emcee said, weeding out the losers. "Now me gonna need da next tree ladies."

Ayana was in this group. She felt nervous. She had never done anything like this before. She looked out over the crowd, making sure that Brandon was still there, and he was. *Showtime,* she said to herself. Ayana was going to work her magic and get their romance back on track.

"Hose Mon, wet 'em down," the emcee announced again.

When the water jetted out, Ayana didn't flinch. She stood there with her hands on her hips like a gladiator ready for battle. When the stream of water stopped, she pressed down on her T-shirt using her hands like a squeegee and stood with her legs spread apart as the water dripped down her thighs. She rubbed the wet material that covered her breasts, but nothing showed through since she was wearing a bikini top.

People started chanting, "Take it off! Take it off!" as they pumped their fists in the air.

The energy emanating from the crowd spurred her on. Ayana reached underneath her wet shirt, untied her bikini top, took it off and tossed it into the crowd. A woman caught it and started swinging the wet top in the air, slinging drips of water with each turn of her wrist. Ayana was in a zone. She closed her eyes and began slowly and sensuously massaging her breasts, focusing on her engorged nipples. The crowd went wild.

She opened her eyes and looked dead into Brandon's handsome face. He had moved from the middle of the crowd and was now standing at the front of the stage. Watching him watch her was making Ayana hot with desire. She kneaded her nipples harder and rotated her hips at the same time, exaggerating her moves like a porn star. The crowd roared!

"Now, dat's what me talkin' 'bout," the emcee said.

The other two contestants were up next, but their performances paled in comparison to Ayana's. When they finished, the emcee told them to step down from the stage, and then he continued. "Lade Numbar Tree, come here." The contestant from the first round stepped up and stood next to Ayana. "When me put me hand above dey head, me want ya to clap. Da lade wit de most claps wins."

He placed his hand above the first woman, and she

received a fair share of claps. He then put his hand over Ayana's head and the crowd started clapping, screaming, yelling and stomping their feet. "I tink we got a winner." He placed a gold tiara on her head. "Congratulations. I crown you Da Queen of Da Wet T-Shirt." She curtsied, blew a few kisses, picked up her bag and left the stage.

Ayana's instant fan club encircled her the second she stepped down, some of the men trying to swipe a feel. She maneuvered out of their grasps, looking for Brandon, but she didn't see him. He was there one second and gone the next.

Damn. Where did he go? Ayana's heart began to sink. Her raunchy display had been to entice him. Obviously, it hadn't worked. He had left and now she felt like a fool. She took the crown off, put it in her tote and slunk through the crowd, feeling defeated even though she had won. As she was walking, someone grabbed her arm from behind. Ayana assumed it was another admirer trying to get her attention. She wasn't in the mood to entertain a stranger. All she wanted to do was go home, get in bed and forget about this night. She'd had enough. If the wet T-shirt contest didn't get Brandon's attention, then nothing would. Ayana swung around to tell whoever was tugging at her to get lost. She turned quickly, breaking the hold the person had on her.

"And where are you going, Queen of the Wet T-Shirts?"

It was Brandon.

Chapter 14

Brandon stood in front of Ayana, staring at the wet T-shirt that was now molded around her breasts, accentuating her nipples. He was finding it hard to keep his eyes focused on her face. As he spoke, his eyes kept darting from her eyes to her chest. Her near nakedness had him mesmerized.

"So, where are you off to in such a hurry?" he asked.

Ayana seemed to notice him staring at her body. She arched her back, suggestively poking her boobs farther out.

"I'm going over to the bar to get something to drink," she replied.

"Mind if I join you?"

"Of course not."

Ayana led the way. Brandon watched her sway her hips from side to side as she moved. He couldn't help but stare at her round rear end in the short-shorts. When they reached the grass-hut bar, people were hanging out, drinking and dancing in the sand.

"Are you having a stout?" he asked.

"Yes, and a shot of rum."

He ordered two shots and two beers. "Here you go," he said, handing her the drinks.

Ayana wasted no time shooting back the rum and chasing it with the beer.

"You want another round?" Brandon asked, looking amazed at how fast she'd drunk the shot and beer.

"Yes, I'd love another round," she said, suggestively licking her lips.

He motioned for the bartender and ordered a second round. "Here you go, Queen of the Wet T-Shirts," he said, handing her the drinks. "Hey, where's your tiara? You deserved to win and should show it off."

Ayana dug the crown out of her bag and placed it on her head, cocking it to the side. "Did you enjoy the contest?"

"Yes, I did. You were amazing. The other contestants didn't stand a chance."

Ayana blushed. "Thanks."

He peered at her shirt again. "Looks like you're drying off."

"Can't let that happen." She bolted back the shot and beer. "Come on—let's go swimming, so I can get wet again." She winked, hoping he'd get the double entendre.

Her words didn't go unnoticed. He smiled, glad that they were on the same page. He didn't like the way things had ended earlier and was eager to start over. "Wet is always good." Brandon wasted no time finishing his drink. He tossed their empty bottles in a trash can, grabbed her hand and led the way through the revelers. They trotted along the shore, down the beach and away from the crowd of people. He wanted to be alone with her without prying eyes watching their every move.

Once they reached a secluded area, he stopped and faced her. He took her face in his hands, looked deeply into her eyes, pulled her to him and said, "I've always wanted to make love to a queen on a beach."

She reached up and wrapped her arms around his neck. "Your wish is my command."

Brandon stepped closer into her embrace and planted his full lips on hers. He slipped his tongue in her mouth and started rotating his hips, grinding his pelvis into hers, intensifying their connection even more.

His manhood rapidly responded, growing inch by inch. He ran his fingers through her hair, bringing her head closer to his. He abandoned her mouth and tenderly kissed her forehead, nose, cheeks and chin. As he covered her face with a series of tender kisses, her crown slipped off.

"Let's go skinny-dipping," she whispered in his ear. "You've got me on fire." Ayana peeled off her T-shirt and shorts and tossed them on the sand.

Brandon untied the string to his trunks and let them slip off, exposing his semierect manhood. "See what you do to me?" he said, stroking himself.

She knelt down on the sand, grabbed the backs of his thighs and brought him closer. Ayana took hold of his penis and kissed the head. She alternated between kissing and licking, flicking her tongue, teasing him with each sensuous stroke.

Brandon closed his eyes and enjoyed her oral talents. After a few minutes of pleasure, he bent down and took her by the elbows, bringing her to her feet. Brandon was on the verge of climaxing but wasn't ready to come yet. He wanted to prolong their foreplay for as long as he could. "Come on."

They raced toward the water, hand in hand, and jumped into the pitch-black ocean, which looked like a Texas oil slick. Ayana splashed the water toward him, creating a rush of waves. Brandon waded in her direction, bobbing and weaving, trying to avoid the onslaught. Once he reached her, he engulfed her in a bear hug and then lifted her high in the air.

Ayana wrapped her legs around his waist, positioning her vagina near his penis. She moved her body rapidly against his, her breasts bouncing up and down with each move.

Brandon took hold of her ass, squeezing her cheeks, bringing her closer. His manhood was like a guiding rod, heading straight to her waiting opening. Entering her sent chills all over his body. His desire for her was stronger than before. He pumped harder and harder, letting the buoyancy of the water aid their synchronized moves. "Oh, baby...you feel like...like..."

"Heaven," she said, completing his sentence.

They rode the waves, holding on and giving in to each other with everything they had. The moon broke through the clouds and beamed a bright ray down on their naked bodies as they each reached a much-anticipated climax.

"That was too good," Ayana said, totally spent.

He held her around her waist, steadying her until she found her balance. "It was better than good."

They held on to each other, ambling arm in arm back

to shore, both weak in the knees. Once they reached the cool sand, they collapsed, consumed from their heated passion. The misunderstanding from earlier was now completely washed away.

Chapter 15

The early-morning sky was pink with shades of lavender streaking through low-hanging clouds as the sun slowly made its appearance. Teal-blue water lapped softly at the shore, creating a melodic rhythm. The beach was serene. Gone were the party revelers from the night before. Brandon was the first to stir. He stretched his long limbs before sitting up. Ayana was still asleep, curled up next to him, looking like a big baby in her birthday suit. He stared at her naked body, admiring her beauty. Her skin was as smooth as satin. Her hair, wet from the ocean, had dried, creating a mass of spiral curls cascading around her head. Their spontaneous romp in the ocean had been both exhilarating and exhausting. They had collapsed on the sand and fallen into a deep sleep before either put on clothes. Brandon's trunks were lying on the sand beside Ayana's clothes and crown. The mere sight of the crown brought a smile to his face. Remembering how brazen Ayana had been onstage, massaging her breasts and showcasing her assets in the wet T-shirt contest, was getting him excited all over again. He could feel his manhood awakening, rising to attention.

Brandon looked around the beach, checking to see if anyone else was wandering about. The strand was deserted with no one in sight. He lay back down and snuggled up close to Ayana, his penis pressing against her bare backside. Brandon reached around, placed his hands on her breasts and began massaging the soft tissue, rubbing her nipples at the same time until they firmed to his touch. He moved her hair out of the way and started sucking her earlobe and then kissing the side of her neck. She began to stir.

Ayana could feel the touch of Brandon in her sleep and thought she was dreaming, but this dream seemed too real. She opened her eyes and saw his hands on her breasts.

"I see somebody has an insatiable appetite," she said, slightly turning her head toward him. She looked over his shoulder to see if anyone was watching them, but no one was within eyesight.

He moved her body closer to his. "You're right. I just can't get enough of you."

With her butt firmly against his crotch, she could feel his thick rod inching between her thighs, making its way to her V-spot, which was getting wetter and wetter by the second. The head of his penis pressed urgently against the lips of her vagina. The feel of him trying to enter her sugar walls made her back arch with desire as they did a sensuous grind, teasing one another with every move.

Brandon turned her over onto her back and moved his body on top of hers, wedging himself between her thighs.

Her toes dug into the sand as she spread her legs apart, allowing him easier access. Ayana wrapped her arms around his back and held on as he made his way into her slippery canal. The sensation of his manhood filling her was exhilarating and sent chills all over her body. She bit her bottom lip to keep from screaming out as she neared orgasm.

He increased his pace, holding on to her, pumping harder and stronger.

As if on cue, the sun broke through the clouds at the precise moment of their dual climax, creating the perfect crescendo to their early-morning loving.

"Now, that was the perfect wake-up call," Ayana said, sitting up and brushing the sand out of her hair.

"Yes, it was." Brandon sat up too and looked down the beach. In the distance, he could see someone walking toward them. "We'd better get out of here." He handed Ayana her clothes. They quickly dressed and made their way back to where the party had been.

"Wait! My crown." Ayana ran as fast as the sand would allow and picked up the golden symbol of her victory. A victory in more than one way—not only had she won the contest, but she'd also won over Brandon. A broad smile spread across her face as she raced back to him.

"Are you hungry?" he asked.

"Yes. I'm starving!"

"I know a great little café not too far from here that serves the best breakfast."

"Sounds good." Ayana wanted to go home first so she could shower and change clothes, but she didn't want to break the momentum. The morning had started off on a good note and she planned on keeping it that way.

"Do you need to…?" He was going to ask if she had to call home before going out, but he caught himself. Brandon didn't want to ruin the day like last time, so he kept his mouth shut.

"What did you say?"

"Uh, I was going to ask if you needed to shower before we have breakfast. If so, we can go back to my place if you want."

"Yes, that sounds good," she said, brushing sand from her arms.

"I drove if you need a ride," he offered.

"I drove too. I'll follow you."

"Okay."

Brandon led the way to the parking lot, where only five cars remained. He walked Ayana to her car, then returned to his rented Fiat, got in and drove off. The ride back to the bungalow was short. He bypassed the main house, where Marigold lived, and pulled around back to the bungalow. He got out, went to Ayana's car, opened the door and helped her out.

Ayana looked around the quiet bungalow. A part of her wondered if Brandon brought other women here. He was such an attractive man who could easily be a player, even though he didn't seem like the type. She casually scanned the room for any evidence of another woman but didn't see anything out of the ordinary. *Stop being paranoid. Obviously he's into you.* Ayana didn't know where these feelings of paranoia were coming from. Probably from the fact that they were bonding really well and she didn't want someone else infringing on her territory.

"You want to shower together?" she asked, walking up close and rubbing her chest against his. Even though they had just made love on the beach less than thirty minutes ago, she was ready for more. Ayana wanted to make sure she was the only woman he craved.

"Hmm, that's a brilliant idea." He lifted her arms over her head and removed her shirt, then leaned down and nibbled on her nipples. "Come on. I'm feeling really dirty," he said, arching his eyebrows.

Ayana took off her shorts and followed him to the bathroom. The previous time she had been there, she had showered in record time, anxious to go home after their disagreement. This morning was completely different. The last thing she wanted was to make a hasty exit.

Brandon turned on the water and then removed his trunks. He stepped in first, the pulsating water beating down on his back as he helped her in. "Turn around."

Ayana moved so that her chest was facing the shower wall. She lifted her arms and put her hands against the pink tiles, slightly spread her legs and waited in heated anticipation for his next move.

Brandon stood and watched as the water dripped down her back and eased between the crack of her butt. "I wish I were that water," he whispered in her ear.

She turned her head over her shoulder and said, "What do you mean?"

He stared intently at her rear end, admiring the view.

"If I were the shower water, I would be dripping all over your body, exploring your hidden treasures."

"You don't have to be water to drip all over me and explore my treasures." She reached for his hand and placed it on her round ass.

Brandon palmed her butt cheeks, caressing them with tenderness. He gently spread them apart, placed his slate-hard cock in between her cheeks and slowly started grinding against her.

Ayana rotated her hips, matching his movements, waiting for him to enter her from behind, but he was taking his time. His slow-motion grind was driving her wild, making her want him badly. She closed her eyes, held on to the shower wall and moaned. "Ohhh...you're making...me...so hot."

He kissed the back of her neck. "Why? We're just taking a shower, that's all." Brandon reached for a bottle in the shower caddy, squirted her back with shower gel and rubbed the substance until it began to lather. He lathered her entire body before putting the bottle back. He slipped his hands over her breasts, down her stomach and in between her legs.

She gasped.

Brandon searched for her clit. Once he found the tiny piece of flesh, he began rubbing his thumb against her pleasure point. He continued rubbing and rubbing and rubbing, increasing the pace until she screamed out.

He bent her forward and began entering her from behind. Even though they had made love earlier, she was still tight, making him work for penetration. Once the tip of his penis was inside her, he pumped slowly, inching himself all the way in. "You feel so good," he said, putting his arms around her waist and pulling her in even closer.

Brandon had been with a fair share of women in his lifetime, but Ayana was by far the best lover he'd ever had. He couldn't get enough of her. Brandon could feel himself falling in love, and it wasn't solely about the sex. Ayana was a good woman. Seeing her outside of New York had shed a new light on the person he knew as Saturday Knight. He tried to hold back, but his body was giving in to her.

They came simultaneously underneath the pulsating water.

"Now, that's what I call a shower," he said.

"I couldn't agree more."

After spending another few minutes showering, they stepped out, toweled off, made their way to the bedroom, fell into bed and passed out. After a few hours of sleep, Brandon made a food run to the main house. Since Marigold was at the shelter, there were no queries to answer while he made two of everything—two jerk-chicken sandwiches on coco bread, two tropical-fruit salads, two slices of rum cake and two ginger beers.

When he got back to the bungalow, Ayana was still curled up underneath the sheet asleep. Brandon didn't wake her. He ate in silence and watched her rest. They never made it out of the bungalow. They spent the rest of the day in bed, eating, sleeping and making love.

Chapter 16

"Of course I'm not dead. I almost checked out, but I had a guardian angel looking out for me. If it weren't for Saturday acting as fast as she did, I would be on the other side, chatting with the Big Guy now." Ed was on the phone talking to Steve, a producer on the show. After two weeks, he was still in the hospital but out of ICU. He had defied the doctor's prognosis and was making a miraculous recovery despite a few setbacks. Once out of ICU, Ed had instructed his assistant to send Saturday three dozen deep pink roses to her apartment as a small token of appreciation for saving his life.

"You can say that again. She jumped into action performing CPR without a second thought. Who knew she'd be the one to resuscitate you? With her bad attitude, I would've thought she was the type of woman to stand by chatting away on her cell phone while someone else did the heavy lifting." Steve had witnessed Saturday's antics up close on the set and wasn't a fan.

Ed didn't say anything right away. He was beginning to feel bad for letting everyone think that the persona he had invented was real. Ayana Lewis was nothing like Saturday Knight. Ayana was sweet and kindhearted, whereas Saturday was just the opposite. He started to tell Steve the truth but didn't want to chance destroying what he had created. The audience loved to hate Saturday, which kept them watching to see what outlandish thing she was going to do or say next. The television business was all about high ratings, and Ed planned to keep his show among the top reality shows for as long as he could.

"Well, you never know who a person really is, now do you?" Ed finally said.

"I guess you're right."

"Mr. Levine, how many times do I have to tell you that cell phones aren't allowed in the hospital?" the nurse said, coming into his private room.

Ed rolled his eyes in her direction. "Steve, I have to go. Nurse Ratched just came in." He disconnected the call and put the phone inside the nightstand.

"I see the heart attack hasn't affected your smart mouth," she shot back.

"Darling Nurse Ratched, I was born with sassiness and will die with sassiness," he said, fingering the pink feather boa that was tied around his neck.

"For the umpteenth time, my name is Nurse Rachel." She walked over to him, flipped back the covers and placed a stethoscope on his chest to listen to his heartbeat.

"Rachel, Ratched, what's the difference?" Ed teased.

Being laid up in the hospital was a bore to him, so he found amusement in ribbing the nurses, and Nurse Rachel—an older, motherly type—was his favorite.

She didn't respond. Most of the time she just ignored him and did her job. She stuck the ends of the stethoscope into her ears and listened.

"How's the old ticker beating?"

"Strong, for someone who had a heart attack less than a month ago and had all the complications that you've had. You're lucky to be alive."

"I was born lucky. So when do I blow this joint?"

She checked his blood pressure, then answered. "Soon, I hope," she said, throwing him a smart line of her own. "But you'll have to discuss that with your doctor."

"When is he coming in? I'm ready to go home. I've had enough of this depressing scene. There are too many sick people in here for my taste."

"This is a hospital. Not that you would notice with all these flowers, balloons and cards everywhere," she said, pointing to the arrangements of roses, gardenias, irises and birds-of-paradise in decorative vases sitting all around the room. Balloons of varying sizes floated on colorful strings, and get-well cards were thumb-tacked to the walls.

"What can I say? I'm well loved by all," he said, with a Cheshire-cat grin.

"Okay, Mr. Well Loved. No more cell phone calls, *especially* business calls. You are still recovering and don't need any added stress, especially if you want to go home."

Ed looked out the window, seemingly ignoring her advice. He felt great, almost 100 percent. He had a show to get back on track and was ready to return to work, even if it only meant calling the shots over the phone.

She snapped her fingers in his direction. "Do you hear me?"

"Of course I hear you. I had a heart attack. I didn't have a cochlear implant for hearing loss," he shot back.

Nurse Rachel shook her head at him as if he were a naughty little boy. "Now open your mouth so I can take your temperature." She stuck the thermometer in his mouth, waited a few moments, took it out and looked at the reading. "All your vitals are normal, so hopefully you'll be out of my hair soon."

"Here's hoping."

"And remember no more cell phone calls. If I see you talking on that thing again, I will have to take it. Understood?"

"Whatever you say, Nurse Ratched."

She rolled her eyes at him and walked out.

Ed waited a few minutes to see if she was going to return. When she didn't come back, he retrieved the phone out of the nightstand, turned his back to the door and made a call. "Hi, it's me again," he said, talking to Steve. "Listen, I want you to call the cast and crew and get them to the penthouse. Since production of the show is on hold momentarily, I want to do a type of reunion show...a special."

"Are you sure? Reunion shows are taped at the end of the season," Steve said.

"I know when they're taped. I want to keep the audience interested in *Divorced Divas,* and running a series of reruns is getting boring. Lying here in this bed, I've been watching the same episodes over and over. If I'm bored with my own show, I'm sure the audience is tuning out. A reunion-type show where we not only focus on this season, but also show some behind-the-scenes clips from last season would pump some energy back into the series. Plus, it's different, and I thrive on being different."

"Now that I think about it, a reunion show would be a good idea."

"Of course it would. We'll call it a *Divorced Divas Divulge* special, not to be confused with the regular reunion show. Now get in touch with the cast and crew and have them report to the penthouse day after to-morrow."

"So soon?"

"Yes. The sooner the better."

"Will you be out of the hospital by then?"

"I plan to be, and if I'm not, I'll leave you with ex-plicit instructions as to how I want the cast to behave." Ed turned back toward the door and saw Nurse Rachel coming down the hall in his direction with a scowl on her face. "I have to go, but be sure to call everyone pronto."

"Okay, you got it," Steve said and hung up.

Ed returned the phone to the nightstand, fluffed up his pillow and laid his head back as if he were resting. He felt better already. Getting *Divorced Divas* back on track was better than any medicine the doctor could prescribe.

Chapter 17

Brandon held on to Ayana's waist as she steered her canary-yellow Vespa through a narrow, tree-lined road. He sat on the back of the scooter with his legs anchored around hers and enjoyed the sights. She was taking him to one of her favorite places—an isolated spot high in the Blue Mountains. As they wove through the secluded mountainside, Brandon gazed up at the trees and spotted one unique-looking bird after another. Some were resting on branches, while others soared through the cloudless blue sky. As many times as he'd been to Jamaica, Brandon had never ventured into these parts before, and he found the journey relaxing.

The day after their indoor lovefest, Ayana had suggested they get out of the house and have a picnic. She had gone home, cooked up a feast, packed it in plastic containers, placed them in the wicker basket on the front of her motorbike, then made her way back to his bungalow. Brandon was surprised to see her zip up the driveway on the scooter, looking carefree with her hair blowing behind her. Initially he was apprehensive about getting on the back because he had never ridden on a motorcycle with a woman before. Not that this was a heavy-duty Harley, but nevertheless, he was hesitant. Ayana assured him that she had been driving a scooter since she was a teenager, which was the best way to get around the island. After some cajoling, he'd agreed and hopped on the back.

"How much longer until we get there?" he asked, looking over her shoulder at the winding road ahead.

"Another few minutes," she answered, slightly turning her head so that he could hear her over the hum of the motor.

"Not that I'm complaining. I like being snuggled close to you," he said, gripping her a little tighter.

Although he couldn't see her face, Ayana was smiling brightly, showing all of her front teeth. She was enjoying being close to him too. Spending the past couple of days with Brandon had been like a vacation within a vacation. They'd been inseparable since the beach party, and she couldn't have been happier. The show's unexpected hiatus had turned into a positive situation for her. Even though it had been only a couple of days, Ayana was falling hard for Brandon. Not only was he an excellent lover, but he also was kind and considerate, a true gentleman. A part of her wanted to pull back and not expose all of her cards, and a part of her wanted to go full throttle and tell him exactly what she was feeling. She knew some men scared easily when confronted with honest emotions, but something told her that Brandon wasn't the squeamish type.

"We're here," she said, pulling over to the side of the road and turning off the motor.

Brandon swung his leg over the scooter, got off, then helped Ayana. He looked around and saw nothing but a mass of trees. "Where exactly are we supposed to have a picnic? I don't see any grass."

"We're gonna climb a tree and eat perched on a branch like squirrels." She laughed.

He came up, tickled the sides of her waist and said, "Oh, I see you think you're funny."

"Stop, stop. I'm ticklish," she said, batting his hands away and laughing.

Brandon went over to the scooter, unhooked the basket and held it in his hand. "So, where are we going?"

"Follow me."

"Are you sure we're not eating in the trees?" he said, looking around at the dense foliage, which resembled a forest preserve.

"No. Come on, silly." Ayana followed a dirt path through the trees, leading the way. She walked a few yards until they reached a clearing. The patch of land looked like a well-manicured grassy knoll surrounded by lush trees.

"What a view," Brandon said, stepping onto the grass and looking out into the distance. From this elevated vantage point, he could see the ocean, which resembled a beautiful, faceted aquamarine, sparkling beneath the midday sun.

"It's amazing, isn't it? This is one of my favorite places on the island."

Brandon put down the picnic basket. "How did you find this place? It's so far off the beaten path."

"I used to come here as a kid with my parents." Ayana went over to the basket, took out a red-green-and-gold-plaid blanket and spread it over the grass. She bent over and untied her beige Timberlands, which she wore with her favorite pair of cutoff blue jean shorts and a pink ribbed tank top, and took them off.

Brandon kicked off his sandals, squatted down on the blanket and flipped open the top of the basket. "What have we here?" he asked, looking inside. He took out four plastic containers and a silver thermos and placed them on the blanket.

Ayana sat next to him and took out two plates, forks and napkins. "I made curry lobster, cabbage with carrots, plantains and beef patties."

"Wow! You made all of this?"

"Yes, I did. Why do you sound so surprised?"

"No offense, but you don't look like the cooking type."

"How many times do I have to tell you that looks are deceiving? I've been cooking ever since I can remember. My mom had me in the kitchen learning how to cook before I started kindergarten. The first dish I ever made was Hawaiian salad."

"Hawaiian salad in Jamaica?"

"Yes, because it's so easy to make, even a five-year-old couldn't mess it up. My parents acted like it was the best thing they'd ever had, and…" Ayana suddenly stopped talking. She realized this was the second mention of her parents, and she didn't want Brandon thinking she was going down the "meet the folks" road again. She didn't want to scare him off.

"And I'm sure it was delicious to them. My parents were the same way. The first time I made them breakfast in bed for their anniversary, I burned the toast and bacon, undercooked the eggs and made watery coffee that looked like tea. I was so proud of myself, and they ate every single bite, like it was brunch at the Four Seasons."

Ayana listened and couldn't believe he was bringing up his parents. *Maybe he's not paranoid about meeting my folks after all,* she thought. Brandon was talking freely. However, she was being cautious, so she just listened as she fixed their plates. "Here you go."

Brandon took the plate and tasted the food. "Hmm, this is delicious."

"Thanks. I'm glad you like it."

He leaned over and kissed her on the lips. "I like it all right."

Ayana could hear her mother's voice in her head. *Da way to a man's heart is thru him stomach. Gurl, if ya wanna land a husband, ya need to learn how to cook.* Looking at the way Brandon was wolfing down her food, Ayana knew her mother was right. "I'm glad," she said, kissing him back.

They polished off lunch and then drank the ice-cold cucumber water she'd made. Brandon stretched out and laid his head in her lap. He looked up at the clear azure sky as a bright green bird with a pinch of crimson streaked across overhead.

"What was that?"

Ayana followed his gaze. "What? I didn't see anything."

"It looked like a parrot but smaller. On the way up here I saw amazing birds."

"You may not know this, but Jamaica is a bird-watcher's paradise. There are more than twenty-eight bird species on the island."

"And how do you know that?" He looked up at her, amazed at her knowledge.

"I was a member of the National Audubon Society. I love bird-watching. It's extremely relaxing."

"You are amazing," he said as he rubbed her leg. "I would have never in a million years thought that Saturday Knight would be a gourmet-cooking bird-watcher. And don't say it—I know, 'Looks are deceiving.'"

They both laughed.

Ayana rubbed his head, and at that moment, she felt close to him. He had shared history about his childhood without any prodding from her. She knew from past experience that when a man opened up freely, it was an indication that he was really into you. Ayana looked up at the sky and said a silent prayer of thanks. She was thankful to finally find a man who valued her as a person. Her ex-husband had wanted a trophy wife that he could control with his money. Brandon, however, seemed genuinely happy just to be in her presence. Again, Ayana contemplated telling Brandon that she was falling in love with him, but it was too soon for true confessions.

"Thanks," Brandon said, looking up into her face.

"For what?"

"For a delicious lunch and sharing your favorite place with me," he said, caressing her leg and snuggling deeper into her lap.

She leaned down and kissed his cheek. "You are more than welcome."

They lounged on the grassy knoll the remainder of

the afternoon until the sun began to set. This had been the perfect day. Good food, a good man and a picturesque view. Life couldn't get much better.

Chapter 18

Brandon was lounging in bed, gazing out the window at the flat calmness of the ocean. The day before, he and Ayana had spent a relaxing afternoon in the mountains, talking and sharing childhood memories. He was feeling closer and closer to her as the days went by. It had been a while since Brandon had been in a committed relationship, and he missed the intimacy that came from bonding with someone. He had thought Jaclene was *the* one, but she turned out to be an opportunist. When she realized that he couldn't help further her career, she dumped him. After that failed relationship, Brandon had focused his attention on work—until now. Although Ayana hadn't mentioned anything about becoming a couple, Brandon could tell by her actions—taking time to cook and giving of herself sexually—that she was becoming attached to him.

Lying in bed alone, with the cool morning breeze blowing through the sheer curtains, Brandon was missing Ayana. She had gone home the night before for a family dinner. She hadn't invited him, and he hadn't invited himself. After being around her and getting to know her better, Brandon was thinking about meeting her parents. As much as she tried not to talk about them, he could tell they were a big part of her life. He knew she shied away from mentioning them because of his initial reaction.

"Maybe I'll call and find out if she has any plans for the day," he said aloud, reaching for the phone.

Brandon looked at the time display on his cell phone; it wasn't even seven o'clock yet. "It's too early. I'm sure she's still asleep."

He put the phone on the bed, closed his eyes and reflected on his time with Ayana. His trip to Jamaica had had a singular purpose—to check on his sister-in-law. Brandon couldn't help but shake his head at the way life threw a curveball when you least expected it. Nearly running into Ayana with his Jet Ski, and her knowing Marigold was indeed fate. Now his Jamaican trip wasn't only about family; it was also about finding an unexpected love. Brandon's cell phone rang, interrupting his thoughts. He quickly picked the tiny gadget off the pillow, thinking it was Ayana.

"Hello?"

"Hey, Brandon, I've been trying to reach you since yesterday," Steve said the second Brandon picked up.

Brandon sat up against the headboard. "Hi, Steve. What's going on? Is Ed okay?" he asked, thinking maybe Ed had had another heart attack.

"Ed is fine. He's almost back to his normal self. He's

still in the hospital but wants everyone back on set tomorrow, so…"

"Tomorrow?" Brandon asked in alarm. Returning
to New York was the last thing on his mind. Being in
Jamaica with Ayana was exactly where he wanted to
be. They were becoming closer and closer every day
and he wanted to remain on the island paradise for as
long as possible.

"Yes, tomorrow. I left you a message yesterday. You
didn't listen to it?"

"No." Brandon hadn't bothered taking his cell phone
on the picnic. Since being on the island, he hadn't bothered much with the phone. It felt liberating to leave it
at home, something he could never do in New York.
He didn't have any pressing business, so he had only
checked his voice mail sporadically.

"Ed is planning a special reunion-type show and
wants the cast at the penthouse for rehearsal."

"A reunion show in the middle of the season? Isn't
that odd?"

"Well, it's not a reunion show per se. It's a *Divorced
Divas Divulge* special taping, and it will focus on this
season and never-before-seen scenes from last season.
Ed wants to revive the audience's interest in the show.
The reruns are bringing the ratings down, so it's a clever
idea."

"I guess you're right," Brandon said, sounding less
than excited.

"I've been in touch with everyone but Saturday. I'm
having a hard time reaching her. I've called and left
messages on her cell, but she hasn't called me back yet.
She's probably sitting in her dungeon brewing a batch
of witches' brew." He laughed.

"I'm sure that's not the case."

"Well, then, maybe she's flying around Manhattan on her broomstick," Steve said, continuing his insults.

"Man, give her a break. Did you ever think that maybe her wickedness is just an act?" Brandon said, coming to her defense.

"I don't think so. Her antics are too realistic to be an act. Anyway, do you know how to get in touch with her? I called Ed to see if he had another number for her, but he hasn't called me back yet."

Brandon thought for a second. He didn't want Steve thinking that he had a direct pipeline to Ayana. With what she had told him earlier about the cast and crew not being aware of her true identity, he didn't want to blow her cover. "I have a list of everyone's cell numbers. I'll give her a call, and maybe I'll get through."

"If you do, tell her she needs to be on the set tomorrow."

"Okay, will do," Brandon said and hung up.

Brandon got out of bed, showered and dressed. He made a cup of Blue Mountain coffee and drank it outside on the patio. It was still early, and he wanted to wait awhile before going over to Ayana's parents' house. He knew where they lived from when he had picked Ayana up for their first date. An hour later, he decided to make the drive.

When Brandon reached Ayana's parents' home, he saw her Vespa was parked out front. Looking at the yellow scooter brought a smile to his face as he thought about cruising through the mountains on the back, holding on to her slim waist. He got out of the car and rang the bell.

"Mornin'," an older, portly-looking woman said as she opened the door.

"Hi, I'm a friend of Sat…uh, I mean Ayana. Is she in?"

"Ya, she in da kitchen makin' breakfast. I'm her muther, Mrs. Tosh. Come in, chile," she said, opening the door wider and stepping aside. "Follow me."

Brandon walked through their quaint home, which was decorated with antiques, overstuffed furniture that was gently worn and traditional Jamaican artwork on the walls. The home was cozy and he got a warm, homey feeling just walking through.

"Ana, someone's here to see ya," her mother said, coming into the small kitchen.

Ayana was standing at the sink with her back to the door. She turned around and nearly dropped the plate she was holding. "Uh…Brandon, what are you doing here?" she asked with a shocked expression on her face.

"Is dat any way to talk to ya friend?" her mother said, scolding her daughter as if she were a five-year-old.

Ayana paused for a moment and took a deep breath. Seeing Brandon standing in her parents' kitchen had caught her totally off guard. While she was collecting her thoughts, her mother chimed in.

"Aren't ya gonna ask him to sit down and have some breakfast? Where ya manners, gurl?"

"Uh…Ma, I'm sure he has better things to do," she managed to say.

"I'd love to have breakfast," he said, pulling out a chair and sitting down at the kitchen table.

Ayana just stood there and looked at him as if he had two heads. *What the hell is he doing here?* She wanted to quiz him, but her mother was standing there watching them both, looking from one to the other.

"Ana, give da young man some coffee."

Ayana followed her mother's instructions and poured Brandon a cup of freshly brewed coffee. She was confused and didn't know what to say. He had gone from acting like a deer in the headlights when she made a mention of her parents to coming to their home unannounced and uninvited. She went about the business of making breakfast until she could think of how to introduce him to her mother. She couldn't say that they worked together because her parents had no idea she worked on a reality television show. She couldn't say he was her boyfriend because technically he wasn't. Ayana didn't like lying to her mother, so she just kept her mouth shut.

"I haven't seen ya 'round here before. So how ya know Ana?" her mother said, sitting across the table from Brandon.

"She knows my sister-in-law, Marigold, and we met at the shelter," he replied.

Good answer! Ayana thought. He hadn't lied, and he hadn't told the entire truth either.

"Oh, me just loves Marigold! She da salt of da earth, helping all thoze battered women and chilren. Me knew her late husband. Him was a good man."

"Thanks. James was my older brother."

"Sorry for your loss. Are ya married too?" Ayana's mother asked, sizing him up.

Ayana swung around. "Ma! Don't start quizzing him."

"It's okay. I don't mind. No, Mrs. Tosh, I'm not married."

"Ya mean, a good-lookin' man like yoself hasn't found a good woman to marry?" She shook her head. "I don't know what's wrong wit ya young people today. Ya tink marriage is a bad ting. Back in me day, we wed as soon as we could and started a family. Don't ya want to get married and have some chilren?" she asked.

Brandon glanced over at Ayana, who had a mortified look on her face, and said, "I'd love nothing more than to marry my soul mate and start a family."

Hearing those words come out of his mouth warmed Ayana's heart, and she smiled. Ayana hadn't known his views on marriage and raising children. Now that she knew he wasn't a man strictly out for a good time, but one who actually had goals, he was becoming more and more attractive. She too wanted a family.

Brandon witnessed Mrs. Tosh glance over at her daughter and smile. He could tell that she was picking up on the fact that they were more than mere friends. Mrs. Tosh had wasted no time asking the important questions.

"Me gonna run some errands. Me be back later. Nice to meet ya, young man."

Brandon stood and shook her hand. "The pleasure was all mine, Mrs. Tosh."

Once she was gone, Ayana went to the kitchen doorway to make sure her mother was out of earshot. Then she walked over to the table and sat down. "So what are you doing here?" she whispered in case her mother was still hanging around.

"Steve has been trying to get in touch with you. He called me early this morning and said Ed wants us to report back to the penthouse tomorrow," he said in a low tone.

"Tomorrow! Why so soon?"

"Ed is feeling better and wants to do a reunion-type show. He's calling it a *Divorced Divas Divulge* special, and he wants to start rehearsals tomorrow."

Ayana hung her head. Being with Brandon the past few days had been a breath of fresh air, and she hadn't given the show or her ugly persona on set a second thought. Sadness began creeping its way into her spirit, and her eyes welled up with tears.

Brandon saw the expression on her face, reached across the table and held her hands. "It's going to be all right."

"How can you say that when you know being back on set is synonymous with me acting like an out-of-control diva?" she said with her face still hanging low.

"Ayana, look at me." He gently raised her chin. "I know the real you now. You're nothing like Saturday Knight. You are a kind, generous person who helps out her family and provides for the shelter. You're a good person."

Hearing his kind words sent tears streaming down her cheeks.

Brandon reached for a napkin in the middle of the table and wiped her tears. "Stop crying. It's going to be fine," he said again, reassuring her. "There's a big difference this time around."

"What do you mean?" she said, blowing her nose.

"This time, while we're taping, your man will be on the set watching your back."

"Are you saying that...?"

He interrupted her. "Yes, I'm saying I'm your man, and you are my woman. Now stop crying and start packing. We have to make reservations and get the next plane back to New York."

Ayana got up, walked over and gave him a tender kiss on the lips. He had soothed her anxiety, and now returning to *Divorced Divas* and reprising her role as Saturday Knight didn't seem so bad. With Brandon in her corner, Ayana knew she could get through just about anything.

Chapter 19

Ayana was able to book a flight from Jamaica to New York with Brandon with no problem. The flight was wide-open with plenty of seats. They sat together in business class, holding hands and enjoying their final hours together before getting back to reality. The time spent in Negril, though brief, had been a dose of paradise. They had become almost inseparable on the island, spending most of their days and nights together. With Ed's grim prognosis before they left New York, returning to the show this soon had been the furthest thing from their minds. As the plane soared through the clouds, getting closer and closer to New York, they sat in silence, mourning their hasty departure from Jamaica. Before leaving, Ayana had called Cedella. They hadn't spoken since the day of the beach party, so Ayana updated her friend on the superb progress she'd made with Brandon and how he had asked her to be his woman. Cedella couldn't have been happier for her and wished her well.

"Would you two care for another cup of coffee?" the flight attendant asked.

"No, thanks. Do you have Guinness Stout?" Ayana asked.

"Yes, we do."

"I'll have a bottle of that and a shot of rum," Ayana replied, wanting to recapture some of their island magic.

"Make that two," Brandon said.

After the flight attendant brought their drinks, Brandon raised his beer bottle and said, "To hot nights on the beach."

"I'll drink to that," Ayana said, tapping her bottle to his. "I still can't believe Ed is well enough to start production again. He was at death's door, barely hanging on, and now he's back in control like nothing happened."

"I guess we can attribute his speedy recovery to modern medicine."

Ayana took a swallow of beer. "I guess."

"Don't sound so sad. Look on the bright side. Ed's heart attack brought us together. If he hadn't gotten sick, the show would have never gone on hiatus, and we wouldn't have been in Jamaica at the same time," he said, sounding optimistic.

"I guess," she responded in the same solemn voice.

"Oh, I hate to hear you sound so glum." He leaned over and kissed her on the cheek. "What can I do to make it better?"

Ayana looked at him and raised her eyebrow. "Uh, I can think of something."

"Name it."

She leaned over and whispered in his ear. "How about joining the Mile High Club?"

"Thought you'd never ask." Brandon peered around the cabin at the other passengers. Some were sleeping, a few were reading, whereas others were entertained by the in-flight movie. "Since there's only one lavatory up here, let's go back to coach, where they have two. You go first, and I'll follow in a few. I'll knock twice so you know it's me."

"Okay!" she said, her mood instantly lightened.

Ayana made her way back to coach, where most passengers were watching the same movie. No one was in line when she reached the lavatories. She opened the door to one, stepped inside and waited. Ayana's heart began to beat faster with anticipation. The thought of getting away with having sex on a plane was thrilling. While she waited for Brandon, she slipped off her jeans and panties, knowing there would be little room to maneuver once he stepped inside the tiny space. No sooner had she folded her jeans and underwear and placed them on the closed toilet lid than the door slid open.

"Hey, sexy," Brandon whispered as he admired her half-naked body before quickly locking the door behind him.

She pulled him by his belt and started unfastening the buckle. "Hey, yourself."

Brandon joined his hands with hers, helping to unfasten his pants more quickly. The expectancy of what was to come had them panting heavily with lust. Once his pants were off, he picked Ayana up and placed her on top of the tiny metal basin.

"Oh, that's cold," she said.

He kissed her on the neck and said, "You won't be cold for long." He then spread her legs apart and wedged himself in between her thighs.

Ayana wrapped her legs around his waist. "You promise?"

"Cross my heart." He reached around, took hold of her butt and brought her closer.

Ayana felt his engorged member pressing alongside the outer lips of her vagina. She wanted to feel the length of him filling her up. "I am so craving you," she whispered in his ear.

Brandon rubbed his growing penis back and forth against her opening, teasing her with each deliberate stroke. "And I want you too."

Ayana opened her legs as wide as the small space would allow, reached down, took hold of his rod and guided him into her wetness. Once he was firmly inside, she hugged him around the neck and held on tight as he thrust deeper and deeper.

"We're…soo…good…together," he whispered in her ear. Brandon picked up the pace, pumping and holding her against him at the same time. Their naughty interlude was fueling his desire for her even more, and he was finding it hard to hold back.

Ayana held on to him with one hand while reaching down and rubbing herself with the other. The dual sensation of her hand and his pulsating penis intensified their lovemaking until she was on the verge of exploding.

They held on tightly to each other in the tiny space and rode the wave of ecstasy to a crescendo, climaxing at the same time. They stayed locked in place, relishing the moment before unwrapping their limbs from around one another. Brandon helped her down from the sink, then reached down, picked her clothes up and handed them to her.

After they dressed, he said, "I'll go out first to make sure the coast is clear. You should wait a few minutes and then come out."

"Okay."

He kissed her tenderly before slipping out the door. Once he was gone, Ayana straightened her clothes and smoothed down her hair. She looked in the mirror and saw that her face was glowing. Brandon had that effect on her. Ayana inhaled deeply and could smell their scent in the air. She smiled and went back to her seat with no one the wiser.

"Feel better now?" he asked, kissing the side of her cheek after she returned beside him.

"Yes, much."

"Membership does have its privileges," he said, winking at her.

"Yes, it sure does." Ayana laid her head on his shoulder, closed her eyes and drifted off to sleep only to be awakened by the sound of the pilot over the intercom.

"Good news, folks. Because of the mild weather, looks like we'll be landing ahead of schedule."

"Well, I guess it's time to make my transformation," Ayana told Brandon.

He looked perplexed. "What do you mean?"

"Say goodbye to Ayana. I have to go and make myself presentable." She stood up, reached into the overhead bin and retrieved her carry-on bag.

"What's wrong with your outfit?" he asked, looking at her jeans and T-shirt. She looked perfectly fine to him.

"I never get off the plane wearing my island clothes. I can't chance reporters and photographers seeing me looking like a country girl. The last time I arrived at the airport, a swarm of reporters and paparazzi were outside, snapping pictures and wanting an interview regarding a scandal I was allegedly involved in. Remember, they are used to seeing the Saturday Knight persona all dolled up, and they know nothing about Ayana Lewis, and I have to keep it that way."

"I understand," Brandon said with sadness in his voice. He wasn't ready for Ayana to turn back into Saturday Knight, but there was nothing he could do about it. He watched her walk into the lavatory, knowing that when she came out she would be a different person, so to speak. Brandon looked down at the cocktail napkin on his tray table, then picked it up.

Fifteen minutes later, Ayana reemerged looking like a celebrity. Gone were the jeans and T-shirt, replaced with a tight black dress that cinched her waist and hips, with black stiletto heels to match. Her hair was no longer in a ponytail—instead, a long platinum-blond wig was cascading loose around her shoulders. She wore dangling earrings that matched a series of necklaces adorning her neck. Her face was made up with bright red lipstick, blush and long false eyelashes.

"Wow, look at you!" he said, having forgotten the glamour of Saturday Knight.

"How's that for a quick transformation?" She put her bag back in the overhead and sat down.

"Here, this is for you," he said, handing her the airline-issued napkin.

Ayana took the napkin out of his hands. "Oh, do I

have lipstick on my teeth?" she asked, assuming he was giving her the napkin to clean her makeup.

"No, read it."

She looked at the white napkin and read the message written in the center. *Blissfully Yours, B.*

"Aww." She touched the napkin to her chest. "That's so sweet. Let me use your pen." She then wrote on the back, *Blissfully Yours, A.* She kissed the napkin, leaving the imprint of her ruby-red lips on the white surface, and handed it back to him.

"I mean it, baby. I am blissfully yours and don't you forget it when we're back in New York on set."

"I promise I won't," she said, snuggling closer to him.

Brandon put the napkin in his pocket and closed his eyes, revisiting their time together in Jamaica. He knew that going back to New York and working on the show as a couple was going to be a challenge, and he wanted to hold on to happy memories for as long as possible.

Chapter 20

Ayana and Brandon went directly to the set from the airport. They arrived at the penthouse on Central Park West together. Riding up in the elevator, Ayana felt her heart sinking. Although she was dressed as Saturday Knight, she wasn't ready to face the cast and morph into character. In her spirit, she was still feeling irie and wanted to return to Jamaica as fast as she could. However, she was under contract and had a job to do.

Standing beside Ayana, holding her hand, Brandon could sense her trepidation. "Are you all right?"

"Yes. I'm fine," she said with coolness to her voice.

"No, you're not. You don't even sound like yourself."

"Brandon, I need to get into character. We'll be on set in a few and I don't want any signs of Ayana show-ing." She eased her hand out of his. "I didn't mention this before, but I think it's best if we keep our relationship under wraps. It wouldn't look too professional if one of the cast members and the director were dating."

"What difference does it make? We're two consenting adults."

"The difference is, I'm supposed to be single on the show, and going through the dating process to find my next husband."

Brandon exhaled hard. "So, you're telling me, I'm supposed to just sit back and watch—wait, *direct*—my woman with another man? Ayana, I don't like this arrangement one bit."

"Yes, until the show goes on hiatus again. My contract will be up by then, and hopefully I will have found another income."

"Since you have everything figured out, when are we supposed to see each other?" he asked, sounding quite annoyed.

Ayana took hold of his hand again, trying to smooth things over. "When we're not taping you can come over to my place, and I can come over to yours."

Now it was Brandon's turn to remove his hand from hers. "So we have to sneak around like teenagers hiding from their parents."

"No, we're not hiding—just keeping our relationship to ourselves. It's nobody's business what we do after the cameras go off."

He exhaled again. "You told me the truth of why you're on the show back in Jamaica, and I accepted it. I guess I didn't factor in the dating component and the premise of *Divorced Divas.* I'm not going to jeopardize your livelihood, but I'm telling you right now, I don't want you kissing on any of these guys."

Ayana chuckled slightly. "Somebody's jealous."

"It's not funny. I'm serious," he said with a straight face.

"Okay," she said and leaned up and kissed him on the cheek.

The elevator doors opened. Ayana stepped off first and strutted into the penthouse ahead of Brandon. The expansive living room was set up with lights and over-head boom microphones. Two plush white sofas were arranged in a row with a white leather chair positioned in the middle. The walls were adorned with copies of artwork by the masters—Van Gogh, Monet and Renoir. Lead crystal vases with fresh-cut flowers were arranged throughout the room. The scene resembled an old-money Upper East Side matriarch's living room, where high tea and finger sandwiches were served. This room, however, served up juicy gossip and plenty of drama.

"Where have you been?" Steve asked, rushing up to Ayana.

She quickly got into character and gave him one of her demeaning looks, complete with an annoying teeth suck. "I was on a plane. Don't blame me for being late when I only had a day's notice."

"I've been calling you for the past two days," Steve said in his defense.

"Whatever," she responded, flipping her hand. Ayana looked around the room, expecting to see the show's creator, but he wasn't there. "Where's Ed?"

"He won't be here until tomorrow, but he'll be calling in throughout the day."

"You're complaining that I'm late, but I don't see anyone else on the set."

"The other ladies are in their dressing rooms waiting for you."

"Well, you can go tell those heifers the star has arrived."

Steve didn't say a word. He just looked at her with disdain. Ayana knew he knew better than to get into a verbal sparring match with the infamous Saturday Knight, for surely he would lose.

"Uh, hey, Brandon," Steve said, diverting his attention from her.

"Hi, Steve. How are you doing?" Brandon asked as he walked toward the executive producer. Brandon strolled right past Saturday as if she weren't there, giving no hint that they were a couple. He shook Steve's hand.

"I'm good. No complaints. Just ready to get the show under way."

"When are we going to start with rehearsals?" Brandon asked, also anxious to begin so that he could get out of there and spend time with Ayana.

"Soon. I'm waiting for Ed to call. He left explicit instructions to wait for his call before we began."

"Well, hello, Brandon," Brooke, the blonde flirt of the show, said as she came into the room. She went directly over to him, ignoring Saturday and Steve, and stood so close to Brandon that her surgically enhanced boobs were almost touching his chest.

Brandon took a step back. "Hello, Brooke," he said in a professional tone.

"So, Mr. Director, how was your time off? Too bad we couldn't get together and hang out. I'm sure we would have had a ton of fun," she said with a wink.

Ayana cut her eyes from Brandon to Brooke. She was seething but didn't say anything. She had laid the ground rules but didn't like this game of nondisclosure.

Ayana wanted to let the world know that Brandon was her man, but she was forced to remain silent. She especially wanted to tell Brooke to keep her paws off of him. Instead, she went over to the sofa, sat down, took her phone out of her purse and pretended to play a game, all the while listening to their exchange.

"I don't think my girl would have liked me hanging out with you," he said, giving Brooke the cold shoulder.

Ayana's ears perked up, and she smiled slightly. *That's right, baby. Tell her you're taken.*

"Oh, I didn't know you had a girlfriend," Brooke said, sounding surprised.

"I do and we're extremely happy. So getting together with you isn't even an option." Brandon cut his eyes at Ayana, who was looking down at her phone but had a pleasant expression on her face. From their close proximity, he knew that she was listening to his every word. Although they couldn't reveal their relationship, he wanted to reassure her of how he felt.

"I can be discreet if you can. We could at least have dinner together. Your girlfriend would never have to know," Brooke said, refusing to accept no as an answer.

"Like I said, getting together with you isn't an option."

Yes! Yes! Inside, Ayana was doing a fist pump and happy dance at the same time. Brandon had put Ms. Thing in her place, and she was elated.

Brandon turned his attention back to Steve, totally ignoring Brooke. "I'll be in the production room. Let me know when we're ready to begin."

"Okay, will do. I'm going to get the other ladies so everyone will be on set when Ed calls."

Once Brandon and Steve had left the room, Ayana

put her phone aside, looked up and started in on Brooke. "Tell me something." She stood and walked over to Brooke. "Why are you always trying to push up on somebody's man?"

"What are you talking about?" Brooke asked, flinging her long blond hair, nearly hitting Saturday in the face.

Saturday quickly moved out of the way. "I'm talking about you coming on to Brandon."

"What's it to you?"

"He's here as the director, not your personal boy toy."

"Once again, I'm going to say, what's it to you? Who I flirt with is none of your business," Brooke responded, not backing down.

Saturday stepped closer and pointed her finger in Brooke's face, nearly touching her nose. "I'm going to tell you what it is to me. He's…"

Brooke slapped Saturday's finger out of her face, interrupting her tirade.

"How dare you hit me!" Saturday raised her arms to push Brooke.

"Whoa, whoa, what's going on here?" Brandon said, stepping between them. He had come out of the production room just in time to stop the fight.

"That whore hit me!" Saturday yelled.

"Who are you calling a whore?" Brooke shouted back.

"Did I stutter?" Saturday countered, trying to reach around Brandon and get to Brooke.

"You both need to calm down. This is a production set, not a boxing ring." He took Saturday by the arm and led her over to the huge floor-to-ceiling window. "What's going on? I step out of the room for a few minutes, and when I come back you're arguing with Brooke," he said under his breath.

Saturday looked past him, leering at Brooke. "She thinks she can just come on to you, like you're here for her personal pleasure."

"Are you kidding me? You're getting all riled up because she flirted with me?"

"I needed to put her in her place and let her know that you're not available."

"Ayana—" he looked over his shoulder to make sure no one was listening "—I already did that. Besides, Brooke is just being Brooke. Remember when she flirted with me a while back? I put her in her place then, and you and I weren't even dating."

"Of course I remember. However, that was then. Now you are my man, and I don't want her trying to sink her claws into you."

"I could go over there right now and tell her that we're dating and put an end to her flirting once and for all. Is that what you want?" He peered directly into her eyes.

Saturday folded her arms across her chest, exhaled hard and said, "You know that's not an alternative."

"Well, then, you need to cool your jets."

Saturday didn't say anything. She couldn't believe how upset she had gotten over a little flirtation. *I must really love this man. I've never acted a fool over any guy before,* she thought. Ayana didn't like the vulnerability that came with being in love. She nearly told her own secret and needed to get a grip. If any of these women smelled a whiff of weakness, they would go in for the kill. Saturday was the vixen of the show, and had to stay in character so she wouldn't lose her job.

"Are you all right now?" Brandon asked when she didn't answer.

She exhaled. "Yes, I'm fine." She crossed the room and returned to the sofa, ignoring Brooke, who was still standing in the middle of the room with her arms folded across her chest.

"Looks like we are postponing today's rehearsal. Ed will be here in the flesh tomorrow and we'll start then. I've already told Petra, Trista and the rest of the crew. Tomorrow's call time is eight a.m. See you guys then," Steve said.

Saturday gathered her belongings and made a beeline for the door without giving Brandon a second look. She needed to go home and formulate a better game plan. Ayana realized that pretending she and Brandon were platonic coworkers was going to be harder than she'd initially thought.

Chapter 21

Ayana hadn't been in her own bed in weeks, and it felt good to relax among the myriad of pillows in varying sizes tossed against the headboard. Her body was sand-wiched between the six-hundred-count sheets, which were as smooth as silk, and a plush down comforter was folded at her feet. The only illumination in the room was the streetlights streaming through the mini blinds and the light of the muted television. She wanted to quiet the chatter in her head and didn't need any additional noise. Ayana ran through the day's events in her mind and didn't like how she had allowed Brooke to push her buttons. Ayana had nearly blurted out that she and Brandon were dating, which would have defeated her plan to keep their relationship under wraps.

"I really need to keep my emotions in check," she said aloud.

Her cell rang, interrupting her thoughts. Ayana reached for the phone, which was lying on the nightstand. "Hello?"

"It's me! I'm back!"

"Hey, Reese! How was your trip?" Ayana was happy to hear from her friend. She had a lot to tell her.

"It was fabulous. We bought some amazing gems, tooled around Capri and ate and drank ourselves silly. We really needed the time away, so we could reconnect as a couple. The first part of the trip was all business— however, the last leg was all pleasure!"

"Nice!"

"So, how's the show been going? I miss my regular updates."

"The show has been on hold for a while. Ed had a heart attack…"

"What! Is he okay?"

"Yes, he's fine now. Tomorrow, we're taping for the first time since he got out of the hospital."

"How long was he laid up?"

"A few weeks."

"What were you doing all of that time?"

"I was in Jamaica. My dad had a slight stroke."

"What? How is he?"

"He's fine."

"Wow. I can't believe all of that happened while I was away."

"It's not all bad news. Guess what? You were right."

"Right about what?"

"Remember when I told you about the new director of the show kissing me?"

"Of course I remember. Wait a minute… Don't tell me that you guys are dating?"

"Yes, we are!" Ayana said, sounding totally elated.

"That's great—now tell me everything."

Ayana went into detail, telling Reese how Brandon had nearly run her over with his Jet Ski, and how he was related to her friend Marigold. She told Reese that Brandon had been standoffish until she revealed the truth of why she was on the show. Ayana told Reese how she and Brandon had fallen in love while in Jamaica.

"That's fantastic! I couldn't be happier. So how is the cast responding to you guys as a couple?"

"No one knows that we're dating. I have to keep our relationship under wraps until the end of the season."

"Why is that?"

"I can't jeopardize my Saturday Knight persona, and risk losing my job."

"Oh, I see. Hold on for a second."

Ayana could hear Reese talking to someone in the background.

"I'd love to continue our conversation, but Joey has drawn me a candlelit bubble bath."

"Aw, that's so sweet. Okay, talk to you later."

Ayana placed the phone back on the nightstand and wondered if she and Brandon would become a happily married couple like Reese and Joey. Although she was falling deeply in love with Brandon, she couldn't allow her feelings to overshadow her judgment. Ayana already didn't like portraying Saturday, but it had gotten even worse. Now she'd have to conceal two lies. The pressure was already getting to her, and the special taping hadn't even gotten under way.

"I have to get back on my game plan."

The time spent with Brandon in Jamaica had been beyond great but had shifted her focus from finding a way out of reality television into a profession that she could be proud of. Brandon had mentioned that she might try her hand at acting, and she thought that was a great idea. Ayana also had branding ideas in mind, but that would probably take longer to facilitate. Presently, she didn't have a talent agent, but getting one shouldn't be a problem because she was already a television personality.

Ayana reached for her cell phone to call Brandon and ask him about his agent. She didn't want to waste another second. She needed to get the ball rolling.

"Hey, are you asleep?" she asked once he picked up.

"Hey, baby. No, I'm not asleep. I'm just lying here thinking about you."

She smiled. "And what were you thinking?"

"How much I miss you. Why don't you come over?"

"I would, but I'm beat. Traveling and dealing with the show has me wiped out."

"Are you too tired for a little phone action?" he asked seductively.

"Hmm? Are you talking about phone sex?" Brandon's question had taken her totally off guard.

"Yes, I am. So tell me, what are you wearing?" he asked, getting right down to business.

Ayana had on a threadbare Reggae Fest T-shirt that was at least ten years old, panties and a pair of sweat socks—the antithesis of sexy. "Uh...I have on a fire-engine-red lace negligee with a matching red thong tucked between my butt cheeks," she elaborated, playing along and getting in the mood.

"Mmm...that sounds so sexy."

"Trust me, it is. You should see how good my body looks in this negligee. My nipples are peeking through the lace."

"Mmm…nice. I can just envision you lying there looking sexy as hell."

"So tell me…what do you have on?"

"My chocolate birthday suit," he said in a husky voice.

"I just love, love, love big, dark chocolate bars."

"Oh, you do, do you? And tell me, what do you like to do with big…dark…chocolate bars?" he asked, speaking slowly.

Ayana deepened her voice into a come-hither tone. "I like to put them in my mouth and…lick them…and suck them."

"And while you're enjoying your chocolate bar, I'll be softly and ever so gently munching on your pink sweet forbidden fruit like a scrumptious treat."

"Hmm, I like the way that sounds."

"Can you do me a favor?" he asked.

"Yes, anything for you, baby."

"I want you to take off your thong."

"Okay." Ayana reached underneath the sheet and took off her white cotton panties.

"Are they off?"

"Yes."

"Good. Now I want you to spread your legs and put your index finger near your clit but don't touch it, just press firmly above the area."

"Okay." Ayana did what he said and waited for further instruction. This unexpected phone sex was making her hot as she anticipated his next command.

"Now close your eyes. Is your finger still near your clit?"

"Yes."

"Are you pressing firmly?"

"Yes."

"Good. I want you to keep it there while you put the phone on Speaker, then set it on the pillow next to you. You're going to need both of your hands for the next move."

Once again she followed his instructions. "The call is on Speaker. Now what do you want me to do?" she asked eagerly.

"Take your other hand, put your first two fingers in your mouth and get them nice and wet." He waited a few seconds and then said, "Take the hand that's near your clit and expose that delicious pink flesh. Now take your fingers and rub your clit until you get nice and wet."

With her eyes closed, Ayana followed his instructions to perfection, rubbing herself, getting wetter by the second. She began moaning. She was in a zone, and it felt good.

"Listening to your moans is making me harder by the second. If I were there, I would taste your kitty cat."

"And I would lick all over your chocolate bar."

"I'm holding my big chocolate bar right now and thinking about you."

"Good. Now I want you to stroke it up and down and pretend I'm there with you."

"Okay. Are you still pleasuring yourself?"

"Yes, and it feels so good."

They were each enjoying the moment, as evidenced by the panting and moaning coming through the speaker. Brandon had coached her to a climax and she was ready to squirt her juices.

Ayana panted heavily.

"Come with me, baby! Yes, yes!" she yelled.

Brandon let out a series of screeching grunts as

he himself exploded. A few seconds later he said in a breathy tone, "Oh, that was good."

"It sure was."

"But I must apologize," he said.

"For what?" She was puzzled.

"I'm sure you didn't call me to get ambushed into phone sex. I barely let you get the word 'hey' out before I started in."

"Baby, you have nothing to be sorry for. Trust me, I more than enjoyed your ambush. It's just what I needed after this afternoon. However, I did call for a specific reason. Remember when we were in Jamaica and you mentioned that I should think about transitioning into acting?"

"Of course I remember. I think you'd be a great actress."

"Thanks. I hope so. The only problem is that I don't have an agent. My attorney brokered the deal with *Divorced Divas.* I remember you saying that you have an agent. Do you think I can call him or her?"

"Sure. I'll give Mario a call in the morning and let him know to expect your call." He gave her Mario's number.

"Great. Thanks so much. I can't wait to leave the show. I don't know how much more of Saturday Knight I can take."

Brandon wanted to tell her he agreed, but he didn't want to offend her, so he kept quiet. "I'm sure he'll take you on as a client. He's well connected in the industry and will have no problem getting you auditions with some of the heavy hitters."

"Brandon, you don't know how much your vote of confidence means to me." Ayana's ex-husband had wanted a wife with no ambition. Shortly after they'd married, he'd insisted that she stop working.

"Ayana, I only want the best for you."

His kind words nearly brought tears to her eyes. "Brandon, I'm so glad you know the real me. I really hate being a diva on the set. I should have never let Ed talk me into portraying such a malicious villain."

"At the time, you didn't have a choice. Don't worry—you'll be out of there soon enough."

Brandon's reassuring words made Ayana feel much better. She now had a solid exit strategy. It was just a matter of time before she could tell Ed and the show *au revoir*.

Chapter 22

Ed was back and in full form. He flounced throughout the penthouse as if he had springy coils in his orange, high-heeled sneakers. His multicolored chiffon scarf floated in the air as he moved about. Ed appeared to be so happy to be out of the hospital and back at work that he could barely contain himself. All morning, he had been talking to the cast and crew, gesturing at a rapid pace, as if trying to make up for lost time. *Divorced Divas* was losing market share and Ed had devised a plan that would surely get the show back on track.

"I want you ladies sitting on the sofa with Moses Michaels in the middle," Ed ordered the cast, pointing his manicured finger at the custom-made two-piece white couch.

Saturday and her cast mates were all dressed fabulously in black. Saturday had on a one-shoulder dress,

Petra wore a halter dress, Brooke wore a sleeveless dress and Trista had on a peplum-style dress. Ed had informed the stylist that he wanted the ladies in black to make a dramatic contrast against the white sofa. They were also in full hair and makeup. Ed wanted them camera ready.

"Why we all dress up? I thought we no tape show, just rehearse," Petra said with a puzzled expression on her face.

"Mr. Michaels only has today available. He's flying to L.A. tonight and won't be back until next week. I don't want to wait until then. We've lost too much time as it is."

"But how we know who to talk about?" Petra asked.

"You mean 'what' to talk about," Saturday said, correcting her as usual.

"I not talking to you," Petra countered.

"Ladies, let's save the bickering for the camera. Now, Saturday, I want you in the center, sitting next to the moderator. Brooke, you're on the other side of the moderator. Petra, you're next to Brooke, and, Trista, you're sitting next to Saturday," Ed instructed.

"Why I no sit in middle?" Petra whined.

Saturday took her seat, spread her arms across the back of the sofa and said, "Because I'm the star of the show. Therefore, I'm front and center. You're just a sidekick."

"What is sidekick?"

Before Saturday could come back with an insulting remark, Brandon, who had been sitting on the side in his director's chair watching the entire exchange, interrupted. "Petra, why do you always let Saturday get under your skin? Just ignore her."

Saturday shot Brandon a look. She wanted to blurt out, *Why are you taking Petra's side?* His remark had taken her totally by surprise, rendering her momentarily speechless.

"You right. I ignore." Petra took her seat without looking in Saturday's direction.

Once the ladies had taken their places, Ed stood in front of them and said, "While we're waiting for Mr. Michaels to arrive, I want to go over a few key points. Remember this is a reunion-type show, so you guys will be discussing what has happened over the past few episodes. Talk about how you felt about your dates, which men really turned you on and which ones you can't wait to see again. The audience loves to hear about romance. I want you to really spice up the conversation. Any questions?"

"Should we mention your heart attack?" Trista asked.

"OH, ABSOLUTELY NOT!" Ed shouted. "This show isn't about me and my health issues. It's about you ladies and your dating issues. Got it?"

Trista looked sheepish and appeared instantly sorry for asking the question. "Uh…okay."

"And one more thing. I have a surprise planned," Ed announced.

"I detest surprises," Saturday told him.

"Well, I hate to disappoint you, love, but there will definitely be a surprise or two during taping, so be ready for anything."

Saturday didn't like being blindsided. She certainly hoped that Ed wasn't bringing back any of her former dates. It was bad enough that she had to sit next to Moses Michaels. Even though she hadn't slept with the famous moderator, they still had a brief history. Now that she and Brandon were an item, she didn't want to bring her past into her present. Before he came aboard as the director, she had cozied up to several men via Ed's instruction. The thought of Brandon hearing about her exploits made her sick to her stomach, but there was nothing she could do about it now. As Saturday was sitting quietly pondering what Ed's surprise could be, in walked the moderator.

Moses Michaels was known around the reality circuit as the host that brought drama to an already dramatic setting. He was the ultimate pot stirrer, asking probing questions that got members of the cast in one heated debate after another. Moses's shrewdness had him in high demand, commanding top dollar to moderate a litany of reality shows.

Saturday watched Moses greet Ed and couldn't help but admire him. Moses stood less than six feet, but he was well built. He was an immaculate dresser. He wore a black Gucci suit, black shirt, black tie and black Gucci loafers—obviously he had gotten the same dress-code suggestion from Ed. He was clean shaven, making his café-au-lait skin look as smooth as silk. Saturday and Moses had made a striking pair, and she could understand why the tabloids had spread rumors that she had broken up his relationship.

"Hey, Ed, how are you?" Moses asked in his signature baritone voice.

"Couldn't be better," Ed replied, shaking Moses's hand. "Thanks for doing this show at the last minute."

"No problem." Moses smiled, exposing his perfect white teeth and deep dimples.

"Did you get my email with the list of talking points?"

"Yes, I did."

That man is still fine, Saturday thought as she watched him. She hadn't seen Moses since their last date months ago. She turned her eyes away before Brandon caught her staring at the handsome moderator.

"Moses, let me introduce you to our new director," Ed said, leading the way to where Brandon sat in his director's chair.

"Brandon, this is Moses Michaels, the best moderator in the business," Ed gushed.

Moses and Brandon shook hands. "Nice to meet you," Moses said.

Saturday watched them exchange pleasantries and felt a bit nervous. She hadn't told Brandon about dating Moses. Really there was nothing to tell because she and Moses had dated only a few times. They had kissed, as she had told Reese, but it was nothing serious.

"Are you guys ready to get started?" Ed asked.

"Ready as ever," Moses said, heading toward the sofa. He sat down in his designated seat between Saturday and Brooke. Moses leaned over toward Saturday and whispered, "Hey there, lovely. You sure are looking good. I've missed those sweet lips of yours." Moses moved his body a bit closer to her as he spoke.

"Hi, Moses," Saturday said, staring straight ahead, ignoring his comment.

"I'm going to Los Angles tonight. When I come back next week, let's do dinner *and* dessert," he said, licking his lips. Moses was a serial dater and had a reputation in the business of sleeping with the beautiful reality stars he interviewed. His once faithful girlfriend had had enough and had left the handsome moderator to his own devices.

"I don't think so."

Saturday glanced over and saw Brandon watching her and Moses. Brandon had an unpleasant look on his face.

"Ready as ever," Moses said.

"Take one. Action!" Brandon announced.

"Hey, everybody. Moses Michaels here on the set of *Divorced Divas,*" he began, peering into the camera. "I'm here with these lovely ladies for a special divulge-all reunion." He looked at the cast to his right and then to his left. "Okay, ladies, let's get down to business. You know I don't like wasting time."

Here we go, Saturday thought, bracing herself for Moses's direct line of questioning. He was known to go right for the jugular. Her heart began beating faster with anticipation.

"So, Saturday, I will start with you. Last season, you made a love connection with one of your dates, didn't you?"

"I make a connection with all my dates," she said flippantly, determined not to be ambushed.

"Well, this particular connection had a special meaning. Why don't we roll tape and refresh your memory?"

The moment he said "roll tape," a huge HD screen dropped down behind them. The screen showed her with Erick Kastell, a high-powered investment banker. Erick was strikingly handsome with thick blond hair and blue eyes. They had had an instant attraction to each other and had gone out on several successful dates. Their last date, a romantic dinner at Jean Georges, had ended with a carriage ride through Central Park.

Saturday watched the screen as they rode with their arms around each other in the back of the small carriage. A tiny video camera attached inside the carriage had captured their every move—her hand resting comfortably on his knee, his arm draped around her shoulders, nearly touching her breast. She was shocked to see this footage because that episode had never aired. Erick had immigration issues and had had to fly back to Switzerland to straighten them out. At the time, Ed didn't know if Erick was ever going to return to the States, so he decided not to air their last date. She had all but forgotten about Erick until now, as she watched him on-screen.

"You are so beautiful," Erick said, leaning in and kissing her on the lips.

Oh, shit! Saturday thought, watching the scene unfold. She kissed him back.

"I know we haven't known each other for long, but I feel a deep connection to you and I know you feel it too."

"Yes, I do." Saturday had been instructed by Ed to play up the romance, so she had.

"Life is short, wouldn't you agree?"

"Yes, I would agree."

"When the producers approached me to be on the show, I was hesitant until they showed me your picture. From the moment I saw you, I was smitten. I've begun to fall for you over these past few weeks, and every time we are together, I fall deeper and deeper in love."

"Ohhh, that's so sweet."

"It's not sweet—it's the truth." He reached into his pocket and produced an aqua-blue Tiffany's box. He opened the lid, and inside was a five-carat diamond engagement ring.

The camera showed a shocked expression registering on Saturday's face before dramatically shutting off.

Moses turned his head to Saturday and said, "Is your memory refreshed now?"

"What do you think? I'm not blind. I can see my date on the screen, just like everybody else," she replied with attitude in her voice.

"Now, now, let's not get testy. You made a love connection with Erick, and that's great. Isn't finding love what *Divorced Divas* is all about?"

Saturday didn't say anything. She was still reeling from seeing that old footage and embarrassed that Brandon had seen it as well.

"You guys at home are probably wondering why you've never seen this footage. It's because this is our first time airing it. Erick had some issues he had to deal with back in his homeland of Switzerland, but he's back now.... Erick, come on out," Moses announced.

The debonair Swiss banker came strolling onto the set.

Saturday was stunned, alarmed and shocked all at the same time and it showed in her expression. Ed had said there would be a surprise or two during taping, but she'd had no idea he'd bring Erick back.

Erick went directly up to Saturday, knelt down in front of her and took the same aqua-blue box that he had had on-screen out of his jacket pocket. "Saturday, will you marry me?"

Saturday gasped and wanted to walk off the set. She couldn't believe that Ed had blindsided her. She'd known he wanted to breathe new life into the show, but she hadn't known it was going to come at her expense. She wanted to rush over to Brandon and explain, but the cameras were rolling. She glanced in his direction and noticed the pissed expression on his face. No doubt he was upset, and she couldn't blame him. She had to do something and quick. Saturday started coughing uncontrollably and patting her chest as if she couldn't catch her breath.

"Cut!" Brandon yelled. "Let's take five," he said.

Saturday immediately walked off set, made a beeline to her dressing room and slammed the door. A few seconds later, there was a knock. She looked at the door before opening it. She didn't know who was on the other side. She didn't want to see Erick, Ed or Moses. She crossed the room and turned the knob.

Chapter 23

Trepidation took hold of Ayana and wouldn't let go as she slowly turned the doorknob. She held her breath and eased the door open.

"Are you all right?"

Ayana exhaled. "Yes, Gabby, I'm fine. I just need a couple of aspirins and a bottle of water," she said to the production assistant. The drama that had just played out on the set had given her a massive headache.

"Okay, you got it," Gabby said, leaving the room and closing the door behind her.

Ayana crossed the room and sat on the leopard-print chaise lounge, leaned her head back against the wall and closed her eyes. Instantly the image of Erick getting down on one knee and proposing appeared. She quickly blinked her eyes open. Ayana couldn't believe that Ed had arranged for Erick to come back on the show and propose. The whole idea was preposterous. She and Erick had known each other for only a few weeks, not nearly long enough to entertain the notion of marriage. When he'd produced the ring box inside the carriage, she had been taken by surprise. The tape ended right before she'd told him it was entirely too soon for a marriage proposal. She'd told Erick to put the ring back in his pocket, which he had. Of course, Ed had stopped the tape for a dramatic effect, right before she'd told Erick that she wasn't going to marry him.

There was a knock at the door.

"Come in!" she called out to let Gabby know it was okay to enter.

"You can't hide out in here forever. We've got a show to do," Brandon said, standing in the doorway. His face was void of expression. He spoke in a monotone, displaying no emotion. Ayana had never seen him look this way before, and his coldness scared her.

She rose from the chaise and went over to him. "Hey, baby, I'm so sorry about that. I…"

"About what?" he interrupted. "There's nothing to be sorry for. This is the way you wanted things, isn't it?" His tone was more robot than human.

"Brandon, you know I have to go along with whatever Ed has cooked up. He's all about the shock factor. As far as Erick is concerned, I told him that I couldn't marry him, but that conversation wasn't shown," she explained.

"You sure did look cozy, hugged up with him on a romantic carriage ride through the park," he said, giving her a stern look.

Ayana exhaled hard. Brandon was right. She and Erick had been huddled together like two sardines in a can. There was no denying that Ayana had enjoyed Erick's company at that time. He was smart, attentive, attractive and rich—a perfect combination. What was not to like? If Erick hadn't had to abruptly leave the country and return to Switzerland, they would probably legitimately be engaged by now. But Ayana would never admit this to Brandon. Things had changed since then, and Brandon was her man now. She wanted to just forget the past, but the past was alive and well and waiting for her on the set.

"What the clip didn't show was me telling Erick that it was too soon for him to propose."

"So you're basically saying that if you had spent more time with him, you'd be engaged *or* married to the dude," Brandon countered.

"No, no! That's *not* what I'm saying."

"Excuse me. Here's your aspirin and water," Gabby said, appearing in the doorway. "And, uh…" She looked from Ayana to Brandon and seemed to sense the tension in the air. "Ed is waiting for you guys. He's ready to resume taping."

"Thanks, Gabby. We'll be right there," Ayana said. She turned her attention back to Brandon. "Honey, please don't misconstrue what's happening on the set. You know as well as I do that Ed has orchestrated this entire reunion to boost ratings." Ayana hoped her explanation was enough to soothe Brandon's insecurities. She watched him intently, looking for a change in his disposition, but the coldness was still present. Ayana didn't know what else to do. She had explained the clip, but it hadn't made a difference.

"We need to get back on set," Brandon said before turning to leave.

Once he left, Ayana took the aspirin and adjusted her attitude. She didn't need to go on set with the feeling of defeat that was lurking in her spirit. She hadn't swayed Brandon and was feeling horrible that her man had to witness her past exploits. She took a few more sips of water and walked out.

"Okay, ladies, resume your positions," Ed said, standing in the middle of the room and giving directions. "Before the break, Erick proposed." He turned to face Saturday. "Saturday, I'ma need you to express happiness—no, make that total elation—when Erick shows you that gorgeous diamond ring."

"Ed, can I talk to you for a second?" Saturday said.

"Can it wait? We're running behind schedule."

"No, it can't." She walked toward the huge floor-to-ceiling windows, away from the rest of the cast, and motioned for Ed to follow her. Once the two of them were out of earshot, Saturday spoke softly. "Why did you bring Erick back?"

"You two had chemistry, and his return to the show makes perfect sense."

"Okay, that might be true, but it makes no sense for him to propose. We haven't seen each other in months. I know you don't expect me to accept his ridiculous proposal," she said, looking across the room at Brandon, who was sitting in his director's chair and talking on the phone. She wanted to tell Ed that she was in love with Brandon.

"The proposal isn't ridiculous and you will accept his ring. Need I remind you that you are under contract, and…"

"My contract doesn't say I have to be forced into

an arranged marriage," she countered, standing her ground.

"No, it doesn't, and I'm not saying you have to marry Erick, but you will accept the proposal," he said with clenched teeth. "This twist will hike our ratings. Remember, you are under contract, and the contract states that the show makes the final call on all artistic decisions. And this, missy, is an artistic decision that I'm making. Got it?"

"Ed, I can't believe you're treating me like this after I saved your life…literally," she said with tears welling up in her eyes.

"Ayana," he said, using her real name, "I truly appreciate what you did for me, but your administering CPR has nothing to do with the show. It's apples and oranges."

Ayana couldn't believe that Ed was being so indifferent and cold toward her. "So, basically, you're saying it's all about the show, and you'll do anything for high ratings."

"Ayana, stop acting so offended. What's wrong with you? You knew what the show was all about when you signed the contract. I need Saturday Knight to show up and show out. Come on. We've got a scene to finish," he said, walking away, leaving her standing there.

Unfortunately, Ed had total control of the situation. Ayana had no choice but to comply. *I can't wait until this contract is over. I'm leaving the show whether I have a talent agent or not. I can't take this anymore,* she said to herself and reluctantly went back to the set and resumed her persona.

"Before the break, Erick proposed. Let's pick it up from there," Ed said, full of enthusiasm.

Erick got down on his knee again. "Saturday, will you marry me?" He repeated the exact same words he had used before her coughing spasm forced the break.

Saturday looked down at Erick and then glanced over at Brandon, who wore a blank expression. She could see Ed out of the corner of her eye mouthing, "Say yes, say yes." She exhaled, put on a phony smile and said, "Yes, I'll marry you."

Erick took the ring out of the box and slid it on her finger. He stood up and kissed her on the lips.

Saturday wanted to throw up. She felt sick to her stomach as his lips touched hers.

"Let's see that rock," Moses said.

Saturday extended her finger toward the camera.

Moses leaned forward, looking at the other cast members, and said, "See, ladies. Love doesn't have a timeline. With some people, it's love at first sight and they don't need a long, drawn-out courtship. Isn't that right, Saturday?"

"Uh…" She stared at Brandon and said, "You're absolutely right." Ayana only hoped that Brandon knew she was talking about him and not Erick.

"Erick, sit next to your fiancée and tell us if you've made any plans for the big day," Moses said, fueling the fire.

"As a matter of fact, I have." Erick turned to Saturday. "My love, I'd like to marry you at The Plaza in a lavish ceremony. We'll take a horse-drawn carriage ride to the hotel as a reminder of where I proposed." He then turned his attention to the other cast members. "Ladies, we'd love to have you in our wedding."

Brooke, Trista and Petra smiled and nodded their heads. Obviously, Ed had made them play along.

"I would love to stand up for you," Petra chimed in, smiling and grinning at Erick. She was blatantly flirting with him and ignoring Saturday.

"So when is the big day?" Moses asked.

"I'm going to need some time to find the perfect dress. You know I have to be the hottest bride ever," Saturday said, trying to skirt the issue.

Moses directed his attention to the camera. "Well, guys, I hate to leave you hanging, but that's the show for now. Be sure to tune in and follow the ladies as they prepare for Saturday's big day. Moses Michaels signing off. See ya when I see ya."

"Cut!" Brandon yelled.

"Great show, everyone!" Ed said, clapping his hands.

Saturday was getting ready to make her way over to Brandon when Erick stepped in her path.

"Hello, my love. I hope you're not too shocked at all of this, but Ed said you wouldn't mind the surprise. I know we haven't seen each other in a while, but I think we really made a connection, don't you?"

Saturday was only half listening to Erick. She was too busy watching Brandon watch them. And Brandon was giving her the evil eye. She could just imagine what he was thinking. "Erick, I'm going to need to talk to you later."

As Saturday was making her way over to where Brandon stood, Ed approached her. "Now, that was GREAT television! If we keep up this type of drama, we'll be sure to beat the competition."

Saturday barely heard what Ed was saying. Instead, she was focused on Brandon, who gathered his notes and walked off the set. She wanted desperately to talk to him but kept getting waylaid. Their brief conversation in her dressing room hadn't convinced Brandon that she wasn't into Erick, and now she was wearing his ring. She started to go after him but reasoned it was probably better to let Brandon cool off first. *I'll call him later,* she thought as Ed continued to sing her praises.

Chapter 24

Brandon walked the crowded streets of Manhattan in a state of disbelief. He was oblivious to the people swarming around him as he plodded along, his steps much slower than the rest. He was well aware of Ayana's duel persona and had accepted her antics as Saturday sparring with the other cast members. But what he couldn't accept was her being engaged to another man. Brandon didn't care if the entire proposal was staged. In his opinion, she should have straight-out said, *HELL NO, I WON'T MARRY YOU!* But she'd smiled and sat patiently while another man slipped a huge diamond ring on her finger. Brandon probably could have accepted the fake engagement if it hadn't been for the tape. Watching her kiss another man was too much. Not only was she lip-locked with him, but from the looks of it—the way she was hugged up with him—she was enjoying every second of their romantic carriage ride.

As Brandon walked aimlessly down Broadway, his cell buzzed. He dug the phone out of his jeans' pocket and looked at the caller ID. It was Ayana. He thought about answering her call but wasn't ready to talk to her just yet. He was still upset that she had accepted the proposal and needed to wrap his mind around what had happened and what he should do about the situation. He needed time to think. He pressed Ignore and put the phone back in his pocket. Brandon didn't feel like going home and watching mindless television or staring at the walls. Instead, he walked into an Italian restaurant and went directly to the bar.

"Hi, what can I get you to drink?" the bartender asked.

"I'll have a bottle of Apothic Red." Brandon planned on being there awhile and didn't want to bother with ordering one glass of wine after another.

"Coming right up."

While Brandon waited for the bartender to return, he looked around the restaurant. Serafina was packed with the after-theater crowd munching on homemade pizzas, delicious pastas, fresh fish and grilled filet mignon. When the bartender came back, Brandon ordered a thin-crusted margherita pizza to complement the wine.

As Brandon enjoyed a glass of red wine, he heard someone call his name. He swiveled around on the stool.

"Hey, B, where the hell have you been?" his friend Jon asked as he walked up to the bar.

"Hey, Jon, I've been meaning to call you." Brandon hadn't spoken to his friend since the shooting started for *Divorced Divas*.

"Man, you did a vanishing act on a brother. The last time we spoke, you were getting ready for your first day on that reality show with them hot chicks," Jon said, licking his lips as if envisioning the cast. "So, how's it going?"

"What are you doing here? Are you meeting friends?" Brandon asked, ignoring Jon's question. There was so much to tell that Brandon didn't know where to start, so he averted the question.

"Yeah, I'm meeting my new girl, Ashley. I haven't spoken to you since I met her. Man, she's so fine it's ridiculous."

"Sit down and tell me how you guys met. You want a glass of wine?"

When Jon sat down, Brandon motioned for the bartender and asked him to bring another glass.

"Man, she's a dancer and is in the ensemble of *Kinky Boots,* the new Cyndi Lauper and Harvey Fierstein musical. She's so good that she ought to have a starring role," Jon said, gushing. "We met through mutual friends one night after the show."

"Wow, you must really like this woman. I haven't seen you this excited about somebody in a while."

"Well…I wouldn't say all that." Jon was a ladies' man and didn't like admitting that he was hung up on one woman.

"Don't deny it. The way you feel about her is written all over your face."

"Okay, okay." Jon threw up his hands in mock defense. "You got me. It's true—she might be the *one.*"

As they were talking, Brandon's cell buzzed. He took the phone out of his pocket and looked at the caller ID.

It was Ayana calling again. He ignored her call and placed his phone back in his pocket.

"The *one?* Wow, I've never heard you say that before."

"That's because I've never felt this way before. Man, we're not getting any younger, and I've been thinking a lot about settling down."

Brandon was floored. Jon, the ladies' man, was actually serious about one woman. Hearing Jon admit his true feelings made Brandon think about Ayana. He had thought that she was the *one,* but now he wasn't so sure.

"So what about you? Have you been dating?" Jon asked.

"Sort of." Brandon didn't feel like baring his soul and confessing that he had fallen in love with the cast member that Jon had gushed over before Brandon started the show. His and Ayana's situation had turned complicated, and it would be difficult explaining that his woman was engaged to another man. Besides, clarifying all the details to Jon would expose Ayana's fake persona, and he wasn't going to jeopardize what she had worked so hard to conceal.

"Oh, I see you're taking a page from my playbook and rotating the ladies," Jon said, smiling.

"Well, I wouldn't say all that."

"Come on, man. Don't be modest. So what if you're dating multiple women? You're single and that's what single men do."

But he wasn't truly single. His heart was with one woman. Even though he was upset with her, he couldn't deny that he was deeply in love with Ayana "Saturday Knight" Lewis.

As they were talking, in walked Jon's girlfriend, Ashley, along with another woman.

"Hey, there's my girl," Jon said, quickly rising from the bar stool and giving Ashley a big hug and kiss. "Man, this is Ashley and her friend Naomi. Ladies, this is my main man, Brandon."

"Hello," the ladies said in unison.

Brandon shook their hands and offered them the two empty bar stools next to him. He had to admit that Jon was right. Ashley was gorgeous, and so was her friend. They both had long, lean dancers' bodies and beautiful faces. Brandon motioned for the bartender and asked him to bring two additional glasses. As he watched the bartender pour the ladies a glass of wine, his phone buzzed. He didn't bother to take his phone out of his pocket this time. He knew it was probably Ayana calling again.

"So, how do you guys know each other?" Ashley asked.

"B and I grew up together in Queens."

"That's ironic. Naomi and I have also known each other since childhood. Ever since we were kids, we both wanted to be dancers. We would put on talent shows in the summer and perform for the neighbors."

Brandon turned his attention to Naomi and asked, "How long have you been dancing on Broadway?"

"This is my first Broadway show. I've been all over Europe and Africa learning different techniques and dancing. I recently came back to the States and landed this gig. So what do you do?"

"I work in television," he said vaguely.

"Oh, really? Where?"

"Brandon is the director for *Divorced Divas*," Jon said, answering for his friend.

"Oh, we love that show!" Ashley and Naomi exclaimed.

"Those women are so sharp. They dress to the nines. I mean, they are put together from head to toe. Do designers donate clothes for the ladies to wear?" Ashley asked.

"I have no idea," Brandon answered.

"So tell me, is Saturday as much of a diva in person as she is on-screen?" Naomi asked.

"Yep," he simply said, not wanting to expound.

He wanted to quickly change the subject. The last person he wanted to talk about was Saturday. So, noticing the bottle of wine was empty, he ordered another bottle and turned to Naomi. "I'd much rather hear about your work."

"There's really not much to talk about. We dance in the chorus line with hopes of one day having a starring role in a show. That's basically it. Your job, however, must be so exciting. I mean, you're the director of a hit TV show. Now, that's something to talk about. Tell me, who's your favorite cast member?" Naomi asked, leaning in closer to him. "Saturday is my favorite. She makes the show interesting. You never know what she's going to say or do. The way she ribs Petra is a hoot. She's always correcting the poor girl's English. Give us a scoop."

"What do you mean? What kind of scoop?"

Naomi moved even closer to Brandon, their bodies nearly touching. "Tell us some juicy insider information. Like which guy out of all Saturday's dates is she going to wind up with? I don't see her with that nerdy-looking guy. And the man she had mad chemistry with, I think his name was Erick, never came back on the show. Do you think he's coming back?"

As Brandon hesitated, he wanted to say, *Her name is Ayana, and she's mine.* But of course he couldn't. As he sat there trying to decide how to steer the conversation away from *Divorced Divas* and Saturday's choice of men, he heard a familiar voice from behind.

"Oh, that's why you couldn't answer any of my calls. You're on a flipping date!"

He spun around and saw Ayana standing there with her hand on her hip, looking from him to Naomi.

"We're not on a…"

"Oh, my God—Saturday Knight! I can't believe it! We were just talking about you," Naomi exclaimed.

Ashley chimed in, "Saturday, is that Erick over there?"

Saturday didn't respond. She stood there and glared at Brandon.

Before Brandon could explain, Ayana turned around and hurried away. He started to go after her, but Ed, Steve and Erick were waiting by the hostess podium. They probably couldn't hear Ayana but they could clearly see her. Brandon watched Ayana as she walked to their table. She had a disappointed expression on her face. He wanted to rush over, take her in his arms and kiss her like he had done in Jamaica. However, one look at Erick, the Swiss banker, and the entire proposal played over in his mind. He got mad all over again. Brandon returned his attention to Naomi. He needed a distraction from his thoughts, and she was the perfect diversion.

Chapter 25

Ayana could barely sit through dinner with Ed, Steve and Erick. She was too busy stealing glances at the bar where Brandon sat with his date. Ed had wanted to go out with his star, her new fiancé and the executive producer to discuss plans for the season finale—Saturday and Erick's lavish wedding.

"You know, I've been thinking. I decided that The Plaza isn't the best venue for the wedding to take place," Ed told the group.

"And why not?" Erick asked.

"Although I love The Plaza, I think it's been done enough. So many celebrities have had their weddings there. I'm envisioning a tropical locale," Ed remarked.

"Like Fiji?" Steve said.

"No, some place closer."

"Like the Bahamas?" Erick asked.

"Actually, I'm thinking Jamaica. It's only a few hours from New York. What do you think, Saturday?" Ed asked.

Although Ayana's body was physically at the table, her mind was elsewhere. She was too busy wondering what Brandon was talking about with the beautiful woman sitting next to him. The woman now had her hand on his arm as she spoke. Ayana was seething. Brandon had all but blasted her about Erick, and now here he was entertaining another woman.

"Saturday, did you hear what I said?" Ed asked when she didn't respond to his question.

Ayana refocused her attention, momentarily taking her eyes off of Brandon and his date. "I'm sorry. What did you say?"

"I said, I think Jamaica would be the perfect locale for the wedding."

"What wedding?" she asked, looking at him strangely.

"Your wedding to Erick," he responded.

"What! Are you kidding? I thought you said the proposal was just for ratings and that I wasn't expected to marry him," Ayana said, slightly raising her voice. She turned to Erick and said, "Sorry, no offense, but we don't know each other well enough to get married."

Erick didn't say anything. He looked at Ed as if deferring the question to the show's creator.

"Don't panic. The wedding will only look real. A marriage license won't be filed. Therefore, you and Erick won't officially be married," he explained.

"Are you sure? I don't want to mistakenly marry a stranger."

"Yes, I'm certain. Your contract is coming up, so

this wedding will be the perfect way for you to exit the show."

Ayana thought about Ed's reasoning for a few moments. "I guess that does make sense."

"I plan to marry off each of you ladies one by one, depending on who wants out of their contract. And then I'll start fresh with a new divorced diva each season. That way the show will remain fresh," Ed explained.

"So you're saying this will be the last antic I'll ever have to enact," Ayana said, warming up to the idea.

"Yes, this wedding will be your final appearance, and then you're off the show—free to do whatever you please."

That was music to Ayana's ears. She could finally see the light at the end of this dreadful tunnel.

"So what do you think about having the wedding in Jamaica?" Ed asked.

"Jamaica!" Ayana shrieked. She had been lost in thought earlier and hadn't heard him mention her homeland.

Steve and Ed, noticing the way she reacted, said at the same time, "What's wrong with Jamaica?"

"Uh…nothing." She couldn't think of a fast answer, short of telling them the truth, which wasn't an option. "Can we shoot in Montego Bay? It's closer than Negril. If we shoot in Mo'Bay, we wouldn't have to transport the cast and crew on a two-hour bus ride into the country." As long as they didn't film the wedding in her hometown of Negril, Ayana didn't feel too anxious about being seen in Jamaica as her alter ego.

"That's a good idea. I want to shoot the wedding as soon as possible. I know Moses said on set that the show will follow you and the girls as you get ready for the wedding, but that's too long to drag this out. The ratings are slipping fast, and this wedding will help salvage our positioning. Steve, can you oversee all of the arrangements?" Ed asked.

"Sure thing. I have contacts at the Grand Palladium, so it won't be a problem to expedite the shoot. The Grand Palladium is a fabulous five-star hotel and will be the perfect venue."

"Excellent!" Ed exclaimed.

As the three men continued to talk about the upcoming wedding, Ayana tuned out again. News of her exit from the show was great, but she still had the fake proposal to deal with *and* the cold shoulder from Brandon. Finding him with another woman had totally caught her off guard. Ayana glanced over at the bar. She watched as another couple sitting next to Brandon raised their wineglasses and toasted with Brandon and his date. It was clear that the four of them were on a double date. Ayana had half a mind to go over there and break up their little party, but she didn't want to cause a scene. Instead, she took out her cell phone and punched in a text to Brandon.

I see you've moved on. So keep on moving. It's over!

She watched and waited for Brandon to acknowledge the text. A few minutes later, she saw him take his phone out of his pocket and look at it. She assumed he was reading her message. He didn't text back—just put the phone back in his pocket and continued his conversation.

Ayana felt hurt and dejected. A part of her—her heart—wanted to keep the relationship going, but another part of her—her pride—wouldn't let her watch Brandon flirt with another woman in front of her face. She thought that after he read her text, he would come over to the table and ask to speak to her, but he didn't. Her sitting there with Erick was probably keeping Brandon from coming over, she reasoned.

The love that she and Brandon had shared in Jamaica seemed like a lifetime ago. Their enchanted time on the island was now nothing more than a distant memory. Ayana was shocked at how quickly everything had changed. She'd thought that Brandon was the *one*. Now he seemed to be the one who was slowly breaking her heart.

Chapter 26

The feel of his muscular arms wrapped around her body, engulfing her in a sensuous full-body hug, felt like a slice of heaven. Every inch of her being craved him. Ayana was hungry for Brandon's touch. He awakened sexuality within her that she hadn't known she possessed.

He nibbled on her earlobe and then whispered, "I've missed you."

"How much?" she asked softly in his ear.

"I can show you better than I can tell you," he said, holding her closer.

Brandon trailed his lips from her earlobe to her neck, where he sucked ever so tenderly, before increasing the pressure, sucking harder and harder.

Ayana closed her eyes and held on to his bald head. "Ohhh…" she moaned.

He didn't stop until his efforts produced a deep crimson spot, branding her with his personalized mark of love. Brandon then trailed his lips to her chest, stopping right between her breasts. He teased her right nipple with his tongue and played with her left nipple until it firmed to his touch. He alternated from one to the other, licking her ample breasts. Brandon continued down her body with his lips, stopping only to tickle her belly button with his tongue.

Ayana lay helpless, enjoying his luscious lips.

He gripped her hips as he slid between her legs, resting his head in the center of her neatly shaven triangle. Brandon eased his tongue between the folds of her vagina and found her clitoris. He positioned his lips around the tiny head and gently sucked.

"Oohh…oohh…"

Brandon was on a mission to bring her to new heights of orgasm. He wanted to ensure she hungered for no other man. He sucked deeper and harder, his wet mouth engulfing her pleasure button. Saliva dripped from his mouth onto his chin and down her thighs as he worked his magic.

Ayana clenched his head tighter as he made love to her clit.

He reached underneath and took hold of her buttocks, bringing her lady lips closer to his mouth. Brandon's deft lips and tongue were working in concert at a rapid pace. Her essence was like sweet cream in his mouth.

Ayana was in a sexual trance and couldn't speak. Her body was doing all the talking. Her head was tilted toward the headboard. Her back was arched and her toes were clenching the sheets as she surrendered to him. She climaxed hard. Her body jerked as she released.

The tension that had been building in her body was now gone.

Suddenly, there was a knock at the door, jolting Ayana out of her delicious dream. She opened her eyes and looked down, half expecting to see Brandon in between her legs, but all she saw was a moistened sheet. The oral encounter with Brandon may have been a dream, but her orgasm had indeed been real. She sighed, frustrated that he wasn't there in the flesh.

"Yes, who is it?" she yelled.

"It's Gabby. Ed wanted me to remind you that rehearsal is in twenty minutes. We're meeting downstairs in the restaurant," she said through the door.

"Okay. Thanks. I'll be right down."

Ayana stretched, climbed out of bed and made her way to the shower. Fifteen minutes later, she was dressed in a white flowing maxi sundress. Her hair was brushed into a ponytail, and her makeup was minimal. Being in Jamaica with the heat and humidity, she didn't feel like putting on the entire Saturday Knight ensemble— wig, heavy makeup, designer duds, jewelry and heels. She would save all of that for the "big day." Ayana put on a pair of oversize sunglasses, took her key card and headed out the door.

When she reached the restaurant with its ocean views and fresh-cut birds-of-paradise, hibiscus and ginger, she felt a sense of home, but that feeling quickly dissipated when Brooke, Trista and Petra came walking into the room. They rolled their eyes in Ayana's direction and went straight to the buffet. Ayana wanted to go over and explain why she had treated them so badly and apologize for her behavior. Unfortunately, she couldn't—not yet. She didn't like being ostracized by the cast and crew, but it was too late now. Ayana walked in the opposite direction, over to the coffee station.

"Where's the groom-to-be?"

Ayana turned around and faced Brandon. She looked through the dark shades into his handsome face and envisioned him making love to her, like he had done in her dream. She wanted to take him by the hand and lead him upstairs to her bed so they could make that dream a reality. They hadn't spoken since that day in New York, and all Ayana wanted to do was make amends. She regretted sending that text when they were at Serafina, but she had gotten upset seeing him talking with another woman and had reacted without thinking it through. The woman at the bar could have just been a casual friend, for all she knew. Being back in Jamaica, where they'd fallen in love, had brought her back to her senses. She truly loved Brandon and didn't want to break up with him. This was all a huge misunderstanding, and she planned on clearing things up and getting their relationship back on track.

She swallowed hard. "Hi, Brandon."

"Look at you in all white." He eyed her from head to toe. "Don't you look like the bride-to-be?" he said with sarcasm in his voice.

"It's not what you think. This wedding isn't…"

Before she could tell Brandon that the marriage was a charade and that she was leaving the show when it was over, Erick came up from behind and hugged her around the waist. "Good morning, sweetheart."

Brandon stood there for a moment, staring at him holding his woman, and then walked away without saying a word.

Ayana saw the disgusted expression on Brandon's

face and knew that he was pissed. She wanted to back out of the arrangement right then and there. This sham wedding was ruining her life. Watching him walk away brought her to tears. Ayana was thankful for the sunglasses so that no one could see her red-rimmed eyes. She wiggled out of Erick's embrace. "Please don't hug me like that again," she told him.

"Why not? We're a happy couple on the eve of our wedding," he said with a huge smile on his face.

"Okay, everyone, finish your breakfast," Ed said, coming into the room with Gabby trailing behind him holding a clipboard. "We'll be heading out to the pool area to rehearse in a few."

Petra rushed over to Ed and said, "Reunion show supposed to be about all of us dating experience, but it the Saturday Knight show. Why she only one get lavish wedding in Jamaica?" she asked in her broken English.

"Cool it," Ed said, waving his floral chiffon scarf in her face. "I plan to marry you off one by one—no worries. You'll get your chance to waltz down the aisle. Now come on, everyone. Down to the pool."

Outside, the pool was enormous and inviting, with crystal clear, ice-blue water. It was the perfect backdrop to the turquoise ocean. A grandiose white-columned gazebo stood at the end of the pool with stunning views of the island.

Ed stepped up on the marble platform of the gazebo. "Saturday and Erick, come up here. You two will stand here with the minister."

Ayana glanced at Brandon, who was standing near the edge of the pool. He was staring into the water, appearing deep in thought.

"Brandon, can you come up here?" Ed called out.

Ayana watched Brandon slowly make his way over. He kept his eyes straight ahead without giving her a second look.

"Stand next to Saturday. I want you to see the vantage point from here. I want a camera at the end of the row of chairs so that it can capture the ocean. A camera will also be in the front to film their faces as the minister conducts the ceremony. Got it?" Ed asked.

"Yep."

As Brandon stood close to her, Ayana became anxious. He still had no idea that the wedding was a sham, and she could see the anger in his eyes as Ed spoke. Ayana was afraid that the longer Brandon went on without knowing the truth, the wider the rift between them would become until it was beyond repair.

"Saturday, I want you looking deeply into Erick's eyes as the minister asks you to recite your vows so that the camera can capture your sincerity," Ed instructed.

The beautiful surroundings were the perfect venue for a wedding. Ayana had always dreamed of having an ocean-side ceremony, but she'd never thought her second wedding would be a sham. Ayana cut her eyes at Brandon and watched his nonexpression as Ed spoke. Brandon looked as though he'd rather be anywhere else but there.

"Excuse me, Ed. Can I talk to you for a second?" she asked.

"Not now, Saturday. I want to run through everything so we'll be ready to shoot tomorrow."

Ayana wanted to tell Ed to ease up and not focus so hard on her reactions during the ceremony. He was talking as if the wedding was going to be the real deal.

The more Ed spoke, the harder it was going to be for her to explain to Brandon the truth about the wedding.

Ayana stepped a bit closer to Brandon so that her arm was touching his. She wanted to convey with body language what she couldn't say with words, but he moved away from her the moment her arm touched his. *What's the use? He's over me.*

The rest of the morning and afternoon was filled with details for the televised nuptials. Ed left nothing to chance. He planned on this being the event of the season. The cast and crew all had their orders, and he expected them to carry out his vision flawlessly. Everyone was excited about the extravaganza except Petra and Saturday. The only thing she could think about was telling Brandon the truth—that the wedding wasn't legal—before she lost him once and for all.

Chapter 27

Ed had hired the best wedding planner on the island, and she arranged everything from ordering the bouquets for the bride and her attendants to selecting the delicious cuisine and champagne for the reception. She even had a designer wedding gown and shoes flown in from New York.

Today was the big day. All the minute details that comprised a wedding were taken care of with all the speed and ease money could buy. To expedite the magical day, Ed used some of his personal funds and told the wedding planner to spare no expense.

Ayana was in her room getting ready to make her grand appearance. She had made up her face expertly, complete with false eyelashes. Hair extensions made her natural hair even longer, giving her a more glamorous look. Ed wanted an attendant to help her dress, but she insisted on being alone. Ayana needed to collect her thoughts before putting on the performance of her life. She stood at the foot of the bed in her underwear and peered down at the pearl-white wedding gown, which was spread out on the bed. There was no denying the dress was beautiful, with its hand-embroidered beading and lace. This was exactly the type of gown she would have chosen if she were marrying Brandon. She sat next to the dress and ran her hand over the duchess silk satin. The feel of the smooth fabric was calming.

Ayana glanced at the clock on the nightstand. "Sixty minutes to showtime," she said out loud and exhaled. A part of her wanted to get the show over with as soon as possible so that she could finally prove to Brandon that the wedding was just for ratings. She planned on showing him that the marriage license was never filed, rendering the union null and void. Ayana reached for the hotel phone. She wanted one last shot at talking to Brandon before he saw her in the wedding dress. The hurt she'd seen in his eyes during rehearsal would be even worse during the actual wedding, and Ayana thought that she could spare him the pain if he knew the truth.

"Hi, may I have Brandon Gilliam's room, please?" she asked the operator.

"Hold on, please." After a few seconds, the operator returned. "I'm sorry, miss, that line is busy. Would you like to call back in a few minutes?"

"Uh…okay, I'll do that." Ayana hung up and thought about calling Brandon on his cell phone, but he would probably ignore the call like he had done in New York. She desperately wanted to talk to him and reasoned that she could get in touch with him if she used the hotel phone. Ayana waited a few minutes and called the operator back.

"Hi, can you try Brandon Gilliam's room again?"

"Sure. Hold on, please."

After a few rings, Brandon picked up. "Hello?"

"Hey, it's me," she said sheepishly.

"Yeah, what do you want?" he asked coldly.

"We need to talk face-to-face before the wedding. What room are you in? I'll come to you," she said, speaking fast.

"You're getting married in an hour. What's there to talk about? This is a done deal. You've made your choice—now live with it. Goodbye, Ayana. Have a good life." Click.

He hung up before she had a chance to explain the situation. Ayana felt like crying. The lie was killing her inside. Ayana had to do something and fast. She considered her options and realized the only thing to do was show Brandon the unauthorized marriage certificate. Maybe once he saw that the document didn't have an official seal, he would believe her once and for all.

Ayana quickly slipped on the gown, zipped it up on the side, stepped into the white satin shoes, grabbed her key card and headed out the door. Ed's suite was on the top floor of the hotel. She made her way down the hall to the elevator and waited impatiently for it to arrive. When the doors opened, she stepped inside. An elderly couple stood near the row of buttons, dressed in matching Hawaiian shirts and khaki shorts and holding souvenir bags.

"Oh, my, what a beautiful bride you are!" the woman said, putting her hand up to her mouth.

"I still remember our wedding day like it was yesterday. You were the most beautiful bride I had ever seen," the man said, turning to his wife and smiling.

"Oh, aren't you the sweetest?"

The husband kissed his wife on the cheek.

"We've been happily married for thirty-seven years. And I wish you and your groom the same type of bliss me and my Walter have found," the lady said, holding on to her husband's arm.

One look at them, and Ayana knew that true happiness was possible. Their love for each other was palpable. Ayana wanted her and Brandon to share that same type of love again. "Thank you. I plan on making that happen."

Once the doors opened, she nearly leaped off the elevator. Ayana picked up the hem of the dress so that she could move faster, and dashed down the hallway. When she reached Ed's suite, a bellhop was wheeling out a white, linen-covered dining cart. She quickly whisked past him. The suite was huge with a long L-shaped entryway. As Ayana was making her way toward the living room, she could hear voices.

"So what are you going to do about the license?"

Ayana stopped in her tracks at the sound of Steve's voice.

"What do you mean?" Ed answered.

"I mean, you told Saturday that the marriage license wouldn't be filed."

"Yes, that was my initial plan, but the officials here said we couldn't have a wedding without an actual license, so I had no choice but to file it."

"The big question is…are you going to tell Saturday and Erick that the marriage is real?" Steve asked.

"I already talked to Erick and he's okay going through

with the wedding. He adores Saturday and would love nothing more than to marry her."

Ayana's knees nearly buckled. She couldn't believe what she was hearing. Her first instinct was to burst into the room and confront Ed, but this was her opportunity to learn what Ed was planning.

"Are you going to tell Saturday the truth?"

Ed started laughing. "Are you kidding? You know as well as I do that she won't go along with this. She didn't want to do a fake wedding, so do you honestly think she'll be okay with an official wedding?"

"I guess you're right."

"Of course I'm right," Ed said with an edge of cockiness to his voice.

And to think I saved his life, she thought, shaking her head. Ayana was hurt and disappointed. She'd thought that Ed was her friend, but the only thing he was loyal to was ratings.

Ed continued, "Besides, if the marriage doesn't work out, they can always get an annulment. People do it every day."

"That's true," Steve agreed.

Ayana had heard enough. She turned around and slowly walked out. As she made her way back to the elevator, she was having a hard time wrapping her mind around the fact that Ed was willing to dupe her into an arranged marriage for the sake of a stupid reality show. At that point, Ayana knew exactly what she had to do.

Chapter 28

The harpist softly strummed her harp strings, playing Bach as the guests arrived. Ed had hired local islanders as extras, so every chair at the ceremony was filled. The outdoor pool area was decorated with white and lavender roses. Large lavender bows were tied to the backs of white chairs and the gazebo was draped with white and lavender chiffon fabric that floated on the midday breeze. The entire scene looked like something out of a fairy tale.

Brandon sat in the last row, taking in the idyllic surroundings. He looked down at the lavender runner and couldn't believe Ayana would be walking down that aisle on her way to marry another man. She had said that the proposal was for ratings and that she had told Erick before that she couldn't marry him. But clearly that was one big lie.

How did things go so wrong? he thought. Brandon reached in his shirt pocket and took out the airline napkin. He gently unfolded it and read the front: *Blissfully Yours, B.* Then he turned it over and read Ayana's writing: *Blissfully Yours, A.* He put the napkin to his lips and kissed the ruby-red lip imprint that she had made. Brandon knew this would be the last time he kissed her lips. His heart ached, but there was nothing he could do about it. Now he wished like hell that he had listened to what she had to say when she'd called his room earlier. She could have been calling to tell him that she wasn't going through with the wedding, but now he would never know. It was too late for should've, would've, could'ves. He refolded the napkin and put it back in his pocket. That memento was all he had left from their time together and he planned on cherishing it forever. As he was sitting there feeling forlorn, his cell phone vibrated. Brandon's heart started racing faster, thinking it might be Ayana. He quickly retrieved the phone from his pocket and looked at the caller ID. His heart stopped racing. It wasn't Ayana; it was his agent.

"Hey, Mario, what's up?"

"Hi, Brandon. My assistant told me you called. Sorry I'm just getting back to you, but I was in Italy on my honeymoon."

Damn! Is everybody getting married but me? "Congratulations, man. I didn't even know you were engaged."

"Well, it wasn't a long engagement. We met at an industry function and had an instant attraction. I just knew she was the woman for me, and I didn't want to wait around and chance somebody else swooping in and stealing my lady."

"Yeah, I know what you mean," Brandon said, looking straight ahead at the altar.

"Well, I didn't call to talk about my honeymoon. I have great news for you."

"Good. I could use some good news right about now," he said.

"It's a good thing you only signed on to work on *Divorced Divas* for one season," Mario said.

"And why is that?"

"I have an awesome deal on the table for you. It's directing a *60 Minutes*–type show for one of the majors. If you want the job, I can start negotiations right away."

"Hell yeah, I want the job! The sooner I leave this train wreck of a show, the better."

"Excellent. I'll contact the executives at the station and get the paperwork going."

"Thanks, Mario, for coming through for me."

"Hey, man, that's why I get paid the big bucks." He laughed and then said, "Oh, I forgot to ask—why did you call?"

Brandon was momentarily so caught up with the news of his new gig that he forgot all about mentioning Ayana to his agent. For a split second he thought about forgetting the favor. Now that she was marrying a rich Swiss banker, she probably wouldn't be interested in pursuing an acting career. However, he had made a promise to her and planned on keeping it.

"Are you taking on any new clients?"

"Yes, I'm always looking for talented people. Why? Do you have someone in mind?"

"As a matter of fact, I do. Saturday Knight is looking for representation. She…"

"Oh, wait right there," Mario said, cutting him off.

"I said I'm looking for talent. I'm not interested in repping a soiled reality-show diva."

"See, that's where you're wrong." Brandon lowered his voice and put his hand over his mouth, careful not to be overheard. "Saturday Knight is a fake persona that Ayana Lewis puts on for the show."

"What? Who's Ayana Lewis?" Mario asked, confused.

"That's Saturday's real name. Ayana is a sweetheart and is nothing like the person you see on television." As Brandon defended his former lover, he realized that he was still in love with her.

"Wow. So you're telling me that whole routine is nothing but an act?"

"Yep, Ayana is a natural actress and would be an asset to your roster," Brandon said, singing her praises.

"I would definitely say so. I really thought that was her true personality. Man, she had me fooled. Have her call my assistant and set up an appointment so we can talk."

"Listen, why don't I just give your assistant Ayana's number instead?" Brandon suggested. He didn't know if or when he and Ayana were going to speak again, and he didn't want to stand in the way of her career.

"That'll be fine. Talk to you later."

"Okay, goodbye." Although he and Ayana were no longer together, he was happy that he could fulfill at least that one promise.

"Why are you sitting all the way back here?" Ed asked, walking up to Brandon.

"What's up, Ed?" he said, looking at the white linen pants and shirt he wore with a lavender scarf draped around his neck. Ed looked like a bride himself in his outfit.

"We're ready to get started, and I need you in director mode. I want to start in five."

Brandon exhaled hard. The moment that he had been dreading was finally here. "No problem."

"I'll have Gabby go get the girls," Ed said, turning and scurrying away, his long lavender scarf floating on the breeze behind him.

Brandon went to his designated position, put on his headset and cued the crew, making sure everyone was in place and ready to shoot. From his position near the altar, but out of the camera's frame, Brandon watched Erick and the minister walk onto the gazebo, which was an indication they were ready to begin.

"Okay, everyone. Ready in five, four, three, two, one. Action!" Brandon announced into his microphone.

On cue, out came Trista in a lavender halter dress, carrying a bouquet of white and lavender flowers. Brooke followed behind Trista, also wearing lavender, but her dress was sleeveless. Next was a tiny flower girl also in lavender. She tossed out white rose petals as she walked slowly up the aisle. Petra was a no-show. Brandon figured that she probably didn't want any part in Saturday's wedding.

Once the bridal party had made their way to the altar, the harpist stopped and the bridal march began. Everyone rose to their feet in honor of the bride.

Brandon watched Ayana glide down the aisle in a gorgeous white beaded gown. She looked like a traditional bride with layers of tulle covering her face. His mouth became dry, and his palms began sweating more and more the closer she got to the altar.

Oh, shit, this is really happening. He wanted to voice his objection before the minister had a chance to ask if anyone had "just cause" to stop the wedding. Brandon took a deep breath. But this was Ayana's choice and there was nothing he could do about it.

When she reached the altar, the music stopped and the minister began speaking.

"Ladies and gentlemen, we are gathered here today to witness the marriage between this man and this woman."

Brandon tuned out the minister's words. Once the minister reached the vow part of the ceremony, a few words caught Brandon's attention, bringing him out of his zone and back to reality. He couldn't believe his ears. *This must be some kind of mistake!* Brandon listened as the minister asked them to repeat after him, and he then watched as they slipped platinum bands on each other's fingers.

"...By the power vested in me, I now pronounce you man and wife. You may kiss your bride."

A lump caught in Brandon's throat as he watched Erick lift her veil.

Erick then kissed his new bride, Petra, on the lips, as the audience clapped. The happy couple then turned around and walked arm in arm down the aisle.

Brandon was dumbfounded. A million questions ran through his head, but most important, where was Ayana?

Once Erick and Petra disappeared inside the hotel, Brandon yelled, "Cut!" He took his headset off and raced toward the front of the hotel. He had to find Ayana and fast. He didn't know what had happened, but he planned on finding out.

Chapter 29

Brandon searched the main floor of the hotel but didn't see Ayana anywhere. He hurried to the front desk and asked the clerk to call up to Ayana's room. He tapped his fingers on the counter while he waited.

"Sorry, sir, there was no answer."

"What's her room number? I can go and see if she's upstairs."

"Sorry, sir, we can't give out the room numbers of our guests."

"But it's urgent that I see her," he said with panic in his voice.

"I'm very sorry, but it's against hotel policy to give out room numbers."

Brandon sighed. He took out his cell phone and called Ayana, but his call went to her voice mail. "Hey, it's me. Please call me as soon as you get this message."

He didn't know what else to do. He was dying to talk to Ayana. First, he wanted to make sure she was okay, and second, he wanted to know the reason she hadn't gone through with the wedding.

Since he couldn't find Ayana, he went in search of Ed, who was no doubt behind switching brides at the twelfth hour. Brandon bolted through the doors of the Grand Ballroom, where the reception was being held, and made his way through the throng of people milling about drinking champagne and eating hors d'oeuvres.

"Where the hell have you been?" Ed asked, rushing up to Brandon. "We should have already started taping this reception. I spent good money to have the entire event filmed, not just the wedding."

"Speaking of…what happened to Ayana?" Brandon asked, totally ignoring Ed's comment.

"Ayana?" A shocked expression appeared on Ed's face. "How do you know her real name?"

"Answer my question first. Where is she?"

Ed waved his manicured hand in the air. "I don't have time to waste talking about her. Get your headset on and direct this reception. You are still under contract, remember?"

Brandon really wanted to tell Ed to shove his contract, but he didn't want to walk off the set on the last day of filming. He was a professional and didn't want the word getting out that he had abandoned a show. Brandon turned his back to Ed and went over to the cordoned-off area that was set up for the crew. He put on his headset and went into action.

The reception was a lavish affair, from a Moët & Chandon champagne fountain, to freshly caught seafood, to delicious Jamaican fare. There was a deejay and one of the island's most popular reggae bands. Brandon could hardly concentrate on his job. His mind was intent on finding Ayana. She was somewhere on the island, but where?

"Would you like a glass of champagne?" Brooke asked, walking up to him with two glasses in her hands.

"No, thank you. I'm working."

"So am I," she said, taking a sip.

"Our jobs are totally different. You're paid to party, and I'm paid to direct the party," he said without making eye contact.

"Why are you so mean to me?" she asked, looking wounded.

Brandon turned and looked at her. "Brooke, I'm not trying to be mean. I'm in love with someone else, and I don't want to lead you on."

"I get it. I was in love once, and it's a beautiful thing when two people are on the same page."

Brandon listened to her words and only hoped that Ayana still felt the way he did. A lot had changed since they had left Jamaica. Brandon just hoped it wasn't too late to win her back. "Yes, love can be beautiful."

"Well, I wish you and your lady, whoever she is, good luck," Brooke said and walked away.

"Hey, Brooke," Brandon called after her.

She turned around and came back. "Yes, Brandon?"

"Have you seen Aya…uh…Saturday?"

"I saw her earlier with her bags. She was outside of the hotel getting ready to board a bus. I guess Ed fired her—she left. I don't really know for sure."

"Fired?"

"That's the word going around. I, for one, am glad to see her go."

"Thanks, Brooke," he said, ignoring her last comment.

Shortly after the reception was over, and the cameras had stopped rolling, Ed thanked the cast and crew for a great season. Brandon immediately rushed back to the front desk.

"What time does the last bus leave for Negril?" he asked the clerk. Brandon had a good suspicion that Ayana had gone home. Whatever had happened to prevent her from going through with the wedding must have been serious. He reasoned that she probably wanted to leave Montego Bay for the comfort of her parents' home.

"Sorry, sir, but the last bus left an hour ago."

"Are there any rental-car companies in the area?" Although the road to Negril was long, winding and dark, Brandon was willing to travel during the night to get the woman he loved.

"All of the rental-car places are closed for the evening."

Brandon slumped against the counter. He was out of ideas. The only thing he could do now was wait until morning. He asked what time the first bus to Negril departed in the morning, then thanked the clerk and went to his room.

Sleep escaped Brandon as he tossed and turned. His mind wouldn't let him rest. He kept thinking about Ayana and how he hadn't given her a chance to explain.

Brandon was up with the sun. He quickly packed. It was still too early to go downstairs and board the bus, so he called Ayana, hoping this time she would pick up.

Her cell phone didn't ring. It went right to voice mail.

"Hey, baby, it's me again. Where are you? Please call me back as soon as you get this message." Brandon was really beginning to panic. Maybe Ayana had fallen ill. Brandon sat on the bed and put his head in his hands. He was racked with worry and guilt.

An hour later, he was on the bus headed to Negril. The ride was long and bumpy. The bus driver wove through the winding roads at a breakneck pace, as if the bus were on rails. Brandon was thankful for the accelerated speed. He couldn't get to Negril fast enough. He was a man on a mission. When they finally reached the town, he asked the driver to let him off at the first hotel stop. Brandon then caught a taxi to take him to Ayana's parents' house.

As Brandon sat in the backseat of the taxi, his heart raced. He was moments from possibly seeing Ayana, and he could hardly wait. He had so much to say to her, but most important, he wanted to apologize for acting like a jerk. Had he listened to her in the first place, he wouldn't be racing all over Jamaica trying to find the love of his life. When they reached the house, he asked the driver to wait while he rang the doorbell.

After a few seconds that seemed like hours, the front door opened.

"Hi, Mrs. Tosh. How are you? I'm Brandon, a friend of Ayana's," he said, his words rushing out.

The older lady surveyed Brandon from head to toe and began to smile. "Yes, chile, I remember ya."

"Is Ayana home?"

"No, chile, she not here."

His heart sank. "Do you know where she is?"

"No, chile. Her left here early dis mornin'."

"Oh, okay. Can you tell her I stopped by?"

"Sure."

"Thanks," he said and went back to the taxi. Although she wasn't at home, he was relieved to know that she wasn't lying in bed sick and was at least still on the island. Brandon asked the driver to take him to New Beginnings.

The shelter was busy as usual with children running and playing in the front yard. Brandon walked through the front door and went to Marigold's office. His sister-in-law was behind the desk doing paperwork.

"Hey, sis," he said.

Marigold looked up. "Oh, me word! Whacha doin' here? Me thought ya were back in New York."

He leaned across the desk and gave her a hug. "I'm here for work. Uh...have you seen Ayana?"

"Ana?" She smiled. "No, I haven't seen her. Whacha want wit Ana? Thought ya said ya were here for work. Ya sweet on dat gurl, aren't ya?" Marigold asked, cutting right to the chase.

Brandon nodded his head. "Yes, I am."

"Me knew it! Me could see dat when ya two were here last time. Ya two were lookin' at each other da way me and James used to. Me glad ya finally found da one."

"Me, too." *I just hope it's not too late,* he thought. "Well, if she comes by, can you tell her to call me?"

"No problem. Ya staying at the bungalow?"

"Yes." He planned on staying on the island until he found Ayana.

Brandon kissed his sister-in-law goodbye. He then headed back toward the taxi. Once he got in, he sat and thought for a moment.

"Where to now, mon?" The driver interrupted his thoughts.

Brandon wanted to go to the bungalow and get his brother's car so that he could do a thorough search of the island. He gave the driver the address, then sat back and gazed out the open window. As he looked at the beautiful countryside with its lush landscape, he spotted a yellow Vespa whizzing by on the other side of the road. It was Ayana.

"Hey, turn around and follow that scooter!"

Brandon sat on the edge of the seat as the driver followed his instructions. Brandon's heart was racing as fast as the scooter. He had finally found her. Now he prayed that she would give him a second chance.

Chapter 30

Ayana's long hair blew in the breeze as she sped along the dirt road on the way to her favorite place. She needed the seclusion of the mountains to clear her head and think about her future plans. As Ayana wove through the mountainside, she replayed the past twenty-four hours in her mind.

After sneaking out of Ed's suite, Ayana had gone back to her room and taken off the wedding dress. There was no way she was going through with the wedding after what she had heard. It was one thing to pretend to marry Erick and another thing entirely to actually marry a man she didn't love. She had put the dress back in the garment bag, returned the satin Jimmy Choos to the shoe box and wrapped the jewelry in tissue paper. At the time, Ayana hadn't had a plan. All she knew was that she wasn't going to marry a man she didn't love. She had sat on the side of the bed, trying to devise a strategy. She knew that Ed would be beyond pissed and would probably threaten to sue her for breaching the contract. After all, she had promised to do a final episode. Time was ticking and Ayana had to think fast.

"I've got it!" she said, hopping to her feet.

Ayana quickly dressed in a pair of jeans, T-shirt and flip-flops. She gathered the bridal gear, putting it in bags, and headed out the door. On the elevator ride to Ed's floor, her heart began beating fast. She didn't know how he was going to take the news. When the doors opened, she stepped out and said a silent prayer as she made her way down the hallway. She knocked at his door and waited. A few seconds later, Ed answered.

He took one look at her and said, "What are you still doing in your street clothes?"

"Can I come in? We need to talk." Ayana hadn't waited for him to answer. She'd walked past him into the suite. As she marched down the long hall, she'd flashed back on Ed and Steve's conversation and had gotten mad all over again.

Once she entered the spacious living room, which was decorated in all white with floor-to-ceiling windows and spectacular views of the ocean, she'd relieved her arms of the dress, shoes and jewelry. "Here you go!"

"What the hell are you doing?" Ed had asked, looking at the bags of bridal gear in the chair.

"I should be asking you the same thing" she'd said, putting her hands on her hips.

"What are you talking about?"

"I'm talking about you trying to pull a fast one on me!" Ayana raised her voice.

Again Ed had said, "What are you talking about? Are you drunk or something?" He'd eyed her closely.

"No, I'm not drunk, but you must think I'm stupid."

"What I think is that you'd better pick up this stuff, go back to your room and get dressed. The wedding starts in less than an hour."

"There's only going to be a wedding if you listen to what I have to say."

Ed had exhaled hard. "There's nothing for you to say but 'I do.'"

"Oh, you mean, say 'I do' and get legally married to Erick!"

Ed had opened his mouth but didn't utter a word when he heard her remark. He was shocked that she knew the truth.

Ayana had looked at the expression on his face. "That's right. I know all about your scheme. The marriage license that was supposed to be unofficial is now the real deal, which means that after this wedding Erick and I will be legally married. But of course you don't care about that. All you care about is your stupid ratings. To hell with everything else! Ed, how could you do this to me?" Tears had formed in her eyes. "I saved your life, and this is how you repay me?"

Ed then had flung the lavender scarf around his neck, cleared his throat and said, "It's not personal."

"Are you kidding me? Marrying somebody I don't love is extremely personal! And I'm not going through with it!"

"Oh, yes, you are! You're under contract…remember?"

As they stood there yelling at each other, Ayana took a deep breath. She needed to get through to Ed, and screaming back and forth wasn't doing the trick. "Ed, can we please sit down and talk?" she'd asked in a calm voice.

He didn't move.

"Ed, if my saving your life meant anything at all to you, you'll hear me out." Ayana had been determined to be heard, so she used the only card she had left.

Ed had crossed the room and sat on the sofa. "Okay, what do you have to say? Make it quick."

She sat in one of the leather chairs. "I know that this wedding is important to you, and I've figured out a way for it to still take place. What if Petra marries Erick instead of me?"

"And how is that supposed to work?"

"You have pull at the official's office where you got the license, right?"

"Yes."

"Well, have them take my name off the license and put Petra's name on."

"I guess I could pay them a hefty bonus to come to the hotel and do the paperwork. That way the wedding won't be delayed too long. But what if she doesn't want to marry him?"

"Who wouldn't want to marry Erick? He's handsome, smart and rich. Besides, they are both European and probably have a lot in common. Why don't you run it past both of them? You are a convincing man, and I'm sure you can get them to agree. And you can also tell them, like you told Steve, that they can always get an annulment if it doesn't work out."

Ed had been silent for a moment, and Ayana could see that he was thinking about the idea. She then added, "Besides, this will be the shocker of all shockers. The audience won't see the switch coming. Talk about increasing ratings. And…" She took a breath. "You can use their wedding as a teaser for next season. The promos could focus on how Petra stole Erick from Saturday."

Ed's face had lit up. "Actually, that's a brilliant idea. You two are always going at it, and this would be the perfect way for Petra to get you back—by stealing your man."

"Yes! That's right! To seal the deal with Petra, emphasize that this will put the spotlight on her and make her and Erick's wedding the most talked about event of the season. Tell her that now she's the star of the show."

"I must say, Ayana—you've thought of everything. Let's call them now," he said, getting up and walking over to the phone.

"Now, if it's okay with you, I'm going to leave. I don't want to stick around for the wedding."

"Yes, I think that's best. I don't want Petra irritated. See you back in New York."

She'd turned to walk away.

"Ayana, wait. I am sorry for putting you through all of this, but you know how crazy I get about the show. Sometimes my judgment gets clouded by the ratings. There are a gazillion reality shows, and the competition to stay on top is extremely stiff. I do appreciate you administering CPR when I had the heart attack, and I promise to give you a glowing reference for whatever you want to do in the future."

"Thanks, Ed. I appreciate that."

They said their goodbyes, and Ayana went back to her room and packed. Before leaving the hotel, she had one more thing to do. She called the front desk and asked for Petra's room.

"Hello?" Petra had answered.

"Hi, Petra. It's Saturday."

"What you want?" she'd snapped into the receiver.

"I just want to apologize for always being so hard on you. It wasn't personal—just a job I had to do."

"I no need you apology. I have you man." Click. Petra had hung up in Ayana's ear.

As Ayana left the hotel and boarded the last bus to Negril, she'd looked back and thought about Brandon. She'd wanted to tell him goodbye, but he was probably in work mode by now. *Hopefully I'll see him back in New York,* she'd thought as the bus pulled off.

Ayana had reached her destination. She pulled over to the side of the road and turned off the motor. She climbed off the scooter and cut through the trees until she reached the manicured patch of land. She sat on the grass. She looked out over the trees at the beautiful mountainside and remembered her last time there. She and Brandon had had a perfect afternoon. She sighed. "If only he were here," she said aloud.

"I am here."

Ayana swung around, and standing there was Brandon. She hopped up. "What are you doing here?"

"I came to get my girl."

She ran to him as fast as she could and wrapped her arms around his neck. "I'm so sorry, Brandon. The wedding was Ed's idea."

He put his fingers to her lips. "Hush. You don't have to explain. The mere fact that you didn't marry that guy says it all."

"I would have never married him. I don't love him. I love you."

Brandon passionately kissed her and then said, "And I love you." He took the napkin out of his pocket and gave it to her.

Ayana read his writing. *Blissfully Yours, B.* "And I am always and forever, blissfully yours."

* * * * *

THE MAID,
THE MILLIONAIRE
AND THE BABY

MICHELLE DOUGLAS

For Millie,
who is ever-generous with her smiles.
We're so happy to welcome you to the family.

CHAPTER ONE

IMOGEN ADJUSTED HER earbuds, did a quick little shimmy to make sure they weren't going to fall out and then hit 'play' on the playlist her father had sent her. She stilled, waiting for the first song, and then grinned at the sixties Southern Californian surf music that filled her ears.

Perfect! Threading-cotton-through-the-eye-of-a-needle-first-time perfect. Here she was on an island, a slow thirty-minute boat ride off the coast of Brazil, listening to surf music. She pinched herself. Twice. And then eyed the vacuum cleaner at her feet, reminding herself that she was here for more than just tropical holiday fun. A detail that was ridiculously difficult to bear in mind when everywhere she looked she was greeted with golden sand, languid palm trees, serene lagoons and gloriously blue stretches of perfect rolling surf.

Still, in a few hours she could hit the beach, or go exploring through the rainforest, or...

Or maybe find out what was wrong with her aunt.

Her smile slipped, but she resolutely pushed her shoulders back. She'd only been here for three days. There was time to get to the bottom of whatever was troubling Aunt Katherine.

Switching on the vacuum cleaner, she channelled her inner domestic goddess—singing and dancing as she pushed the machine around the room. This was the *only* way to clean. Housework was inevitable so you might as well make it as fun as you could.

She'd been *so* quiet for the last three days, but the lord of the manor, Jasper Coleman, didn't like noise, apparently.

Each to his own.

She shrugged, but the corners of her mouth lifted. At eleven o'clock every day, however, he went for an hour-long run. A glance at her watch told her she had another fifty minutes in which to live it up before she'd have to zip her mouth shut again and return to an unnatural state of silence—and in which to dust, vacuum and tidy his living and dining rooms, his office and the front entrance hall. She meant to make the most of them.

She glanced around at the amazing beach-house mansion. While she might refer to Jasper Coleman as lord of the manor, his house didn't bear the slightest resemblance to an English manor house. The wooden beams that stretched across the vaulted ceilings gave the rooms a sense of vastness—making her feel as if she were cast adrift at sea in one of those old-fashioned wooden clippers from the B-grade pirate movies starring Errol Flynn and Burt Lancaster that she used to love so much when she was a kid. A feeling that was solidly countered by the honey-coloured Mexican tiles that graced the floors, and the enormous picture windows that looked out on those extraordinary views.

She angled the vacuum cleaner beneath the coffee table. She should *love* this house. But the artfully arranged furniture and designer rugs looked like something out of a lifestyle magazine for the rich and famous. Everything matched. She repressed a shudder. Not a single thing was out of place.

Now if *she* owned the house… *Ha! As if.* But if she did, it'd look vastly different. Messier for a start. Her smile faded. There were shadows in this house, and not the kind she could scrub off the walls or sweep out of the door. No wonder Aunt Katherine had become so gloomy.

And those two things—Aunt Katherine and gloomy—just didn't go together. The weight she'd been trying to ignore settled on her shoulders. She had to get to the bottom of that mystery, and not just because she'd promised her mother. Aunt Katherine was one of her favourite people and it hurt to see her so unhappy.

Another surfing song started and she kicked herself back into action. She had a house to clean, and she'd achieve nothing by becoming gloomy herself. She turned the music up and sang along as if her life depended on it, wiggling her backside in time with the music and twirling the vacuum cleaner around like an imaginary dance partner. While the rooms might be tidy, they were huge, and she had to get them done before Mr Coleman returned and locked himself away again in his office to do whatever computer wizardry he spent his days doing. In a suit jacket! Could you believe that? He wore a suit jacket to work here on an island that housed precisely four people. Just…wow.

The second song ended and her father's voice came onto the recording. This was one of the joys of her father's playlists—the personal messages he tucked away in among the songs. 'We miss you, Immy.'

She rolled her eyes, but she knew she was grinning like crazy. 'I've only been gone three days.' She switched off the vacuum cleaner, chuckling at one of his silly stories involving the tennis club. He recommended a movie he and her mother had seen, before finishing with, 'Love you, honey.'

'Love you too, Dad,' she whispered back, a trickle of homesickness weaving through her, before a movement from the corner of her eye had her crashing back to the present. She froze, and then slowly turned with a chilling premonition that she knew who'd be standing there. And she was right. There loomed Jasper Coleman, larger than life, disapproval radiating from him in thick waves, and her mouth went dry as she pulled the earbuds from her ears.

Her employer was a huge bear of a man with an air of self-contained insularity that had the word *danger* pounding through her. A split second after the thought hit her, though, she shook herself. He wasn't *that* huge. Just…*moderately* huge. It was just… He was one of those men whose presence filled a room. And he filled this room right up to its vaulted ceiling.

A quick sweep of her trained dressmaker's eyes put him at six feet one inch. And while his shoulders were enticingly broad, he wasn't some barrel-chested, iron-pumping brawn-monger. Mind you, he didn't have a spare ounce of flesh on that lean frame of his, and all of the muscles she could see—and she could see quite a lot of them as he'd traded in his suit jacket for running shorts and a T-shirt—were neatly delineated. *Very* neatly delineated. *That* was what gave him an air of barely checked power.

That and his buzz cut.

So…not exactly a bear. And probably not dangerous. At least not in a 'tear one from limb to limb' kind of way. None of that helped slow the pounding of her pulse.

'Ms Hartley, am I right in thinking you're taking personal calls during work time?'

He had to be joking, right? She could barely get a signal on her mobile phone. She started to snort but snapped it short at his raised eyebrow. It might not be politic to point that out at this precise moment. 'No. *Sir*,' she added belatedly. But she said it with too much force and ended up sounding like a sergeant major in some farcical play.

Oh, well done, Imogen. Why don't you click your heels together and salute too?

'Not a phone call. I was listening to a playlist my father sent me. He's a sound engineer…and he leaves little messages between songs…and I talk back even though I know he can't hear me. So…' She closed her eyes.

Too much information, Immy.

'I expected your aunt to have made it clear to you that I demand peace and quiet when I'm working.'

Her eyes flew open. 'She did!' She couldn't get Aunt Katherine into trouble. 'But, you see, I thought you'd already left for your run.'

She glanced at his office door and had to fight the urge to slap a hand to her forehead. She was supposed to check if that door was open or closed. Open meant he was gone and she could clean this set of rooms without disturbing him. If it was closed that meant he was still working… and she had to be church-mouse quiet. Biting her lip, she met his gaze again. 'I'm sorry. I forgot to check your office door. It won't happen again, Mr Coleman, I promise.'

He didn't reply. Nothing. Not so much as a brass razoo. Which was an odd expression. She'd look it up…if she could get an Internet connection. She eyed him uncertainly. He might not be a big bear of a man, but he fitted her image of a bear with a sore head to a T. Which might not be fair as she didn't know him, but she wasn't predisposed to like him either, the horrid old Scrooge.

He turned away, and she sagged with the relief of being released from those icy eyes. But then he swung back, and she went tense and rigid all over again. 'I'm going for my run *now*, Ms Hartley. In case my attire had slipped your attention.'

His sarcasm stung. Her fingers tightened about the vacuum cleaner, and suddenly it was Elliot's voice, Elliot's mocking sarcasm, that sounded through her head. She thrust out her chin. 'Did you just call me stupid?' She might only be the maid, but she didn't have to put up with rudeness. 'Look, I made a mistake and I apologised. It doesn't mean I'm stupid.'

'Oh, Imogen!' She could practically hear her mother's wail. *'What about Aunt Katherine? You promised!'*

Jasper Coleman had been in the act of moving towards the front door, but he turned back now with intimidating slowness. Rather than back down—which, of course, would be the sensible thing to do—she glared right back at him. She knew she might be a little too sensitive on the topic of her sharpness of mind and her reason—her *intelligence*—but she wasn't being paid enough to put up with derogatory comments directed at it.

At least, that was what she told herself before she started quaking in her sensible ballet flats. Her sense of self-righteousness dissolved as Jasper drew himself up to his full height. Any idiot knew you didn't go poking bears.

'I don't know you well enough to make a judgement call on your intelligence, Ms Hartley.' He gestured to his office door. 'A question mark does, however, hang over your powers of observation.'

She bit her tongue and kept her mouth firmly shut. Thankfully it appeared that he didn't expect an answer, as, without any further ado, he strode from the room. A moment later she heard the click of the front door closing. He didn't do anything as uncouth as slam it.

'Of course your attire hadn't slipped my attention,' she muttered, pushing her earbuds into the pocket of her skirt. She was a dressmaker. She noticed what everyone wore.

Though for some reason she'd *really* noticed what he'd been wearing. Which didn't make a whole lot of sense because his attire had been so very generic. Those nondescript running shorts had come to mid-thigh and were neither ridiculously tiny nor ridiculously tight. His T-shirt, though, had hugged his frame as if it'd been spray-painted on, highlighting the flex and play of firm muscle.

Oh, Imogen, who are you trying to kid?

It wasn't his clothes but the body inside the clothes that had held her attention so avidly.

Scowling, she pushed the image of her perplexing boss from her mind and completed the rest of the cleaning as quickly as possible, vacuuming and dusting immaculate surfaces. But, as her aunt said, they were immaculate because they were cleaned five days a week. Without fail. Because it was what the lord of the manor decreed, apparently.

Jasper's office was as immaculate as the rest of the house. And just as cold. Unlike her workspace at home, he didn't have any photographs sitting on his desk, no sentimental knick-knacks or anything personal. His room was functional and blank. He was supposed to be some kind of computer *wunderkind*, though how on earth he could create in a space that was so *beige* was beyond her.

She gave a final flick of her duster to the enormous desk, glanced around the room with a critical eye, and was about to leave when her gaze shifted to his computer... for the third time in about as many minutes. She bit her lip. She'd bet—given all the fancy tech gadgetry he had in here—he could log onto the Internet without a single problem.

She'd been trying to find out—for three days now—if the waters surrounding the island were safe. Aunt Katherine had no idea. She preferred the calm waters of the lagoon to the surf.

Jasper swam in his twenty-five-metre pool twice a day—from six to seven each morning and again in the evening. The man was obviously a fitness freak—three hours of cardio a day. Imagine? 'Kill me now,' she muttered. Not that she disapproved of fitness. She just couldn't do fitness for fitness's sake. She had to do something fun or it just wouldn't happen. Give her a Zumba or dance class, or the surf. She loved swimming in the ocean.

If it was safe.

Not giving herself any time to hesitate, she slid into her boss's chair, woke his computer from sleep mode and clicked the Internet browser icon. Surely he wouldn't mind? It'd be in his best interests to keep his staff safe, right? Occupational health and safety and all that.

She recalled the look in his eyes less than thirty minutes ago, and her own churlish, 'Did you just call me stupid?' and grimaced. He might make an exception in her case and feed her to the sharks.

'So just hurry up and find out what you need to find out,' she ordered, typing in: Swimming in Brazilian waters.

The search engine results loaded onto the screen. 'Eureka.'

She leaned forward, intent on clicking the link to a website that looked as if it would give her the information she needed.

'Do *not* move a muscle, Ms Hartley,' a deceptively soft voice said from the doorway.

Imogen froze. She moved nothing but her eyes to meet her employer's gaze. 'Is there...?' She swallowed. 'Is there a snake or a scorpion about to pounce on me?' Her voice came out hoarse, but she was too afraid to cough and clear her throat in case she incited some animal to attack.

'Don't be ludicrous. Of course there isn't. Unless you call yourself a scorpion or a snake,' he added, striding towards her with a purposeful step, his lips pressed into a thin line.

Danger. The word whipped through her for the second time. This man was dangerous. She should've followed her first instincts. Leaping to her feet, she shot around the farthest side of the desk, keeping its wide expanse between them. She grabbed a paperweight in one hand, and then seized a pen and held it like a dagger in her other.

He slammed to a halt so quickly he swayed where he stood. 'What are you doing?'

'I don't like the look in your eyes.'

For some reason, her words made him pale. His chest lifted as he dragged in a breath. 'I don't like undercover journalists.'

'I'm not a journalist,' she spluttered, 'undercover or otherwise!'

'I hold the same contempt for industrial spies.'

She pointed the pen at his computer. 'You think I'm snooping in your personal files or…or your work files?'

Lips that shouldn't look quite so full twisted. 'The thought had crossed my mind.'

Wow, was this man paranoid or what? No wonder he lived on a desert island. And no wonder her aunt had warned her to be circumspect around him—*difficult* and *temperamental* had been the words she'd used.

'We seem to be at an impasse, Ms Hartley. I never for one moment meant for you to think that you were in physical danger from me.'

Oddly enough, she believed him.

'But I want to look at that computer screen to see precisely what it was that had you grinning like a Cheshire cat and shrieking "Eureka".'

That was probably a very good idea. 'How about I go this way until I'm standing in front of your desk?'

'And I'll go this way—' he gestured in the opposite direction '—until I'm behind my desk.'

'I want it on record that I take exception to the charge of shrieking, Mr Coleman. I don't shriek.'

'Duly noted, Ms Hartley.'

'Right, well…let's call that Plan A, shall we?' Imogen Hartley's lips lifted, but that didn't assuage the acid burning in Jasper's gut. The fear in her eyes as he'd started towards her had nearly felled him. What kind of brute did she take him for?

'Do you want me to count?' He didn't want to give her any further cause for alarm. 'On the count of three—'

With a frown in her eyes, as if he puzzled her, she shook her head and started moving around the desk. He kept his own steps measured and unhurried as he moved in the opposite direction.

Once they'd switched places, rather than looking meek and mild, or guilty and ashamed, Imogen Hartley made an exaggerated flourish towards the computer like a model in an infomercial.

He muffled a sigh and took his seat. At least she didn't look frightened any more. Steeling himself, he turned to his computer. He stared at it for several long moments, blinked, and then eased back, his shoulders unhitching. 'You're checking the surf conditions?'

She nodded.

He tried to keep a frown from forming. 'Did you really think Ilha do Pequeno Tesoura—' he used the full Portuguese name of the island '—would be in the database of some surfing website?'

'Well, no, not exactly. But we're only a leisurely thirty-minute boat ride from the coast. Which means it'd be quicker by speedboat,' she added with a shrug, as if that explained everything.

A speedboat would reach the island in less than fifteen minutes. And her shrug explained nothing.

'So I thought that checking the surfing conditions on the coast might tell me what I needed to know.'

'Which is?'

She gestured, presumably towards the Atlantic Ocean on display outside his office window. 'If it's safe for me to swim on your beach.'

'Why?'

Two vertical lines appeared on her brow as if he'd just asked the most ridiculous question ever put to her—as if two seconds ago she'd considered him a sensible man and now she didn't.

Two minutes ago, she'd thought him a scary man. He'd never forgive himself for that.

Still, those lines on her brow were oddly cute…and kind of disturbing. Disturbing in the same way that seeing her dancing and singing while she'd been vacuuming had been disturbing. This woman was full of life and energy and spontaneity—full of unguarded reactions. It reminded him of normal people, and the outside world, and life. It was why he'd been so unforgivably short with her. The ache she'd unknowingly created inside him—an ache he'd thought he'd mastered a long time ago—had taken him off guard. It was why he'd come back early from his run—so he could ask Katherine to apologise to the girl on his behalf.

Apologise yourself now.

He opened his mouth. He closed it again. Katherine had rolled her eyes when she'd spoken of her niece—had said she was flighty and impulsive…recovering from the latest in a string of unsuitable relationships…had hinted, without saying as much, that her niece would find him irresistibly attractive. Be that as it may, while she might be irresponsible this girl was untouched by all the ugliness that surrounded him. And he'd like to keep it that way. It'd be better for all concerned if she considered him a temperamental grump rather than a reasonable human being.

He watched, fascinated, as she forced her face into polite lines. 'The reason I was checking the surf conditions is because I want to swim on the beach out there. My aunt couldn't tell me. She doesn't like the surf. If she wants a dip, she swims in the lagoon. You only swim in your pool. So…'

It took an effort of will not to lean towards her. 'So?'

'So I wondered if there was something wrong with it. Is there a great white shark colony camped just off the reef? Are there hidden rips or strange jellyfish? I mean, I've not noticed anything unusual, but...'

She trailed off with a shrug, her meaning clear. She'd evidently grown up with the same 'swim safe' messages that he and most other Australian children grew up with. The main beach here on Tesoura was a sheltered haven with rolling breakers created by the offshore reef, but the thought of her swimming alone disturbed him. 'Are you an experienced surfer?'

'I'm not a board rider, but I swim a lot at the local beaches back home.'

He searched his mind for where it was that Katherine's family called home.

'Wollongong and Kiama way,' she clarified. 'The beaches an hour or two south of Sydney.'

He'd swum those beaches once upon a time. A lifetime ago. A life that felt as if it had belonged to somebody else.

He shook the thought off. 'The beaches here are similar to the ones you'd be used to back home.' Tesoura's beaches were probably safer than most.

'Thank you.' The smile she flashed him pierced beneath his guard, making that damn ache start up in the centre of him again. Her smile faded, though, when he didn't smile back, and he did his damnedest to not feel guilty about it. 'I'm sorry, I should've asked your permission before using your computer.'

Which raised another question. 'I don't want you touching any of the equipment in this room, Ms Hartley.'

She nodded and apologised again, hesitated and then said, 'I guess there's no chance of you calling me Imogen, is there?'

'None whatsoever.' He did his best not to feel guilty

about that either. 'Didn't you bring a laptop or tablet to the island?'

For some reason that made her laugh. 'Ah, but, you see, I haven't been given the keys to the kingdom.'

What on earth was she talking about?

'The Wi-Fi password,' she clarified.

Why on earth not?

'Apparently I don't have the right security clearance.' Her lips twitched irresistibly. 'It must be above my pay grade.'

She quoted that last sentence as if it was a line from a movie, but he wasn't familiar with it. Then again, he couldn't remember the last time he'd watched a movie.

He pushed that thought aside. Why on earth hadn't Katherine given her niece the password?

None of his business. He knew Katherine was keeping secrets from her family, but he had no intention of getting involved. Without a word, he wrote the login details down and pushed them across to her.

She glanced at them and her eyes started to dance. 'Does that mean I just got a promotion?'

He resisted the urge to smile back. 'It now means you can log onto the Internet using your own devices rather than mine, Ms Hartley.'

The smile dropped from her lips. Again. Banter with the boss wasn't going to happen and the sooner she understood that, the better.

Something rebellious and resentful at the strictures he'd placed upon himself prickled through him, but he squashed it. It was for the best.

She shifted from one leg to the other. 'Look, I wanted to apologise again about earlier. I—'

'It's all forgotten, Ms Hartley.'

'But—'

'I'd appreciate it if you'd close the door on your way out.'

He turned back to his computer and opened a fresh spreadsheet. She stood there frozen for a moment, and then shook herself. 'Yes, of course, sir.'

And if her *sir* held an edge of sarcasm, he didn't bother calling her on it. He wasn't interested in winning any Best Boss of the Year awards. Imogen was only here temporarily while Katherine sorted a few things out. She'd be gone again in a flash. And peace would reign once more.

The moment she left he closed the spreadsheet. He'd only opened it to look busy and get Imogen to leave his office. Ms Hartley, he corrected. *Not Imogen.* He checked his Internet browsing history more thoroughly.

She'd started precisely one search. That was it. She'd wanted to know the surf conditions. As she'd said. She wasn't a journalist. She hadn't lied.

Good. He hadn't relished the thought of telling Katherine her niece was a thief, liar or cheat. He eased back in his seat, glad that the open friendliness of Imogen's face wasn't a front for deception. He was glad his instincts hadn't let him down.

You could've made an effort to be a little friendlier.

He squashed the notion dead. No, he couldn't. It started with a couple of shared jokes, and evolved to shared confidences, and before you knew it a friendship had formed—a friendship you'd started to rely on. But when it all went to hell in a handbasket you found out that you couldn't rely on anyone. Not your friends, not your girlfriend and sure as hell not your family. He wasn't walking that road again.

It was easier to not start anything at all. He'd learned to rely on nothing beyond his own resources. It'd worked perfectly for the past two years, and if it wasn't broken...

A sudden image of Imogen's face—the fear in her eyes as she'd edged away from him—speared into his gut, making a cold sweat break out on his nape. Who was he kidding? *He* was broken.

And a man like him needed to stay away from a woman like Imogen Hartley.

Shooting to his feet, he strode to the window, his lip curling at the tropical perfection that greeted him. He should've chosen the site of his exile with more care— picked some forlorn and windswept scrap of rock off the coast of Scotland or...or Norway. All grey forbidding stone, frozen winds and stunted trees.

Two years ago, though, all he'd cared about was getting as far from Australia as he could, as quickly as he could.

He wheeled away from the window. He'd never cared that the island was beautiful before, so why wish himself away from it now? He should never have cut his run short—that was the problem. Running and swimming kept the demons at bay. He should've stuck to his routine. And a hard forty minutes' worth of laps would rectify that.

He flung the door of his office open at the exact same moment the front doorbell sounded. He blinked. He hadn't known that the doorbell even worked. It hadn't rung in the two years he'd been in residence. All deliveries—food and office supplies, the mail—were delivered to the back door and Katherine. The villa was huge and sprawling, and the back entrance was closer to the jetty, which suited everyone. Nobody visited Tesoura. *Nobody*.

He'd bet his life it was Imogen Hartley. She'd probably rung it for a lark. She was exactly the kind of person who'd do that—just for the fun of it, to see if it worked. He waited for her to pop her head into the room and apologise. She'd probably feed him some story about polishing it or some such nonsense. He'd even be gracious about it.

Imogen came rushing through from the direction of the kitchen. 'Was that the—?'

The doorbell rang again.

'—the doorbell?' she finished.

He gestured towards the front entrance, his gut clench-ing. 'I'd appreciate it if you'd answer it, Ms Hartley.'

Those vivacious eyes danced as she started for the door. 'Butler is definitely a promotion.'

Even if he hadn't put his 'no smiling' rule into place, he couldn't have smiled now if he'd wanted to. Somebody ringing the front doorbell here on his island miles from civilisation could only mean one thing—trouble. 'If it's the press…' he managed before she disappeared into the front hall.

She swung around. 'Short shrift?'

'Please.'

She gave him a thumbs-up in reply before disappearing, and despite himself a smile tugged at his lips. The woman was irrepressible.

He stayed out of sight but moved closer so he could listen.

'I understand this is the residence of Jasper Coleman,' a pleasantly cultured male voice said.

'May I ask who's calling, please?'

He couldn't fault Imogen's tone—courteous, profes-sional…unflappable.

'I have a delivery for him.' There was a series of dull thuds, as if things were being dropped to the ground, and then a softer click and scrape. 'Don't worry, he doesn't have to sign for it.'

Unflappable disappeared when Imogen yelped, 'That's a baby!'

What?

'Hey, wait! You can't just leave a baby here.'

'Those were my instructions, miss.' The voice started to recede. 'Just following orders.'

Jasper shot out from his hiding place in time to see his *butler* accost a man almost twice her size and pull him to a halt. 'What is wrong with you? You can't just go around dumping unknown babies on people's doorsteps.'

'The baby is neither unknown nor am I dumping him. I was hired to escort the baby to Mr Coleman. And I'm rather pleased to have managed it before his next feed is due. As far as I'm concerned, my job here is done.'

Ice trickled down Jasper's spine. Ignoring it—and the baby capsule sitting on his doorstep—he forced himself forward. 'There has to be some mistake.'

'No mistake,' the man said, turning towards Jasper. 'Not if you're Jasper Coleman.'

Imogen released the man's arm and stepped back to let Jasper deal with the situation, but she didn't disappear back inside the house and he didn't know whether to be glad of her silent support or not.

'You *are* Jasper Coleman, right?'

He wanted to lie, but there was a baby involved. 'Yes.'

'Then there's no mistake.'

His gut clenched. There was only one person who would send him a baby, but... It was impossible! She'd said she hated him. She'd said he'd ruined her life.

The man gestured to the baby capsule. 'Mr Coleman, meet your nephew.'

On cue, the baby opened his eyes and gave a loud wail.

Jasper couldn't move. 'What's he doing here?'

'Your sister hired me to escort the baby here from Australia.' He pulled a card from his pocket and handed it across. 'Belforte's Executive Nanny Service, sir.'

'You're a nanny?'

'One of the best. If you check with the office, you'll see that everything is in order. I believe you'll find a letter from your sister in one of the bags. I expect it'll explain everything.' And then he frowned as if suddenly recalling something. 'Mrs Graham did say that if I saw you to say the word *Jupiter*. She said you'd know what that meant.'

His gut twisted. Jupiter had been their password as kids.

The baby's cries grew louder and more persistent.

He was aware of Imogen glancing from him to the nanny and back again, but he couldn't meet her eye. He couldn't move.

'You'll have to excuse me. I'm expected in Rio for my next assignment by nightfall. Have a nice day.' And then he turned and strode away, evidently washing his hands of them all. And who could blame him? It wasn't *his* baby.

It didn't stop Jasper from wanting to tackle him to the ground and force him to take the baby back. *Damn!* What game was Emily playing now? He swallowed down his panic and channelled the coldness he'd spent the last two years perfecting. He would find a way to deal with this and—

Imogen pushed past him to sweep the crying baby up into her arms and cuddle him. 'Hey there, little dude, what's all this fuss about? You feeling a bit discombobulated? I don't blame you.'

The baby batted his face into her shoulder a couple of times, rubbed a fist across his eyes, while Imogen cooed nonsense, and then he finally looked up at her. She sent him a big smile before blowing a raspberry into his hand. To Jasper's utter astonishment the baby not only stopped crying but smiled back, as if Imogen was the best thing he'd seen all day.

And Imogen Hartley visibly melted.

Right, she'd said she'd wanted a promotion. He wondered how she'd feel about the position of nanny?

CHAPTER TWO

IMOGEN BOUNCED THE baby on her hip and winced at Jasper's white-faced shock. A baby turning up on his doorstep was obviously the last thing he'd expected. Cool eyes darkened and a bitter resignation twisted his lips, making her heart thump. She fought an urge to go over and put her arm around him, to try and comfort him the way she did the baby.

But why should he need comforting?

She moistened her lips. 'This is your nephew?'

He nodded.

She waited, but he didn't offer anything else. 'What's his name?'

'George.'

It was too hard to look at Jasper, so she smiled at George instead. 'Hello, gorgy Georgie!'

Jasper swore. Not particularly badly, but with a venom that made both her and the baby jump. *Okay.* So he *really* hadn't expected the arrival of this baby. And he was *really* unhappy about it.

But little George stared at his uncle with wide fear-filled eyes and looked as if he was about to start crying again. So she bounced him gently and started singing, 'I'm a little teapot.'

The baby turned to her again and his face broke out into a big smile. He waved his hands and made lots of inarticulate noises. What an adorable bundle of chubby-cheeked cuteness!

'Hey, you going to be a singer, little guy?' She glanced at his uncle. 'How old is he?'

'Nine months.' Jasper stared at her oddly. 'You're very good with him.'

'Back in the real world I'm Auntie Immy to four of the cutest babies on the planet.'

'I thought you were an only child?'

Ah, so Aunt Katherine had told him a little about her, then. What other confidences had she shared? 'An honorary aunt.' She stuck her nose in the air. 'Which everyone knows is the best kind.'

He stared at her for a moment before one side of his mouth hooked up. Her heart stilled mid-beat, before pounding again with ferocious abandon. That half smile transformed him completely—the stern mouth curved with a sensual lilt that chased away some of the shadows in his eyes. It made her think of summer and fun and…ice cream. She fought to catch her breath. From the first moment she'd clapped eyes on Jasper, everything about him had screamed undeniable maleness. But now he was also unmistakably gorgeous.

He sobered, the frown returning to his face, and she dragged her gaze away. Dear God, please don't let him have misconstrued her scrutiny.

She scuffed a toe against the ground and tried to hide a grimace. What was there to misconstrue? She'd been ogling him, which was seriously poor form. But it didn't mean she had designs on him or anything, and—

'Are you feeling all right, Ms Hartley?'

She realised she'd scrunched her face up, and immediately set about un-scrunching it. 'Thought I was going to sneeze.'

He raised an eyebrow.

'It didn't seem like a good idea with an armful of baby,' she improvised. She wanted—no, needed—him to stop looking at her in that way. She gestured to the series of bags that George's minder had dropped to the doorstep. 'I guess we should get these out of the sun.' Without another word, she grabbed the baby capsule at her feet and strode through into Jasper's impeccable living room.

She grinned at the baby. 'Oh, you're going to mess this up perfectly, master George.'

'How is he going to mess it up?' Jasper said, coming in behind her. 'Is he old enough to walk?'

'Unlikely, though he might be crawling. Hey, little dude, are you speeding around yet?' She sent Jasper a grin. 'I'll show you what I mean.' She went to hand him George, but he took a physical step away, a look of horror speeding across his face.

Whoa.

She gulped down the words that pressed against the back of her throat. There was something going on here that she didn't understand, and the last thing little George needed was for her to make it worse. So she instead pointed to the bags. 'In one of those there are bound to be some toys and a baby blanket.'

Without another word, he started rummaging and eventually found what she'd asked for. Handing her the blanket, he held a toy out in each hand—a plastic set of keys on a key ring in primary colours, and a plush bunny rabbit with long ears. With a squeal, George reached for the keys.

Very carefully, Jasper handed them over.

Imogen spread the blanket on the living room's thick designer rug and then upended the rest of the contents of the bag across it.

'What the—?'

Setting a boomerang pillow in the middle of it all, she very gently settled George into its curve before pulling the toys closer. He threw the keys, waved his arms about and started making *broom-broom* noises.

She reached for a toy car. 'Is this what you're after, little guy?'

He grabbed it, immediately shoving one corner of it in his mouth.

Imogen rose and gestured to the baby, the rug, and the assortment of toys. 'Hey, presto, your living room isn't quite so immaculate.'

He eyed her carefully. 'You sound as if you approve of the change.'

'It's very hard to disapprove of babies, Uncle Jasp—Mr Coleman,' she amended in a rush, heat flushing through her cheeks.

What on earth…? Just because there was a baby in the house didn't mean she could dispense with normal boss-employee formality.

He let her near slip pass, just continued to stare at her. Um…?

Oh! She was supposed to be working. He was probably wondering what on earth she was still doing here lingering in his living room as if she owned it. Swallowing, she backed up a step. 'I guess I better get back to work and—'

'No!'

She halted, mentally tutoring herself on the appropriate levels of deference due to an employer. 'Sir?'

'I have a proposition to put to you, Ms Hartley.'

She glanced at baby George, who was happily banging a plastic hammer against his foot, and she started to laugh. 'I just bet you do.'

Damn! Couldn't she maintain a semblance of polite dutifulness for even thirty seconds?

He eyed the baby and then her. 'You did say you wanted a promotion.'

She'd been joking! And while it hadn't been a joke that'd

made him laugh, or even smile, she knew he hadn't taken her seriously. 'Is nanny a promotion?'

'Absolutely. It comes with a higher pay grade, for a start.'

She didn't care about the money. The money wasn't the reason she was here.

'With all the associated security clearances.'

Had he just made a joke? She grinned—partly in shock but mostly in delight. 'Now that *is* an attractive fringe benefit.'

'Is that a yes, then?'

She glanced at the baby. It'd be way more fun to look after George, but it wasn't why she was here.

'You're hesitating. May I ask why?' He gestured to the baby. 'You seem a natural. While I understand there may be some allure to dancing with vacuum cleaners, you did seem to enjoy singing nursery rhymes too.'

She'd definitely rather look after George than dust and vacuum, but she'd promised her mother she'd find out what was troubling Aunt Katherine. Looking after a baby 24/7 could put a serious dent in the amount of time she could give to that.

'Ms Hartley?'

'Mr Coleman, I have a feeling that your idea of what being a nanny involves and my idea of the same are worlds apart.'

He blinked.

She nodded at the letter he held—the letter from his sister that he still hadn't opened. 'You don't know how long George is here for. You don't know what his mother's wishes are and—'

'How will our ideas about a nanny's duties differ?'

She eyed him uncertainly. 'I think you'll expect me to be on duty twenty-four hours a day, seven days a week. And I'm sorry, but I'm not interested in working those kinds of hours. That's not the reason I came to Tesoura. I'm here to spend some time with my aunt. And in my free time I plan to lap up all of the tropical gorgeousness that I can.' Until she returned home, and her real life started. A thrill rippled through her at the thought…along with a growing thread of fear. 'The former is going to prove difficult and the latter impossible with a baby in tow.'

He tapped a finger against his lips. 'Asking you to work those hours would be completely unreasonable.' He said the words with such a deep regret that in other circumstances she might've laughed.

She didn't laugh. She edged towards the door before she weakened and did what he wanted—became a full-time carer to that gorgeous bundle of baby.

'Where are you going?'

His sharp tone pulled her to a halt. 'To go and perform the duties you're currently paying me for.'

'You can't leave me alone with the baby.' Panic rippled across his face. *'Please.'*

That *please* caught at her, tugged on all of her sympathies and completely baffled her. 'Why not?'

'I don't know a single thing about babies.'

George had been staring at them as if aware of the tension that had started to zing through the air, and he promptly burst into tears. She didn't blame him. She swooped down and lifted him in her arms, patting his back as he snuffled against her neck. 'Well, lesson number one is to not yell around them. It upsets them.'

Aunt Katherine came into the room with her brisk step. 'Goodness, I thought I heard a baby. So the cot and pram that were just delivered weren't mistakes, then?'

Jasper gave a curt shake of his head and gestured towards George. 'Emily's baby.'

Her aunt's eyes widened. 'Well, now, that's a turn up for the books.' She moved across and clasped one of George's hands. 'Hello, little man, it's nice to meet you. I knew your mummy, back in the days before you were born.' She glanced back at Jasper. 'Poor little tyke looks tired. How long is he here for?'

He shook his head. 'I don't know.'

Imogen refrained from pointing out that if he read his sister's letter, they might get an answer to that particular question.

Katherine pursed her lips. 'Right.'

Imogen glanced from one to the other, trying to make their relationship out. Katherine had been on the island for the past two years. Before that she'd worked for the Coleman family for seventeen years. Were they friends? She bit her lip. Were they lovers? The question disturbed her, though she couldn't have said why. At forty-nine Katherine was still young, and she was certainly attractive. While Jasper would be what—mid-thirties? It didn't seem outside the realm of possibility.

Her aunt was keeping secrets. Every instinct Imogen had told her that. Was Jasper one of those secrets?

If he were either a friend or a lover, though, he'd have given Katherine the week's leave she'd requested at Christmastime.

Her aunt's laughter hurtled her back. 'Don't look at me like that, Jasper, because the answer is a big fat no. If I'd wanted to look after a baby, I'd have had one of my own.'

That made Imogen smile. Katherine didn't have a maternal bone in her body.

'But—'

'No buts,' Katherine said without ceremony. She glanced at Imogen and then Jasper again, and her eyes started to gleam. 'I'll let you continue your negotiations with Imogen, shall I?'

'What negotiations?' he grumbled. 'She's as hard-headed as you.'

Imogen surveyed her perplexing boss. For someone who'd been shocked into white-faced silence at the arrival of the baby, he seemed to have taken it into his stride now, seemed almost…resigned. Why—if he didn't want the baby here—wasn't he making arrangements to send the child back?

Katherine turned and patted Imogen's arm. In a low voice she said, 'Get him to help with the baby,' before disappearing into the kitchen.

If she did what her aunt asked, would Katherine stop avoiding her and tell her what was wrong?

'What did your aunt just say to you?'

She did her best to smooth out her face. 'Only that lunch is ready.'

His eyes narrowed, but he didn't call her on the lie. She pulled in a breath. 'Mr Coleman, I think between the three of us we can work something out.'

He widened his stance. 'You heard your aunt—she'll have nothing to do with him.'

'She won't change dirty nappies or bathe George. But she'll give him a bottle and be happy to keep an eye on him when he's napping.'

'There's one other thing you need to take into consideration, Ms Hartley, and that's the fact that I'm *not* looking after that baby.'

'Mr Coleman,' she said very gently, 'that's not my problem. It's yours.'

He knew he was being unreasonable—not to mention irrational—but he could barely check the panic coursing through him. It'd smashed through the walls he'd put up to contain it, and while part of him knew the panic was illogical, another part understood all too clearly that he had every reason to fear the consequences of his nephew's visit.

Aaron wanted revenge, and Jasper didn't doubt that his

brother-in-law would use George as a weapon—to hurt him or extort money from him. That was the best-case scenario he could come up with—that Aaron wanted money. And Jasper would give money—a lot of money—to keep this child safe.

But he'd learned to not rely on best-case scenarios. With his luck in another day or two police would show up and arrest him for allegedly kidnapping the baby. And then he'd be charged, and there'd be court proceedings…again. The thought had exhaustion sweeping through him.

Ms Hartley was right, though. This wasn't her problem. It was his. He dropped to the edge of the nearest sofa. *Focus.*

Fact number one: the baby was here now, and arrangements needed to be made for his care. Fact number two: he didn't want the press getting wind of this—whatever *this* was. Instinct warned him it'd be wiser to scotch any rumours before they started. He had to keep this as quiet as possible, which meant the fewer people who knew, the better. *Those* were the important facts for the moment. He could worry about the rest later.

'Can…can you just stay there with the baby while I make a phone call?'

She frowned but nodded. Not giving her a chance to change her mind, he grabbed his phone and speed-dialled his assistant in Sydney. He needed information. 'Evan, my sister has just had a nanny service deliver her baby to my house without warning.'

Two seconds of silence greeted him before Evan said, 'What do you need me to do?'

'Can you find out what Emily and Aaron's movements are at the moment? *Discreetly.*'

'I'll be in touch as soon as I find anything out.'

'The sooner the better, please.'

He tossed his phone to the coffee table and scratched a

hand across his head. It was entirely unreasonable to ask Imogen to be on call with the baby all the hours of the day and night. It contravened every workplace agreement he subscribed to. It was unethical. He'd taken great pains to ensure his company's workplace practices were above reproach. It was especially important now to continue in the same vein.

Besides, neither Katherine nor Imogen were the kind of women to be browbeaten by a domineering boss. Not that he was domineering, but he wouldn't be able to cajole either one of them into doing something they didn't want to do. There was a part of him that was glad about that. It indicated that they had integrity. It was important right now to surround himself with people of integrity.

The sofa dipped a little as Imogen sat beside him. 'I want to pat your back much the same way as I am little George's at the moment.'

He met warm brown eyes flecked with green and filled with sympathy. He straightened. 'Please don't.' The thought of her touching him…

He cut the thought off.

George had nestled his head in against her shoulder and noisily sucked a dummy, while she rubbed slow, soothing circles to his back—lulling and hypnotic. It took a force of will to lift his gaze back to her face. Up this close he could see the light spattering of freckles across her nose.

'Of course I'd not do anything so forward. But it's obvious your nephew's arrival has come as something of a shock.'

Understatement of the century.

'I think I should leave you in peace for the next hour or so to read your sister's letter, and to take stock of the situation. I'll keep this little guy with me for the present.'

That was kind, but…

'Wait,' he said as she started to rise.

She subsided back to the sofa. He let out a low breath. He wasn't ready to read Emily's letter yet. He wasn't sure he'd be able to believe a single word it said. 'You honestly believe that between the three of us, we'd be able to look after the baby?'

'Yes.'

'How would you see that working?'

She shrugged, and her chin-length hair—a mass of dark curls—bounced and bobbed. 'A little bit of give and take on all sides, I expect. Though probably mostly from yours.'

He didn't like the sound of that much. Still…needs must. 'In what way?'

'You'd need to cut down on some of your working hours to help out with George.'

He'd expected that.

'Mind you, that could be a good thing. Seems to me you work too hard anyway.'

The moment the words left her mouth, she shot back in her seat. 'I can't believe I just said that. It was way too personal and completely out of line. I'm sorry.'

She was holding his nephew, rubbing his back—and she spoke the truth—so he let it pass. He worked long hours because, like the swimming and the running, it helped to keep the demons at bay. Keeping busy kept him sane. For the duration of the baby's stay he'd simply be busy helping look after him instead of wrestling with complicated computer code. It wouldn't have to be any different from his current routine.

'And while George is here, you might need to…'

He raised an eyebrow.

'Lower your standards of cleanliness.'

He blinked.

'If I'm looking after George for part of the day and night, I'm not going to have the same amount of time to devote to cleaning your house.'

'That's fine with me.' In fact, it was more than fine. 'Ms Hartley, you've vacuumed and dusted these rooms every day since you arrived. Now far be it from me to question your work practices—I've never been to housekeeping school, so I don't know what the norm is—but don't you think vacuuming every day is overkill? I'm tidy in my habits, don't tramp mud into the house on a regular basis, and don't have children or dogs—' He broke off to glance at the baby in her arms. 'I don't *usually* have children or dogs to stay.'

'But Aunt Katherine said you had the highest expectations when it came to—' She broke off, biting her lip.

What on earth had Katherine been telling her niece?

He pushed the thought away. He had more pressing concerns at the moment. 'I'm happy to relax the current cleaning standards.' He pulled in a breath. 'There's just one other little problem in your proposed plan.'

'Which is?'

His stomach churned. 'I don't have the first idea about babies. I don't have a clue how to feed them or what to feed them or how to prepare whatever it is that you do feed them. I've never changed a nappy. The thought doesn't fill me with a great deal of enthusiasm, admittedly, but evidently it's a chore I'm not going to be able to avoid. And precisely how do you bathe a baby without drowning it? Don't they get slippery and hard to hold? That sounds like a disaster waiting to happen, if you ask me.'

She smiled, the green sparks in her eyes dancing, and the impact of it hit him in the middle of his chest, making his heart thump.

'I can teach you all of those things easy-peasy. But there are a couple of other things you'll need to learn too, like cuddling and playing. Both are vital to a baby's development.'

Before he knew what she was about, she'd leaned forward and set the baby on his lap, and he wanted to yell at her to take him back. But recalled, just in time, that he wasn't supposed to yell around the baby. He wanted to shoot to his feet and race away. But he couldn't because he had *a lap full of baby*.

He wasn't sure how the kid would've reacted if he'd been fully awake—with a loud verbal protest he suspected—but, drowsy as he was, he merely nestled in against Jasper's chest. The warm weight made his heart thud, made him wonder when was the last time he'd actually touched someone? *Hell!* He—

'Stop frowning,' she chided gently from where she'd moved to kneel in front of him, adjusting his arm so it went fully around the baby with his hand resting on the child's tummy. 'We don't want George glancing up and being frightened out of his wits by the scary man glaring at him.'

The thought that he could so easily frighten his nephew sickened him.

'I mean, that's hard enough for a grown-up to deal with.'

Her voice held laughter, but that didn't stop his gaze from spearing hers. 'I'm sorry I scared you earlier. I really didn't mean to.'

'I know that now. I overreacted, but—'

He looped his fingers around her wrist. 'Never apologise for trusting your instincts and being cautious. It's better to feel a little foolish than it is to get hurt—every single time. No exceptions.'

She stared at his hand on her wrist and nodded. She'd gone very still. Had he frightened her again? He didn't hold her tightly. She could move away at any time... Her tongue snaked out to moisten her lips and something hot and sweet licked along his veins.

He let her go in an instant.

She eased away, colour high on her cheekbones. 'Do

you mind if I check the bags?' She gestured to the muddle of bags that apparently came with a baby.

'By all means. Are you looking for anything in particular?' If she took the baby back he'd look for her.

'George's schedule.' He must've looked clueless because she added, 'Feed times, nap times…those sorts of things.'

He tried to do what she was doing—focussing on the situation with the baby rather than that moment of…

He didn't know what to call it. A moment of awareness that had taken them both off guard. He pulled in a breath and counted to ten.

Emotions were running high, that was all. He was holding his nephew, for heaven's sake. A nephew he'd thought he'd never get to meet, let alone hold. It was making him hyper-aware of everything. What he didn't need to notice at the moment, however, was the silkiness of his housemaid's skin or the shininess of her hair. He gritted his teeth. Or the beguiling shape of her mouth.

He forced his gaze to the baby who, with half-closed eyes, continued to suck on his dummy with a kind of focussed fierceness. His chest clenched. What kind of unfairness or…or whim had turned this little guy's life upside down? The innate fragility and helplessness of the baby, the sense of responsibility that suddenly weighed down on him, had his former panic stirring. How could he do this? How—?

'I didn't go to housekeeping school either,' Imogen said out of the blue. 'Just so you know. In case you hadn't worked that out for yourself yet.'

She sat cross-legged on the rug, going methodically through each of the bags. And she was telling him this because…?

'I wouldn't want you accusing me at some distant point in the future of being here under false pretences.'

He recalled how she'd puffed up earlier when she'd

thought he'd been slighting her intelligence. Did she feel lesser because she'd not been to the right school or wasn't properly qualified or something? Focussing on her issues was certainly better than focussing on the baby he held. 'It doesn't necessarily follow that you're not a hard worker, though, right?'

'Exactly!' Her smile was so bright it could blind a man. He blinked but he couldn't look away. And then she grimaced. 'I don't have the subservient thing down pat yet, though.'

His lips twitched. 'I hadn't noticed.'

'Ooh.' Her grin widened and she pointed a finger at him. 'You just made a joke.'

He ignored that. Making jokes at the moment was no doubt highly inappropriate. For heaven's sake, *he was holding a baby.* 'Ms Hartley, let me put your mind at rest. I trust Katherine's judgement.'

'Even though I'm family?'

She's a bit flighty and irresponsible.

He didn't see any evidence of that. 'Even then,' he said. He spoke without hesitation. He'd trust Kate with his life. He knew she was keeping secrets from her family, but they were harmless enough. He couldn't blame her for protecting her privacy when he'd all but exiled himself to a remote island.

She's a bit flighty and irresponsible. He suspected Kate had lied about that to put an invisible wedge between him and her niece. He didn't blame her for wanting to protect Imogen from a man like him. He didn't consider himself a good prospect either.

Imogen halted from her rifling of bags. 'I want to apologise for my rudeness earlier.'

She'd been rude?

'I shouldn't have jumped on you like that for calling me stupid.'

'I did *not* call you stupid.'

'You know what I mean.'

She'd only been responding to his rudeness. 'I shouldn't have been so short with you.'

One shoulder lifted. 'I'm a bit sensitive on the subject, and I shouldn't have flared up like that.'

He stared at her for a moment. 'Why are you sensitive?'

She ducked her head. 'It doesn't matter.'

He had a feeling it mattered a great deal.

He wasn't sure what she saw in his face when she glanced back up, but whatever it was had her heaving out a sigh. 'I don't think I'm stupid, Mr Coleman. I know I'm not. I'm just a bit sensitive about it at the moment because last week, before I came here, I ran into an old boyfriend— my high-school sweetheart.'

From the look on her face he'd been anything but a sweetheart.

'When he found out I had no plans to go to university— like him—he told me I was…'

'Stupid?'

'I believe the words he used were *uneducated yokel.*' She shrugged. 'Naturally I kicked his sorry butt to the kerb.'

'*Smart* move.'

'But, you know, that was seven years ago, and people grow up, so when I saw him last week I said hello.' Her lips thinned. 'That wasn't quite so smart.'

A hard ball settled in the pit of his stomach. 'He called you stupid again?'

'Implied it.'

What a jerk! 'Why?'

She shook her head. 'It doesn't matter.'

He didn't believe that for a moment.

'I'm *not* stupid and what I'm doing with my life *isn't* stupid or risky. It's just…his voice has wormed its way inside my head, and I haven't been able to shake it. I'm sorry you were the one who had his head snapped off, though.'

'I have broad shoulders.' He shrugged. 'And if you want the truth, I came back early from my run to apologise for being so grumpy.'

She folded her arms and stared at him. 'You know what? You're not the slightest bit difficult or temperamental.'

What on earth had made her think he was?

Katherine. The answer came to him swiftly. Katherine didn't want him messing with her niece, and he had no intention of giving the older woman cause for concern. He might not be difficult and temperamental, and Imogen might not be flighty and irresponsible. But their lives were poles apart. And he had every intention of keeping them that way.

CHAPTER THREE

THE MYRIAD EXPRESSIONS that chased themselves across Jasper's face pierced Imogen with unexpected force. Her heart beat too hard—a pounding that rose into her throat and made it ache.

She didn't bother tempering the sympathy that raged through her. She doubted she'd be successful even if she tried. He'd stared at his nephew with a mixture of such shock and wonder, pain and hope and desolation, that it had almost overwhelmed her. She understood the shock and the hope, but not the pain and desolation. And certainly not the fear.

A bit of panic—yes.

Worry and anxiety—absolutely.

But not that bone-crushing fear that had seemed to be directed both inwards and outwards at the same time. She'd been desperate to rid him of that expression, so she'd overshared. Again.

But that was better than staring at his awful expression and doing nothing about it. The lines fanning out from serious grey eyes were still strained and the grooves bracketing his mouth were still deep, but he no longer looked so worn or overwhelmed.

The grey of those eyes was quite extraordinary. She'd never seen eyes like them—silver in some lights, they held a hint of blue in others, but could deepen to charcoal and concentrate so intensely you felt spotlighted…and seen, *really* seen.

'All right, Ms Hartley, let's try your suggestion and see if, between the three of us, we can manage. I'll increase your and your aunt's salaries for as long as the baby is here and—'

'Oh, that's not necessary.' He was already paying her a generous salary.

'You'll both be taking on extra duties and I have no intention of taking advantage of your good natures. We'll do things by the book. You'll be compensated accordingly.'

He wanted this to be a work arrangement, rather than a favour between friends. Which suited her fine because they *weren't* friends. She recalled the awful expression that had overtaken his face and couldn't help thinking that the one thing Jasper Coleman could do with at the moment, though, was a friend.

She glanced at George, noting the way he worried at his dummy. 'He's due for his bottle.'

'You'd better take him, then.'

She suspected that if he'd had more confidence in handling babies, he'd have simply handed him over, and she'd have had no choice but to take him. As it was, he stared at her expectantly, evidently expecting her to obey him immediately, and she had to fight her instant response to do exactly that. 'I will, but first I want to make a request.'

His brows rose. Yep. He'd expected her to jump to do his bidding immediately.

It's what he's paying you for, Imogen.

'Is it possible for us to drop the Mr Coleman and Ms Hartley and call each other by our first names? I know I'm only a housemaid with a promotion to a third of a nanny's position while you're a genius billionaire, but I can promise you I won't forget the distinction. The thing is, I've never worked in an environment that maintained such formalities, and I just know I'm going to slip up and call you Uncle Jasper to little George here at some point. "Go to Uncle Jasper, Georgie,"' she sing-songed to demonstrate what she meant. 'It'd be really nice if we could eliminate that worry right now.'

She couldn't work out if he was trying not to smile or trying not to frown.

'You don't look particularly worried, Ms Hartley.'

Was that a no? 'I can assure you that I'm shaking on the inside.'

She bit back a sigh when he didn't smile. Mind you, he didn't frown either. She tried again. 'You and my aunt call each other by your first names. I promise not to take any liberties just because we move to a more informal mode of address.'

He stared at her for several long seconds. 'Are you familiar with the movie *The Sound of Music*?' he finally asked.

'Intimately.' It was one of her favourites. 'An oldie but a goodie.'

'I'm vividly reminded of the moment in the film where the captain asks Maria if she was this much trouble at the abbey.'

A bark of laughter shot out of her. 'And she answers, "Oh, much more, sir."' She glanced at the baby in his arms. 'I have to say I'm *very* glad you weren't just landed with seven children.'

As if they couldn't help it, his lips lifted. Her pulse shimmied and all the fine hairs on her arms Mexican-waved.

'Very well, Imogen, first names it is. Perhaps now you'll be good enough to take the baby?'

He angled the side holding the baby towards her, and she moved closer, ordering various parts of herself to stop tripping the light fantastic. 'Hey there, beautiful boy.' George came willingly, but not before Imogen had sucked in a deep breath of Jasper-scented air.

He smelled of the sea and the sweat from his run and

something darker and spicier, like cardamom. The smell of sweat especially should've had her nose wrinkling, but it didn't. She edged away before she could be tempted to drag in another appreciative lungful.

His sister's letter still sat unopened on the arm of the sofa. Why hadn't he torn it open and devoured its contents yet? She adjusted her weight from one leg to the other. 'May I make a suggestion?'

'You may.'

'I think you should read your sister's letter. And before you accuse me of taking those liberties that I promised I wouldn't, I want to assure you that I'm not trying to pry. Your family's concerns are none of my business. But we need to know if George has any medical issues or medications that he's taking or any allergies.' She lifted the schedule of feeding and nap times she'd found in the same bag that held some ready-made bottles of formula. 'None of those things are mentioned here, which probably means that there's nothing to worry about,' she added quickly at the look of absolute horror that passed across his face. 'But with knowledge being power and all that,' she finished on a weak shrug.

Surely no mother would send her baby somewhere so remote—so far from medical facilities—if he had a known medical condition like asthma, though. At least…not a good mother. She glanced at the baby in her arms. Sympathy, compassion, pity and foreboding all churned in her stomach. Why on earth would *any* mother send her child away? Was Jasper's sister a good mother or—?

'Why are you frowning, Imogen?'

She started. 'Oh, I…'

'I'd rather know. Especially if it pertains to the baby.'

He hadn't called *the baby* by his name yet—not once. What was that about? Though she wasn't silly enough to ask that question either…yet.

'Your sister would tell us if there were any issues we should be aware of where George is concerned, right?'

She waited for him to reassure her. He didn't. His shoulders didn't slump, but it felt as if they ought to, that they were only remaining in place due to some superhuman effort on his behalf. 'I don't know. My sister and I have been estranged for the last two years.'

Why?

She didn't ask that either. He didn't look as if he had the heart for it. She focussed her attention on the baby instead. 'How about we make a pact, little George? While you're here you're only going to get all good things. What do you say to that?'

He spat out his dummy and gave a grumpy grunt that reminded her so much of his uncle it made her laugh. 'I'm glad we got that sorted. It's going to be nothing but sun and fun and kisses and cuddles and good times, right?'

He nodded, copying her, and he looked so darn cute she found herself automatically swinging back to Jasper to share the moment. She found him staring at them with an arrested expression on his face, and it had her smile freezing and all of that shimmying and Mexican-waving happening all over again.

She had to get that under control because *that* wasn't going to happen here. Instinct told her that if Jasper thought for a single solitary second that she was attracted to him, he'd boot her off his island faster than she could sew a side seam. She couldn't let *that* happen until she'd found out what was troubling Katherine.

She swung away, grabbing up the bag with the bottles and formula. 'I'll go and warm up George's bottle.' And she didn't glance back once as she marched from the room. She kept her gaze trained on little George, who clapped his hands together and chanted, 'Yum, yum, yum.'

Both she and George were chanting, 'Yum, yum, yum,' as they entered the kitchen.

Katherine glanced up from where she sat at the table with a glass of iced tea. 'I expect you're both hungry.'

'Ravenous,' she agreed, pulling a bottle from the bag and setting it in the microwave.

'Here, give him to me,' Katherine said when the bottle was ready. 'I'll feed him while you eat your sandwich.'

Imogen did as she bid. Maybe little George here could be the icebreaker she needed with her aunt?

They both watched as the baby fed greedily, his eyes closing in bliss. 'Eat up, Immy, because you're burping him. I don't do vomit. Or nappies.'

Imogen grabbed her sandwich from the fridge—chicken salad, her favourite—and started eating too.

'What's been decided?'

'I told Jasper that between the three of us, we'd be able to manage. I thought he was going to explode.' She winked. 'But he eventually saw the wisdom of my suggestion.'

Katherine snorted.

'We're both being paid higher duties for the duration of George's visit. And before you ask, I've no idea how long that's likely to be.'

Katherine raised an eyebrow. 'He's really agreed to help with the baby?'

She bit into her sandwich and nodded. 'He wasn't what you'd call enthusiastic—' *resigned* might be the appropriate term '—but he agreed to let me teach him what he needs to know.'

'Good for you.'

He hadn't been the least bit unreasonable or temperamental. She glanced at her aunt before feigning interest in her sandwich again. 'While I'm more than happy to pull my weight and do the job I'm being paid for, I'm not prepared to be turned into an on-call round-the-clock drudge. I came here to spend time with you, Auntie Kay.'

Katherine's face shuttered at her niece's words, and Imogen set her sandwich down and gripped her hands in her lap to counter the painful tightening of her throat. Had she done something to disappoint her aunt, to alienate her somehow? She swallowed hard and did what she could to keep a cheery expression on her face. 'Why did you tell me to get Jasper to help with George? When I dumped the baby on his lap, I thought he was going to pass out. What's the deal with his family?'

Her aunt gave her one of *those* looks. 'Imogen, I don't gossip about my employer.'

'I'm not asking you to. It's just…he seems a bit hung up about it.'

'People's lives can be complicated.'

Was her aunt's life complicated? Was that the problem? 'You think well of him, though, right? I'd even go so far as to say you care what happens to him.'

'I've known him for nearly twenty years. I worked for his family for a long time. Of course I care what happens to him. But he's shut himself away for far too long. It'll do him good to have a bit of contact with the outside world.'

'Are the two of you more than friends?'

Shocked eyes met hers. 'Are you suggesting what I think you're suggesting?'

'I know it's none of my business, but—'

'It most certainly isn't. But, me and Jasper? The idea is ludicrous.'

That made her frown. 'Why? You're both young and attractive. And you're stuck out here together all on your own and—'

'I don't feel *that* young, Imogen, I can assure you. The idea is preposterous. I've known the boy since he was twelve years old.' Katherine's eyes narrowed. 'And I'd advise you not to get any ideas in that direction either. Jasper Coleman is a troubled man. Like the rest of his family.'

'Is there anything I ought to know? Is he...' she hesitated '...dangerous?'

'Of course not. I wouldn't hire any young woman to work here if I thought that, and certainly not my own niece.'

Of course she wouldn't.

'It's just that young women have always fallen all over themselves to impress him. I'd rather not see you join their ranks.'

'Oh, you don't need to worry about me, Auntie Kay. I have plans and I'm not letting any man derail them.' Plans she and her best friend and now business partner, Lauren, had staked their entire life savings on. Elliot could take his *stupid* comments and choke on them, because Imogen *was* going to succeed.

She glanced at her aunt again, swallowed. 'I've been playing around with some new designs and I'd love to show them to you after dinner—get your opinion, throw around some new ideas.' Katherine was the reason she'd learned to sew as a fresh-faced nine-year-old. She'd always encouraged Imogen's creativity.

'I'm sorry, but I have to keep going over the household accounts. I promised Jasper's accountant I'd have them to him by the end of the week.'

It was the same excuse she'd given last night. Imogen did her best to stay chipper, to give her aunt the benefit of the doubt. Maybe she *wasn't* purposely avoiding her. 'Can I help?'

'I expect you're going to have your hands full tonight.' She handed George over. 'Time for me to get back to work.' With that, she strode in the direction of her office.

Imogen watched her go and pursed her lips. As soon as her mother had found out that Katherine was looking for a temporary maid, she'd badgered Imogen to take the position and make sure all was well. And for the first time

Imogen was glad she'd promised to do what she could. Because her mother was right—something was wrong.

She stared down at the now content baby. 'I'm going to get to the bottom of this, George.' Her aunt was acting out of character, and she was going to find out why.

'Are you sure this is the first time you've changed a nappy?' Imogen demanded, moving in to run a finger around the waist and legs of the nappy Jasper had just put on the baby.

She smelled of oranges and vanilla. He frowned; dumbfounded that he'd even noticed what she smelled like. 'The very first time,' he promised, edging away a fraction.

Chagrin flashed across her face and it almost made him smile. So far today he'd learned how to prepare a bottle of formula, though he'd managed to get out of feeding and burping the baby. She'd accepted his 'I'd prefer to watch the first time' excuses, though he doubted he'd get away with that at lunchtime, especially as she'd given him a free pass for the entirety of yesterday. He'd told her he'd needed to put some work measures in place before he could concentrate more fully on helping her with the baby.

It had been a lie, mostly. He owned the company. He employed other people to manage its day-to-day operations. He didn't need to check in daily. A simple email had taken care of business.

But he'd needed the solitude—had needed to get his head around the events of the previous day. He'd need a whole lot more than a day and a half of solitude to make that happen, though.

He forced himself back to the present moment to find Imogen still staring at his nappy attempt. 'What? There's nothing wrong with it.'

'I know. That's the problem.' She wrinkled her nose. 'You're one of these perfect people who get everything spot-on first time, aren't you?'

Nope, that didn't describe him at all. 'I'm good with my hands.' He'd allow that much. He'd spent far too much time as a kid making paper planes and kites. He'd eventually graduated to assembling model airplanes and ships, and then disassembling computer motherboards and putting them back together—activities that had kept him out of sight and out of the line of his father's fury.

The baby chose that moment to wave his hands in the air with a series of excited gurgles, and Imogen swooped down to kiss those little fists and tickle his tummy, making him chortle. He was a sturdy and happy little chap. *Not* what he'd have expected from Emily's child.

Imogen sent Jasper a sidelong glance, the green in her eyes sparkling with devilment. 'So, you're *good with your hands*, huh?'

He didn't have a collar on his T-shirt, so it had to be an imaginary collar that tightened about his throat. 'I, uh…'

She straightened, laughing outright. 'When I first met you, I dubbed you Mr Cool and Mysterious, but I think I need to revise that to Mr Clueless and Out of His Depth.'

He stiffened, trying to resist the pull of her teasing. 'I *am* still your employer, remember?' But his words didn't carry even a quarter of the weight he'd meant them to.

'Yes, sir!'

She saluted and all he could do was shake his head. Where did all of her irrepressible sense of fun come from?

She stepped away from the change table. If nothing else, the baby had certainly arrived well equipped.

His jaw suddenly clenched. A change table. In his house. On an almost deserted island. It'd look as if he'd planned for the arrival of this child.

Try explaining that to a jury.

'Right, seeing as though you're so good with your hands, you can carry George through to the living room.'

He crashed back and pushed his dark suspicions to the back of his mind.

He hadn't had to pick the baby up yet. Other than the time she'd plonked him on his lap, he hadn't touched him until the nappy change. Jasper had spent the last two nights at the other end of the house from Imogen and the baby, but Imogen had been adamant this morning that they set up a proper nursery in one of the upstairs guest bedrooms. At *his* end of the house. He'd wanted to protest, but on what grounds?

He couldn't keep taking advantage of Imogen's good nature. And the light in her eyes had told him not to bother trying. She might have an irrepressible sense of fun, but if she was anything like Katherine, she'd have a will of steel too. And instinct told him she was definitely cast in the same mould as her aunt.

So, he'd helped to shift all the associated baby paraphernalia, had unpacked tiny romper suits and little short sets into a chest of drawers. There'd been something about those tiny clothes that'd had his chest clenching. He'd done his best to ignore it. He couldn't afford emotion and sentiment. Not in this situation.

Swallowing back an automatic objection, he took a step closer to the baby.

'What are you afraid of?' she asked softly at his elbow.

Too many things, and all of them too personal to share. But he had to say something. 'I don't want to drop him. I don't want to hurt him.' Both of those things were true.

She didn't laugh, and something inside him unhitched. He suspected he deserved mockery, but he was grateful to be spared it all the same.

'George isn't a newborn, so you don't have to support his head when you lift him. His neck muscles have developed enough to support that weight on their own.'

'Okay.'

'Once you pick him up, you can either balance him on your hip, like you've no doubt seen me doing.'

She seized a teddy bear to demonstrate. He did his best not to focus on the shapely curve of her hip.

'Or you can hold him against your shoulder.' The teddy went to her shoulder where she patted his back. 'Or you can hold him in front of you with his back against your chest.'

The teddy bear was pressed to her chest. But it was smaller than a life-sized baby and holding the toy there highlighted her, uh…curves. Rather deliciously.

Don't ogle her chest.

'Of course, you shouldn't hold him too tight.'

She demonstrated by pulling the soft toy hard against her and it was all he could do not to groan. He would *not* notice her physical attributes. It'd be wrong on so many levels. He was her employer, for heaven's sake. He might've been stuck on this island for the last two years, but he read the news, kept up with what was happening in the world—the *#metoo* movement had *not* passed him by. And he was not going to join the ranks of men who used their positions of power to prey on young women sexually. The thought sickened him.

He forced his mind back to the task at hand. 'Isn't he going to squirm and throw himself about and…?' He trailed off with a shrug.

'Have you ever held a puppy or kitten?'

'No.' He and Emily hadn't been allowed pets when they were growing up.

He turned to find her mouth had fallen open. A beat started up somewhere in his chest. Her eyes softened and she lifted her hand as if to touch him, and then seemed to recall herself. Stiffening, she eased back. 'Not everyone is an animal person.'

'I'd have loved a dog as a kid.'

Where on earth had that come from?

But it earned him a smile and he couldn't regret it.

'All I was going to say is that puppies and kittens wriggle a lot when they're excited. George here is a whole lot easier to hold than an overexcited puppy.'

'Okay.'

'So…' She gestured for him to pick up the baby.

He and the baby stared at each other. Carefully, he eased forward and slid his hands beneath the baby's armpits and lifted him. The weight of the baby was somehow reassuring. He dangled him at arm's length, getting used to the weight, noting how large his hands looked around the baby's middle. Little legs kicked as if they had an excess of energy, but they didn't make him feel as if he'd drop the child.

Swallowing, he moved him to rest against his chest and shoulder. The kid grabbed a fistful of Jasper's shirt and bounced, but Jasper kept a hand at the baby's back to steady them both, and then slowly let out a breath. 'Okay, that wasn't so bad.'

He turned to Imogen, expecting to find her smiling, but she wasn't. She was staring at him, hands on hips. 'What?' he asked, suddenly defensive.

'Do you know you haven't spoken to him yet?'

He scowled. Yeah, he knew. It was another one of those threshold moments, and he'd had enough of them for one day. 'Did you have a lot of pets growing up?'

Her face relaxed into a smile. 'I can't imagine not having a dog.'

'You have a dog…*now*?'

She started to laugh. 'Relax, Jasper, I've neither abandoned my dog nor brought her with me and hidden her in your garden shed. She's the family pet, and lives with my parents and has done so for the last ten years. Lulabelle the Labrador cross is adorable and spends most of her days dozing in the sun. I couldn't imagine not having a dog,' she repeated.

He'd ached for a dog as a kid, but he hadn't thought

about that in years. He rolled his shoulders, keeping a firm grip on the baby. 'Why not?' What was so good about having a dog?

'They're great company.'

Yeah, well, he didn't need any of that. He liked his own company.

'They're a lot of fun.'

He didn't need fun either.

'And they don't judge you. They just love you uncon-ditionally.'

He couldn't think of anything to say to that.

She started to laugh again. 'And in addition to all of that they'll keep you on your toes as they chew your shoes, dig up the garden, traipse mud into the house and pee on the carpet. A lot like kids, I guess.'

'Oh, now I'm really going to rush out and get a dog,' he said wryly, trying not to notice the way the ends of her hair danced whenever she laughed.

She sobered and nodded at the baby. 'You're going to need to talk to him.'

Damn. He'd thought he'd distracted her from that. 'Why?' Why did he have to talk to the kid? It'd be in ev-eryone's best interests if he could maintain his distance. He'd make sure the baby's physical needs were met—why couldn't that be enough?

'Because he needs to know he can trust you. Besides, it's friendly and polite.'

He wanted to stop his ears and close his eyes.

'He needs to feel comfortable around you, not fright-ened or intimidated.'

He pulled in a breath. Okay, her words made sense. He could make small talk with the kid, right? It wouldn't kill him. It wouldn't bring the walls he had firmly in place crashing down. He glanced down to find the baby staring at him. 'Hello, baby.'

George shoved a fist in his mouth and eyeballed him.

'George,' she sighed. 'His name is George.'

A scowl shuffled through him. Who'd chosen the name—Emily or Aaron? 'George is too big a name for a baby—too adult.'

'Which is why I sometimes call him Georgie…or Gorgy Georgie.'

The baby pulled his fist from his mouth to smile at her, but Jasper shook his head. 'I am *not* calling him that.' He must've spoken too loudly, because the baby gave a start. 'Sorry if that offends you,' he muttered, patting the nappy-clad bottom. 'What about kid?' he said, hoping to avert some very loud crying. 'Are you all right with me calling you kid?'

To his utter amazement, the little guy threw his head back and laughed. As if Jasper had just told him the funniest joke he'd ever heard. He tried to stop his chest from puffing up, tried to not feel so pleased when a little hand slapped his chest, right above his heart. 'He's a happy little guy, isn't he? Doesn't seem to cry much.'

Her lips curved into the most bewitching smile that he did his best to ignore. 'You sound surprised.'

'I am.'

'Not all babies fuss and cry a lot.'

But he'd never thought for a single moment that Emily's baby would be one of the contented ones. He pushed the thought aside. 'What now? What are we doing next?'

'We're going to the beach.'

He stiffened. 'You just want to go for a swim. You're going to abandon me on a beach with a baby I barely know, while you get to live it up.'

He took one look at her face and he wished he could haul the words back. He'd planted that idea well and truly in her head, and he could see now that she meant to run with it.

'How very perspicacious of you,' she said, mock sweetly. 'I've been on call with the baby ever since he arrived. I deserve a swim. And I'm not exactly abandoning you. I'll be within shouting distance.'

He tried not to scowl.

'And while I'm swimming you might want to give some thought to how you'd like our schedule to work.'

'What do you mean?'

'I'm not leaving Aunt Katherine with all the housework. I'll need a few hours each day to dedicate to my housekeeping duties. I suspect you'll want a few hours each day to work too.'

Um. 'I…' He didn't know what to say, what to suggest.

'For the moment, I'm just saying think about it.'

She turned and left the room. 'Where are you going?' he hollered after her.

'To put my swimmers on,' she hollered back.

'What am *I* supposed to do?'

She moved back to stand in the doorway. She glanced at the baby and then around the room. 'You'd better pack him a bag—some toys, his teething ring, a blanket…and a hat.' She glanced at him, her eyes tracking across his head, and he had to fight the urge to run his hand across his buzz cut. 'You might want one of those too. I'll bring the sunscreen and some cold drinks,' she tossed over her shoulder before disappearing.

Jasper huffed out a breath. 'You wouldn't believe it from the way she speaks to me, kid, but I'm *her* boss.'

He set the baby carefully into his cot while he gathered a few things together. He found a tiny cotton sunhat and set it on the baby's head.

The baby frowned and pushed it off. 'So…it's going to be like that, is it?' Jasper's hands went to his hips. 'She's going to insist on it, you know.' Shoving the hat in the pocket of his cargo shorts, he hiked the bag over his shoulder, lifted the baby out of the cot, and went to find a hat for himself.

CHAPTER FOUR

IMOGEN CHANGED INTO her swimming costume and tried to make sense of the expressions that had flashed across Jasper's face whenever he'd glanced at his nephew. Consternation was ever present, which she got. But she didn't understand his... She didn't know what to call it—calculation, maybe? As if he viewed his nephew as a piece of problematic computer code he needed to decrypt. Or a to-do list he needed to tick off.

Beneath that, though, she also sensed the wonder George stirred in him. And the fact it was an ever-present threat to his detachment. It was as if Jasper was afraid to care even the slightest little bit for his baby nephew.

Maybe he was, but why? Because of his sister?

She slathered on sunscreen. It was none of her business. She knew that. But if George's sister was an irresponsible piece of work or in some kind of trouble, then little George was going to need someone to rely on. Someone like Jasper.

She snapped the tube of suncream closed with the heel of her hand. Surely Jasper didn't mean to abandon George at the end of all this—just hand him back to his mother when the time came and be done with him? Not without some follow-through. Not without making sure George was going to be okay. He had to maintain some contact with his nephew, even if it proved difficult. Right?

But even as she thought it, she was far from convinced Jasper saw it the same way. In fact, she was almost certain he saw it in a completely opposite light.

'He's a troubled man.'

Her aunt's words played in her mind, and she found herself nodding.

'He's demanding and difficult.'

That had her shaking her head, though. He valued his privacy, and she doubted he'd suffer fools gladly, but he wasn't unreasonable, and while he could be remote and aloof he wasn't surly or supercilious. Those things gave her hope because she hadn't imagined the surprise in his eyes, or the pleasure, when George had smiled at him.

If it hadn't been for those glimpsed flashes of warmth, the thawing she sensed him trying to fight, then she'd...

She jammed a hat to her head.

Then you'd what? She mocked her reflection, rubbing in a dollop of cream still left on her nose. She wasn't making a dent in Katherine's aloofness at the moment, so what impact did she think she could have on Jasper?

The one thing she *could* do was to ensure little George's stay here was as lovely as possible. And she meant to do that to the best of her ability.

Grabbing a tote, she tossed in a T-shirt and the sunscreen, before stalking into the kitchen to grab some cold drinks and a bottle of cold boiled water for George. Katherine, sitting at the kitchen table, gave a start and pushed the letter she was reading back into its envelope and slid it beneath the newspaper.

Imogen's chest tightened, but she pretended she hadn't seen the furtive movement. 'We're heading down to the beach. Want to join us?'

'Imogen, I'm working!'

She seized a couple of pieces of fruit. 'You're entitled

to some R & R. And I bet Jasper wouldn't mind. In fact, I expect he'd welcome your company.'

'I'm sorry, Imogen, but even if I wasn't busy, I'm not a fan of the beach and all of that sand.' She eyed the fruit Imogen still held. 'And if you're going to feed any of that banana to the baby, you better pack some wet wipes.' She pointed. 'In that cupboard to the left of the sink.'

With a sigh, she grabbed them and then gathered up her things. She paused in the doorway. 'Auntie Kay, is everything okay?'

'Of course it is,' Katherine said brusquely. 'Why wouldn't it be, you silly child? Now, you'd better get your skates on. Jasper won't like kicking his heels for too long. Enjoy your swim.'

She had no choice but to submit. But as she walked away, her mind raced. She needed to find a way to break through her aunt's atypical reserve. Doing housework and looking after a baby were all well and fine, but she had to remember the real reason she was here on Tesoura.

They spread the blanket in the shade of a stand of palm trees that swayed gently in the breeze like something from every hopeful daydream she'd ever had about tropical islands. 'Smell that glorious sea air, George. Feel how warm it is. Hear the sound of the waves.'

She closed her eyes and inhaled. *Glorious.*

When she opened her eyes, she found Jasper staring at her as if she'd lost her mind. George was clapping and beaming. George was the easiest to deal with, so she kept her gaze on him and clapped too. While she might've addressed the baby, her words had been aimed at the man. She wondered if Jasper ever did relaxed and casual. He might've changed into shorts and a T-shirt, but for all intents and purposes he might as well have still been wearing a suit jacket for all the relaxation he radiated.

Pointing that out, though, would be impertinent, and it'd achieve absolutely nothing. So, she kept on clapping her hands. 'This was the game George and I played last night. For a very long time.'

'Looks riveting.'

'It's just as well babies are so cute, because so much of their care falls into the categories of the mundane and downright boring.'

'Which is the real reason you didn't want to take on the job of full-time nanny?'

There was no censure in his voice, just curiosity, and she found her gaze swinging up. 'Do you think housework is any less boring?'

One shoulder lifted. 'Given the way you do it—dancing and singing off-key at the top of your voice—perhaps.'

His words made her laugh, but his almost-smile had things inside her wobbling. She dragged her gaze away. 'Like I said, I just don't want to lose all my leisure time.' She needed the time and headspace to keep chipping away at her aunt.

'So what now? I get the great good fortune to play the clapping game while you enjoy your said leisure time?'

The question could've sounded sulky and petulant, but it didn't. He just looked—and sounded—at a genuine loss. She made a mental note not to swim for too long. She had no intention of abandoning him, not when he evidently felt so out of his depth. 'There are lots of other games too. For example, we like playing choo-choo trains.' She seized the bright red plastic train and pushed it across the blanket, making train noises.

George pursed his lips and made *choo-choo* sounds too, and then clapped and grinned.

Jasper shook his head. 'I'm *not* doing that.'

Imogen gurgled a laugh at George. 'Uncle Jasper thinks choo-choo trains are beneath his dignity.'

George bent at the waist, leaning towards her to laugh too, laughing because she was laughing. He was the sweetest little guy.

Her employer glared. 'I'm wondering how you got to twenty-five years of age without someone throttling you, Ms Hartley.'

'I'm guessing it's because of my sparkling personality.' She hummed a few bars of 'How Do You Solve a Problem Like Maria?' from *The Sound of Music*. Without giving him time to respond, she pulled the bag he'd packed towards her. 'Right, you have a couple of books here—' the thick cardboard ones that were almost indestructible '—so you can read one of those to him. But you have to point to the picture and say the word. Making the appropriate sound will earn you bonus points.' She pointed to a chicken and made chicken noises.

He opened his mouth, but she pushed the book into his hands before he could speak. 'It also makes the game last longer and that can be a blessing when your hands are sore from the clapping game.'

He didn't sigh, but it looked as if he wanted to.

'First and foremost, you need to keep him safe.'

His shoulders immediately tensed. 'What dangers am I guarding against?'

'Well, he isn't crawling yet, but he can roll and he can do a funny kind of tummy crawl. So he can get himself to the edge of the blanket…and there's all of that sand…and everything he picks up goes in his mouth.'

He nodded. 'No sand eating.'

'Once babies begin to move, they can do so surprisingly quickly.' She pointed to the water behind her.

He pointed a finger at her and then the water. '*Not* going to happen.'

'I know. You'll keep an eagle eye on him.'

He blinked.

'Insects can be a problem too. We don't want him bitten by an ant or stung by a bee or anything along those lines.'

He immediately traced the blanket's perimeter with eyes that made her think of laser beams. She pulled in another of those wobbly breaths. His worry, his vigilance, his desire to do this thing—a thing he apparently didn't want to do—to the very best of his ability, touched something inside her, made it soft and breathless. 'And…um… finally…the sun. We don't want him getting sunburned.'

His hands slammed to his hips. 'Then why don't we just take him back inside where it's safe?'

'Jasper,' she said gently, 'he's *your* nephew. You're free to take him back into the house whenever you want. But how would you feel cooped up inside all day? Besides, there are things you need to protect him from in there too—the sharp edges of coffee tables, making sure he doesn't put something he shouldn't in his mouth.'

He dragged a hand down his face, making her heart twist. 'I'm sorry. It's just…there's a lot to consider.'

And he'd never expected to be in this situation. That much was apparent. She forced her lips upwards. 'If it's any consolation, vitamin D is most excellent for growing bones, and sunscreen will help take care of the sunburn.' She raised an eyebrow. 'As will a hat.'

'It's in my pocket,' he muttered. 'He doesn't like wearing it.'

She didn't say anything, simply poured some sunscreen into her hand. 'I've never put this stuff on a baby before, so it could prove interesting.'

He looked as if he wanted to run away. 'How can I help?'

'I don't know. You might need to hold him. Let's see how we do first.'

She smeared a line of the lotion down George's nose and across each cheek, and started to rub it in. He gave a squeal of outrage and tried to turn his face away, but she was too quick for him. When she did it again, he frowned at her and then he opened his mouth and…well, he yelled at her to stop. It was the only way she could think to describe it, and she found herself laughing. 'He reminded me of you then.'

'I don't frown like that.'

'I beg to differ.'

'And I would certainly never yell at you.' He then seemed to recall that moment in his study when he'd found her sitting in front of his computer, and winced, scrubbing a hand across his hair.

She took pity on him. 'Not without provocation,' she agreed. 'And in George's eyes, sunscreen apparently provides ample provocation.'

His nose curled. 'I can understand that. The stuff is sticky.'

If she didn't still have a handful of sunscreen she'd have slammed her hands to her hips. 'Are you telling me you're not wearing sunscreen?'

'I…' His mouth opened and closed. 'There wasn't time.'

Without thought, she reached across and deposited a liberal amount of lotion to his face. George let loose with a long, 'Ooh!'

'Exactly, Master George, Uncle Jasper needs to set you a good example.' But as she said the words, her stomach was clenching up tighter and tighter. She should never have touched him. What on earth had she been thinking?

She hadn't been thinking. She'd acted on impulse. And in this instance, impulse was bad. *Really bad.*

Or really divine. Depended on which way you wanted to look at it. Beneath her fingers Jasper's skin felt warm and vital, vivid, and the strength of him seeped into her fingers and all the way through to her bones, making her feel buoyant and alive. Which was crazy. The scent of him—warm cotton and cardamom—had an unfamiliar yearning stretching through her.

She couldn't look at him; afraid she'd betray the need racing through her. She stared doggedly at George instead. 'I'm really sorry. I shouldn't have drowned you in suncream, but your nephew is watching this exchange intently. And I'm thinking that if I dab a final bit on your forehead and rub it in, then maybe he'll be a bit more amenable and let me do the same to him.'

'Right.'

That was said through a clenched jaw, and she did her best not to wince. She tried to not feel *him* as she did it, but her fingers were tingling by the time she'd finished.

Little George blinked when she repeated the procedure on him, and frowned, but he didn't squeal or holler.

'Okay.' She gritted her teeth. 'Let's try arms next.'

Without a word, Jasper held out an arm, but she couldn't help noticing the way his eyes had turned remote and distant. Cold. It was all she could do not to shiver.

To her amazement, though, George also held his arm out in imitation of his uncle. Holding her breath, she squirted lotion on both arms—man's and child's. 'Quick,' she murmured to Jasper. 'Give me your other arm.'

Again, George copied, and she laid a line of cream down both arms—one strong and tanned, the other tiny, plump and pale. 'Right, we're ignoring your arms for the moment, Jasper. You take one of George's arms while I do the other. You can rub yours in once we're done.' Which meant she wouldn't have to touch him again.

Without a word, and with quick efficient movements that made her own efforts seem clumsy, Jasper gently rubbed the cream into George's right arm. Wanting to distract George while she did his legs, she said, 'Help Uncle Jasper rub the cream on his arms.'

She gave a quick demonstration, not actually touching Jasper, just pretending to, and George immediately leaned forward and started patting his uncle's arm. Jasper turned to her, his eyes wide. 'He...he understood exactly what you wanted him to do!'

'He's smart...and utterly adorable. And that—' she pointed to his arm '—will keep him occupied for ages.'

While the lotion on Jasper's other arm was about to drip onto the blanket. With an apologetic grimace, she reached across and rubbed it in. The action brought her face in close to his and she wondered if the consternation—the turmoil—in his eyes was reflected in hers. She edged back, her mouth going dry, and the shutters slammed down over his eyes, leaving her confused and flailing.

'I think it's time you went for your swim, Imogen.'

'I think that's a very good idea.' She nodded. 'Before you throttle me.'

Did she imagine it or did his lips just twitch?

She started to untie her sarong and his gaze immediately swung away to focus on the baby. It made her heart thump too hard. She swallowed and forced herself to focus on the reason she'd brought him and the baby out here. 'What are you going to do if he cries?'

Jasper did his level best to keep his eyes on the baby. Imogen's touch—on his face and his arm—had been innocent, almost absent-minded. But it had woken something inside him, and he desperately wanted to lull it back to sleep. Ogling her, near naked in a swimsuit, would *not* help him achieve that particular objective. Besides, he didn't ogle. He'd never ogled. And he wasn't starting now.

'And here's a hint. Calling for me is the wrong answer.'

Her voice was filled with laughter and he wanted to lean into it, play along, but experience warned him not to. While he might have to face the fact that he could like Imogen Hartley—quite a lot actually—there was no place in his life for her. He'd trusted a woman once—had foolishly come to rely on her, had thought they were a team.

But she'd left, frightened off by his father's threats. He didn't blame her for leaving, not for a moment. But it'd taught him two hard lessons. The first—that he couldn't rely on anyone but himself. The second—that it'd be wrong of him to put any woman in a position where she could be hurt by his father.

'Jasper?'

She could whisper his name in a way that made the surface of his skin come alive.

She knelt back down to the blanket in front of him and the baby. 'If you're that uncomfortable with this, I'll stay. I don't have to go for a swim.'

'No, you go for your swim.' He didn't want to deprive her of such an innocent pleasure. She'd been looking forward to it—had definitely earned it—and he'd do whatever he could to facilitate it. He made himself swallow, pulled his face into neat lines. 'I'm just...out of practice at talking to people. Evidently I've been spending too much time in my own head.'

He couldn't believe he'd said that out loud. He wanted to check his words, choke them back, but it was too late. Gritting his teeth, he forced his mind back to her original question. 'If the baby cries, I'll make sure nothing is hurting him, and then I'll check his nappy.' Um... 'I saw a bottle of something in your bag...?'

'It's just cold boiled water.'

Right. 'Well, I'll see if he wants that.'

'And if that doesn't work?'

He tried not to scowl—neither she nor the baby deserved his malcontent. 'I'll distract him by playing choo-choo trains or something equally inane.'

The green flecks in her eyes shone bright and clear. She stared at him steadily now and he didn't know if she was amused by him or concerned.

Don't be an idiot.

If she was concerned about anyone it'd be the baby.

'And if that doesn't work,' he added, doing his best not to frown, 'I'll sing to him.'

Her lips parted. 'What a lovely idea.'

He stared at those parted lips and that monster he'd been trying to lull roared back to life—fierce, hungry and primal. Her eyes widened at whatever she saw in his face, and her tongue eased out to moisten her lips. They stared at each other, lost in some strange in-between world— but in between what he couldn't say—and then the baby squealed, and she jerked back, and he could breathe again.

She leapt to her feet. 'If he cries, pick him up and give him a cuddle. That might be all he needs—a bit of reassurance that he's safe.' And with that, her sarong floated to the ground and she set off towards the water.

He did his best not to notice her bare legs and arms or the curve of her hips. She wore a seriously sedate swimsuit, and a sun shirt. It shouldn't make a man's mouth dry with longing.

It shouldn't.

Keep your head.

He'd been on his own too long, that was all. This was just an…adjustment.

A squeal at his elbow snagged his attention. He glanced down to find the baby pointing a wobbly arm after Imogen and frowning. 'Immy's going for a swim.' He called her Immy to the baby because it was what she called herself. *Come to Immy; Immy's getting your bottle now.*

George looked as if he might cry. 'She'll be back soon. It's not worth getting upset about, kid, believe me. Look—' he held out his arm, shuffling closer '—we haven't rubbed all of this goop in yet.'

The baby gave a toothless grin and started patting Jasper's arm with an enthusiasm that tugged at the older man's heart. He was a clever little kid. Were all babies this smart? He'd bet they weren't.

They spent a leisurely few minutes making sure it was all rubbed in, and then George stared at him expectantly. Right… He cleared his throat. 'Do you want to play the clapping game?' He clapped his hands together a few times. Nothing. 'What about your train?' He seized the train. 'Would you like to play with that?' No way was he making *choo-choo* noises, though.

The train was tossed across the blanket. Uh-huh…

The hat! He pulled it from his pocket and set it on the kid's head. The kid immediately sounded a protest and went to pull it off, but Jasper whipped out his own cap and waved it about.

'Look, I have a hat too.'

And he set it on his own head.

The baby pointed to it and bounced. 'Um! Um! Um!'

He wanted Jasper's hat? He handed it over. The kid pulled his own hat off and gave it to Jasper, and then tried to put Jasper's cap on. He finally managed it, with a bit of help from his uncle, and did his best to look up at Jasper, but the brim covered his eyes. Fat hands lifted the brim, and when he finally made eye contact with Jasper, he laughed hysterically. Jasper couldn't help but laugh too. The kid had a weird sense of humour. And that was the game they played for the next twenty minutes—swapping hats and laughing.

Boring and mundane? Perhaps. But he'd attended board meetings that had dragged worse and achieved less. And at least he was sitting in the sun on a beautiful beach.

The thought gave him pause. Since when did he care where he was or what the weather was like? Though a bit of sun was good for the baby. Imogen had said so. Personally, he didn't care about either the beach or the sunshine. At least that was what he told himself.

He glanced back at the baby. Okay, this whole 'looking after a kid' thing wasn't rocket science. It was something he *could* learn. He could make sure all the kid's physical needs were met, and be friendly with the little guy, *and* keep his distance. He didn't need to engage his emotions towards the baby any more than he did towards his staff back in Sydney. He cared about their well-being, naturally, but it didn't matter to him on a personal level if they decided to leave his employment or anything. Just as it wouldn't matter when Emily demanded the return of her child.

And as far as Jasper was concerned, that was the best-case scenario he could think of.

'Look.' He pointed down the beach. 'Here comes Immy.' She moved with an unconscious grace that had his chest drawing tight, making it hard to get air into his lungs. He swallowed and looked away. 'I hope she enjoyed her swim, kid. She's earned it.' He had to do better where she was concerned. She'd gone above and beyond these last two days.

George glanced up at Jasper, eyes wide, and then his face split into a grin and he clapped his hands. Jasper found himself smiling back and clapping his hands too.

'How was the water?' he asked when she reached them, doing his best to look—and feel—unaffected.

'Freezing!' she said with her usual irrepressible cheerfulness, grabbing her towel and drying her face. 'Makes you tingle all over.'

Tingling was the last thing he needed to think about, but she literally glowed from her swim. Something inside him responded to it. And there was nothing he could do about it. Other than try and ignore it.

'Hey, Georgie, did you have fun?' And then she squeezed a drop of water from her hair and let it fall to the baby's foot.

George squealed. And when she made as if to drip more water on him, he squealed louder, seized a handful of Jasper's shirt and hauled himself upright on wobbly legs. He'd have fallen, would've pitched forward to smack his face against Jasper's knees, if Jasper hadn't caught him. The kid then stood balanced on Jasper's lap, and he bounced and chortled and waved his arms in glee that he'd evaded Imogen and her antics.

Jasper could barely draw breath. The baby had *trusted* him to catch him—to protect him and keep him safe.

George laughed up at his uncle now as if they'd shared a joke. Jasper's mouth dried. That…that was just fanciful, right? Nine-month-old babies couldn't share a joke with you.

The baby's legs gave way, and he plopped down on Jasper's knee, snuggling into him…and then he wrapped an arm across Jasper's tummy and he cuddled him. Every hard thing inside Jasper's heart melted to a puddle, and his arms went around little George of their own volition.

He stared down at his nephew, his heart filling with too much emotion. He said the rudest word he knew. Very softly.

He glanced up to find Imogen watching. She didn't remonstrate with him for his bad language. Instead, she asked, 'What just happened?'

The soft warmth of her voice helped to soothe the ragged edges of the panic pounding through him.

He didn't bother trying to deny it. 'I'm falling for him.'

She wrapped her towel about herself and sat on the edge of the blanket. 'What's wrong with that?'

His chest ached. His throat ached. And his head pounded. 'I have absolutely no jurisdiction over this child, Imogen. When one of his parents demands his return, I have to hand him over. I won't be able to keep George here.'

She sucked her bottom lip into her mouth, her gaze never leaving his. 'But you can visit him, can't you? And he can come for holidays here to Tesoura, right?' She searched his face. 'I'm not getting something. What am I not getting?'

A breath rattled out of him. 'My sister is married to a man who beats her. I tried to help her break free of him, but she didn't want that. Instead, she cut *me* from her life and said she never wanted to see me again.'

Her hand flew to her mouth. When her gaze lowered to the babe in his arms, her eyes filled. He wanted to hug her for her concern, for the way she worried about George. For her kindness.

'No matter how much I might want to, I can't protect George. Not from his own parents.' And yet how on earth could he abandon George to a lifetime of fear and abuse?

Nausea churned through him. History was going to repeat, and he was powerless to stop it. The thought nearly broke him.

'Despite all of that,' Imogen said slowly, 'your sister still sent the baby to you. That has to mean something, don't you think? What did her letter say?'

'Next to nothing!' It hadn't provided him with an ounce of reassurance. George jumped at his tone and started to fidget, Jasper soothed him the way he'd seen Imogen doing—holding him against his shoulder and rubbing his back. '"Dear Jasper,"' he recited through gritted teeth, '"I know you've probably not forgiven me, but there are some things I need to take care of. In the meantime, I need someone to look after George. Please keep him safe until I can come for him. Emily."'

She hadn't signed off with 'love' or 'best wishes' or 'sincerely' or anything else. And she hadn't given him any further explanation. He wasn't sure why he'd expected more. His lips twisted. Hope sprang eternal, he supposed.

Imogen had stiffened. She stared straight at him as if

expecting something more from him—in the same way he'd expected something more from Emily. 'What?'

'It sounds like she's in trouble.'

He hated the way her words made his gut clench. 'What makes you think that?'

Her hands lifted. 'What makes you think there could be any other possible explanation?'

'Experience.'

She blinked and eased back. He was going to have to explain, and he didn't want to. But George needed all the allies he could get, and Jasper had no intention of ostracising a potential ally as kind and generous as Imogen. She made his nephew smile and she made him feel safe. That was worth more than gold.

He did what he could to find his equilibrium. 'My father and brother-in-law are both shaped in the same mould.'

Her bottom lip wobbled. 'They're both…violent?'

'They're both miserable excuses for human beings.'

Her eyes filled again, and it made his chest twist. 'I can't stand either one of them,' she said with quiet vehemence, and for some reason it warmed up parts of him that had started to chill.

'My father wanted all of my mother's attention. He resented Emily and me for taking up so much of her time. Sometimes, when it all got a bit too much for her, she'd farm us out to relatives for a couple of weeks or would send us off to some holiday camp.'

He'd hated it, but at the same time he'd welcomed the reprieve from his father's anger.

Imogen worried at her lip. 'She was probably trying to protect you.'

His head felt too heavy for his shoulders. 'Or saving her own skin.' And he didn't blame her. But when he'd offered her a chance to escape her husband—when he'd offered her refuge and a chance to start a new life—she'd spurned it, had rejected him. Just like Emily.

'That's what you think Emily is doing with George?'

'I know that on the day she sent George here, she and Aaron attended a big charity ball in Sydney—one of the biggest events of the social calendar—filled with all of the powerful and well-to-do. I also know that in the coming week Aaron is going to the States. No doubt Emily will be going with him.'

She pressed a hand to her brow. 'What if you're wrong? What if she's in trouble and trying to break away from her husband? Him going to the States could provide her with the perfect opportunity to do that. Does she have anyone she can turn to? Would your parents take her in?'

'My father would order her to return to Aaron.' The two of them had always been as thick as thieves.

'Friends?'

'Aaron vets all of her friends—in truth he's probably isolated her from them all by now.' In the same way his father had his mother.

'So she has no one to turn to?'

She had him! She had her brother. He broke out in a cold sweat. Despite everything she had to know that, didn't she?

CHAPTER FIVE

'I'VE BEEN THINKING about what you said.'

Jasper came striding down the path towards her and Imogen halted in her pegging out of George's tiny clothes, momentarily transfixed. The back garden was a riot of shrubs, palms and flowerbeds, but none of that could hold a candle to the man moving with such easy grace towards her.

He carried George in his arms, completely at ease as if he'd been born to it. The image of a little baby held against a pair of broad, sigh-worthy shoulders—all of George's small helplessness contrasted with Jasper's power and strength—had the potential to do crazy things to a woman's insides. Protectiveness and nurturance all wrapped up in a single glorious package. Was there anything more attractive—?

She broke off, realising that Jasper was staring at her expectantly. She tried to click her mind into gear. 'You've been thinking about what I said?' she parroted, hoping she didn't look completely at sea.

'About Emily.'

She eased back to survey him more fully. 'About the possibility of her being in trouble?'

He nodded.

She glanced at George, currently fascinated by a bird singing in a nearby shrub, before turning back to Jasper with his serious grey eyes and mouth that was made for smiling but so rarely did. She was becoming too invested here, but how could she not? The way these two had bonded in the last couple of days amazed her. They adored each other. And it made her fear for them both.

She swallowed. 'And…?'

'I have a favour to ask.'

Her heart leapt. Which made no sense. She bent down to retrieve a tiny pair of shorts from the laundry basket. 'Okay.'

He took the shorts from her and handed her George. 'I need your help.'

'Okay.' She focussed on the variety of romper suits, bibs and singlets that waved in the breeze like colourful bunting and tried to get her racing pulse under control.

He pegged out the shorts and then reached into the basket for a bib and pegged it out too. She wanted to tell him that she was paid to do the laundry, but didn't because… well, he was the boss and she guessed he was also paying her to hold the baby.

'Does that mean you'll help?'

'Of course I will.' A woman could be in trouble, and there was a baby involved. How could she refuse?

And just maybe the warmth from a pair of grey eyes as they rested on her didn't hurt either.

That's shallow, Imogen. Seriously shallow.

But Jasper's eyes *weren't* shallow. They hinted at depths she found intriguing…fascinating.

He reached out and clasped her forearm in silent thanks. The heat of his touch penetrated through skin, muscle and sinew, making her want more. She sucked in a breath as the ground beneath her feet shifted. It took her so off guard she didn't have time to hide her reaction. His gaze narrowed and his nostrils flared. She recognised the same need and hunger coursing through his eyes.

Everything inside her clenched. She forgot to breathe.

He stepped back, distancing himself behind a mask of stern calmness, and she gulped in a breath, reminding herself that he was her employer and she was his employee. And even if that weren't the case she wasn't getting involved with someone who'd marooned himself on a desert island.

She had plans. Lauren was relying on her. She was relying on Lauren. As soon as she left here she was throwing herself wholeheartedly into those plans. If she didn't she and Lauren would lose everything they'd worked and saved so hard for—it wasn't just her money they were risking, but Lauren's too. They'd made a solemn promise to give this new business of theirs every chance they could—to give it their very best efforts. She squared her shoulders. She wasn't letting Lauren down, and she *would* prove the naysayers wrong.

Tesoura was idyllic for some holiday R & R, but there was no way she'd ever live in a place like this.

Not that he'd ever ask her to.

Which was exactly as it should be.

She retreated to a nearby stone bench and busied herself bouncing the baby. Tried to quieten the clamour flooding her veins.

'I didn't realise how much laundry a baby could generate.'

Jasper surveyed George's clothes flapping in the breeze, obviously not finding it difficult to move on from thoughts of touching her. Well, she could move on too—with the same super-duper ease. She pasted on a bright smile, which admittedly was a little difficult when she was gritting her teeth, and tickled George's stomach. 'Messy little tyke, aren't you?'

Jasper continued pegging out the clothes. She kept her gaze trained on a nearby hibiscus flower in bright red.

'Is there a trick to it?'

Jasper, with the now empty basket clasped to his side, stared at her. She moistened dry lips. 'A trick to what?'

'Washing George's clothes.'

She tried to stop her eyes from staring. 'You want to do the laundry?'

'*Want* is too strong a word, but you said you'd teach me everything I needed to know. I want to know how to do it *all*. And it doesn't seem fair that you get landed with all the boring, mundane bits.'

That was the problem. Right there. In that one gloriously generous sentence. He said something like that, and it turned her to mush. He acted all lord of the manor one moment, and then…and then the opposite of that. It could knock a girl sideways if she was taken unawares. She did what she could to stiffen a backbone that wanted to melt. 'Jasper, stuff like doing the laundry is what you're paying me for.'

'But if something were to happen to you or Katherine— say you both got a tummy bug—or were simply busy with other things, I'd need to know how to do something as basic as wash George's things.'

She knew he came from a privileged background, but surely he knew the fundamentals. 'You, um…have done a load of washing before, right?'

He looked momentarily horrified, and then he laughed. 'It's true that my family had household staff when I was growing up, but seriously, Imogen. Your aunt was my family's housekeeper for nearly twenty years. What do you think?'

She bit back a grin. 'I expect she made sure you and your sister learned a few life skills.'

'Precisely. I know how to operate my washing machine. I do my own laundry when your aunt takes her annual leave.'

Why hadn't he granted her leave at Christmastime? The more she learned about him, the more of a puzzle that became. She couldn't imagine him denying her aunt any request for leave.

Which maybe meant Katherine had lied to them. It

maybe meant her aunt hadn't wanted to spend Christmas with her family.

She swallowed.

'Imogen?'

She shook herself. 'The only difference is in the laundry powder. We use a milder detergent for George's things. A baby's skin is more sensitive than an adult's.' She led him into the laundry room where she pointed the relevant washing powder out to him.

He nodded. 'Okay, got it.'

The laundry was generous by laundry room standards, but far too small to be confined in with Jasper and her own see-sawing hormones. Especially when he leaned in close to take George from her arms. The scent of warm spice invaded her senses. She took a hasty step back and spun on her heel to lead the way into the kitchen. 'So how can I help? What's this favour you want to ask?'

'I want to set up a fake social media account. I've spent the last two days trying to contact Emily, but with no luck. It could be that she's simply wanting to avoid me.'

The worry in his eyes belied that, though, and it tugged at her heart. 'You think you'll be able to reach her via social media?'

'It's worth a shot. I suspect Aaron monitors all her phone calls and social media accounts. He'd never allow her to friend me or anyone associated with me.'

She still wasn't a hundred per cent sure what this had to do with her.

'But he probably wouldn't look twice if she received a friend request from Jupiter Collins, who attends the same gym.'

The penny dropped. 'You want me to pose on social media as Jupiter Collins.'

'Complete with a profile pic, history and a social calendar filled with all the things young women your age like to do.'

'I already have social media accounts, though. My picture is already out there in cyberspace. Won't that...' she lifted her hands '...cause problems, blow our cover?'

'I have computer programs that will help with that. When I'm finished with your picture, you won't recognise yourself.'

'Okay, let's do this.'

They left the baby with Katherine. Once in his office, the first thing Jasper did was position Imogen against a wall without windows, so there was no possibility of the view giving away their location, and took a photo.

She watched in amazement as he hunkered down at the computer with her image before him on the screen and changed her dark brown hair—all wild curls—to a sleek blonde shoulder-length bob. Her hazel eyes became blue and he lightened her skin tone. She tried not to grimace as he then did odd things, like lengthen her face, widen her smile and enlarge her eyes.

She pressed her fingers to her face, to reassure herself that everything there was unchanged. 'Me, but not me. It's amazing.'

Jasper studied the image on his screen. 'I like the real you better.'

'Yeah, right,' she snorted. 'She's thinner, has beach-blonde hair and big baby blues. And is a gym junkie!'

Jasper laughed, and for a moment it felt as if she were catching a big wonderful wave that rolled you gently all the way to shore. 'While you're sassy, funny and cute. And a surf junkie.'

He thought she was cute? Really?

She tossed her hair. 'Sassy is just another word for "lack of subservience", right?'

He chuckled again, his fingers typing away furiously.

'I'm not all that interested in subservience, Imogen. Your good heart is of far more value to me.'

Don't melt. Don't melt.

He suddenly froze. 'This—' he gestured to the screen '—isn't some weird male fantasy of mine. I wouldn't want you thinking that this is a… I mean…'

She took pity on him. 'That's good to know, Jasper.'

He eyed her uncertainly and then turned back to his computer. 'I made up a short bio for our Ms Collins last night.'

Jupiter Collins's biography appeared on the screen, and Imogen leaned in closer to read it.

'I have her living in a neighbouring Sydney suburb to Emily, and she goes to the same gym. I made her five years younger so they can't be old school friends.'

She read the bio, and something tugged at her. 'Give her a baby too.'

'Why?'

'So, we can tell her how George is doing.'

He swung to her. 'That's a really nice idea. Boy or girl?'

'Girl.'

'Name?'

'Georgia,' she said immediately. 'Georgia… Jas…' She tried to think of a feminine version of Jasper. 'Jasmine! Georgia Jasmine.'

He huffed out a laugh but sobered almost immediately. 'A baby will provide another point of contact. They both go to the gym *and* have babies of a similar age. Jupiter's friend request shouldn't raise Aaron's suspicions.'

His fingers flew across the keyboard. They looked sure and capable and she'd never realised before how sexy a man's hands could be. The thought of those hands on her body—

Heat exploded through her and she had to look away.

Inappropriate. Seriously inappropriate.

'How…um…?' She cleared her throat. 'If you and your sister are estranged, how do you know what gym she goes to?'

'I rang her best friend yesterday.'

He'd been busy.

'Aaron hates Prue. Has forbidden Emily from having anything to do with her.'

Imogen's nose curled. 'I *really* don't like this man.'

'I hate him.'

He slumped as if all the energy had drained from him at that admission. Imogen found herself reaching out to clasp his hand.

'You're doing what you can. You're keeping George safe and you're giving Emily a way to contact you if she needs to. One step at a time.'

His hand tightened about hers. 'I shouldn't have leapt to conclusions so quickly—shouldn't have been so caught up in my own bitterness that I discounted the possibility that she might be in trouble.'

He glanced at their joined hands and then released her so fast it made her blink. She pulled her hand into her lap, her heart starting to pound. 'What matters is that you're doing something now.'

He went back to his typing, his mouth set in a straight line. 'Emily and Prue *accidentally* bump into each other every once in a while. Prue makes sure of it. She agrees with you, by the way. She said the only reason Emily would send George away was if something was wrong.'

And he'd immediately leapt into action to help a sister who hadn't spoken to him in two years.

'I'm giving Jupiter three months' worth of history.'

'How on earth can you do that if you're only creating the profile today?'

He glanced at her from beneath his brow. 'It's probably better not to ask.'

Right.

'Any suggestions for things Jupiter might've posted?' he asked.

'Absolutely.'

The corners of his mouth twitched. 'You didn't hesitate.'

'I'm a very social person. I have a phone full of photos that I've shared on social media.'

'Social, huh?'

'I take pictures of movies I've seen, books I'm reading— usually for my book club—pictures of my toes after I've had a pedicure. Cocktails make great pictures to share. And the beach. I share oodles of pictures of the beach. And my softball team's scores.'

'You play softball?'

'Yep. It's off-season at the moment, but I'm a halfway decent hitter and—' she waggled her eyebrows '—I'm third base.'

'You don't say?' Those delicious lips curved upwards. 'You lead a full life.' The smile faded and his brow knitted together. 'You must hate it here.'

What on earth…? 'Of course I don't hate it. Tesoura is paradise, and Aunt Katherine is here. It's the perfect spot for a mini-break.'

'But you'd never settle in a place like this for good?'

'No way. I'd holiday here again in a heartbeat. But I couldn't live the kind of life you do, Jasper. I love my softball team and my book club. I'd miss my family and friends too much. I love my life. Why would I give all that up? Even for an island paradise?'

I love my life. Imogen's words rang through Jasper's mind. Had he ever loved his life?

The answer came swift and sure. *No.*

He'd been fiercely glad when, at the age of eighteen, he'd broken away from his father's control. In retaliation, Keith Coleman had refused to pay for his son's university studies, had refused to introduce him to the so-called 'right people' and had refused to put his name forward at his exclusive gentlemen's club. Jasper didn't regret any of it.

He'd used the modest legacy his grandmother had left him to help fund his studies. He'd worked part-time and had flat-shared with three other guys. He'd got by just fine.

He'd loved being free of his father. But he hadn't loved his life. His victory had been bittersweet. Neither his mother nor Emily had ever managed to escape, despite all of his begging, despite the detailed plans he'd given them to prove they could make it work. He'd had to continue watching from the sidelines as his father had directed their lives with a filthy temper and an iron fist.

At the age of twenty-five he'd invented a universal print drive that had made him millions. He'd renewed his petitions to his mother and Emily to come and live with him, or to let him buy them houses of their own away from Keith and Aaron. He'd promised them money and whatever else they needed, had sworn to protect them. But again, they'd both refused.

And then everything had blown up in his face and…

And he'd come here.

Luckily he'd had the means to do that!

But while he'd been free, he hadn't been happy.

His money meant he'd been able to put together a crack team of computer programmers. His company made some of the market's bestselling computer games. That gave him satisfaction. There'd been a couple of women he'd imagined himself in love with over the years. Those affairs had been exciting. But he'd never experienced the kind of bone-deep contentment with his life that Imogen evidently did with hers.

And while a part of him envied it, he also suspected a life like that could never be his. A person needed a better childhood than he'd had to achieve that kind of happiness—the sense of security that such happiness could last and was worth investing in.

It was a timely reminder of the gulf that lay between him and his intriguing part-time nanny. He was in danger of finding her too interesting, too…*desirable*. And he needed to annihilate all thoughts in that direction. Mentally girding his loins, he glanced across to find her scrolling through pictures on her phone.

'I can't use photos you've already uploaded to social media,' he felt bound to point out.

'But there are oodles and oodles that I haven't used. I took some of the gardens in the local park.'

They'd be suitably generic. Jupiter could be interested in gardening. Excellent.

'Here's a lovely glass of Sémillon.'

She liked Sémillon?

'Wait, what was that?' He touched her wrist as a couple of photos whizzed past.

She went back and a picture of a formal dress appeared. 'This?' She turned the screen more fully towards him. 'We're not sharing that. It's one of my new designs. I've been snapping the odd shot to share when I open my school in May.'

He sat back. He didn't know why he was so shocked. 'You're a designer?' On some level he'd always known she wasn't actually a housemaid, but… 'You're opening a design school?'

'I'm a dressmaker,' she corrected. 'And it's more a sewing school than a design school. We'll teach sewing, dressmaking, pattern making and so forth. We'll also offer a bespoke dressmaking service.' She shrugged. 'We're hoping it'll keep us busy.'

'Us?'

'A girlfriend and I are going into partnership.'

'Why are you waiting till May? Why not now?'

'The premises we've leased don't become available until then. And Lauren is on contract in the UK until March, so…'

He didn't know what to say. 'I had no idea.'

'There's absolutely no reason why you should.' That cheeky smile peeped out, making things inside his chest fizz like champagne. 'So maybe now you can see why I have such a problem with subservience. I actually want to be the big kahuna.'

She winked as she said it, though, and he knew she was simply teasing him. But… 'Launching a brand-new business. It's—' He snapped his mouth shut.

None of his business.

Those green sparkles in her eyes dimmed as if she knew exactly what he was going to say. 'Why aren't I back home frantically preparing for the launch of my school?' She started flicking through her photos again, but her knuckles had turned white. 'Lauren and I have been working towards this launch for two years. We've got everything in place, ready to go. I'll be back home in March, maybe sooner, to do all the pre-launch stuff.' She glanced up as if she was going to say more, but then shrugged. 'This will be my last chance for some R & R for some time to come, I expect. I mean to enjoy it while I can.'

But she wasn't getting R & R, was she? She was working as a maid and nanny. He glanced at his watch.

The woman opposite him gurgled back a laugh. 'Is there somewhere you need to be?'

He liked her laugh, and he liked it when he could make her laugh. He pulled in a breath—mentally pulling back. He had no intention of getting too used to that laugh. It was a temporary treat, like ice cream or cake.

When was the last time you had ice cream?

He rolled his shoulders. That didn't matter. It just proved how easy it was to give up unnecessary treats—like ice cream, cake and a woman's smile—and not miss them. And he had no intention of missing Imogen when she was gone either.

In one sudden swift movement, she pushed away from his desk. 'Oh, you probably are busy! Probably have video conference calls planned and all manner of things. I—'

'Not today,' he assured her. 'I just wanted to make sure we weren't running late for your daily swim.'

She eased back down into the chair. 'You don't have to work that into your schedule, Jasper. It's my job to work around yours.'

She was already going above and beyond. And he didn't like the thought of her swimming on her own. He didn't say those things out loud. He simply said, 'George enjoys his time on the beach.'

She looked as if she wanted to say something but turned back to her phone instead.

'What were you going to say?'

The green lights in her eyes caught the sun pouring in at the windows, and it made him suddenly glad that he'd chosen to live on a tropical island rather than some frozen rock in the North Sea.

'Just that we can take it in turns if you like? Swimming, I mean. You have this amazing beach at your disposal. Why not take advantage of it? It's way more fun than laps.'

For the past two years he'd exercised—hard. But he'd chosen the gruelling and effective over the fun. He hadn't felt like having fun. But today her suggestion appealed. 'You wouldn't mind?'

Luscious lips broke into a broad smile. 'Would I mind sitting on the beach, here in paradise, playing with George while you have a dip in the ocean?' She shook her head. 'You're a seriously hard taskmaster, Mr Coleman, but I'm up for that particular challenge.'

He tried not to grin. And failed.

She rested her chin on her hands and pursed her lips. 'I don't have the subservient thing down, but you don't really have the boss thing down either, do you?'

'My philosophy is to hire the best people, tell them what I want, and then leave them to get on with it. I find that works ninety-nine per cent of the time.'

'Nice philosophy.'

She gazed at him with frank admiration and it made perspiration gather at his nape. 'It doesn't mean I can't pull rank when I need to.'

'I already know this about you.'

Damn. Was she never going to let him forget that unfortunate morning when he'd growled at her? He opened his mouth to apologise—*again*—when he recognised the teasing laughter in her eyes and something inside him eased. 'Very funny, Ms Hartley. Now if you'd be kind enough to send me some of those photos…?'

She turned her attention back to her phone. 'I'm sending them with captions.'

'Because you don't think I can manage a twenty-five-year-old woman's voice?'

'Because it'll be quicker, and I want to get down to the beach.'

'That definitely wasn't subservient.'

He was rewarded with a tinkle of delighted laughter as he watched his email program and waited for the first of her photos to come through. They hit his inbox in quick succession. Her captions were short and sparky and the voice was better—younger—than he could've ever managed.

'So?'

She stared at him with an angled chin, evidently waiting for feedback. He was a firm believer in giving praise where it was due. 'These are perfect.'

'I should've been a writer.'

For a fraction of a second, he stilled. Did she know

Katherine's secret? Had her aunt finally confided in her? Whether she had or hadn't, it wasn't his place to give the game away. 'It's not too late,' he said instead. 'Though you might be pressed for time with the opening of your new school.'

'Yeah, nah.'

His lips twitched. 'Was that a yes or a no?'

'It's a maybe.'

She'd gone back to her phone and an influx of new pictures arrived, along with suggestions for status updates. All spot on and useful. He suddenly frowned. 'Would it be asking too much for me to have a look at your profile?'

'Friend me.'

Not a good idea.

Her fingers stilled. She glanced up. 'You don't have a profile on social media, do you?'

'No.'

'Of course he doesn't,' she murmured, before gesturing to his keyboard. He opened another browser window and handed the keyboard over, careful to glance away when she typed in her password. Her feed promptly appeared on his screen and as he scrolled down it, he found it as fun and vibrant as the woman herself.

He let out a breath. 'You and Jupiter don't sound anything alike.' It was the reason he'd wanted to check her account.

Liar. You wanted a voyeuristic glimpse into that life she loves.

'You made it pretty clear you didn't want anyone being able to trace Jupiter to me—or to link us together in any way.'

'I wish some of the people I work with were as quick to read between the lines as you.'

'Ooh, do I sense a promotion to Marketing Manager?'

'Not a chance.' He channelled his best Captain Von Trapp impression to counter the overwhelming desire to reach across and slam his lips to hers. 'Way too much trouble for the abbey.'

She didn't laugh as he'd expected. Her gaze was focussed on the computer. She pointed. 'That's my family. At Christmas. The holiday is a big deal for us.'

She had a big extended family. And every person in the photograph wore a big grin and a silly paper hat—the kind that came from Christmas crackers. There were pictures of huge platters of king prawns sitting either side of a baked ham that held pride of place on a table groaning with baked vegetables and salads. There were pictures of a game of backyard cricket and a water fight. It was about as far from the Christmases of his childhood as one could get.

He thought of George and his heart burned. What would his nephew's future Christmases be like?

'Of course, Aunt Katherine wasn't there, which put a bit of a dampener on things.'

Katherine hadn't been there? Why not? She'd told him—

He gulped the question back and glanced up to find Imogen... Well, she wasn't actually glaring at him, but it was only one level away. There was definitely puzzlement in those eyes, and a lurking resentment.

Katherine hadn't been at the Hartley family Christmas. And Imogen blamed him for it. *He's difficult and demanding.*

'What do you do for Christmas, Jasper?'

'Nothing.'

She straightened. 'What, really? Nothing? No roast turkey or ham or...or a plum pudding or presents?'

'Nothing,' he repeated, a bad taste coating his tongue.

'You don't have your bachelor buddies come to stay or...or...?'

'Nothing.'

The single word sounded stark.

It *was* stark.

He glanced back at the photographs on the screen. All that laughter and fun... He could never re-create that in a million years—he wouldn't know where to start—but in the future he could at least make an effort. He had to. For George's sake.

'What happened to you, Jasper?'

He glanced across at her whispered words. Her eyes had welled with such sadness he reached out to touch her cheek, aching to offer her some form of comfort. He wanted to tell her not to cry for him, but the words wouldn't come.

He pulled his hand back and lifted his chin. 'Nothing of any note.' It'd be better for her to not get involved in his life. Much better. 'C'mon, it must be time for that swim.'

CHAPTER SIX

IMOGEN SLATHERED SUNSCREEN across her cheeks, surreptitiously watching her aunt as the older woman jiggled George on her knee. Despite Katherine's no-nonsense briskness and seemingly cheerful demeanour, it couldn't hide the tired lines stretching from her eyes or the occasional slump of her shoulders when she thought no one was watching.

Ever since Imogen had arrived on the island, she'd told herself to go slow, that there was time for her to win her aunt's confidence, but she was coming to the conclusion that she'd chosen the wrong approach.

Except...

Her chest squeezed tight. Except the expression on Jasper's face when she'd blurted out her question not ten minutes ago—*what happened to you?*—had shown her the folly of the direct approach.

The darkness that had stretched through his eyes... It had made her throat burn and her eyes sting. She'd have done anything in that moment to make him feel better.

That's not what you're here for.

With a sigh, she glanced at her aunt, who was playing some game with George that involved his fingers and toes. 'Auntie Kay, what made you come to Tesoura?'

Katherine raised an eyebrow. 'I didn't want to work for Keith Coleman any more. I liked his wife, and I'd liked both Emily and Jasper, but they'd left home by then...' She ran a gentle hand over George's hair. 'And after the blow-up, I thought Jasper could use a friendly face.'

She plonked herself in a seat. 'What blow-up?'

'Honestly, Imogen, it was in all the papers at the time.' Her aunt turned to face her more fully. 'Your lack of interest in current affairs is appalling.'

She wrinkled her nose. 'I keep abreast of world affairs. And two years ago, I was in Paris.' She'd been doing an internship at one of the big fashion houses there. Australian news didn't rate much more than a line or two in the European papers. She racked her brain for what her mother must've told her at the time, but she'd been so full of the excitement of living and working in Paris—all that she'd been learning and experiencing—that if her mother had told her anything, it certainly hadn't stuck.

'There was a falling out between Jasper and the rest of his family. His brother-in-law accused him of assault and Jasper was charged—it was all set to go to court—but the charges were dropped.'

Her heart hammered against her ribs. 'And?'

'And that's all anyone knows. Other than the fact that none of them have spoken to Jasper since. Or he to them.'

Had Jasper given his brother-in-law a taste of his own medicine? She hoped so. She *really* hoped so.

'But as Keith is one of Australia's leading politicians, the tabloids had a field day with the story—it seemed that every day there were front pages splashed with claims and counter claims. It was ugly, and an unpleasant time for the family.'

No wonder Jasper had leapt to the wrong conclusion the day he'd found her sitting at his computer chortling, *Eureka*.

'Don't you find yourself going—I don't know—a bit stir-crazy here?'

Real amusement lit her aunt's eyes. 'You've only been here a week. You can't be bored already.'

'Of course not! This place is amazing, beautiful. But I couldn't live here for good. It's so…' *Empty.*

'I enjoy the peace and quiet.'

'But don't you miss catching a movie whenever you want, and seeing your friends—' she went straight for the jugular '—and browsing bookstores?'

'Are you trying to steal my staff, Ms Hartley?'

She swung around to find Jasper striding into the kitchen wearing a pair of brightly coloured board shorts, and both her and her aunt's mouths dropped. Her pulse did a funny little cha-cha. 'I, uh…' She swallowed. 'Well, I'd be fibbing if I said the family wouldn't love it if Aunt Katherine came home.'

'I'll offer you double whatever she's offering, Kate.'

'Very funny.' Katherine's gaze raked up and down his length. Imogen tried not to follow suit. 'But let me see if I have this right. You're going swimming? With Imogen?'

'Not at the same time.' He flicked a glance in Imogen's direction but just as quickly looked away again. 'We'll be taking it in turns to sit with George on the beach.'

Katherine's brows rose. 'But you're going swimming… for fun.'

He stretched his neck first one way and then the other. 'Imogen pointed out, quite rightly, that I have a perfectly good beach sitting on my front doorstep that I hardly seem to use. So I thought I'd…use it.'

Katherine took them in with one glance before giving a smile so blindingly bright Imogen had to blink a couple of times to clear her vision. 'I see Imogen has been working her magic on you.'

Heat flushed up Imogen's neck and into her face. What on earth…?

'I'm glad to see you finally taking a bit of a holiday, Jasper.'

'It's not exactly a holiday. We—'

'The two of you look the picture of youthful holiday fun.'

In her head, she begged her aunt to stop.

'Why don't you leave George with me and go enjoy yourselves?'

The look she sent the two of them was so arch Imogen prayed for the ground to open up and swallow her.

'Wouldn't dream of leaving you with the baby, Kate,' Jasper said, not looking at Imogen. 'Besides, George loves his daily romp on the beach.'

Without another word, Imogen grabbed her tote and the baby bag and led the way to the front door and outside. She didn't want to meet Jasper's gaze but ignoring him would only make things more awkward.

If that were possible.

She glanced up, but instead of derision or embarrassment she found laughter in those cool grey depths.

A breath whooshed out of her. 'Wow!' Jamming her hat to her head, she pulled it down low on her forehead. 'Just. Wow. That was so not subtle.'

'You can say that again.'

'She used to be the coolest person I knew, but now...' She shook her head.

Spreading the blanket beneath the palm trees in what had become their usual spot on this glorious stretch of beach, she scattered several of George's toys across it, her mind racing. 'It doesn't make sense.'

Jasper lowered George to the blanket. 'Why not?'

She started, realising she'd spoken her concern out loud. 'It's just... I could've sworn when I first arrived that she was warning me off you.'

He eased down onto the blanket too. 'How?'

No way was she telling him that. She adjusted her hat and sat. 'Just telling me to be careful not to bother you. Things like that.'

'She told you I was difficult and demanding, didn't she?'

Damn.

'She told me you were flighty and irresponsible.'

Her mouth fell open. His gaze lowered to her lips for a fraction of a moment, his eyes darkening, before snapping away again. Heat flared in her stomach before charging out to her extremities, making her swallow compulsively. If the man could create that kind of heat in a woman, just from a single smouldering glance, could you imagine—?

Don't imagine.

'You're not flighty and irresponsible any more than I'm difficult and demanding.'

'Exactly.' With a superhuman effort she reined in her pulse. 'So why…?'

'Your aunt is a clever woman. I suspect she's been hoping we'd keep our distance from each other, but George's arrival has put paid to that plan.'

'So why do such an about-face now and literally throw us together?'

He quirked an eyebrow, and she rested back on her hands. 'She *wasn't* trying to throw us together,' she started slowly. 'She was hoping to embarrass us and make us feel so awkward that we'd barely be able to look at each other.'

'That'd be my guess.'

'Why on earth would she do that? I know how well she thinks of you, while I used to be her favourite niece.' But maybe she wasn't any more. She rubbed a hand across her chest. Maybe somewhere along the way she'd lost her aunt's love and respect.

'Imogen, she could think well of me and yet at the same time not think we'd make a good match. She knows the kind of family I come from. I don't blame her for not wanting that for you.'

'Auntie Kay doesn't judge people on their families. She—'

'Go for your swim, Imogen. You've earned it. It doesn't matter why Katherine would prefer not to see us hooking up together, because it's simply not going to happen. It's one of those ridiculous hypothetical scenarios that we needn't concern ourselves with.'

A short sharp jab of pain went through her. It took an effort to keep her voice quiet and measured. 'I don't need warning off, Jasper.'

'That's not what I was doing.'

'Yes, it was.'

He opened his mouth, hesitated and then dragged a hand down his face. 'I'm sorry. I didn't mean to offend you. And it's probably closer to the mark to say I was warning myself off.'

That didn't seem very likely and her disbelief must've shown. He picked George up and held him in front of him—almost as if he were using him as a human shield. 'You're an attractive woman, and you make me laugh. Now, I don't mean to make your aunt sound asexual, but I've known her since I was twelve years old. She practically feels like *my* aunt.'

She frowned, not sure where he was going with this.

'So, in essence, I've spent the last two years on this island without any female company that I'd classify as beguiling or tempting.'

He thought her beguiling and tempting?

'I can't deny that I enjoy your company. I also appreciate all you've done to help George. I'm just reminding myself not to enjoy it too much.'

He thought her beguiling and tempting?

She moistened her lips, and just for a moment wondered

what it'd be like if they did allow themselves to enjoy each other's company *too much*.

She tried to shake the thought off. It was crazy—and crazy-making. She wasn't interested in a fling, and instinct told her he wasn't a fling kind of guy either. Neither of them needed that kind of complication in their lives. He needed to focus on his little nephew—and she wanted to help with that, not become a hindrance.

'You know what?' She rose. 'I might go for that swim now.'

He didn't say anything, just nodded, but she was minutely aware of her body as she untied her sarong—her fingers fumbling with the knot. Jasper thought her beguiling and tempting? The thought awakened something inside her—a sexy siren who wanted to tempt and beguile and make a man lose control—and while she did her best to ignore that siren call, she was unable to keep the sway from her hips as she walked towards the water.

She did her best to lose herself to the push and pull of the waves, to the invigorating assault of cold water on overheated flesh, and to the thrill of catching perfectly formed waves until she'd worn that siren out—or, at least, had numbed her with cold and exercise. Only then did she emerge back on dry land—out of breath and ready to drop.

Jasper tossed her a towel. 'How was that?'

The siren snapped to attention and Imogen could've wept. She dried off her arms and legs extra vigorously. 'Brilliant. Just give me a moment and you can tag-team me.' She pulled her sea shirt over her head and reached for the dry T-shirt she had in her tote but froze at the hunger that blazed in Jasper's face. Every desire she'd ever had roared to life in an instant.

With a tensing of his jaw, he dragged his gaze away, and, giving herself a mental slap, she scrambled into her dry shirt, wound her sarong back around her waist—not bothering to tie it, knowing her fingers wouldn't work—and knelt on the other side of the blanket from him, careful to keep her eyes fixed on George.

'Your turn!' Her voice emerged too loud and the brightness she injected into it jarred. She'd meant to physically tag him—slap her hand to his—but she changed her mind. One touch and he'd realise she was burning up.

Blowing out a breath, she smiled at George, picked up his teddy bear and danced it along the blanket. 'Water's great once you get in.'

Jasper shot to his feet as if he couldn't wait to be away from her, and she was really careful to keep her gaze from him as he shucked off his shirt, but couldn't resist glancing behind her as he jogged straight into the water without breaking stride, the shock of the cold barely seeming to register.

'Oh, my, George,' she murmured, pushing his toy train towards him and fanning her face. 'Your uncle is hot, hot, hot.'

But off-limits. Definitely off-limits.

Her employer swam for a good twenty minutes.

He's your boss. Don't forget he's your boss.

'Water's pretty damn fine, right?' she said, doing her best to look unaffected by the perfect line of his chest when he stood by the blanket again. The way the towel rubbed across defined pecs and honed abs made her mouth dry.

'Imogen, it's freezing!'

He dragged that towel over his hair before pulling his shirt back on and hiding all of that gloriously masculine muscularity.

That was a good thing.

He sent her a grin and she was relieved to see the strain had faded from his face. It helped ease the tension that had her wound up tight.

'But I know what you mean. I forgot how invigorating

that could be.' He spread his towel out beside the blanket and collapsed onto it. 'Did you and young George here have fun?' He tweaked his nephew's toes.

'I had a good think while you were swimming.' Was it her imagination or did he tense at her words? 'About Aunt Katherine,' she added quickly. She didn't want him thinking she was referring to anything else. 'I'm worried about her.'

He sat up, giving her his full attention. 'Why?'

'She told us all back home that she couldn't get the time off at Christmas, that she was needed here on Tesoura. I know that you're not going to give me an answer to this, but I'm starting to suspect that you did give her the time off, and she simply chose not to spend it with us.'

He watched her carefully but didn't say anything.

'She's been avoiding me since I arrived. During the day it's all work, work, work, and at night she tells me she has to get the household accounts into order for your accountant.'

She was doing what?

That was an outright lie. Not that Jasper could say as much to Imogen.

'I think the real reason she's trying to keep us apart is so we don't start comparing notes, realise there *is* something wrong and put our heads together to try and figure out what it is.'

That made a disturbing amount of sense. He knew at least one thing that was troubling Katherine. But was there anything else?

Shame hit him. He hadn't been paying attention. He'd been far too focussed on... He swallowed. He'd been too focussed on himself. Misfortune made some people more empathetic. He, though, had become more self-absorbed.

Look at the way he'd immediately jumped to the conclusion that Emily had sent George to him as part of an elaborate plan of revenge. It still might be, but that didn't change the fact that it shouldn't have been his first concern.

'Jasper, I have a feeling you know more about this than you're letting on.' She stared at him for several long seconds. 'Relax, I'm not going to ask you outright. I understand you have a duty as Katherine's employer and friend to keep her confidences.'

He let out a careful breath.

'But I am going to ask you if I should be as worried as I am.'

His gut clenched at the anxiety reflected in her hazel eyes, at the way her teeth worried her bottom lip. He wanted to ease her mind. He'd do just about anything to make her smile again. But he couldn't lie to her. 'I don't think you should be as worried as you are.'

She let out a long breath and closed her eyes. 'Thank you.'

'But I'm not a hundred per cent sure.'

Her eyes sprang open.

'Would it help if I had a word with your aunt?' He could at least urge Kate to confide in her niece.

She nodded without hesitating. 'Thank you.'

Jasper didn't approach Kate until after dinner, after he'd put George down for the night. Only then did he set his feet in the direction of the kitchen and Katherine's domain, but raised voices had him halting short of the doorway.

'For heaven's sake, Imogen, for the last time nothing is wrong! I'm getting tired of you harping on the subject.'

'But I'm worried about you.'

'That doesn't give you the right to pester me or pry into my personal life.'

What the...?

'Pry? I haven't pried.' Imogen's incredulity mirrored

his own. 'Auntie Kay, we're family. I know Mum's worried about you too, and—'

'While *I* know your mother sent you here to try and pressure me to return home. She's always known how to play the guilt card, but I'm not falling for it this time.'

'That's not fair!'

'It's more than fair. And you coming here as her proxy… It disappoints me, Imogen. I thought better of you.'

'What on earth are you talking about? I—'

'Enough! Yes, your mother and I have had a falling-out, but it's not your place to make me feel guilty about that or to play go-between. I have the right to live my life as I see fit. You're here to work—end of story. I'd appreciate it if you did that without interfering in my personal life.'

Jasper's head reared back. He'd never heard Katherine use that tone before, and he moved forward without thinking, aware of how gutted Imogen must be, and then had to take a step back when Imogen pushed past him with her head down. But that didn't prevent him from recognising the devastation on her face or the betraying sheen in her eyes.

A moment later the front door slammed. He wanted to go after her, make sure she was all right.

He shot into the kitchen and glimpsed Katherine's troubled expression before she quickly masked it again. She wiped the kitchen counters down vigorously. 'Did you want something, Jasper?'

He didn't bother pussyfooting around. 'That seemed unnecessarily harsh.'

'I don't appreciate Gloria's tactics.'

Gloria was her sister—Imogen's mother. 'Imogen isn't Gloria.'

'But she's acting as Gloria's envoy.'

He considered the charge. It didn't add up, not after

their conversation earlier on the beach. 'Are you sure about that? Because I'm not.'

Katherine's eyes flew to his. She straightened, setting the dishcloth in the sink. 'What other explanation is there? Why else would Immy be here?'

'For all the reasons she's stated—that she's between jobs, that she wanted to see a little more of the world, that she wanted to spend some time with her favourite aunt.'

'But she keeps asking annoying questions and saying she's worried about me, and—'

'Because she *is* worried. I know that for a fact. Look at it from her perspective. She's come all this way to see you—it's obvious that she adores you—and you're refusing to spend any time with her. And you're using the lamest excuses to avoid her. Now *I* know why you're busy, and *I* know why you're worried, but Imogen doesn't have a clue. And neither does Gloria.'

She pressed a hand to her forehead.

'Is it possible her mother didn't tell her about your argument?'

She blew out a breath. 'Yes.'

'So...?'

'So I'll apologise when she returns and smooth things over.'

'Why don't you tell her the truth? She'll be thrilled for you.'

'Because that will simply give her mother another weapon to use against me. She'll say I don't need an outside job to support myself any more, and that I can just as easily move back home and write there.'

'You can ask Imogen not to tell her.'

'That doesn't seem fair—asking Imogen to keep secrets from her mother.'

'She's a grown-up, Kate. I suspect there are lots of things she doesn't tell her mother.' He hesitated. 'Is there anything other than the book that's bothering you? Because I can—'

'Of course not!'

Her reply came too quickly. Unease circled through him, though he couldn't explain why.

'I can see, however, that you're worried about Immy.'

His shoulders went tight. He didn't like being so easy to read.

'Why don't you go after her and make sure she's okay? Let her know I'm sorry and fill her in on my secret. It's been exhausting to keep it and I'll be glad for her to know the truth.'

'Wouldn't you prefer to do that yourself?'

She shook her head. 'Off you go.' She shooed him out of the kitchen. 'I'll keep an eye on the baby.'

He found Imogen walking along the beach, her hands shoved into the pockets of her shorts and her shoulders hunched. The water lapped at her toes, but she barely seemed aware of it. He moved in next to her, and they walked in silence for a bit. The faintest blush of mauve lingered in the sky to the west as the last of the day's light faded.

'Did you hear all of my exchange with Aunt Katherine?'

She didn't look at him, just kept her eyes trained straight ahead. 'I heard enough to get the general gist.'

A huge golden moon hung low on the horizon, casting a path of dancing light on the water and turning the sand silver except for where the silhouettes of the palm trees made dark shadows. 'I didn't know that she and my mother had fallen out.'

'A fact that occurred to her only after you left.'

She stopped then, her eyes searching his face. The hurt mirrored inside them made his heart burn. 'Really? Or are you just trying to make me feel better?'

He crossed his heart.

Her gaze raked across his face again before something inside her seemed to relax. 'And I'm guessing she perhaps reached that conclusion with a little gentle persuasion from you?'

He didn't answer and she started walking again.

'She is sorry, you know?' he ventured.

She nodded, but still didn't speak. He touched her arm to make her halt. The silk of her skin an invitation hard to resist. 'I saw how upset you were when you left the house, Imogen. I…' He didn't know what it was he wanted to say—that he was worried about her, or that he was sorry she'd argued with her aunt, or that he thought her the most beautiful woman he'd ever laid eyes on?

He tried to dismiss that last thought to some dusty dungeon of his mind. It was just the moonlight talking.

'It's sweet of you to worry about me, Jasper, but I'm fine. To be perfectly honest I'm a bit cranky with both of them for turning me into piggy in the middle.'

She stared out to sea, her hands on her hips. 'Do you know what they fell out about?'

He stared into the dark waves. 'All she said is that she was tired of Gloria pressuring her to return home for good.'

'They've always been chalk and cheese, you know? Mum's the extrovert who's super social while Katherine's the one who has always relished peace and quiet. Mum's also seven years older and still sees Katherine as her little sister who needs brisking up.' She wrinkled her nose. 'It makes her bossy. I don't blame Katherine for getting her nose out of joint and telling Mum to pull her head in.'

'But?'

She shrugged. 'Despite all that, they're really close. I mean, they bicker, but it really rocked everyone when Katherine didn't come home for Christmas. It sent Mum into one of her panics. She was convinced something was wrong.'

And she'd infected her daughter with her own anxiety. 'About Christmas…'

She glanced at him. 'What about it?'

'Your aunt does have something on her mind, and she's given me permission to share it with you.'

She turned to face him fully and it made him hyper-aware of the warm breeze brushing against his calves and the lazy, languid elegance of the nearby palm trees and the rhythmic sound of the sea.

'Which is?'

He snapped back to attention. 'She wants to keep it just between us for the time being. So if you have a problem keeping things from your mother…'

Her eyebrows rose. 'I'll respect my aunt's confidences.'

This really should be coming from Katherine, but he knew how much the older woman hated fuss of any kind. He sympathised with that. He preferred to avoid the spot-light too. 'Well, the truth of the matter is a couple of years ago your aunt had a novel accepted for publication.'

Imogen stared at him in incomprehension for a mo-ment and then everything inside her seemed to electrify. She straightened, her shoulders shot back and she stared at him with huge eyes. 'She's been writing a book?'

'Well, a series, actually. She's had three books accepted so far and is working on her fourth—pulp fiction.' He grinned because he couldn't help it. 'Imogen, you have to read her stuff. It's so much damn fun. A crazy blend of zombie horror and romance, but it works.'

Her jaw dropped. 'You've read them?' And then she thumped his arm. 'I'm *so* jealous.'

'But now you can read them too.' Warmth radiated from where she'd touched him. He tried to ignore it.

She jumped up and down then, clapping her hands. 'Oh,

this is the best news. So exciting.' She stopped bouncing to purse her lips. 'She's been keeping it a secret because she thinks my mother will poke fun at her. Mum's a high school English teacher with a high regard for the classics, but she's not a literary snob. In her spare time she reads…'

'Zombie horror?'

A laugh gurgled out of her and it washed over him, rich and warm. 'Cosy mysteries and family sagas. I bet she'd love Katherine's stuff.' She lifted her chin. 'But you know what? They can sort that out for themselves. I'm not getting involved.'

Good for her.

Her face clouded. 'So that's why she didn't want to come home at Christmas?'

'Not exactly. Her publisher wants her to make significant changes to her latest manuscript before they'll agree to publish it. She's been trying to make those changes and struggling with it big-time.'

Comprehension dawned across her face. 'And that's what she's been doing in the evenings—not working on the household accounts but working on her book.'

He nodded because it was too hard to speak when he was fighting to get air into his lungs. The play of emotions across her face in the moonlight, the bounce of her hair and the vulnerable mobility of her lips all held him spellbound.

'Jasper, thank you. I—'

She broke off as their gazes caught and clung.

CHAPTER SEVEN

JASPER WANTED TO kiss her. She recognised the desire alive in his face. It shimmered like the light on a piece of Thai silk—prisms of luminescence arcing delicately against fragile cloth to form rainbows of luxuriant colour. Her every atom yearned towards him. She didn't just *want* him to kiss her—she *ached* with it.

Hovering between breaths, she waited, but he blinked, and she saw him fight to find the strength to gather his resources and step back.

A protest keened through her, but she understood why he did it. He was her boss. Making a move on her would be dishonourable, even though her employment status in his house fell firmly in the temporary category.

But she could make a move on *him* first, right?

She moistened her bottom lip. His gaze zeroed in on the action, hunger darkening his eyes and making his breathing ragged. The pulse at the base of his throat raced.

Why, yes. Yes, she could.

A thrill raced through her. 'Have you ever seen a more glorious moon?' she whispered, pointing to it though her gaze didn't leave his.

His gaze didn't leave hers either. 'No.'

'I once strolled along the Seine in the moonlight on a warm spring night, and I didn't think there could be a more romantic setting in the world. But I was wrong.'

His nostrils flared. 'You think my island is romantic?'

She nodded. 'Standing here on this beach now with a moon like that—all bright and vibrant—hovering just above the horizon like some kind of jewel, and with a warm breeze playing across my bare skin, that gorgeous perfume I've never smelled before drifting across from the forest and mingling with the scent of the sea...'

His Adam's apple bobbed.

'It feels like magic. And *very* romantic.'

His eyes throbbed into hers.

'I want to kiss you, Jasper.'

'Imogen.' Her name was barely more than a groan wrenched from his throat.

'I won't if you don't want me to.'

He closed his eyes, all the muscles in his jaw bunching.

'You know those moments you wished you'd taken, but you let slip away? And then spend the rest of your life kicking yourself for?'

His gaze returned to hers.

'This feels like one of those moments.'

A slow breath eased out of him, drawing her attention to the strong column of his throat and down to broad shoulders that made her mouth dry.

She forced her gaze back to his, not bothering to hide her need. 'I know it can't be anything more than a kiss. I'm not usually impulsive like this. I'm not into flings. But once I leave your gorgeous island, I'm starting a new phase of my life. This might be my last chance...'

He edged closer. 'To?'

'To seize the perfect moment—to live in it—without worrying about the consequences. To revel in a moment out of time one last time.'

His face gentled. 'A moment out of time?'

'A moment that, even when we're old and grey, will still put a smile on our faces whenever we remember it.'

His knuckles brushed across her cheek, firing her every nerve ending with heat and lust. His smile, when it came, made her thighs tremble. 'Then we'd better make it memorable.'

Her pulse started to gallop. She did what she could to get it under control—at least a little—because she didn't want to rush this moment. She wanted to savour it and imprint it on her mind for all time.

Which sounded crazy and overly dramatic, but she didn't care. She was following her gut all the way on this one.

Lifting her hands to touch his face, she revelled in the feel of his day-old growth as it scraped across her palms. He held still, waiting. 'What?' he eventually whispered, and she realised she'd been staring.

'There's something else that makes this moment incredibly romantic.'

'What's that?'

'You,' she murmured. She couldn't believe that she was touching him; that she was going to get to kiss him. 'You're beautiful, Jasper.' She could've chosen any number of words. *Gorgeous. Hot. Sexy.* They all fitted. But the one she'd uttered felt perfect. 'Beautiful inside and out.'

His lips parted as if in shock. His eyes had grown soft. 'Imogen…'

But she was done with talking. She slid her hands around his neck and pulled his head down to hers, reaching up on tiptoe to touch her lips to his.

The spark that ran through her made her tremble, but his hands at her waist held her steady. It gave her the security, and the boldness, to lean farther into him and move her lips across his more firmly. He was an intoxicating mixture of softness and strength, and kissing him was as invigorating as swimming in wild surf. It electrified her. And it must've electrified him too because it was as if their blood started racing at the same speed and to the same beat; their mouths opened at the same time and their tongues tangled as they tried to devour each other.

Wind roared in her ears, blocking out the sound of the surf. One of his hands pressed against the small of her back, urging her closer. The other flattened between her shoulder blades, hauling her against him. Every inch of her from the hips up could feel all of him. She wrapped her arms around his neck and tried to get even closer. The kiss went beyond anything she'd ever experienced. As if together they'd become the sea, sand and sun. As if crashing against each other, washing against each other, and heating each other up was what they were designed for.

She wrapped one leg around his waist to angle her pelvis more firmly against his. One large hand splayed beneath her thigh to hold it in place, and with a guttural groan he thrust against her. She threw her head back with a cry of pure need, arching into him.

She didn't know who stilled first. The way it felt—as if the moon had cast some spell on them and had cosmically attuned them to each other—they might've stopped at exactly the same moment. They stared into each other's stunned eyes. At least, she expected she must look as shell-shocked as him. She felt as if she were in a snow globe and someone had just shaken it—and the landscape of her life would never settle into the exact same contours again.

He let go of her leg. She lowered it to the ground.

He unwrapped his arm from her waist. She removed her hands from his shoulders.

She touched her fingers to her lips. He swallowed. 'Did I hurt you?'

She shook her head. 'No, but…wow.' Heat continued to spark across her skin like a tropical storm. 'I mean…wow!'

He nodded.

'No.' She shook her head. 'I mean a real *wow*.'

'Imogen—'

'I really wasn't expecting *that*.' She knew she was babbling but couldn't stop. 'I thought it was going to be some really sweet kiss that…' She shook her head at his pulsing, dark-eyed silence. 'But that wasn't *sweet*. I was ready to tear your clothes off and do things to you and with you that I've never—'

He reached out and pressed his fingers to her mouth with a low curse that made her close her eyes. Eventually she managed a nod. 'Sorry. Too much information.'

'For the record, I wasn't expecting things to get so intense so quickly either.' His hands clenched. 'I've been on this island too damn long.'

She gulped in air. 'Oh, no, you don't. You're not taking *all* the credit for that. It had just as much to do with me as it did with you. And I don't care what stupid excuses you want to make, but together we…*rock*.'

Bracing his hands on his knees, he huffed out a laugh. 'That's one way of putting it.' He straightened and met her gaze. 'But we both know it can't go beyond that, right?'

'I know.' She scratched both hands back through her hair and then frowned. She bit her lip and stuck out a hip. 'Why not?'

Her question slipped out without her meaning it to. Maybe the kiss had short-circuited her thought processes. His face grew grim and for a moment she thought he might revert to the wounded bear she'd met when she'd first arrived here, that he'd turn around and stalk off without another word. But then his face gentled again and he almost smiled. 'Because you're not romantically impulsive?'

And neither was he?

'You don't do flings.'

And he wasn't offering anything more.

Got it.

'You're only in Tesoura for a short time. You have big plans for your life. Exciting plans.'

She did. And she'd never be so foolish as to sacrifice those plans for a love affair. 'That's right.' She slapped a hand to her forehead. 'I remember now.' She eyed him carefully. 'And you have no plans to leave Tesoura?'

'None. This is my home now.'

She pulled in a breath. 'You're right. This can't go beyond that kiss. Sorry—' she shot him what she really hoped was a smile '—the oxygen is finally reaching my brain again.'

He laughed, and she wished she couldn't feel its rumble all the way to the centre of her being.

'There are other reasons too, Imogen. Many reasons. I'm going to tell you a story so you can understand what I mean.'

A story?

He pointed at the moon, and she turned to look. 'It still looks amazing,' he said.

But not as amazing as it had a moment ago. As it had moved farther into the sky, it had diminished in both size and colour. It looked neither as big nor as vividly yellow, as if it had lost some of its heat and energy.

Jasper surprised her when he moved behind and wrapped an arm about her shoulders and drew her back against him. She didn't resist, just let his warmth surround her. It was a protective gesture, a gesture of camaraderie, and it was kind. He didn't want her to feel alone, and he didn't want her to feel rejected.

The moon blurred and her throat ached.

'Do you remember asking what had happened to me?'

She nodded, not trusting herself to speak.

'I think if I tell you that story, you'll understand—and agree—that it's better for me to be on my own.'

She frowned out at the dark water, lifting a hand to

squeeze his forearm in a show of silent support. She couldn't see how she was ever going to agree that he should be *on his own*. Not forever. She got the fact that he might not want to be with her, but this self-imposed exile? He deserved better than that.

'I've already told you my father was physically abusive. He had a big leather belt that he wielded with great… authority. When he wasn't using his fists.'

She flinched, and his arm tightened about her.

'My mother copped most of his anger, though she's spent her entire life trying to placate him. I stepped in when I could…when doors weren't locked.'

She closed her eyes, but the image of the young boy he must've been was burned onto the insides of her eyelids. She forced her eyes open again. 'And then *you* copped it.' He didn't say anything. He didn't need to. 'Emily?'

'Mum and I did our best to protect her. She's a couple of years older than me, but she's always been a tiny little thing.'

Her heart burned.

'They say history never repeats, but they're wrong. In Emily's case it did. I never really liked Aaron all that much—thought him kind of smarmy—but I figured Emily was better off with him than at home where Dad was liable to lash out without warning. I'm guessing that's what she thought too.'

If Emily had never had a strong female role model like Imogen, then…then she'd have never really stood a chance.

'I dropped in on Em and Aaron unexpectedly one evening. I could hear raised voices upstairs, so I let myself in and followed the ruckus to its source. Where I saw Aaron backhand my sister. I saw red.'

'What happened?'

'I punched him, but evidently not hard enough because he got up and came at me. Emily was screaming at us to stop.' He paused. 'He charged. I sidestepped. Don't get me wrong, I had every intention of beating the living daylights out of him, but not in front of Emily. She'd been traumatised enough.'

He went so still she started to worry. She wrapped both her hands around his forearm and held on tight, pressed back against him, wanting him to know that he wasn't alone.

A breath shuddered out of him. 'His momentum sent him crashing across the landing and down the stairs.'

She gave a slow nod. It evidently hadn't killed the guy as he was still making Emily's life a misery... 'I'm finding it hard to feel any sympathy for him.'

A low chuckle broke from his throat, disturbing the hair near her ear and making her break out in gooseflesh. 'I can't say I felt too much of that at the time either. He broke his leg badly in two places. He walks with a limp and still needs a stick to get around. He's lucky to not be in a wheelchair apparently.'

She had a feeling he was lucky Jasper hadn't managed to get his hands on him good and proper.

'He accused me of assault. I was charged and a trial date was set.'

All Aunt Katherine had told her earlier came back now. She spun in his arms. 'But it didn't go to court.'

He stepped away and she immediately missed his warmth. His laugh held a bitter edge. 'He knew his charges would never stick. His fall down the stairs was an accident of his own making, not mine.'

So he'd dropped them, but... 'Why didn't Emily break free of him when she had the chance?'

This time his laugh held even more bitterness. 'Believe me, I wish I knew. I tried to get her to leave him.'

Her heart pounded so hard her chest hurt. 'But?'

'She told me she still loved him. She said he'd only forgotten himself that once, had only hit her that one time, and that it had been her fault for goading him into it.'

Imogen covered her face with her hands.

'She told me her relationship with Aaron was none of my business, that she hated me for what I'd done.'

She pulled her hands away to stare at him in disbelief. She felt suddenly and utterly exhausted. He must feel at least a hundred times worse.

'She said she'd never forgive me for hurting Aaron, and that she never wanted to see me again.'

And he'd not heard from her until last week? 'Your parents?'

'They took Aaron's side. My father and Aaron were always as thick as thieves, and my father had been looking for an excuse to sever all ties with me for years. He seized this one when it came along, lost no time in telling the tabloids my temper had always been a problem.'

'What an absolute pig of a man!'

'He forbade my mother from having any contact with me.'

It wasn't her place, she knew that, but she was angry with his mother too—*livid*. She pressed her lips together as hard as she could for a moment before releasing them. 'Do you miss them?'

'I don't miss my father.' He glanced at her with shadowed eyes. 'I have no love left in me for him. He destroyed that a long time ago. But my mother and sister...'

He missed them. She could see it. He'd banished himself to this island in despair because he hadn't been able to save them.

'I call my mother twice a year. I ask her the same questions. Can I come and get you? Is there anything I can do to help you get away from him?'

He was keeping the lines of communication open. Letting her know she had an escape route if she needed it. Imogen wanted to hug him.

'She refuses every single time. She tells me she likes her life.' He was quiet for a moment. 'I made her memorise my phone number in case she ever needs to call.' He shook his head. 'Emily still refuses to speak to me.'

For the last two years he'd been on his own, with no one to talk to about any of this. It had to have been festering away inside him like poison. She wanted to cry for him. 'Jasper, I'm so sorry.'

He nodded. With what looked like a concerted effort, he pushed his shoulders back and smiled. The sadness in his eyes, though, pierced her soul. 'So you can see why I think it best that I remain on my own.'

She didn't bother fighting her frown. 'Actually, I'm afraid I don't.'

His jaw went slack. 'Imogen—' he leaned towards her '—my family is complicated...ugly.'

'So what? It's not who you are. If a woman cared about you, she wouldn't give two hoots about your complicated family. She'd care about you—that's what would matter. I'm sorry, Jasper, but I don't get that reasoning at all.'

Jasper pinched the bridge of his nose, tried to ignore the way his heart leapt at her words. 'I missed out one important thread in my story.'

He called it a story because he desperately wanted to put some distance between it and him. But it didn't seem to be working.

Imogen pressed her hands to her abdomen as if she were fighting nausea. 'There's more?'

'I had a fiancée.' He forced himself to straighten. 'It wasn't public knowledge—we hadn't announced it yet. Bronwyn was, and still is, a cellist with the Sydney Symphony Orchestra. My father threatened her career—told her he'd have her dismissed from the orchestra—if she didn't break things off with me.'

Bronwyn's betrayal was still a raw ugly wound, though he'd never blamed her for her decision to walk away from him—not in the least. His father had threatened her career, her livelihood…her dream. 'He told her he'd see to it that she'd never play again.'

'So…she broke up with you?'

'I don't hold her responsible for that.'

Her eyes filled and his throat thickened. 'I can see that. Though, I'm not sure I'd have been so forgiving in your place.'

Imogen thought she'd act differently, but she didn't know Keith Coleman. She didn't understand how dangerous he could be. And Jasper had no intention of her ever finding out.

'*That's* why I need to be on my own, Imogen. *That's* why I can't have any ties. My father will go after the woman I love and do whatever he can to destroy her.'

'So you're not even prepared to risk it? Even if this hypothetical woman you love—and who loves you—not only has her own resources to rely on, but yours as well?' She leaned towards him. 'You're a wealthy man. That gives you a measure of power and protection.'

'It's not worth the risk. We're not just talking about someone's livelihood here, but their dreams—things they've been working towards their entire lives.' He could never ask a woman to give that up for him. 'My father has political power. His connections include key industry and business figures. He wields his influence with about as much care—and as much gusto—as George does his toy train. I will never put a woman in a position where she could be hurt by him.'

'Then your father has won. You're letting him win.'

Her words had a resonance that sounded through him.

Maybe she was right, but at least he could prevent his father from hurting another woman.

'No woman needs that hassle in her life. It's not a war she should be forced to fight. It wouldn't be fair. I refuse to be the catalyst for that kind of damage. It wouldn't be fair,' he repeated, before drawing himself up. 'Have you heard the mantra "do no harm"?'

She stared out at the water for three beats and then turned back with a nod.

He slapped a hand to his chest and met her gaze. She pulled in a breath as if she understood everything he was trying to say. For some reason that only made his heart burn harder.

'Life isn't fair, Jasper. No matter what you do, life isn't fair. It's not fair that you have such a father. It's not fair that a jerk of an ex-boyfriend of mine calls me stupid. It's not fair that my mother—'

He jerked to attention. 'Your mother?'

She shrugged. 'It wasn't fair that she and my aunt had to watch my grandmother die from breast cancer.'

Some sixth sense told him it wasn't what she'd originally meant to say. She turned on him, though, before he could challenge her. 'The thing is, whatever you do—you're not going to be able to protect everyone from everything. And you don't know what unforeseen consequences your attempts to keep everyone safe—your attempts to *do no harm*—could have either.'

'What are you talking about?' The decision he'd made was the right one, damn it.

'The day after you'd broken up with her, Bronwyn could've just as easily tripped and fractured a wrist. Hey presto, she can no longer play in the orchestra. That stuff happens all the time. But if you'd still been together and you'd been walking beside her, you might've caught her. And hey presto, no broken wrist.'

He rolled his eyes. 'You're being ridiculous. You're creating imaginary scenarios that may or may not happen and—'

'So are you!'

His head rocked back. He felt as if she'd slapped him.

'You're saying *if* you let a woman close, and *if* your father finds out about it then he *might* threaten her in some way. And *if* that happens, you're saying she's going to walk away from you…and *if* she doesn't then she's going to get hurt because you and her don't have the power to fight your father.'

His teeth ground together.

'That's a lot of *ifs* and *mights*, Jasper.'

He counted to ten. 'You haven't lived the life I've lived. And you don't know my father the way I do. This is no longer up for discussion.'

'But—'

'Look, I know that kiss was spectacular. But spectacular kisses don't necessarily lead to spectacular relationships.'

She drew herself up to her full height, which meant she reached the top of his nose. 'This isn't about me.'

'Are you sure?' He knew it wasn't, but he asked the question to deliberately anger her, to distance and alienate her. It'd be much better that she think him a jerk than for his father to—

His hands clenched. He would *not* let his father hurt her. He would not allow that man to dim this woman's fire or to crush her dreams.

Her soft laugh jerked him back. 'You're being a deliberate jackass now.'

His jaw clenched before he forced it to relax again. 'We really need you to work on that subservience thing.'

'You're being a deliberate jackass, *sir*.'

He had to cover his mouth to hide a smile.

She turned and started back along the beach in the direction of the house. He fell into step beside her, doing his best to not breathe in the notes of vanilla and citrus that seemed to be a part of her. Water foamed up suddenly around her ankles, making her smile. It was such a simple pleasure, and in that instant he felt bad for being, as she'd put it, a jackass.

'That kiss, Imogen...'

Was it his imagination or did she stiffen? 'Hmm...?'

'You're right, you know? It's not the kind of kiss one forgets.'

'Burned on my brain,' she agreed.

He envied her that cheerful candour. 'And when I'm old and grey and I remember it, it's going to make me smile. Every single time.'

'Me too.'

She sent him a smile full of warmth, but a new distance lurked at its edges, a distance he'd created, and his heart protested. A defiant part of him wanted to smash the barriers he'd forced her to put into place. But to what end? So he could hurt her more?

He clenched his hands. Sometimes spectacular kisses did lead to spectacular relationships, but mostly they didn't. He and Imogen didn't have a relationship—not in that sense—and they weren't going to. A man who couldn't find a way to protect his own mother and sister didn't deserve love and romance. His chest burned. He wasn't worthy of a woman like Imogen.

He pulled in a breath and steeled himself. He couldn't kiss Imogen again. He *had* to resist.

CHAPTER EIGHT

IMOGEN HAD HEARD about raging emotions—had read about them in books, and had even experienced them a time or two, but not like this. She felt as if she were being battered by cyclonic winds and stinging rain. A part of her wanted to seek shelter, to lick wounds that had started to throb with a nagging persistence that made her temples ache.

Another part of her wanted to seize Jasper and kiss him again, to drag him into the maelstrom with her. If he kissed her back it would make all those aches go away. She knew that on a primal level.

But if he didn't kiss her back…

She pulled in a breath and swallowed. If he didn't kiss her back it'd make everything hurt twice as much. And she couldn't kiss him again. Not after he'd told her he didn't want her to.

When they reached the edge of his garden, she halted and closed her eyes. 'That birdcall is lovely,' she said on the pretence of listening to something rather than calling attention to the effort she was making to calm the storm raging inside her.

She needed to compose herself before she spoke to her aunt.

She could feel Jasper's eyes on her, assessing her, so she did what she could to smooth out her face. 'Do you know what it is?'

She opened her eyes to find him shaking his head. She resisted the urge to point out that he demonstrated a remarkable lack of interest in his idyllic island retreat—the place he now apparently called home. She'd bet a therapist would have something insightful to say about that.

She pressed her lips together to stop herself from playing therapist.

He opened the front door and ushered her ahead of him. She refused to notice the warm spicy scent of him—or his beguiling heat—as she slipped past.

Don't think about Jasper. Focus on Aunt Katherine.

Katherine and George were in the living room, and, with the windows dark now from the night, the room reminded Imogen even more of a ship. George, looking sleepy on his blanket on the floor, cuddled his toy rabbit with its super-long ears. Katherine, looking worried, leapt up from the sofa the moment they entered.

'Imogen, honey, I'm sorry about earlier,' she started at the same time Imogen spoke.

'You've written a book!'

And then they both laughed and hugged.

'I shouldn't have said what I did,' Katherine said, pulling Imogen down to the sofa beside her.

George saw his uncle and let go of his soft toy to kick his legs and lift his arms to be picked up. With a smile that caught at her stupid, susceptible heart, Jasper lifted him and cradled him against his shoulder. She now knew how strong those arms were, how broad and solid those shoulders.

'I should've known Gloria hadn't told you about our tiff.'

Imogen hauled herself back, studiously averting her gaze from man and baby.

'My only excuse is that I've not been sleeping well and…'

Imogen reached for her aunt's hand. 'Jasper tells me you're having trouble with your latest book.'

'It's a hot mess, but I think I'm finally starting to make progress.'

Katherine's smile didn't quite reach her eyes, so Imogen didn't believe her, and while she didn't want to add to her aunt's stress, she didn't want to keep secrets from her any longer either. 'I didn't know about your falling-out with Mum, Auntie Kay, but there is something you probably should know.'

Katherine stared at her—and so did Jasper as he lowered himself into the armchair opposite. She could feel his attention like a laser beam and she really, *really* wished she could just not be aware of it…not be aware of *him*.

Katherine seized Imogen's shoulders, her face losing all colour. 'Immy, please tell me she doesn't have breast cancer.'

It hit her then how much her grandmother's death had affected the two sisters. 'I promise you, she doesn't have breast cancer.'

Katherine sagged. 'You frightened me out of my wits.'

'I'm sorry, I didn't mean to. There is an issue, but it's not as serious as cancer. Back in November Mum found out she has macular degeneration.'

Katherine stared at her. 'She's going blind?'

Imogen's eyes filled and she nodded. 'She has time yet. They can delay it by giving her injections into her eyes, but eventually…'

'Why didn't she tell me?'

'She was going to tell you in person at Christmas.'

'But I didn't come home.' Katherine tapped a finger against her mouth. 'So that's why she's been so passive-aggressive recently and telling me that my being so far away isn't fair to your grandfather.'

'You know what she's like. She's focussing all of her worry on who's going to look after Granddad if she's blind.'

Katherine stiffened, and then without warning burst

into tears. Imogen wrapped an arm about her shoulders, her throat thickening. 'She's going to be fine, Auntie Kay, I promise you. Like I said, there's time. It could be years before her eyesight becomes truly bad. There's time for everyone to adjust, to put strategies into place. And there's no need for you to come home—not for good. Dad and I can look after Granddad—'

'Darling girl, that's not your job.' Katherine lifted her head and wiped her eyes. 'The thing is…'

Katherine's expression had ice fist-bumping down Imogen's spine. Jasper leaned towards them. 'What is the thing?' she croaked.

'Just before Christmas, I found a lump in my breast.'

Imogen's hand flew to her mouth. Her heart pounded so hard it was nearly impossible to breathe. 'You spent the holidays getting tests?'

Oh, please, don't let Auntie Kay have cancer, please—

Katherine's gaze dropped. 'No.'

No? But… Grandma had *died* of breast cancer. Katherine had seen the effects, had—

'I went to a little village on the mainland and worked on my book. And waited for the lump to go away.'

Her mouth went dry. 'Auntie Kay…'

Jasper shot to his feet, his face set, though his eyes blazed. He still held the baby against his shoulder as if it were the most precious thing in the world—cradling him there as if he wanted to protect him from all hurt.

Katherine glanced from one to the other. 'I meant to.' Her bottom lip trembled. 'But I was afraid. I didn't realise that's the way I'd react. I couldn't face the thought of…' She covered her face briefly. 'But if I do have breast cancer and if I die and if Gloria goes blind then…who will look after your grandfather? Your uncles won't know what to do. And I—'

'Kate.' The quiet authority in Jasper's voice had them

both turning to him. 'That's an awful lot of ifs on very little evidence.'

Had he meant to repeat the words she'd said to him earlier?

His brows drew down over his eyes. 'Why didn't you tell me?'

'We don't talk about personal matters, Jasper.'

'But this is your health!'

'I was hoping it'd go away. I know that probably sounds stupid to you both, but—'

'No,' Imogen said. 'I get it. But, Auntie Kay, we have to get you examined.'

Katherine hesitated and then nodded. 'I'll make an appointment tomorrow.'

Jasper widened his stance. He looked suddenly immovable. 'We can do better than that. I'll organise a seaplane for first thing in the morning, and I'll have you seen by a team of Brazil's best medical professionals ASAP.'

Katherine thrust out her jaw. 'Don't come over all highhanded with me, Jasper. You can't force me into anything I don't want and—'

'Kate, I would never force you into anything against your will. *Never.*'

Jasper wasn't his father. She could see now how he'd modelled himself to become the exact opposite—the protector rather than the abuser. She wanted to leap up and hug him—for his kindness to Katherine, but also for all the constant restrictions he placed on himself, for the sacrifices he made without asking for anything in return. A man like Jasper deserved to be surrounded by family and love.

The fight drained out of her aunt. 'I know. I'm sorry. It's just that things are going to start moving so quickly now and it feels as if everything will start spinning out of my control.'

Imogen seized her hand. 'As soon as we have answers,

it'll stop the spinning.' She tightened her grip. 'You know that in the majority of cases lumps are benign.'

'But what if it's not? With my history...'

Fear clutched at Imogen's heart.

'We take it one step at a time,' Jasper interspersed calmly. 'If it isn't benign, then we'll make a plan. You'll take a deep breath and consider all your options. We'll find a way forward, Kate. You're healthy and still young. I promise, you won't be on your own.'

Katherine pulled in a deep breath and nodded. Imogen could see her mentally steel herself to face whatever the future had in store. Jasper fumbled with his phone and Imogen leapt to take the baby.

'He was fussing earlier,' Katherine murmured, 'so I brought him downstairs. But he seems to have settled again now.'

'I'll go put him down.'

It took her next to no time to put the sleepy baby to bed. She started back towards the living room but halted in the shadows at the top of the stairs when her aunt said, 'Jasper, I can't afford the kind of treatment you're talking about.'

Jasper's head lifted from where he furiously texted on his phone. 'Healthcare benefits were part of your employment package.'

Katherine snorted, and Imogen didn't blame her. The man was a *terrible* liar.

He dragged a hand down his face. 'Okay, I have a lot of money. It's just sitting there doing nothing. Please let me do this for you. Let me do something good with it.'

The room blurred, and Imogen's throat thickened.

'You've been a rock—one of the few stable elements in my life. You mean a lot to me. You're like...family.' He gave a half laugh. 'The family I wished I had. Not the messed-up excuse that I got. Please let me do this one thing for you.'

'You can't refuse that, Auntie Kay.' The words burst from Imogen as she flew down the stairs. *Accept his offer*, she wanted to yell. It had been made with a good and pure intent.

'Immy's right. I can't refuse you when you put it like that. Thank you, Jasper. I'm grateful…and touched.'

Katherine rose and gave him a hug. Her eyes were wet when she released him several moments later and his were suspiciously bright at well.

'So you'll be ready to leave at six in the morning?'

Katherine nodded.

Imogen eased forward. 'Can I help with anything?' She'd sit up all night and hold her aunt's hand if it'd help.

'Thank you, Immy, but no. I'm going to pack a few things and then do some breathing exercises. A bit of quiet now is what I need.'

She watched her aunt leave the room before swinging to Jasper. 'Thank you. A million times, thank you.'

'It's nothing.'

'It's everything! To know we'll have an answer one way or another soon…' Didn't he know what a big thing that was? 'Knowing will help. I know she's been hiding from it, and I know she's afraid.' Imogen was terrified so it must be a thousand times worse for her aunt. 'But getting an answer—knowing—is good. And you're making sure that happens as soon as possible.'

'It's the least I can do.'

It was more than most would've done. She didn't say as much, though. It was taking all her strength and concentration not to get caught up in the clear grey of his eyes and the beguiling breadth of his shoulders.

'You'll be okay here on your own for a couple of days with George while Katherine and I go to the mainland?'

She wished she could go too but she swallowed and nodded. 'Of course. Eduardo's here if I need help with anything.' She lifted her chin. She wasn't adding to the expense or the hassle of the trip. She could talk to her aunt every day on the phone.

Those eyes didn't leave her face. 'You want to be with your aunt.'

It was a statement, not a question. 'I wouldn't be human if I didn't want that. But it's neither here nor there. You're…'

She trailed off when he punched a number into his phone and lifted it to his ear. 'Antonio, is there room for another two passengers—one adult and one baby?'

Imogen's heart thumped.

'Excellent. Thank you.'

'It's really not necessary,' she whispered.

'Your aunt will be happier if you're with her. And it's your aunt we need to think about.'

'I swear to God you just became my new favourite person, Jasper.'

Just for a moment his eyes crinkled. And she wanted to hug him so badly things inside her hurt. As if he read that thought on her face, he took a step back. 'Pack light. One small bag. Plan for a two-night stay. If we need anything else, we can buy it on the mainland. I'd better finish making the arrangements and pack for me and George.'

She watched him leave. 'Goodnight, Jasper,' she murmured once he'd disappeared from view.

Her new favourite person? She swallowed. She hadn't been joking.

She was in trouble. Big trouble.

Jasper had made arrangements for the seaplane to take them to the port of Santos—an hour away—and from there a limousine took them to São Paulo. He'd ordered Evan to find him the best darn medical facility in the city. His assistant had gone above and beyond. Not only had he shortlisted five hospitals with excellent reputations, but he'd also managed to book Katherine into one of them for a biopsy that very morning. He didn't know what strings Evan had pulled or how much money it was going to cost, but he didn't care. Kate deserved the absolute best.

He sank into a chair in the hallway outside her door, dropping his head to his hands. Why hadn't he taken better care of Kate? Why hadn't he insisted on taking her and Eduardo to the mainland once a year for medicals?

He'd become unforgivably self-absorbed since arriving on Tesoura. He'd lost a part of himself when Bronwyn, Emily and his mother had turned their backs on him. He'd shut himself off emotionally, fooled himself into thinking that large donations to women's refuges could replace emotion and caring. But he'd been wrong.

The door to Kate's room opened and he straightened. He didn't want either woman to see how worried he was. He needed to be strong for them. Imogen's ashen face as she walked out squeezed his chest tight. He drew her down to the seat beside him. George continued to sleep in blissful ignorance in the nearby stroller. 'Your aunt is in excellent hands.'

'I know. And I'm so grateful to you, Jasper.' She sent him a brave little smile that twisted his insides. 'They're about to take her down for the biopsy, but she wants a word with you before she goes.'

With a nod, he shot to his feet and strode into Kate's room. 'How are you feeling? Is there anything I can get for you?'

'Now that I'm here, I'm feeling remarkably calm.'

He sat on the edge of her bed. 'Is there anything you'd like me to do?'

'Actually, there is.'

He leaned towards her, all attention. 'Name it.'

'I'm going to be busy with tests all day, Jasper. I don't want Imogen fretting any more than she already is. Besides, a hospital waiting room is no place for a baby. I want you to take her out to see the sights—get her mind off things for a while. I don't want to see either one of you until visiting hours this evening.'

'But—'

She raised an eyebrow and he swallowed back his protests. 'I've a novel I wouldn't mind finishing. I have a pen and notepad because a new story idea has come calling, which is far from convenient considering I haven't finished my current one yet but playing around with that will keep me busy. And I have a playlist full of my favourite songs. I've everything I need to keep me calm and occupied.'

He read the subtext. Him and Imogen fussing and hovering would add to her stress—their anxiety would feed hers. He flashed to Imogen's pale face and nodded. Sitting here worrying wouldn't do her any good either. He fished out his phone and brought up a list of current 'things to do' in São Paulo and scanned the offerings. His lips lifted, and he met Kate's gaze. 'Done. Now is there anything I can get or do for you before I whisk Imogen away for the day?'

'I have everything I need, thank you. You've gone above and beyond.'

He rose, hesitated and then leaned across to press a kiss to her cheek. 'We're just a phone call away. If you need us…'

She nodded, blinking hard, and then she rolled her eyes as two orderlies came into the room pushing a wheelchair. 'Honestly, is that necessary? You are aware that I haven't lost the use of my legs?'

Jasper hid a smile. She pointed a finger at him. 'Now, I'm looking forward to being regaled with your adventures later this evening, so don't let me down.'

He saluted and left the room. Imogen glanced up and he forced a cheerfulness he was far from feeling. 'Come on.' He took the stroller and started to wheel it down the hall. 'We've been banished.'

She rose automatically but she didn't move. 'By who?'

He linked an arm though hers and urged her forward. 'Who do you think?'

'Oh, but—'

'Imogen, Kate is going to be busy with tests all day. It's not like we're going to get a chance to see her between those tests or to sit with her.'

'I know. I just… I want to be close in case she needs us.'

'She has both our numbers on speed dial.' He forced himself to release her. Touching her made him…actually it unmade him. 'Do you know what she's looking forward to?'

'What?'

'Us regaling her with our adventures for the day.'

'But—'

'Wondering what we're getting up to is one of the things that will help her get through today.'

She worried at her lip.

'And you know how she hates fuss of any kind.'

She worried harder and he wanted to wrap her in his arms and tell her everything would be all right. Only he didn't know if it would be. Panic tried to let loose inside him, but he reined it in. 'And this isn't a place for a baby.'

She glanced at George and her shoulders slumped. 'Okay, but if you think some cathedral or museum is going to take my mind off what's happening here you have rocks in your head.'

'That sounds like a challenge.' He pushed the stroller into motion again, and her eyes widened at what he expected was the smug expression on his face. 'I'll bet you lunch at an authentic Brazilian eatery that it does.'

Her jaw dropped. 'You're on,' she said with a glare.

Twenty minutes later a taxi set them down at their destination—the museum of contemporary art. Imogen watched the taxi depart. 'Your Portuguese is very good. When did you learn?'

'When I first arrived on Tesoura. It seemed the polite thing to do.'

He'd banished himself to an island and had learned a language he hardly ever used because he never went anywhere, and he never saw anyone. What kind of sense did that make?

He shook the thought away as she glanced at the building in front of him. 'So this is a…museum.'

'Not just any museum. Here, you take the top and I'll take the bottom.' He gestured to the stroller and together they manoeuvred it up the stairs.

'What's so special about—?'

She broke off when she saw the sign advertising the current exhibition, and he grinned at her expression. 'You mean besides the fact that there's currently a costume exhibition showing here?'

The woman was a dressmaker, a seamstress—she'd worked in Paris and was opening her own sewing school in a couple of months. He figured the one thing in this entire amazing city that had the potential to charm her, to fire her enthusiasm and imagination, was a historic collection of amazing clothes.

She slammed her hands on her hips, and he could see her try to work up some righteous outrage. 'You exploited my weakness for a free lunch?'

'Hey, whatever works.'

She glanced at the sign again. 'Well, it looks as if lunch is definitely on me.' She threaded her arm through his and he had to grit his teeth against the rush of warmth that sped through him. 'C'mon, I can't wait to see this. When Aunt Katherine hears about it, you're going to get the biggest gold star.'

The next two hours flew by. The clothes on display were utterly amazing—everything from indigenous ceremonial robes, intricate Renaissance ball gowns, to costumes used in popular soap operas. There were hats and shoes, under-clothes and tools of the trade that meant very little to him. It wasn't the items on display that held his attention, but Imogen's rapt delight. Her explanations of the techniques used and her appreciation for the fine craftsmanship had him transfixed.

'Your sewing school is going to be amazing.'

She stilled but didn't look at him. 'What makes you say that?'

'You have a real passion for all of this. And passion is the thing that makes the difference. People are drawn to it. It gives you the energy and drive to succeed. It means that when you hit a road bump, you'll find a way around it.' He could almost sense the doubts piling up inside her. 'And you shouldn't let that stupid ex-boyfriend of yours convince you otherwise.'

She swung to him, her mouth dropping, but then she turned back to the displays and he let the matter drop. Her passion challenged him in ways he hadn't expected. He'd been passionate once—passionate about building his company into a globally recognised brand; passionate about doing all he could to help his mother and sister; passionate about neutralising his father and the harm he did.

He'd let his passion die. And in the process, he'd become a robot. His chest cramped. His passion for life and justice might've died, but it didn't mean he had to become a miserable excuse for a human being.

He shook the thought off and picked up George's tossed bunny for the fifth time. George squealed in joy when Jasper handed it to him...again.

He was convinced Imogen would've happily spent the entire day perusing the collection, but George's eventual protests warned them he'd had enough of being cooped up in his stroller.

She turned with a smile. 'Lunch?'

'I know the perfect place.'

Her lips twitched. 'I just bet you do.'

He took her to Ibirapuera Park. At 158 hectares, it was one of the largest urban parks in Latin America. They bought *pastel de queijos*—delicious deep-fried snacks stuffed with savoury fillings—and meat patties formed around wooden skewers called *kibe*, and sat on the grass to eat them. They spread out a small blanket for George, and he belly-crawled between the two of them, munching on a rusk and cooing his delight at being freed from his pram.

Buskers started up nearby and Imogen leaned towards them as she listened. 'My father would love this so hard.'

Her sound-recording father? He straightened from where he'd been leaning back on his elbows. He'd been trying to think of a way to keep her occupied for the afternoon, and he might've just found it. 'Would you keep an eye on George for ten minutes while I slip off?'

'Sure.'

It took him fifteen minutes, but it was worth it when he lowered his bag of purchases to her lap. She pulled out the mini cassette recorder and the stack of tiny tapes he'd bought, and she turned to him with a question in her eyes. 'I thought you might like to record these guys for your dad…and maybe send your parents a kind of São Paulo diary. I mean, I know you can do that stuff on your phone, but reception is pretty dodgy at Tesoura, and if you wanted to continue the diary there… Anyway, I thought your father might enjoy the older technology.'

'Oh, Jasper, that's a brilliant idea!' She leaned across to George, who sat between them, and tickled his tummy. 'Your uncle has the best ideas, George.' She glanced up, her eyes shining. 'Thank you, it was the perfect thing to do.'

He didn't know how she did it, but she made him feel like a superhero.

She slipped a tape into the recorder and immediately

gave the date and location, introducing both George and Jasper and making them say hello into the machine. George's hello was inaudible as he tried to eat the recorder. She rescued it with a laugh and then rested back on one hand and gave her impressions of the city. She recorded the nearby buskers—but not until she'd bought their CD and asked their permission. When they found out she was from Australia they played a Brazilian version of 'Waltzing Matilda' that absolutely delighted her.

Her fun and excitement infected both him and George. Though eventually George snuggled down on his blanket with his bottle, his eyes growing heavy as the afternoon began to lengthen. Imogen collapsed to her knees beside Jasper, gesturing to the buskers. 'They're amazing. My father will love them. This day has been amazing, Jasper. It shouldn't have been but...*you're* amazing.'

And then she leaned forward and pressed her lips to his in a brief, exuberant kiss that had every pulse in his body thumping.

She eased away, still smiling, but it faded as she stared into his eyes. Her lips parted and a yearning he couldn't refuse stretched across her face. In that moment he was lost. Curving a hand around her nape, he drew her head back down to his again and he kissed her with a hunger he didn't bother trying to conceal. Somehow, she ended up in his lap, curled there as if she belonged, her fingers threading through his short hair, her tongue tangling with his and driving him mad with need.

He only came to when a group of passing youths catcalled. *Damn.* What on earth was he thinking? They were supposed to be looking after a baby, not necking like a couple of teenagers!

He set her away from him with more speed than grace. 'I'm sorry. I promised that wouldn't happen again.'

She paled at whatever she saw in his face. He pulled in a deep breath, tried to moderate his voice. 'Are you okay?'

'I'm fine.' She lifted her chin. '*I'm* not the one who's sorry that happened.' The green in her eyes flashed. 'I *like* kissing you, Jasper. I... I like you.'

He saw then how invested she was becoming—in him... in them. But there was no them. And if he let her continue thinking that, he'd hurt her. Badly. With a force of will, he hardened his heart. 'I like kissing you too, but it won't happen again. Emotions are running high today.'

Her gaze narrowed. 'It's more than that and you know it.'

'And I don't need the complication in my life,' he continued as if she hadn't interrupted. He hated the swift shaft of pain that darkened her eyes. 'Your aunt would never forgive me if I scratched that particular itch with you, especially if I let you think it meant more than it did.'

He waited for her to call him a jackass, but she didn't. She merely turned her back on him and her attention back to the park.

Damn! His life was on a Brazilian island. Hers was in Australia. Their lives were going in totally opposite directions. Perhaps that in and of itself wasn't such an insurmountable obstacle if it weren't for other things. But there *were* other things—his father, his own reluctance to trust again, his lack of faith and hope. Just...*no*! He wasn't prepared to go through any of that again.

He couldn't give her the kind of long-term relationship she wanted and deserved, so he had no business kissing her. What she deserved was a wholesome, undamaged man who wasn't carrying a ton of baggage and didn't have a family like his waiting to close its jaws about her. She deserved a man who could commit to forever. A man who could protect her rather than one who would bring trouble to her door.

And that man wasn't him.

CHAPTER NINE

IMOGEN STARED AT the doctor the following morning. 'The lump is benign?' she repeated.

'We're ninety per cent certain it's benign,' the doctor clarified. 'We only have the preliminary results—it'll be another five days before the full report is available—but the signs are good.' The doctor smiled. 'But, *sim*, I am confident all is well.'

Jasper leaned towards the statuesque white-coated woman. 'So you don't think Katherine has cancer?'

'That is correct.'

With a whoop, Imogen hugged her aunt, though she was careful not to hug her too tight in case Katherine was still sore from her biopsy. 'Best news ever!'

She turned back to find that Jasper had seized George from his stroller and was holding him aloft like some kind of victory trophy. George loved every moment of it, squealing and kicking his legs.

Katherine seized the doctor's hand and pumped it up and down. 'Thank you so much, Doctor. I can't thank you enough.'

'It will be thanks enough, *minha amiga*, if you keep up to date with your mammograms and promise to make an appointment with your doctor if anything ever again gives you cause for concern.'

'I've learned my lesson. So… I can go now?'

The doctor consulted Katherine's chart. 'I'm afraid not. Mr Coleman has booked you in for a complete medical check. But you should be done by four o'clock this afternoon.'

Katherine turned to Jasper as soon as the doctor left and raised an eyebrow. Imogen did her best not to think about how she and Jasper would survive another day in each other's company.

Not after he'd kissed her. And then acted like a jerk. When prior to that he'd been...

She swallowed. When he'd been every dream she hadn't known she'd wanted. He'd been kind and fun, warm and witty, he'd made her laugh when she hadn't thought that possible. He'd given both her mind and her hands something to do, and while that hadn't rid her of worry for Katherine, it had made it bearable.

Until he'd kissed her, that was. She'd forgotten everything then—Katherine, George, herself. The kiss had been perfect.

Until it wasn't.

'Imogen, help me out here.'

She snapped back to find an exasperated Katherine staring at her. She'd missed the beginning of the conversation, but she could guess it. 'What's the harm in getting the tests done, Auntie Kay? Mum's wishing she'd gone for an eye test earlier.' She glanced at her watch. 'It's only another six or so hours. I'm happy to hang here and keep you company.'

She didn't want to spend another moment with Jasper, thank you very much. Their stilted conversation and taut silences were wearing on her nerves. After yesterday's kiss he'd retreated with so much unholy speed it'd left her feeling tainted and ugly. And stupid.

It shouldn't matter so much. It shouldn't *hurt* so much. But it did.

Katherine blew out an exasperated breath. 'Fine, I'll

have the tests, but I don't want either one of you hanging around the hospital. Go out and see the sights. Have fun.'

Ha! Fun and Jasper no longer went together in the same sentence.

Jasper cleared his throat. 'I actually have some work I need to do.'

He didn't look at her as he spoke.

'Work when you get home,' Katherine protested. 'You and Imogen should go enjoy yourselves.'

'That's okay, Jasper doesn't need to act as my tour guide,' Imogen inserted in her most cheerful voice—so bright it bounced off the walls like a shiny new ten-cent piece. 'What I'd really like to do today is hit the shops. I want to buy souvenirs for everyone back home. I was reading about a market that's under one of the art galleries and it sounds fab—I'm hoping to pick up some pretty, locally made jewellery, maybe find a fabric store or two. I doubt it'd be Jasper's thing.'

'I'd be happy to accompany you.'

But he said it with such a lack of enthusiasm it made even Katherine roll her eyes. Imogen did her best to stop her insides from shrivelling. 'Not necessary. And I'm happy to take George so you can concentrate on your work.' George would be a welcome distraction.

'I can manage.' He set George back in his stroller.

She folded her arms. 'You know he hates being cooped up inside all day.'

His eyes flashed. 'So I'll take him to the park.'

Ha! So he wasn't as cool and reserved as he'd like her to think.

Katherine glanced from one to the other, and Imogen immediately curbed her impulse to get another rise out of him. It was childish. And it'd only make her feel better in the short-term. It'd be best to do what he was doing—put him out of her mind completely. 'Are you sure you wouldn't prefer a bit of company, Auntie Kay?'

'Absolutely not.'

'Then is there anything you'd like me to get for you while I'm out?'

Her aunt made a list, and Imogen didn't know why Jasper hung around if they were going their separate ways for the day. 'You didn't have to wait,' she said as they walked to the elevator.

'I wanted a word with you before you took off.'

But when several people joined them in the elevator he didn't speak again until they stood alone in the wide hospital foyer. The waiting made things inside her clench up. 'It's great news about Katherine's results,' she finally prompted when he'd remained silent for too long.

He turned to her as if he'd forgotten she was there. Which was great for a girl's ego. She pressed her lips together hard and didn't say a word.

'Look, Imogen, about what happened in the park yesterday—'

'Are you just going to apologise again?' she cut in. 'And remind me you're not interested in a relationship again, blahdy-blah?'

His eyebrows rose. 'Blahdy-blah?'

She lifted an eyebrow of her own, and eventually he nodded. 'Pretty much.'

She gave an exaggerated roll of her eyes designed to annoy him. 'Then *puhlease* spare me and take it as read, okay?' She had the satisfaction of seeing his jaw clench, but it didn't help, not in the slightest. Just as she'd known it wouldn't. 'Was there anything else?'

'Yes,' he snapped, drawing himself up to his full height and becoming a stranger—an autocrat—and it reminded her fiercely that he was her billionaire boss and she was nothing but his lowly maid. 'Can you cook?'

That made her blink. 'I'm no chef, but I can cook a meal without burning it.'

'I want to give Katherine a week's holiday. I'd like to reassign your duties to meal preparation. You've taught me enough now about how to look after a baby that I'm confident I can take care of George without assistance. Needless to say, I'm grateful for all the help you've given me where he's concerned.'

But her help was no longer required. She heard that message loud and clear. This was Jasper Coleman reasserting his authority. She wanted to tell him he was being a pompous jackass. But he wasn't. He was drawing strict and rigid boundaries between them, leaving her in no doubt that he'd meant all he'd said about relationships and complications.

And the sooner her heart got that message, the better. She folded her face into polite lines. 'That won't be a problem. I'd be delighted to assist, sir.'

He blanched at her *sir*. She refused to let herself feel anything. She simply waited for him to either give her further instructions or to dismiss her. Actually, this subservience thing wasn't too hard once she put her mind to it.

'Have a pleasant day, Imogen.'

'Thank you, sir.' She bent down to tickle George's tummy and then turned and walked away before she cried.

After her third day of being Tesoura's head chef, Imogen told herself that she'd finally found her equilibrium. She and Jasper hadn't been able to maintain such an intense formality with each other, not with Katherine playing spectator. But as they hardly spent any time in each other's company, maintaining a polite facade proved no great hardship.

As long as she didn't look at him. As long as she didn't remember the way he'd kissed her in the park. As long as she recited, *You're just the maid* over and over in her mind.

What was proving harder to ignore at the moment was a baby's insistent crying. She turned her clock to face her—2:38 a.m. It appeared Mr I'm-Confident-I-Can-Look-After-George-on-My-Own-Without-Assistance wasn't doing so well in the parenting stakes at the moment.

She was tempted to roll over and pull a pillow over her head, and if it was only Jasper who'd suffer she would. But George…

With a sigh, she hauled herself out of bed, mentally checked what she was wearing—a baggy T-shirt and a pair of tracksuit bottoms, which were far from glamorous but at least covered her decently enough—before heading in the direction of George's wails.

She found Jasper pacing the living room with a distressed George, who was refusing to take his bottle.

Jasper's eyes flooded with relief when he saw her, but he said, 'I'm sorry I disturbed you. I needed to heat up a bottle and he cries even harder when I put him down.'

She ignored Jasper—it seemed wise—to focus all her attention on the baby. 'Hey, little man. What's the problem?'

He lifted his head to stare at her and held out his arms, his cries easing. She took him and cuddled him close. 'Aw, poor baby. You're hot.'

He opened his mouth and made angry noises and she cooed back soothing sounds as she ran her hand over his damp hair. 'I know, you're trying to tell me what's wrong, aren't you?'

His crying subsided into hiccups and she took the opportunity to run a finger along his gums. Poor little guy had a tooth coming through. Without glancing at Jasper—it was better not to look at him or to think about him, especially not at this time of night—she started for the nursery.

'What are you looking for?' Jasper said when she tried to search one of the bags one-handed.

'His thermometer.'

He took the bag, found the thermometer and handed it to her. She took George's temperature, crooning to him the entire time.

'Do I need to call a doctor?'

She shook her head, finally risking a glance his way. He looked deliciously dishevelled and heartbreakingly worried. 'His temperature is only up a tiny bit. How long has he been like this?'

'Nearly two and a half hours.'

No wonder he looked so frazzled. 'Why didn't you come and get me?'

'Because I didn't want to come across all feeble and pathetic. But you were my next port of call. How did you get him to stop crying?'

She grimaced. 'I'm going to try and break this as gently as I can—this is a temporary respite. George is teething.'

The nursery was too small, too intimate, too much. She moved towards the door, nodding at the bag Jasper had discarded. 'Let's go back downstairs, but bring that with you.'

She put teething gel on George's gums. But it evidently brought him little relief, as he soon started crying again.

She watched Jasper pace the floor in growing agitation, biting the inside of her lip. 'Would it help if I told you this was entirely normal?'

'A little.' But his eyes said otherwise.

Whatever else had happened between them, she couldn't deny that he loved his nephew. She flashed to the day of Katherine's scheduled biopsy—the way he'd taken her to the exhibition and had then urged her to record a message and playlist for her parents, the way he'd helped draw her mind from her worry. She needed to find a way to distract him like that.

'Can you access Jupiter's social media account from your phone?'

'Yes.'

'I think we should post something to her timeline now.'

He pulled out his phone. 'What do you want it to say?'

'Pacing the floor with a teething nine-month-old. Have tried a bottle, teething ring and teething gel so far, and lots of walking and rocking. So far nothing has helped. Any tips?'

He glanced up and she couldn't read the expression in his eyes. 'If you say one thing about bed hair,' she warned.

'There's absolutely nothing wrong with your hair, Imogen. You're hoping Emily reads this, aren't you?'

She shrugged.

'You're a genius.'

'*Not* a genius. Just not afraid to ask for help. There's a wealth of experience out there on social media. Why not tap into it?' If, at the same time, they could pique a mother's maternal concern…

His phone pinged.

'Guardian Angel 27 says "Pray".'

'Helpful.'

More pings sounded. 'Janice sends "lots of hugs".'

It was nice of her, but not exactly helpful either.

'"Iced water",' he read out.

Her lips twitched. 'That's a little ambiguous. Are we supposed to give it to him to drink or douse ourselves in it?'

His gaze didn't leave his phone. 'Um… "Hang him upside down whilst you drink a margarita."'

'Just…no.'

He scanned through the replies that were evidently pouring in, and then stilled. 'You won't believe this, but Emily has just responded.'

She leaned towards him. 'What does she say?'

'That last time her bub was teething, putting him in his stroller with his comfort toy and pushing the stroller back and forth helped.'

'I'm putting him in his stroller.' She started for the front foyer, which was where the stroller was currently parked.

'I'll grab his bunny.'

Jasper's heart pounded as the baby's cries started to abate.

Imogen nudged his foot and he realised she'd been talking to him and he hadn't been paying attention—hadn't heard a word.

'Tell her George's crying is easing and that it looks like it's working.'

He started typing on his phone.

'Georgia!' she corrected. 'Say Georgia.'

He backspaced, heart and head both racing. He nearly handed her the phone, his fingers feeling like thumbs, but...

But he was finally talking to Emily. His sister. After two years she'd finally spoken to him again, and he hadn't realised it would mean so much.

A personal message hit his inbox, and he immediately opened it. Need help.

He wanted to ring, but if Aaron was nearby... 'What can I do?' he typed back.

His phone rang. 'Emily?'

'Jasper.'

He didn't bother with preliminaries or pleasantries. 'What do you need?'

'I need to get away from Aaron. If he gets hold of me now, he'll kill me.'

He doubted she was exaggerating. 'I can get you on a plane first thing in the morning, for either Rio or São Paulo. Hold on...' He strode into his office, aware of a silent Imogen coming to stand in the doorway with the stroller to watch and listen as he made the travel arrangements on his computer. 'Have you got pen and paper there, Em?'

He gave her the flight details. He organised a bodyguard

to accompany her from Sydney to Rio. He organised a private charter from Rio to Tesoura.

'Are you safe from Aaron tonight?'

'I'm at a safe house. He's away on business but will be back tomorrow. Look, Jasper, he's involved in some kind of money-laundering racket, and I've been helping the police with their enquiries. It's about to come to a head soon…'

'Does he know that?'

'I don't know, but I don't want to be anywhere near him when he does.'

'I won't let that happen. Give me the address of where you're staying. I'm sending that bodyguard tonight.'

'I'm going to have to ditch my phone. He'll be able to track me on it.'

'I'll have a new one couriered to you.' She needed to be able to contact him in case anything happened.

'How's…how's George?'

'He's the sweetest, happiest little guy, Em. I don't know how you've managed it.'

'I've missed him so much, but Aaron has been so…unpredictable lately.'

Jasper closed his eyes.

'I needed to send George somewhere safe—away from everything that's happening here—in case things blew up earlier than expected.'

'Where does Aaron think he is?'

'With Auntie Pat. I told him I wanted to go and stay with her for a few days while he was away on business.'

He'd bet Aaron hadn't liked that. Pat was their mother's sister, and she loathed Keith. Which meant she probably loathed Aaron too.

'Tomorrow you and George will be reunited and safe, I promise.'

'I can't thank you enough, Jasper.'

'No need.'

They rang off. He turned to meet Imogen's gaze. She looked as if she meant to take a step towards him but pulled back at the last moment. 'Emily is coming?'

He nodded.

'That's…that's amazing news.'

She glanced down at the stroller, stopped pushing and lifted crossed fingers. Not a peep came from George. He'd finally fallen asleep.

With a brisk movement, she turned and headed upstairs. Jasper eased past the pram and followed her. 'What are you…?'

He trailed off when she checked the two currently vacant guest rooms. 'We'll give her this one.'

It was the room next to George's and had its own en suite bathroom. She grabbed a fresh set of sheets from the linen cupboard and started to make up the bed. He immediately kicked forward to help. 'There'll be time to do this tomorrow, you know?'

'I know, but I'm awake now.'

She shot him a grin and it made things inside him burn. He'd missed that smile. And her sense of fun. He shook himself. It didn't matter how much his heart protested. The distance he'd deliberately put between them was still for the best.

'I warn you now, though, breakfast is going to be a lacklustre affair.'

'Forget breakfast. I'll get some cereal and toast when I'm ready. Sleep as late as you like. I plan to.'

'Liar. You probably won't sleep a wink until Emily is here.'

She was probably right.

He followed her gaze as it ran about the room. 'What?'

'This is a nice room, but I'm wondering how we can make it more homey. I'll put a vase of flowers on the dresser.' She glanced in at the en suite bathroom. 'I bought some pretty toiletries while I was on the mainland. They'll do nicely in here.'

His chest hitched. 'You don't have to give your things away, Imogen.'

'I don't mind. Besides, I think your sister deserves a little pampering. And I know you'll want her to feel...'

'Safe? Unafraid?'

She nodded. 'But also at home. As if nothing bad could possibly happen to her here. That it's okay for her to let down her guard and rest.'

She put it into words better than he ever could have.

She glanced at him then with unabashed admiration. 'You thought of everything—on the fly—without a moment of panic, when she rang and asked for help. You were confident and in command of the situation—which must've been so reassuring for her. It was amazing to witness. She's lucky to have you, Jasper.'

An itch started up between his shoulder blades. Nothing could happen between him and this woman—he would not let his family destroy her the way it had him and Emily. But he owed her. And he could give her something now—a part of himself he'd never given to anyone. 'Immy, I've played that scenario—Emily ringing me like that—in my mind hundreds, maybe a thousand, times.'

Shortening her name seemed natural and right, so he didn't bother questioning it. 'Ever since I arrived on Tesoura I've wanted Emily to call and ask me to help her break free from Aaron.' He gave a low laugh. 'Which probably means I have some kind of saviour complex.'

'Nonsense.' She moved a step closer, her hands pressed to her chest. 'It means you love your sister and you want her to be safe and happy.'

He tried to not look at her chest, at the way her hands—pressed against thin cotton—highlighted curves that made him ache. He forced his gaze back to hers. 'On the outside

I might've appeared calm during that phone call, but on the inside, I was anything but.'

Her eyes softened and her lips parted. Wind roared in his ears and fire licked along his veins. He eased back a step, feeling anything but calm now. She glanced at him and then at the freshly made bed and colour mounted high on her cheeks. Everything inside him clenched. *No!* He would not take advantage of this lovely woman. 'I've been meaning to ask, when are you returning to Australia?'

She stared as if she hadn't heard him, and then her head rocked back. 'I... I hadn't set a firm date.' She swallowed. 'You evidently think I should.'

He forced himself to nod. 'You have the launch of your sewing business to prepare for, and...' His mind went blank as he fought the urge to take his words back and beg her to stay.

Her chin lifted but the sparkle in her eyes had dulled. 'I'll talk it over with my aunt and let you know.' She edged towards the door. 'I'm going back to bed. George?'

'I'll take care of him.'

She left, but it was a long time before he could move, before he could rid himself of the foul taste that coated his tongue.

The reunion between Emily and George was a revelation. The way George's face lit up...the love in Emily's face... It made Jasper's throat thicken and he had to clear it a couple of times. Imogen, who hovered nearby ready to leap in and help with anything if it was needed, swiped at her eyes.

She went to disappear back into the kitchen, but he caught hold of her hand. 'Emily, this is Imogen. And heaven help us all if she hadn't been here to help with George—teaching me all I needed to know about babies.' And about being an uncle, he realised now. She'd helped to thaw some of the frozen parts inside him. So had George.

'He's been a perfect doll,' Imogen assured Emily now. 'Haven't you, little man?' she said, tickling his tummy and making him gurgle out a delighted laugh.

Jasper froze. The tableau that the two women and the baby made...the fact his sister was *in his house*...

He recalled a time when he'd once gone skiing. He'd become so cold that when he'd walked back inside the warm lodge, his face and extremities had burned and ached for a full ten minutes before they'd started to feel normal again. That was how he felt on the inside now.

'I know how long that flight is from Sydney,' Imogen said. 'I'm thinking you'd probably love a chance to freshen up. Why don't I show you to your room?'

He trailed along behind them. So many emotions pounded through him in such quick succession it left him feeling disembodied. Happiness, grief, anger, protectiveness, relief—they all wrestled inside him.

'It's a beautiful room.' Emily's gaze zeroed in on the photo of George sitting on the bedside table. Imogen had taken it on her phone and had sent it to Jasper to print out before she'd placed it there in a pretty frame. 'Oh, Jasper, thank you so much!'

She threw an arm about his neck—her other held George clasped to her hip. George cuddled Jasper's arm and something that had been broken inside him started to knit back together.

When Emily released him, Imogen moved across to the bedside table and opened the top drawer. 'I took the liberty of grabbing you a few personal items.'

Emily moved across to glance inside. She stilled before meeting Imogen's gaze. 'Thank you.'

Curiosity shifted through him and he started to move across, and then stopped. They were probably referring to feminine hygiene products. Not that he was the least squeamish or embarrassed about such things, but a woman was entitled to her privacy.

'Is there anything else you need? Anything else I can do?' Imogen asked.

Emily shook her head. 'You've been so kind, thank you.' She glanced at them both, hesitating. 'I'd just love an hour to rest and…and to spend some time alone with George.'

She looked scared—as if she was afraid he would refuse her that…as if she'd started to equate all men's attitudes and behaviours with Aaron's and their father's. It pierced him to the core. 'Take as long as you want. Let me—' it occurred to him then that she might be more comfortable around another woman '—or Imogen know if there's anything you need or anything we can do.'

She nodded, and he left the room, stumbled down the hall to his own bedroom. Slumping down to the bed, he dropped his head to his hands and tried to stem the tears that scalded his eyes.

There was a soft sound in the doorway, and then a pair of arms went around him and pressed his head gently to the softness of her stomach. Imogen. He didn't need to open his eyes to know her. He knew her by her scent, by the sound of her movements, and by the way his every atom came to life at her nearness. He wrapped his arms about her middle and held her tight until the burning stopped. Only then did he ease away.

'Sorry.' His voice came out gruff. He felt vulnerable, exposed…embarrassed. 'What a big baby. I—'

She cupped his face and lifted it to meet her gaze. 'This is a normal human response to an overload of emotion. You've been on this island on your own for far too long, have kept too much bottled up.' She bit her lip, her eyes troubled. 'And despite her make-up, I know you saw her bruises too.'

He had. They were old bruises and were fading, but it

hadn't stopped him from wanting to punch something—preferably Aaron. 'She's so thin.'

She swiped the pads of her thumbs beneath his eyes. 'That, at least, is something we can fix, right?'

He nodded. She dropped her hands and eased away. 'It's time for me to get back down to the kitchen.'

With a smile, she was gone.

Over the course of the following week, Emily did put on weight—her cheeks filled out and her eyes started to lose their shadows. Katherine received her full test results, which verified the findings of the preliminary report—she didn't have breast cancer. It gave her the impetus to finish her book and send it off to her editor, and to resume her housekeeping duties. Meanwhile, Jasper desperately tried to think of a way to tempt Imogen back into the water for her daily swims.

She hadn't been for a single dip since they'd returned from São Paulo. He had an uncomfortable feeling he was to blame, but he didn't know how or why, and he desperately wanted to make amends. She'd arranged her return flights to Australia and now only had another week before she left. That was all—*one single week*! He wanted to make it as pleasant for her as he could.

And he definitely didn't want to think about how he'd feel once she was gone.

'What's on your mind?' Emily said from her spot on the floor where she played with George.

'Imogen.'

'Hmm…'

He glanced up at the knowing note in his sister's voice when the front door crashed open with a bang that made them all jump. Aaron appeared in the doorway. His shadow seemed to darken the room. Emily gave a strangled cry, her hand flying to her mouth. Jasper shot to his feet. Little George pulled himself up on unsteady legs and hurled himself at Jasper, clinging to his leg and hiding his face against it.

'I knew this was where you'd be, you traitorous cow!'

Jasper fought the urge to move across and punch the other man. Emily and George had seen enough violence, had been through enough.

At that moment Imogen came walking down the stairs with an armful of dirty linen. 'Do we have another visitor?' she called out cheerfully. 'Should I make up another room?'

'No need,' Aaron said with a snarl as she reached the bottom of the stairs. 'My wife, son and I won't be staying.'

'I see.' She pursed her lips, staring up at him. She looked tiny beside him. 'I take it you're Aaron?'

He gave a thin-lipped smile that made Jasper's heart pound so hard it almost hurt. He handed Jasper to Emily and started across the room, but before he could reach them, Imogen calmly lifted an arm and sprayed Aaron full in the face with something that had the other man immediately screaming and dropping to his knees. 'Agh, help! She's thrown acid in my face!'

She stepped over him and handed the can of spray to Emily. 'I knew that was going to be a good investment. Pepper spray,' she added for Jasper's benefit. 'I know it's not legal in New South Wales, but when I saw a can of it in São Paulo I figured it wouldn't hurt to have some.'

He didn't know what to say. He couldn't believe how... how *efficiently* she'd handled a potentially deadly situation.

Katherine came through from the kitchen. 'I've called the police. They're on their way.' She tossed Jasper a roll of duct tape. 'Tie him up for his own safety. Before Imogen is tempted to hurt him some more. And, Jasper,' she added, 'I wouldn't be too gentle about it if I were you.'

As much as he wanted to, he couldn't hit a defenceless man, and at the moment Aaron was nothing but a helpless, snivelling mess.

The police arrived an hour later and took him away. Emily and George retired to her room for a rest. Katherine returned to the kitchen. Jasper stared at Imogen. 'You really are something.'

She shrugged, but it didn't hide the way her hands had started to shake. 'I was pretty amazing, huh?'

He pulled her into his arms, pressing his lips to her hair. 'You scared me half out of my wits.'

CHAPTER TEN

KEITH COLEMAN ARRIVED two days later.

'Jasper,' Katherine called out from the living room. 'Your father is on the supply boat. It'll have docked by now, so he'll be here any minute.'

Jasper came out from his office where he'd been digitising Imogen's tapes for her. He couldn't decide if he was surprised by this turn of events or not. He glanced across at Emily, who'd paled, but she kept a resolute angle to her chin. Beside her, George crab-walked the length of the sofa, holding on to it for balance. The kid was going to be a runner when he grew up—a top-class athlete.

When he glanced back up, Imogen had appeared at her aunt's shoulder. Everything inside him clamoured at the mere sight of her. Ever since he'd watched her approach Aaron, fear had filled his soul. He'd wake in the middle of the night in a cold sweat from dreams where she was in trouble and he couldn't get to her in time.

Not that she'd needed him to come to her rescue two days ago. She'd rescued all of them instead.

The fact was she didn't need *him*.

The front door rattled and then shouting and pounding followed when it didn't open.

George fell to his nappy-clad bottom. Emily picked him up and cuddled him. Katherine's brows rose. 'The door's locked?'

'Oh, didn't I mention it? I've taken to locking it.' Imogen shrugged with an utter lack of concern.

Jasper wanted to smile at her complete disregard for his father's impatience—growing louder by the second. And then he wanted to hit something. Was she afraid to stay here since Aaron's unexpected arrival? Was—?

'Should I get it?' She pointed to the door.

He blew out a breath and nodded. 'Chin up, Em. I won't let him hurt you.'

'I know. It's like this is the final hurdle, and then I'll be free.'

He kept his gaze trained on Imogen as she moved towards the door. She opened it with a scolding, 'Heavens, what a racket. Really, sir, the doorbell is in perfect working order. Now, how can I help you?'

'I'm Mr Keith Coleman, and I demand to see my daughter and son. I *will* see them and no damn servant is going to stop me.'

Jasper moved into view before Keith could push Imogen out of the way. If his father touched her, he knew he wouldn't be able to think straight. And it'd be better for all concerned that he kept this as civilised as possible. From behind Imogen, he met Keith's glare. 'If you so much as lay one finger on any person here on my island, I will beat you to a bloody pulp and then take you a mile out that way—' he pointed seawards '—and drop your sorry butt overboard.' He kept his voice pleasant for George's and Emily's sakes.

Keith's mouth worked, but no sound came out.

Imogen glanced at Jasper and he nodded. She opened the door wider. 'Why don't you step inside, Mr Coleman?'

Keith straightened his suit jacket before stalking into the living room.

Emily stood and Jasper went to stand beside her. Imogen moved back beside her aunt. Keith sneered at them all. 'You think you have the upper hand, but you're wrong.'

Once upon a time a veiled threat like that would've had Jasper turning cold with dread. Now he saw through the bluster to the ugly bully beneath.

Keith stabbed a finger at Emily. 'I demand you return to your husband immediately.'

'You want her to return to a dangerous criminal?' Jasper kinked an eyebrow. 'How very egalitarian of you.' He couldn't believe his father hadn't washed his hands of his son-in-law and put as much distance between himself and Aaron as he could, given Aaron's allegedly illegal activities.

The older man dismissed that with a wave of his hand. 'It's all a misunderstanding. And one that will be more quickly cleared up with Emily at home by her husband's side.'

'That's not going to happen.' Emily lifted her chin. 'I won't be returning to Aaron. Ever. I'm filing for divorce, and I hope he rots in prison.'

Keith's eyes narrowed to slits. 'If you don't do as I say I'll have you declared an unfit mother. I'll sue for custody of George.'

'You can try, but you won't succeed. I've been planning my escape for months. I know my rights. I've photographic evidence of the bruises Aaron's given me. And I think it's safe to assume that Jasper will provide me with the very best family lawyers available.'

'Goes without saying,' Jasper murmured, proud of the way she held her ground.

'And if you do take this to court, Father, I'll tell the police that you and Aaron wanted me to perjure myself in court and say that Jasper's attack on Aaron two years ago was unprovoked.'

'Why, you little—' He broke off, his eyes narrowing. 'Your mother will pay for your disobedience.' He clenched a hand, that fist leaving none of them in doubt as to how he meant to make her pay. From the corner of his eye, Jasper saw Imogen flinch and had to bottle down his instant desire to plant a fist in his father's face.

He wasn't his father.

'Mother doesn't deserve the way you treat her, but I can't take responsibility for that any more.'

Emily's words made Jasper blink. Had she stayed with Aaron all this time to protect and support their mother?

Giving a derisory snort, the older man turned his attention to Katherine. 'I know what you've been up to. I've been keeping tabs.'

Katherine's eyes went mock wide. 'How thrilling for you, Keith.'

'I could make you a laughing stock—expose the ludicrous stuff you write to everyone you know.'

Jasper's gut clenched, but Imogen gave a barely stifled giggle. 'He has no idea about the world of genre fiction, does he, Auntie Kay?'

'None.'

Imogen winked at Jasper, who must've also looked at a loss because she added, 'Katherine's more likely to be swamped by adoring fans than mocked. I mean, there's bound to be the odd literary snob, but—'

'But not anyone we need concern ourselves with,' Katherine said.

'I know who your agent is. I know the name of your editor. Your publisher is a member of my club.'

Ice tripped down Jasper's spine. Keith would ruin Kate's career? The sense of déjà vu, of helplessness, rose up through him.

Katherine folded her arms. 'The thing is, publishing houses can be sold. I'm quite certain that Jasper could be prevailed upon to buy a publishing house, and to maybe even make me one of his lead authors.'

His panic dissipated, his heartbeat steadied. 'I've always fancied becoming a patron of the arts.'

The smile Imogen sent him was worth the price of two publishing houses.

'I know all about *you* too, Imogen Hartley. And you needn't think you're out of my reach.'

Jasper's every sense went on high alert.

'If you and your aunt don't want any trouble, you'll both leave this island now...*today*.'

'Or?' she inquired with a polite lift of her brows.

'Or you'll find the lease for your business premises has disappeared and the space mysteriously let to someone else. Or maybe the zoning laws will have changed...and then your planning-permission paperwork might go astray.'

She glanced at Jasper. 'He really is an unpleasant piece of work. You and Emily have my sympathies.'

Acid burned his chest. She was leaving in five days anyway. Her leaving today would make no difference. This wasn't her fight. She had a life to get back to. He steeled himself for her nod of acceptance and tried to control the nausea swirling through him.

She folded her arms. 'You're a slimy eel of a man, Mr Coleman.'

Jasper stiffened. What was she doing? Couldn't she see the danger of kicking the hornets' nest?

'You don't see it, do you?' she continued. 'The tables are turning...the power is shifting. Jasper would buy me the perfect premises and hire a business lawyer on my behalf—just to make sure all my paperwork was in order—if I asked it of him. And I'd rather take my chances with him than with you, thank you very much.'

He stilled. It hit him then—Imogen would always choose to do what was right rather than what was easy. She wasn't like Bronwyn. She was a woman who would stay and fight for him. For a moment he could barely breathe.

And then his heart swelled.

'But he won't be able to prevent the bad publicity of a smear campaign. I'll make sure word gets around that your workmanship is substandard and your ethics questionable.'

The threat rocked her, Jasper could see that, but her chin didn't drop. 'Like I said, I'll take my chances.'

'You're fools, the lot of you. You—' he swung back to Jasper '—will return to Australia at my side tomorrow and help me fix this sorry mess or I'll destroy them all.'

Jasper's mind raced. Imogen's words going round and round in his mind—*the power is shifting.* Why hadn't Keith disassociated himself from Aaron? Why hadn't he claimed ignorance of the man's activities and thrown him to the wolves? Keith had done that more than once in his political career to so-called trusted colleagues. Unless…

Jasper widened his stance. Unless he was involved in Aaron's illegal activities too.

All the pieces of the puzzle fell into place. The reason Keith had championed Emily and Aaron's relationship. The reason he'd renounced Jasper before his son could work out what was going on. His desperation now.

Jasper no longer feared his father. He might not be able to nullify all the harm Keith could do, but the women in this room had just shown him how he could mitigate it.

He didn't want to mitigate it, though. He wanted to *demolish* it. He recalled his father's threats to Imogen, and his resolve hardened to tempered steel. He wasn't letting the man get away with that. He was *not* going to let him hurt Imogen. Not now. Not ever.

His every thought sharpened—honed by years of imagining all the ways he could bring Keith to justice. An image fixed itself in his mind. He'd been digitising Imogen's tapes. That recording equipment was sitting in the top drawer of his desk.

Keith obviously interpreted Jasper's silence for apprehension because he gave a triumphant laugh that made Jasper's skin crawl. 'You always were a soft touch. It was your downfall. You'll do what's right by these women.'

'Why don't we take this discussion into my office? Katherine, could you organise refreshments, please?'

Katherine didn't so much as blink, but Emily grabbed his arm and stared up into his face with earnest eyes. 'Don't do this, Jasper. *Please.*'

It hurt that she had so little faith in him, but he couldn't blame her—not given her experiences with their father and Aaron.

He ignored Emily's plea to glance across at Imogen. 'Make up a guest room for my father.'

Her brow pleated. 'What are you doing? Why don't you just boot him off the island and—?'

'I'm doing what's necessary.'

'But—'

He moved across to her. 'Don't make things harder than they have to be.' He made sure the words carried across to his father. He made sure his next ones didn't. 'Slap me across the face and flounce off to the kitchen.'

She took a step away from him her eyes going wide, and then her face darkened, and she did as he'd requested— she slapped him.

The imprint of her hand burned against his cheek and he wanted to kiss her. He squashed the impulse as the kitchen door slammed behind her. Emily raced off after her with George in her arms, while he gestured for his father to precede him into his office.

'She's a fiery little piece,' Keith said.

'And fired after that little display,' Jasper returned.

'Pity, you could've had some fun taming her.'

His father's words made his stomach turn, but he didn't betray it by so much as a flicker of an eyelash. He waved to a drinks cabinet on the other side of the room. 'There's a very good aged single malt there. Help yourself.'

While his father's back was turned, he moved behind his desk, opened his top drawer and placed a blank cassette into the mini-recorder before slipping it into the pocket of his jacket. This morning when he'd pulled on a suit jacket, he'd told himself it was an attempt to return to a sense of normalcy—that he was once again ready to take a conference call if the occasion required it. Imogen had taken one look at him and had shaken her head. He was glad now he'd taken the trouble, though. The jacket felt like armour.

His father returned with two glasses of whisky. Jasper took one and sat, gestured for his father to take a seat too. 'You ought to know I'm not the inexperienced boy I once was. The business world has taught me a lot. It's not possible to achieve the amount of success I have while keeping all of one's ideals and scruples...intact.'

He pretended to sip his Scotch as he let his father draw conclusions—undoubtedly unfavourable—about his son's business practices.

Imogen's face rose in his mind, solidifying his intent. 'I'm not easily browbeaten. And I'm not going to pretend I am now.'

'If you don't do as I tell you, those women will suffer. I'll make it a personal crusade. While I'd be a fool to say such things in front of witnesses, accidents can be arranged.'

'Yes, they can.'

He let those words sink in before continuing. 'However, while your threats have little impact on me, I *am* a businessman. I like to make money. And I find myself growing tired of island life.'

Keith's eyes narrowed. 'What are you proposing?'

'I won't make Emily return to Aaron.'

His father started to rise. 'But—'

'The man's a fool for getting caught. I'm sure there's a way to…deal with him.'

Keith subsided, his eyes starting to gleam. 'Deal with him how?'

'I'm sure you can think of something. I'll only agree to return to Australia if you cut me in on whatever scheme you and Aaron have going.'

Keith started to laugh. These were the kinds of deals his father was used to making. 'You think I'd trust you with anything of that kind?'

'Money can buy a lot of things. Including information.'

Keith leaned back as if he held all the cards. 'Are you offering me money?'

'No, I don't owe you a thing. You owe me. And if I return to Australia…' He let the sentence hang for a moment. '*If* I return to Australia it'll be on an equal footing, *not* as your dogsbody.'

Keith's face twisted, and he slammed his glass down. 'You want to cut me out—take control of everything!' Because that was the way his father's mind worked.

Jasper gave a negligent shrug. 'Just like you, I find I have a taste for power. I want to be top dog.' He wanted to make sure Keith could never threaten Imogen again.

Keith thumped his chest. 'I'm top dog. I'm the one who has the contacts and knows how everything fits together. If I cut you in, it'll be on my terms.'

'But that said,' he continued, as if his father hadn't spoken, 'I'm sure my money could be put to use in advantageous and creative ways that would be in everyone's best interests.'

He broke off when a knock sounded. Katherine entered with a tray bearing coffee and warm scones. She set it on the desk. 'Will there be anything else?'

Jasper glanced at his father and let his lips lift as if in expectation that a deal would be struck soon. 'I think we'll have the fillet steak for dinner tonight, Katherine.'

It was his father's favourite, and predictably the older man preened as if he'd somehow won. Stupid man. Keith was going to find out exactly what happened when he threatened the people his son loved.

Katherine closed the door on her way out. Jasper set a mug of coffee in front of Keith. 'I'll need some kind of guarantee before I commit any money to the project.'

Keith seemed to think that over, knocked back the rest of his Scotch before setting it down with a nod. 'I can tell you enough to realise any financial investment you make would be well rewarded.'

Jasper lifted his coffee to his lips. 'I'm listening.'

'Let me get this straight,' Emily repeated. 'Jasper *asked* you to slap him?'

Imogen nodded. 'He's up to something. He has a plan, so don't lose heart. Your father doesn't frighten him.'

Emily let George scramble down from her lap to retrieve his bunny. 'I hope you're right.'

She was right. Jasper had a plan. She just prayed he could pull it off.

'I must say, Immy, you certainly responded to his request with…enthusiasm,' Katherine said.

'I wanted to be convincing.'

Had she channelled all her anger into that slap? Anger that he'd kissed her and then rejected her. Anger that it continued to mean so much. She swallowed. 'Do you think I hurt him?'

Katherine's eyes danced. 'Let's just say that I think it'll keep him focussed.'

She'd hated hitting him. The moment after she'd struck him, she'd wanted to take that beautiful face in her hands and kiss it better—it was why she'd flounced away in such a rush. Instinct told her that Jasper was playing some deep game, and the stakes were high. She'd help him in whatever way she could—because she trusted him and wanted to support him—and he'd be grateful. But she had to be careful not to read anything more into it than that.

She wasn't giving him any further reason to tell her that while he was attracted to her, he didn't want anything more. He'd been honest with her from the start. Why couldn't she have got that straight in her head? Why did she have to go and fall for him?

'Right, Imogen, you'd better go and get that room ready.'

Emily twisted her hands together. 'I don't want to sleep in the same part of the house as my father.'

Imogen didn't blame her. 'My room has twin beds if you want to bunk in with me. I mean, it's nothing fancy, but…'

The relief that raced across Emily's face was all the answer she needed. 'C'mon, I'll make up a room for Sir Keith the Jackass and then we can move your things downstairs for the night.' Including that can of pepper spray.

The rest of the afternoon dragged by, the suspense that hung in the air making it hard to concentrate on anything. Emily had her dinner in the kitchen with Imogen and Katherine. Jasper and his father ate in the dining room where Imogen couldn't help noticing how at home Keith made himself.

Ha! What did she mean, *couldn't help noticing*? She was spying. Of course she could help noticing. She was *deliberately* noticing.

And what she deliberately noticed was that Keith did most of the talking—all of it bragging and big-noting himself, name-dropping and blowing his own trumpet in relation to his access to Australia's highest political powers. The slimy toad. Jasper, on the other hand, kept calmly plying the man with a very good burgundy—four bottles of the stuff, to be precise—and very little of it made its way down its owner's throat. She crossed her fingers and hoped that whatever Jasper's goal happened to be, he achieved it.

'Your father can drink a lot,' she said, closing the

kitchen door quietly and returning to the table where Katherine had brought out a deck of cards and told them they were playing gin rummy. George had long since been put to bed in his cot in Imogen's room.

'Like a fish,' Emily agreed. 'Jasper's going to need a lot of wine if he's hoping to get him drunk.'

Katherine dealt out the cards. 'Then it's just as well your brother keeps his cellar well stocked.'

They played cards for nearly two hours. The next time she peeked, Imogen watched Jasper half carry his very drunk father upstairs, presumably to bed. When he came back downstairs, he went straight into his study without so much as a glance in the direction of the kitchen.

She shifted her weight from one foot to the other, biting the inside of her cheek. She really wanted to go to him, but on what pretext? If he wanted her, he knew where to find her.

Acid burned her stomach. He didn't want her, though. As much as she might want to, she couldn't lose sight of that fact.

Katherine gave her a nudge. 'Go and find out if there's anything else he needs, and tell him we're locking ourselves in.'

She turned in surprise.

Katherine held up a key. 'The staff quarters lock.'

'Is that necessary?'

'It'll make Emily feel safer.'

She was halfway to Jasper's office when she realised her aunt hadn't actually answered her question. Which was probably an answer in itself. Stomach churning, she tapped on the open office door. Jasper glanced up from where he furiously typed on his computer. 'There's nothing else I need for the evening, Imogen,' he said, pre-empting her. 'You're free to retire.'

Lucky her.

'Emily is bunking in with me tonight. And George.'

He nodded and returned to his computer. 'Was there anything else?' he finally said, not looking at her.

Her chest tightened. He wasn't going to tell her what he was up to? What his plan was? She frowned at a spot on the carpet. 'Katherine told me to tell you we're locking ourselves in.'

He swivelled to face her. 'That's not necessary. But if it makes you feel better…'

What would make her feel better was if he swept her up in his arms and kissed her, told her he'd die without her. Her lips twisted. But that evidently wasn't going to happen.

His eyes swept across her face, and his jaw clenched. He turned back to his computer. 'Goodnight, Imogen.'

She turned and left without uttering another word.

'What did he say?' Emily said the moment she marched back into the kitchen. 'How did he seem?'

High-handed. Remote. Autocratic. She bit the words back. They weren't fair. 'Preoccupied…and uncommunicative.'

'Never mind.' Katherine marshalled them towards the staff quarters. 'Tomorrow may reveal all.'

Imogen tried to rein in her confusion, her hurt. Jasper didn't owe her anything beyond a fair wage and decent working conditions. Her pique faded, but she refused to let hopelessness take its place. Her future held lots of good things—oodles of them. It just didn't include Jasper.

She lifted her chin. Being here on the island had taught her an important lesson. Sometimes you had to take a risk—and if you worked hard and planned well it paid dividends. Some risks *were* worth taking. Look at Aunt Katherine—she'd dared to dream, and it had led to a publishing deal. Emily had risked her own safety to forge a new life for her and George.

Katherine and Emily had faced their fears and both their lives were the better for it. She could face her fears too.

She *wasn't* stupid. She *wasn't* naïve and unprepared. She and her business *would* thrive. As for Jasper…

Instinct told her he was taking a big risk now. With all her heart, she hoped it paid off, hoped he vanquished his demons where his father was concerned. And that he had the chance to lead a good and happy life. Her eyes burned. It was what he deserved.

CHAPTER ELEVEN

EDUARDO APPEARED THE following morning as Imogen served breakfast in the dining room. He hovered by the kitchen door, evidently waiting for her.

The scent of freshly cooked bacon—normally a smell she relished—made her stomach turn. Or maybe that was simply her employer's guest. She finished refilling Jasper's and Keith's coffee mugs before moving across to him. She listened as he gave his message in halting English.

'Is there a problem?' Jasper demanded in some kind of boss voice that set her teeth on edge.

She moved back to the table, hands folded at her waist. 'Eduardo tells me there's a boat here. The skipper claims he's been hired to take someone to the mainland.'

Keith smirked. 'Now you'll get your comeuppance, missy. You might think twice before losing your temper again.'

The passage to the mainland was for her? But…she had another four days before she had to leave. She wasn't ready to go yet. She—

'Call the others in, Imogen.'

As Eduardo hadn't left the doorway, and Katherine and Emily had come to stand behind him, Imogen didn't need to call anyone over. They all moved to stand beside her.

'I have something here I think you'll all be interested in hearing.'

Jasper pulled her mini-recorder from his pocket and hit

play. She listened, at first in confusion, but then in growing comprehension as Keith's voice droned on, bragging about offshore bank accounts, complex financial transactions designed to camouflage where money came from, Ponzi schemes and the killing to be made in digital currencies. On the tape, Jasper asked leading questions about how Keith saw his son fitting into this mini-empire of white-collar crime, and Keith gave detailed explanations. She couldn't believe the man had fallen for it! His enormous ego and inflated sense of his own power—his stubborn belief that he could still cow and manipulate Jasper—was his undoing.

'You recorded me?' Keith leapt to his feet, ejected the tape and ground it beneath his heel on the tiles, before shredding the roll of plastic film that had recorded his damning words. He bared his teeth, his breath noisy in the silence. 'You're going to pay for this.'

Jasper didn't appear the least bit perturbed by Keith's actions so she chose not to be either.

'You were so confident you could get me onside. And so ridiculously sure that you were safe telling me everything because there was no one else to bear witness—your word against mine. And as you'd already discredited my character back in Australia, who'd believe an embittered son over a respected politician, right?'

Keith gave an ugly laugh and held up the shredded tape. 'And without this, it's still your word against mine.'

'The tape you're holding is a copy. After I put you to bed last night, I spent the rest of the evening digitising the contents of the tape and sending the electronic file through to the Australian Federal Police. The original is in my safe.'

Keith's face turned purple and then grey.

'As we speak, your house in Sydney is being searched. I've spoken to Mother and told her what's happening, and she's decided to throw her lot in with me rather than take any more abuse from you.'

'She wouldn't dare! I'll—'

'You'll do nothing, because more likely than not you'll be banged up in a jail cell next door to Aaron. You're in no position to do anything.'

'The ungrateful—'

'When you hit someone enough they'll eventually bite back.'

Imogen watched the scene play out in front of her and wanted to cheer…and throw up…and hug Jasper, Emily and George…and the Australian Federal Police.

'You're now a person of interest and a warrant has been issued for your arrest. Police officers will be here in—' he glanced at his watch '—an hour or two, I suspect. So you can wait for them, or you can take your chances evading them on the mainland and leave on the boat that's just arrived. Up to you.'

The older man slammed to his feet. 'I'll make you pay for this. All of you.'

He raced upstairs—presumably to pack. 'Don't let him out of your sight,' Jasper said to Eduardo.

Less than thirty minutes later, the boat pulled away from the dock with Keith Coleman on board.

'Why did you let him go?' Emily almost wailed as she stared after the departing vessel.

'I didn't let him go, Em. Two of the local *policía* are on board, as he'll find out soon enough. They'll hold him until someone more senior arrives to deal with him. I just wanted to prevent any further unpleasantness happening on my island.'

They returned to the house, and Jasper explained how his plan had formed and how he'd executed it. While Keith hadn't been so unguarded as to give up the names of his associates, he'd given enough information that the police were sure they'd be able to make further arrests in the near future.

Emily laughed and cried.

Imogen let herself out of the house and made her way along the beach, keeping to the shadows of the palm trees. She should be feeling exultant—and a part of her was. But it also felt as if a line had just been drawn in the sand. It brought home to her the fact that she'd be leaving in four days and would never see Jasper again.

She scrambled up the steep track of the headland at the end of Jasper's beach. Ever since arriving she'd been meaning to climb it. *No time like the present.*

She was breathing hard when she reached the top, but the view rewarded her efforts. A sapphire sea glistened in the sun, ruffled here and there by a playful breeze. That breeze might stiffen later this afternoon, creating white-caps, but for now it merely caressed and stroked. A few giant rocks rested between the island and the horizon, giving depth and definition to all the amazing blue.

Turning to survey the vista behind, she was greeted with lush greenery. The wooded hill that was Tesoura's interior hid the far coastline from view. Birdcalls rang throughout the forest, hinting at the abundant life hidden there. Below to her left, Eduardo's pride and joy—the garden—reigned in emerald splendour with Jasper's mansion gleaming white and magnificent in the midst of it. Beyond that stretched the lagoon with its tiny dock and barely a ripple disturbed its surface.

If only she could channel some of that tranquillity into her own soul. Finding a flat rock, she sat and stared out to sea. Wasn't there some poet who'd claimed beauty could heal the hurts of the world? She rested her chin on her hands and glared at the glory spread before her, waiting for it to weave its enchantment and magically glue her heart back together.

Stupid heart.

Stupid her for giving it away so easily where it wasn't wanted.

Stupid.

Her eyes burned but she forced her chin up. Falling in love with Jasper wasn't stupid. It seemed almost…inevitable. He was wonderful. Falling in love with him simply went to show what excellent taste she had. It was just a shame he didn't love her back.

She didn't know how long she sat like that before she heard Jasper beating up a path towards her. Cool reason told her it had to be Jasper. Katherine would simply wait until Imogen came down if she wanted to speak to her. Emily would be busy with George, and Eduardo with his garden.

There was nothing cool about how she felt at the thought of seeing him now, though. She tried to school her features. She told herself to be cheerful. She might be in love with a man who didn't love her back, but she still had her pride.

'Hey!' she said, leaping to her feet when he broke through the undergrowth and crested the summit. With a superhuman effort she kept a grin on her face. 'Here's to the man of the moment!' She gave him a round of applause. 'You were amazing back there—all cool, calm and focussed—like some white knight on his charger.'

'I—'

'I mean—' she knew she was babbling but couldn't stop '—how good did it feel to slay that particular dragon?'

'I…'

She skipped forward to high-five him, but rather than slapping his palm to hers, he caught her hand, lacing his fingers with hers, and not letting go. 'You left.'

The hurt in his eyes nearly undid her. She couldn't tell him the truth—that she'd needed time alone. She couldn't tell him that in vanquishing his father he'd forced her to face the fact that he didn't love her. She could no longer pretend that he was trapped by his family and circumstances.

But that was her problem, not his.

His fingers curled around hers as if they'd never let her go.

Wishful thinking.

Everything inside her throbbed. Her smile had fled, but she refused to let her chin drop. 'I wanted to give you and Emily some time alone together. To process all you've managed to achieve, to celebrate the fact you've broken from your past.'

'You left,' he repeated, his brows lowering over his eyes. 'You don't see it, do you?'

'See what?'

'Without you, Imogen, there wouldn't have been anything to celebrate.'

What was he talking about?

'Without you, I don't want to celebrate.'

Her heart all but stopped.

Jasper swallowed. He'd screwed up, hadn't he?

This lovely woman had offered him a glimpse of another life—a life he desperately wanted—and he'd flung it back at her. She'd offered him her heart. Not in so many words, but they both knew that had been the subtext of their conversation on the beach that night after their kiss.

She'd been prepared to see where things between them might go, but he'd dismissed the idea. Ruthlessly. He winced, imagining how hard-hearted she must've thought him. She'd accepted his rejection with equanimity—hadn't tried to change his mind, had respected his wishes.

And then he'd kissed her again in São Paulo and had rejected her all over again. That had been unforgivable. He didn't blame her for locking her heart up tight against him now.

She pulled her hand from his, her brow wrinkling as if she was trying to make sense of what he'd said. 'I can't take credit for what happened this morning.'

She might've closed her heart to him, but he could open his to her. 'This morning had everything to do with you.' He clenched his hand, trying to keep a hold of the feel of her, wanting it imprinted on his mind. 'If it weren't for you, I might never have believed that Emily was in trouble in the first place.'

'I know you believe that, but I don't. It was you who worked out how to contact her. And when she did make contact, it was you who got her to safety.'

'It was also you,' he pressed on, 'who made me fall in love with George.'

She rolled her eyes. 'I think you'll find George was responsible for that himself.'

'You taught me how to be an uncle.'

It appeared he'd finally shocked her into silence. Her mouth opened, but no words came out.

He widened his stance. 'Yesterday afternoon when my father threatened Emily, I was angry. When he threatened Katherine, I was outraged. But when he threatened you, I wanted to kill him.'

Even now the memory had everything inside him clenching up tight. 'I knew I could counter the harm he threatened. You all showed me how to do that—and I'd have been happy to do it. But the thought of you having to put up with his spite, being persecuted for no other reason than the fact that you're a good person…' Both his hands clenched. '*That* was the moment I decided to take him down.'

The green highlights in her eyes seemed to alternately flash and dull, like the sun on a moving sea. She moistened her lips and an ache started up inside him. 'Why?'

His mouth dried, but he was through with lies and deceit. 'Because I love you.'

She froze. She blinked. She didn't utter a single damn word.

Give her more, you idiot.

Reaching out, he touched her cheek. 'I know I've given you no reason to believe me—that I've run hot and cold. And I don't blame you if you don't return my feelings, but I can't let you leave this island believing you don't mean anything to me.'

Her lips parted. He wanted to kiss her so badly he started to shake with it. But then she backed up a step and the hope he'd stupidly let loose drained away and the day darkened as if a cloud had just passed across the sun.

He glanced up at the sky. Not a single cloud marred the endless blue—not even on the farthest horizon. Turning back to Imogen, he pressed his lips together to stop from begging her to give him another chance. He didn't regret telling her how he felt; he didn't regret telling her he loved her, but he wouldn't harass her. He'd had enough of men hassling women to last him a lifetime.

She thumped down to a rock as if her legs had given way. She swallowed and gestured to another rock nearby. He took it, hating how much distance it put between them. From here he couldn't reach out and touch her.

That's the point.

'If you'd prefer to be alone, I can leave.'

'I don't want you to leave, I'm just… I know my silence must sound deafening to you, but…' Her eyes narrowed. 'I'm trying to decide if I believe you or not.'

He froze. Did that mean…? Was she saying…? He didn't bother trying to rein in his hope. 'Why do you doubt me?' If he knew that, he might be able to allay it.

She covered her face with her hands, and he understood they weren't playing games here—they were in deadly earnest. 'Because it's what you do, Jasper—it's your modus operandi.' She pulled her hands away. 'You want to protect women… And children.'

She thought that was a bad thing?

'After meeting your father—' she shuddered '—I can see why you don't want to be anything like him.'

He remained quiet, focussed.

'You know that I'm not immune to you. I know you know that.'

His heart pounded.

'And I'm worried that if you think you're hurting me, you'll give me what you think I want regardless of the cost to yourself.'

He leaned towards her. 'You think I'd tell you I loved you to make you happy rather than because it's true?'

Her tongue snaked out to moisten her lips. 'That's the thought that's crossing my mind.'

Damn. He tried not to notice the shine on her lips, tried not to let it distract him. 'You're right insofar as the thought of hurting you makes me feel physically ill.'

Although the sun beat down on them with benevolent warmth, she'd gone pale. His heart gave a sick kick.

'But you're wrong too,' he forced himself to continue. 'I would never lie about loving you. It would hurt you tenfold in the long run because you'd eventually work it out. How could I do that to you—a woman with so much love in her heart and so much joy for life and so much to look forward to?' He shook his head, praying she'd believe him. 'If I thought you loved me, but I didn't return that love— I'd have to tell you. It'd be a clean break. Painful at first, no doubt, but I know you'd move on.'

She blinked.

'That kind of lie—the kind you're accusing me of—is a trap. It'd be a trap for the both of us and I've seen what traps do to people. I don't want that. Not for me. And I sure as hell don't want it for you.'

She rested her elbows on her knees, her chin in her hands as she stared—almost glared—at him. It shifted her towards him fractionally and he wasn't sure if she was aware of that or not. There had to be some other way he could convince her, something he could—

'You told me that Tesoura is your home. That you have no plans for ever leaving.'

'I was wrong.' He spoke without hesitation. 'Running away like I did was the coward's way out.'

She straightened. 'That's not fair! You had every reason for needing a bolt-hole. You are *not* a coward.'

Her defence warmed him. He wanted to take it as a good sign.

She thrust out her chin. 'And you're not an emotional coward either. You just told me you loved me without knowing if I'd say it back. That was pretty brave.'

He still didn't know if she was going to say it back. But he didn't point that out.

'Regardless of what happens between me and you, Imogen, I'm returning to the real world. I want to be close to my family. I have my heart set on living in Wollongong, but if that's not possible then I'll get a place somewhere in Sydney.'

Her eyes widened at his words.

'I know you don't see it, but you've made me a new man.' *Please let her see that.*

'You helped me deal with the bitterness and resentment I'd let fester inside me. But that's not all. You've given me hope.' He wanted her to feel the truth of his words in her bones. 'I'm not talking about the hope that something might happen between the two of us. I'm talking about the hope that I can live a good life again—that I can be an uncle to George, a brother to Emily, a son to my mother, and maybe even a husband and father myself one day. I'm planning to reconnect with the friends I've shunned these last two years, and I'm going to get hands-on again with my business.'

She straightened; her hands pressed to the spot above her heart. Tears sparkled on her lashes.

'You want to know the exact moment I realised I was in love with you?'

She nodded.

'The moment you appeared in the living room in the middle of the night to help me with George when he was teething. I'd never been so darn happy to see anyone. And before you say otherwise, it had nothing to do with George. Seeing you simply made the hard stuff easier to bear. Seeing you made me feel that some piece inside me that had been missing had just been found. I felt…whole.'

Her lips parted.

'When did I *actually* fall in love with you?' He shook his head. 'Probably the moment I saw you dancing with that stupid vacuum cleaner.'

'But…you yelled at me.'

'I didn't yell!' He grimaced. 'Though I was admittedly less than cheerful at the time.'

She kinked an eyebrow at his understatement.

'That was the moment everything started to change, and I didn't want it to. I was pushing back against it, trying to maintain the status quo. I'm sorry I was so bad-tempered. You didn't deserve it.'

The expression in her eyes made his heart beat hard. 'You want to know when I first realised I was in love with you?' she asked.

Every cell inside him fired to life at her words. He tried to keep his feet on the ground, not to get carried away. Her confession didn't mean she still loved him. But her smile…

'It was the moment you made arrangements for me to travel with you and Aunt Katherine to São Paulo. I told you that you were my new favourite person.'

He remembered the exact moment.

'As soon as the words left my mouth, I knew they were true. I think it all started, though, that day on the beach.'

'When we kissed?'

'No. Though *that* was a revelation.'

She could say that again.

'I'm talking about the day you fell for George. When he grabbed on to you and you just couldn't hold out against him any longer. I think that was the moment when my heart waved a white flag and surrendered.'

But he'd rejected her twice since then. Had he trampled so hard over her heart that she didn't have any love left for him now? He wanted to drop to his knees in front of her but forced himself to remain where he was. 'Imogen, I've just spoken about the future I want. What I want more than anything is for that future to be with you. I don't expect you to trust me immediately.' Desperation clawed at him. 'But please let me see you a little when I'm back in Sydney. Let me prove to you—'

Her smile transformed her face and he couldn't speak as his throat closed over.

'No, Jasper, that's not a deal I want to make.'

But she smiled in a way that lifted rather than felled him.

'The deal is that you see me a lot. *A whole lot.* Didn't you hear what I just said?' She surged to her feet, and so did he. 'I love you too.' She moved across to stand in front of him, reaching up to touch his face, her eyes soft and her lips even softer. 'I love you.'

And then she was in his arms, her arms wound tight around his neck and her hair tickling his face. He wrapped his arms around her waist and closed his eyes, giving thanks to whatever deity had sent her into his life.

She eased back, her mouth millimetres from his. 'Deal?' she whispered.

'Deal,' he murmured, catching her lips in a kiss that promised a lifetime. He'd finally found the one place he belonged—with Imogen—and he meant to treasure it, to treasure her, forever.

EPILOGUE

Three years later

JASPER GLANCED AROUND the monstrosity of an open-plan kitchen/diner that Katherine had told him was an utter necessity and had to pinch himself. It was crammed to its vaulted ceilings—ceilings Imogen had swooned over—with Christmas cheer, with excited chatter and laughter, and with all the things he'd known Christmas could hold for other people but had never expected to experience for himself.

Several people toasted him as he came into the room and he grinned. It was official—he and Imogen had been added to the Christmas hosting rota. He had to pinch himself again.

His wife hadn't been kidding when she'd said the holiday was a big deal for her family. Tonight, they were hosting the Christmas Eve party; tomorrow Imogen's parents—two of the nicest people he'd ever met—were hosting the traditional all-day Christmas lunch, while the day after that her uncle Robert and aunt Sarah were hosting the Boxing Day wind-down.

And he loved it. All of it. With a passion that almost seemed unholy.

And the house he and Imogen had designed for the ten-acre block of land he'd bought in Wollongong—with its extraordinary ocean views—provided the perfect back-drop for all this warmth and belonging. Everything was... *perfect*.

Almost perfect. His father had another five years to serve on an eight-year jail term, but as far as Jasper could tell not a single person missed him. Aaron had already served his eighteen-month sentence and had relocated to Darwin. Jasper's lips tightened. But only after striking a devil's bargain. In exchange for start-up funds for a bar and restaurant, Aaron had signed away all his custody rights to George. Jasper still couldn't believe the man had sug-gested such a thing—George was a joy, a delight, a trea-sure. But if that was the way Aaron felt, then it was better for George to have nothing to do with him.

He pushed the sombre thought away. Tonight was for fun and laughter and giving thanks. Moving behind Imo-gen, who was putting the finishing touches to a cheese and fruit platter, he slipped his arms about her waist. 'Anything I can do to help?'

She gave a delicious shiver when his lips touched her nape. 'I don't think so—the food's all ready.' They'd pre-pared a buffet-style feast and had set up picnic tables and blankets on the lawn outside. The evening was balmy and the sky full of oranges, pinks and mauves as the sun started to set. 'But please tell me someone is supervising the chil-dren in the pool.'

'Your aunt Fiona and aunt Stacey are keeping a close eye on proceedings while your uncle Jordan and uncle Dennis discuss the merits of different car motors.'

Imogen laughed. 'If they keep that up my aunts might just push them in the deep end.'

'And your cousins are teaching George how to dive.' George, who was nearly four and utterly fearless!

'Good for them.' She set a final bunch of grapes to her platter with a flourish and then turned and looped her arms about his neck. 'So how are you enjoying our very first party in our gorgeous new house?'

'I love it. When can we have another one?'

He didn't try to temper his excitement, his enthusiasm… his joy. He knew it must be shining from his face, but he didn't have to be wary or guarded here—not among these people who'd embraced him and claimed him as one of their own.

Her face softened. 'You deserve all of this, Jasper. All of the fun and holiday spirit and love.'

'I don't know about that.'

'I do,' she said, her voice a soft whisper against his skin.

They'd married eighteen months ago, and he hadn't known it was possible for one man to feel so lucky—loving her was the smartest thing he'd ever done. That love filled his chest now, making him feel weightless, as if he could float up to the highest point of the ceiling.

She glanced beyond him, her luscious lips curving into a smile. 'It's nice to see your mother and Emily enjoying themselves.'

He followed her gaze to the terrace outside, where his mother and sister were firmly ensconced in a circle of Imogen's family—all of them laughing and seemingly talking at once. It'd taken time for the shadows to retreat from their eyes. They'd bear scars forever, he knew that, but it didn't mean they couldn't be happy in the here and now.

He'd had three cottages built on this ten-acre block, each with its own private garden. Emily and George were in one, Katherine in another, and the married couple he and Imogen had hired as housekeeper and gardener were living in the third. He'd wanted to build one for his mother but she hadn't let him. She'd sold the house in Sydney to buy a modest unit in Wollongong's town centre, within easy access to them all. He hoped that, given enough time, both Emily and his mother would find a love like his and

Imogen's—a love that healed and renewed; a love that made the world a place full of hope and possibility.

Imogen reached up on tiptoe to press her lips to his and a familiar surge of heat licked along his veins. Whatever she saw in his face made her chuckle. 'Hold that thought until the party's over.'

He had every intention of doing exactly that. For now, he contented himself with reaching for his phone and selecting a song from his playlist. He spun her in his arms as sixties Southern Californian surf music poured from the speakers. 'Pretend I'm a vacuum cleaner and dance with me.'

She threw her head back and laughed, her dark curls bouncing with effervescent good humour. 'Best offer I've had all night!'

He made a mental note to better that offer when they were alone.

His heart nearly burst when the entire kitchen and dining room erupted into a storm of dancing. Katherine and Imogen's mother, Gloria, started a complicated dance that had them both breathless by the end and everyone else clapping madly. Katherine's writing career was going from strength to strength and Gloria, in her spare time, had taken it upon herself to become Katherine's marketing manager. He suppressed a grin. So far the arrangement was working beautifully even given the occasional inevitable bump along the way.

'Food's up,' Imogen hollered when the song ended.

They ate. They socialised. They sang Christmas carols for the children. At nine o'clock the fireworks he'd arranged—with all the associated council permits and fire safety precautions in place—created a magical display that delighted child and adult alike.

After that, sleepy children were put to sleep in spare bedrooms or on the sofas in the lounge room while the adults continued to revel for another couple of hours. Eventually, though, the guests started to excuse themselves. Jasper saw the last of them off and then wandered back through the house to find his glorious wife.

She stood outside on the terrace, staring at a moonlit sea. She turned to greet him with a smile as big as her heart, and full of love. For him. The knowledge awed him. 'That was one of the best Christmas Eve parties ever, Jasper. If we're not careful we might just find ourselves hosting it every year.'

'I wouldn't mind.'

She poked him in the ribs before sliding an arm about his waist. 'You'd *love* it.'

He grinned, tucking her in more firmly against his side. 'That was the best Christmas Eve ever.'

'Which is what you said last year…and the year before that,' she teased.

'And I'll probably say it again next year.' He sobered, glancing down at her. 'They keep getting better. I don't know how, but they do.'

She sobered too. Moving out from beneath his arm, she took his hand in both her own. 'I think this one is extra special.'

'It's the first time we've hosted one of the Christmas events.' *That* was a big deal. 'And we did it in our dream home.' To be honest, though, wherever Imogen happened to be was his definition of dream home.

'Not just that—this whole year has been amazing.'

Her and Lauren's sewing business had become a soaring success. They now ran a very exclusive fashion house— The House of Tesoura. Emily had started her own PR company, and the fashion house had been her first client. Both businesses were thriving. 'You've achieved amazing things this year, Imogen. The House of Tesoura is the toast of the town.'

'I'm ecstatic about that, of course—' her eyes danced '—and over the moon that I can blow raspberries at all of the naysayers, but that's not what I'm talking about. I'm talking about the plans we discussed a few months ago. I feel as if we're on the cusp of an exciting new adventure.'

He swallowed and his heart started to thud. 'You mean…about starting a family soon?' He was almost too afraid to hope. He already had so much.

'That's exactly what I'm talking about.' She bit her lip and then took his hand and laid it flat against her abdomen, her eyes shining and her lips trembling.

A jolt shot through him like electricity—he went rigid, and then a wild, glorious excitement coursed through him. 'You're…?'

She nodded. 'I found out yesterday. I wasn't going to tell you until tomorrow. I thought it'd be the best Christmas present ever. But I've been bursting with the news… and now seemed like the perfect time.'

He couldn't push a single word past the lump in his throat. *Imogen was pregnant.*

His hand curved against her in wonder. *They were going to have a baby.*

'Happy?' she whispered.

With a superhuman effort, he swallowed down the lump. 'I thought I was happy two minutes ago. This—' he shook his head '—it's almost too much.'

'No, it's not, darling Jasper.' She reached up to touch his face. 'It's just right. It's exactly as it should be.'

'I'm the luckiest man alive.' Cupping her face, he lowered his mouth to hers and told her in a language that needed no words exactly how happy he was.

* * * * *

CARIBBEAN ESCAPE
WITH THE TYCOON

ROSANNA BATTIGELLI

For my beautiful daughter, Sarah,
a strong, shining star.

CHAPTER ONE

"YOU SIT HERE and don't move, Adrien," Chanelle heard a deep voice say at the table across from hers. She had just been looking out at the coast from the deck of the luxury cruise liner *Aquarius*, a ship she'd never dreamed she'd be a guest on.

"I'll be right back with something yummy for the both of us," the man said with a laugh. "I'll give you a hint: it rhymes with *nice dream…*"

Chanelle looked up, curious to see the face that matched the voice. But she only saw the back of the man's head. And below the golden-brown hair that curled at the ends, a firm neck and muscled shoulders that were distractingly discernible under his turquoise shirt. His perfectly fitting black linen trousers emphasized his strong legs.

Before he turned toward the ice cream machine, a young lady passed by wearing a red bikini and a filmy white cover-up that barely covered anything, and gave the man a big smile. She said something to him, and Adrien's father stopped to talk to her, giving Chanelle a glimpse of his chiseled profile and groomed shadow. And his quirky smile and narrowed eyes.

Chanelle's stomach muscles contracted involuntarily, and her pulse quickened, followed immediately by a feeling of guilt for her physical reaction to a guy who was married and yet flirted with other women.

Despicable. And practically in front of his child...

Her attention was diverted by the *vroom, vroom* sounds of the man's son as he moved his miniature racing car along the table. Adrien was a cute little boy, with bright blue eyes and short, golden brown hair, the same shade as his dad's. At one point, he backed the car up and let it go. The car skidded off to the far end of the table, and the boy immediately jumped on his chair to reach across to get it. Chanelle turned in alarm toward his father, but he was now concentrating on filling two cones, the woman gone.

Chanelle's heart skipped a beat. Adrien was so close to the ship railing... What if he took a tumble over the edge? Her heart leaped into her throat when she saw him begin to straighten, and without any further hesitation, she closed the distance between them in two strides and clasped his arm.

"You need to come down—"

"What exactly are you doing?"

Chanelle heard the deep voice directly behind her. Only this time it lacked the light, playful tone he had used with his son. Before she could react, the child had wrenched himself away and was scrambling off the chair and running to his father.

Chanelle turned to face them awkwardly, feeling a flush bloom across her cheeks. The man had set down the cones and was embracing Adrien with one arm while staring at Chanelle, his eyebrows furrowed above icy blue eyes. "Why were you grabbing him?"

Because you weren't there, making sure your son didn't end up losing his balance and tipping overboard, Chanelle wanted to retort.

She felt her jaw muscles tensing. "I wasn't grabbing him." She looked at the man steadily, willing herself to sound calm and not defensive. "He had jumped up to get his toy car, and I was worried that he'd lose his balance and fall." She gazed at the boy, whose face was puckering as he looked at his shoes. "Or topple over."

"He was in no danger. I had my eye on him." The man's eyes narrowed, and Chanelle felt as if she were staring at two brilliant blue laser beams.

Your eye was on a red bikini, she wanted to retort. She felt her cheeks fire up as the stormy blue of his eyes intensified.

"I was closer to him than you," she said, trying to keep her voice steady, "and from where I stood, he looked perilously close to the edge." Chanelle bit her lip. "Look, I was just trying to protect him. One wrong move and he could have—"

"I get the point," he said, putting up a hand. His tone lacked its previous gruffness, and his eyes seemed to have softened. "Thank you for your valiant gesture."

Chanelle's eyebrows lifted as she stared at the man who was staring down at her. His eyes were a startling turquoise, matching his golf shirt. Gazing at his bronzed features, perfectly shaped lips and a jawline that reminded her of the sculpted perfection of Michelangelo's *David*, Chanelle felt an inner jolt. A series of jolts. As her gaze slipped downward, she had the crazy thought that with his looks and build, he should be modeling for a living. The top buttons of his shirt were undone, revealing an inverted triangle of golden-brown hair. When her gaze returned to his face, she started at the piercing intensity of his eyes. She looked away, her cheeks feeling like molten lava. He stepped forward and took his son firmly by the hand. The child lowered his gaze again, aware that his actions had caused concern.

"What is going on here?" A thirty-something young woman with bouncy strawberry-blond hair, and clothes and shoes that screamed *designer*, approached them and took Adrien protectively by the hand. She threw a concerned look at her husband.

"Nothing to worry about," he drawled. "I'll take care of it."

Chanelle couldn't help glancing at his left hand. *No ring.* She almost snorted. *No wonder.* He obviously preferred to *look* single… Chanelle's gaze flew to the petite woman. Did she have any idea that her husband was a playboy?

A rich playboy, from the look of her diamond of at least two carats.

"I'm going to our stateroom. Come on, Adrien," she said brusquely. She lifted an eyebrow imperiously toward her husband. "Vance?"

"I'll join you shortly, Mariah," he said. He released Adrien's hand.

Chanelle stood by awkwardly as the man's wife strode past her stiffly, ignoring her completely. When she and her son had disappeared past the automatic glass doors, Chanelle glanced warily at the man. *Vance.* Nice name. Too bad it didn't match his character.

He had taken a few steps closer, and his brows were furrowed again. Her nose picked up spicy notes of his cologne. A woodsy and exotic fragrance that reminded her of sandalwood and cedar. Chanelle wondered uneasily if, now that his wife and child were not present, he was about to give her a blast for interfering in their business.

Why *hadn't* she minded her own business? The cruise hadn't even begun, and already she was feeling a surge of anxiety. She took a deep breath, bracing herself for a verbal onslaught.

And then his brows unfurrowed. "Have you considered applying for a job on the ship, watching over the children?" he said with a quirk of a smile, blue eyes crinkling at the corners. "I don't believe this cruise line comes equipped with a guardian angel."

Chanelle blinked, distracted by the way the turquoise of his eyes had darkened to lapis and not knowing how or what she should reply. She patted her hair down self-consciously. It had been rather humid in Tampa, and in such conditions, her hair had a tendency to fluff out and get frizzy.

Her emotions at this moment felt just as frizzy, with the unnerving way that he was gazing at her...

"I—I was just trying to prevent a tragedy," she said, unable to keep the defensiveness out of her voice. She straightened, trying to boost her confidence. She was not going to let this—*this womanizer*—try to appease her with his charm. How many other women had he referred to as an angel? "And I'm not sorry I interfered," she added, jutting out her chin.

He stared at her wordlessly for a moment, his eyes narrowing, before shifting his gaze to her engagement ring. His jaw muscles flickered and he seemed lost in thought, and Chanelle had to resist the urge to whip her hand behind her back. Finally he looked up, and pinned her with a curious gaze. "Your fiancé is a helluva lucky guy to have such a caring wife-to-be. He won't have to worry about your future children, with *you* protecting them like a lioness." He gave a husky laugh and then stared at her intensely. "So tell me, since this is a Zodiac cruise, *are you* a Leo?"

Vance watched the extraordinarily long eyelashes of the woman opposite him flutter over green-hazel eyes that sparkled like gemstones. Her glossy lips parted briefly and then shut, drawing his eyes to their perfect dimensions—not too thin and not too wide. And from having observed her stature as he approached—or more specifically, the way she fit into her white jeans and fuchsia T-shirt—it was obvious she either worked out or was just born lucky. He watched as she ran her fingers through her lustrous auburn hair, the movement sending a hint of her perfume drifting toward him, a candy-like scent of raspberry and plum…

She blinked at him as if his question were the last thing she had expected to hear him say.

What the hell was he doing? He didn't really want to know her sign, did he? *No, of course not.*

Vance wished he could take the question back. It was something he might have asked in a more flirtatious situation. And he had no intention of flirting with this lovely but rather overreactive—*and engaged*—passenger. He shifted as a couple strode past them. He should have followed Mariah back to the stateroom immediately. And now he had to think of an appropriate way to end this—

"Sagittarius."

She said it defiantly, her green eyes flashing a silent warning.

He had no choice but to continue this now. "Ah…the Archer," he murmured. "The healer whose intelligence forms a bridge between earth and heaven." He raised an eyebrow. "Let me guess. You're either a nurse or a teacher…or in some kind of caring profession." He stroked his jaw. "Or I'm completely off the mark and you're an astrophysicist," he added with a chuckle.

She wrinkled up her face and rolled her eyes, an attempt—*possibly?*—to conceal her amusement. A tingling sensation spiraled through him. The dimples that had appeared briefly in her cheeks were charming. Whether he liked it or not, she was igniting feelings that he did not want ignited. He forced himself to come back to earth. "Well, are stars your thing, or what?" he said lightly.

Her lips parted, and she had that look of *Why would you even want to know?* She gave him a measured glance. "I don't have time for stargazing," she retorted, "and my job is much more down-to-earth. With no sparkle or glitter."

She hesitated for a moment, and her eyes seemed to darken. He caught the slight crease of her forehead before it disappeared.

"I'm a social worker," she said matter-of-factly. "In child protection." She took a deep breath, and her eyes seemed to blaze in the late-afternoon sunshine. Her mouth opened slightly as if she were about to say something more but then promptly closed again.

Vance surveyed her flushed cheeks. No wonder she had been so quick to act with Adrien. And he had been too quick to jump to the wrong conclusion, asking her why she was grabbing him... "Protectiveness is in the nature of a Sagittarius," he said gruffly, nodding.

She didn't respond, but something flickered in her green eyes before she lowered her gaze.

Vance knew that Adrien hadn't been in danger, but he could understand that from where she had been sitting, it had looked like Adrien was in a very vulnerable position. And she hadn't hesitated in reacting...

Something in Vance's gut told him that if Adrien *had* tumbled over, this vigilant Sagittarian would have plunged right in after him. He had seen that fierce protectiveness in her eyes as she had quickly reached out to stop him. Vance had no doubt that on the job or not, she saw herself as a champion of children, on constant alert to ensure their safety and well-being.

His gaze shifted again to her hands, where she was unconsciously twiddling her ring.

He felt his jaw tensing. "I should let you get back to your—"

Her head jerked up.

"Fiancé."

Her eyes shot green sparks at him before dropping to her left hand. "Thank you," she replied stiffly, her voice sounding far from grateful. She tossed her hair back and turned away.

It was quite the mane, he thought, watching the way the sun made her auburn hair look like copper gold. He had a sudden urge to run his fingers through it. And to talk to her longer, despite the voice in his head urging him not to.

"Hey, there," he called. He waited until she turned around and then flashed her a smile. "I realize I must have sounded harsh initially," he said. "I apologize. I'm protective, too, when it comes to family."

Her eyes widened. For a moment she said nothing and then shook her head dismissively. "No need to apologize. I probably should have minded my own business."

"Well, allow *me* to at least apologize for addressing you as 'Hey, there,'" he said, smiling. "I'm Vance. And I'd like to make it up to you by buying you a drink. What do you say, Miss—?"

She blinked at him wordlessly. When a few seconds had passed and she still had not responded, he frowned. "Is something the matter?" Was he imagining it, or was she giving him a look of disdain?

"I don't have drinks with married men," she said coolly. "And I believe you told your wife you'd join her shortly…"

Vance blinked, momentarily confused, but before he could reply and tell her he wasn't coming on to her, she had turned on her heels and disappeared.

Way to go, Kingston. How obtuse to be offering to buy a guest a drink, given that she was engaged and that she had presumed he was married. From the look on her face, it was obvious that she considered him a creep. Shaking his head, Vance headed inside and pressed the elevator button for the ship's upper level—Deck Thirteen.

He glanced at the time on his phone. The cruise director would soon be announcing the emergency assembly drill. All the passengers would be called to make their way to their assigned deck to undergo the required safety routine in the event of an emergency. And soon after that, the ship would set sail.

He had enough time to have a quick talk with Mariah and Adrien and then relax with a glass of wine at the Mercury Bar on Deck Ten. No, he would head to the bar first. Mariah would probably be wondering what was taking him so long, but until she texted, he was just going to take advantage of having some time to himself.

As the elevator opened on Deck Eight, Vance caught a flash of auburn hair among a group of people walking down the hall. He felt his pulse jack up. And then another flash of fuchsia above snug-fitting white jeans. It *was* her. He smiled apologetically when he realized that several elderly women were waiting for him to move to the back of the elevator so they could enter.

Moments later, Vance leaned back in a lounging chair in the Mercury Bar, savoring one of the ship's premium wines. It would kick off his week-long holiday after an intense nine months taking over Zodiac Cruises, his parents' company. Even though he had initially balked when his mother had mentioned plans for a special cruise to formally hand over the reins of the company to him, Vance was looking forward to finally having some time to unwind.

Nine months ago, the life Vance had known and enjoyed had shattered. His father had had a heart attack after a family dinner. Before he had taken his last breaths, he had managed to tell his family that he loved them.

Vance swallowed hard. The man who had spent so much

time away from home—and had relinquished parenting to build his business—had looked at him with piercing clarity for a few moments and rasped, "I'm sorry, son. For everything I said or didn't say to you. For not being there for you as you were growing up. I… I wanted to build the company for my family. Now I leave it in your hands… Will you take it on, son?"

Vance had felt a sharp twinge in his own chest at his father's words, and he had instinctively realized that he needed to forgive his father. The wall he had constructed around his heart over the years, brick by brick, had to give. But something had lodged in Vance's throat, preventing him from expressing any feelings, and when his father passed seconds later, Vance was flooded by guilt that he had not given his father the satisfaction of knowing that he had forgiven him—or at least that he would try to forgive him— and that he would carry on with the company.

That was what his dad had always wanted, to have him working alongside him, learning the ropes and eventually taking over when he decided to retire. But Vance had balked from the beginning, always feeling a disconnect with the man who had barely been around in his youth.

And how could the concrete barrier around his heart even begin to give after decades of reinforcement? His father's quickly uttered words to him as he approached the end of his life were too little and too late.

Getting involved in the company had been the furthest thing from Vance's mind. In high school, when his father had urged him—on one of his rare home visits—to do his community service hours at Zodiac Cruises' headquarters, Vance had declined, preferring to volunteer at a nearby art gallery. His time there had reinforced his interest in the art world, and the sketches he had shown his father to prove his intentions to pursue art at university had met with barely concealed scorn.

"You've got to be joking." His father's sharp laugh as he had tossed Vance's scrapbook aside dismissively had struck him as if he had lunged a fist into his chest. Vance still remembered how he had wobbled backward a couple of steps, slack-jawed and speechless.

"Are you telling me you'd rather be a starving artist?" His father's eyes, resembling gray storm clouds, had bored into Vance. "Don't be a fool." And then he had abruptly left, telling his wife that he had lost his appetite and wasn't going to stay for dinner.

Vance winced at the memory. His father had been harsh with him, but Vance had refused to buckle and eventually graduated with a master of fine arts degree, receiving the highest honors and a substantial monetary prize from the department. His mother had been at his graduation ceremony, and the look of pride in her glistening eyes had moved him, but her effusive words of praise and congratulations could not make up for the fact that his father had not bothered to show up.

Within a few months, a prestigious art gallery in Toronto's historic Distillery District had hired Vance as assistant curator, and his work there, along with his travels, had kept him quite occupied, with very little time to visit his mother save for the occasional Sunday dinner.

The dinner that had proven to be his father's last had turned out to be the same as previous occasions—the atmosphere tinged with tension, stilted conversation and a formality that was never present when he was alone with his mother. Seeing his father—whom he had always categorized as tough and uncompromising—reduced to such a vulnerable and conciliatory state had been a shock. His father's deathbed request had immobilized him, and Vance had barely had time to process the request before his father passed.

Vance took a gulp of wine. He had never wanted to get involved in the family business, but the irony was that after the funeral, Vance had spent every waking moment trying to prove himself worthy of following in his father's footsteps. For his mother's sake, he had tried to convince himself repeatedly. He was doing it for her, to keep the business running as smoothly as possible. And maybe to assuage the guilt that had surfaced knowing he hadn't given his father the satisfaction of a positive response to his last request as he had taken his last breaths.

And to do the job properly, it meant that he had had to temporarily give up the lifestyle he had previously enjoyed, which his father had not approved of. And his job at the art gallery.

It had been too late to make a vow to his father, but not too late for Vance to carry out his promise to himself.

So for the last nine months, Vance had worked twelve-hour days at headquarters in Toronto and had undertaken several cruises, mentored by every department head of Zodiac Cruises. He had been surprised at how much he had enjoyed learning the workings of the business, and he had started to think of ways that he could put his art and history background to good use in the company...

His mother had planned *this* cruise to officially acknowledge Vance in his new position. "Your father wanted this, remember?" she had reminded him several times when he had claimed that he didn't have time. "His dream was to pass the reins as president of Zodiac Cruises over to you himself one day..."

Vance felt a fresh stab of grief and the familiar swirl of guilt in his gut. What had he really known about his father's dreams? His feelings toward his father were so convoluted. He was sure that he had felt every possible emotion when it came to his dad: bitterness, disappointment, abandonment, even hate in his adolescent years. He had never understood the man…a man who had chosen work over family.

What's done is done, he told himself. He had another drink of his wine and willed the memory of his father's last moments to vanish. As soon as that image had dissipated, green-hazel eyes flashed in Vance's memory. Why did his thoughts keep returning to *her*? For nine months, he had stayed clear of women, focused entirely on the company. He hadn't agreed to take a break and go on this cruise with the notion of resuming his past lifestyle…

And yet he had impulsively told her he'd like to buy her a drink. What the hell had he been thinking? And he had completely ignored the clear fact that she was engaged. Vance scowled. It was obvious that his playboy habits hadn't been completely extinguished…

He couldn't help wondering what her fiancé was like. Did he run his fingers through that blaze of hair? Did it get wild and tangled when they—?

Taking a deep breath, Vance forced the image out of his mind. He should have never agreed to this cruise. It was frivolous, considering the projects that needed his attention back at Zodiac headquarters…

Vance rolled his neck to one side and then the other. Maybe after the emergency drill, he'd relax in his private whirlpool. He felt tense around his shoulders, and the warm jets would be a welcome relief… A bit later on, he'd either order room service for dinner or they could dine at one of the specialty restaurants if Mariah preferred.

And then they would proceed to the Milky Way Theater, where the ship's troupe of dancers and singers would be performing a medley of songs from the '60s to the '80s.

Classic hits from iconic singers. It was a great first-night show, and he would be giving a brief welcome to the audience before it started.

And maybe the Sagittarian might not be there to distract him…

CHAPTER TWO

CHANELLE STOOD BY the railing on Deck Eleven, her gaze shifting from the lapping waters of the bay to the magenta-and-gold sunset as the Tampa Bay skyline receded in the distance. She had decided against joining the cruise director and other staff and the probable swarm of guests at the Sail Away party on Deck Twelve after the emergency drill. She wasn't in the mood to mingle just yet…

Chanelle closed her eyes, letting the repetitive sound of the waves soothe her. Her thoughts were interrupted by a soft giggle in a far-off corner. Two darkened forms exchanged a kiss and wandered off hand in hand. She sighed. Could she not have picked a holiday where she wouldn't be reminded at every turn of her failed relationship?

She bit her lip. Much as she had wanted to blame Parker for not being sensitive enough to her work commitments, she had had to face the truth: that she had invested more time and energy in her job and not enough with him.

"I've met somebody at the gym…" He had dropped the bombshell seven months ago. And he'd told her he would be back the next day to get his things. Everything but the engagement ring he had given her.

If all had worked out with Parker, she might have been planning her wedding now, or even enjoying her honeymoon…instead of cruising alone, Chanelle mused, taking a deep breath.

But it hadn't worked out, and she had to admit—if she were to be totally honest—that she was relieved.

Not that she had felt that way at first.

Hurt and feeling betrayed, she had wanted to analyze what had gone wrong with their relationship and had checked out the self-help section of a local bookstore. One title had immediately caught her eye, as Parker had often accused her of being overly sensitive. And soon after delving into the book, Chanelle had discovered that she had many of the traits that the book identified…some that she had been aware of and some—she had realized in wonder—that she had exhibited even in childhood.

She'd also learned things she hadn't known: that highly sensitive people had nervous systems that were more easily activated by sensory stimuli. Which had explained why certain smells were unbearable, or why intense sunlight or loud music or people could be so jarring…and why her skin couldn't tolerate certain fabrics. No lace or wool for her! Or most synthetic materials. All this had illuminated her as to why she'd ended up with a skin rash or migraine at times…

Chanelle had learned that highly sensitive people—or HSPs—processed their experiences and feelings with greater depth and emotional intensity.

Given such sensitivities—not only physical, but emotional also—was it any wonder that her line of work had pushed her coping mechanisms to the max? And that Parker hadn't been able to cope? The book had outlined how challenging it could be for others to understand and empathize with an HSP. It was challenging enough for an HSP to deal with their sensitivities, and relationships could present even greater testing grounds…

Her relationship with Parker hadn't passed the test. Neither one of them had been solely to blame, though. She had been too focused on her work—there was no denying that—but Parker could have at least been honest with her and broken things off *before* getting involved with someone else. That would have been the *decent* thing to do.

And it had been this last thought that had finally convinced Chanelle that Parker hadn't been the right man for her. After the initial shock and sting of betrayal, Chanelle had accepted the fact that Parker was not the guy she was meant to have a happy-ever-after with.

He had betrayed her trust. She deserved better.

This realization had come before the acknowledgment that she had burned out on her job. And her parents, who were on the other side of the globe on an extended trip to visit relatives in Australia, hadn't been there to comfort her for either her breakup with Parker or her lingering emotional distress after a traumatic case involving two siblings and their neglectful parents. Meredith, Chanelle's employer, had kindly advised her to consider a leave even months before this particular case, having observed the classic signs of burnout becoming more prevalent in Chanelle. But Chanelle had insisted she was fine, telling herself that she needed her work more than ever after Parker had left…

She had been wrong, of course. She should have heeded Meredith's advice from the beginning. Chanelle sighed. After consulting with her doctor, Chanelle had taken a leave, "to be assessed on a regular basis." This was not a sign of weakness, her doctor had asserted gently, but a step toward ensuring her emotional well-being. Having a job that dealt with the trauma of others required particular diligence in maintaining physical and emotional health and balance in one's own life.

Enough! Chanelle was tired of thinking of the circumstances that had brought her here. And she needed to keep Parker out of her thoughts. She didn't want him on this cruise with her. She was over him.

She had tucked the engagement ring he had left her in her purse months ago and had slipped it on her finger momentarily, wondering what she was going to do with it. And then, before she could put it back in her purse, she had become distracted by the incident with the child and his distracted father.

Perhaps what she really hadn't gotten over was the fact that another man had dumped her. The first one had been her biological father. Her mother had revealed the story to her when she had felt Chanelle was ready. His name was Trevor, and upon hearing that his girlfriend Katie—Chanelle's mother—was pregnant, he had promptly broken up with her, claiming the baby wasn't his. He had accepted a job out of town right after college graduation and never returned, leaving Katie heartbroken. Fortunately, Chanelle's grandparents hadn't abandoned Katie, and Chanelle had grown up missing a father in her formative years, but living with a set of grandparents who cherished her.

She had just turned twelve when her mother married a furniture dealer called Martin, and although Chanelle had initially been reluctant to trust him—there had been a couple of men Katie had dated before him who had caused Chanelle some anxiety—Martin's easy and joking manner and obvious devotion to her mother eventually won her over. Chanelle's faith in men had been temporarily restored, but now she had to admit to herself that Parker's decision to break up had stirred up a flurry of latent feelings that could be associated with her father's rejection of her. Her social work and psychology studies had not been for nothing, she thought, her mood darkening as she watched the swirling waters from the deck.

Two men had abandoned her. One, her father, who hadn't even wanted to acknowledge that he'd had anything to do with her conception. Who had chosen to run away from his responsibilities to her and her mother. And Parker, who had left her for another woman. Both had run away from the promise of what was to come—the birth of a baby and the birth of a marriage, respectively. Neither the baby nor the marriage had been given a chance...

Chanelle's work had helped take her mind off the latter. She had pushed herself to the limit, convincing herself that the children she was protecting, or rescuing from a parent or parents who were unfit, depended on her. And she had no intention of abandoning them.

She had tried to be a superwoman, she realized, and had driven herself into a state of burnout. And she was having a hard time coming to terms with not being able to do her job.

Who am I? She shook her head and gripped the deck railing. Her job had been everything to her. *What do I do now?*

Chanelle squeezed her eyes tightly at the prickly sensation behind her lids but wasn't able to stop a few tears from slipping down her cheeks.

"Hey, there..."

Chanelle didn't need to make the quarter turn to see who the approaching footsteps belonged to.

The distracted father/playboy.

"I can't have anyone on my ship looking so sad." He stopped a couple of feet away from her.

Had she heard correctly? *My ship?* No, it couldn't be...

Chanelle quickly wiped her eyes. How embarrassing that he had seen her in such a state. She looked beyond him, expecting to see his wife.

"Has something happened on board to upset you?"

Why did he care? And what could she possibly tell him?

"I—I'm okay," she managed, her voice wavering.

His eyes swooped down on her and narrowed. "No, you're not."

She stared at him, startled by his directness. Something

thudded in her chest. "It's not something I feel comfortable discussing with—"

"A total stranger?" He raised an eyebrow. "Look, you don't need to discuss anything with me. But now that I'm here, I'd like to set the record straight." He took a step closer. "I wasn't trying to come on to you earlier…and seeing someone in tears on a cruise concerns me."

Chanelle looked beyond him again, the butterflies in her stomach rising in a swirl. What would his wife think if she suddenly showed up? She took a step back. "I appreciate your concern, but you don't need to worry about me." Actually, she *didn't* appreciate his concern, but the words had left her mouth before she could stop them.

"The expression on your face worried me." He rested an arm on the railing and glanced at the water before meeting her gaze again. "It was more than sad—it was almost a look of desperation."

Chanelle's eyes widened as his words hit her. *Hard.* "You thought I was going to…" She glanced at the black depths of the bay. She had been momentarily sad, yes, but desperate, no. *No.*

"I would have stopped you," he said huskily. "Or dived in after you, new suit and all."

"You wouldn't have had to." She held up her chin defiantly, trying to prevent herself from gazing at him from the neck down.

His piercing blue eyes had a hawklike intensity, as if he were trying to determine if she was lying. "Good to know." His brow smoothed out. And then his eyes narrowed again. "I don't mean to pry, but if there is a problem between you and your…" He glanced at her ring finger.

It suddenly hit her. He had noticed her engagement ring during their first encounter…

His words struck a nerve. Chanelle bristled. Was this…

this Romeo…actually implying that she was having issues with her fiancé? What business did he have to butt into her life? She felt an inner heat surge through her veins and upward into her cheeks.

"Look, I hate to be blunt, but I don't appreciate you trying to find out if there is a problem in my relationship. It's really none of your business." She felt her cheeks tingle. Usually the precursor to their becoming flaming red. "And if you don't mean to pry, then don't."

"*Touché.* I apologize, Miss…or Ms.…"

She threw him an incredulous glance. Did he not realize that she didn't want to keep talking to him? He just raised his eyebrows and looked as unruffled as she was ruffled. It didn't help that a portion of her brain was registering how good-looking he was in his charcoal-gray suit and salmon-colored shirt and black tie. She heard herself sigh in frustration.

"Chanelle." There! Now maybe he'd go away and leave her alone.

He opened his mouth to respond but closed it when his cell phone buzzed. He retrieved it from his pocket to glance at it. He messaged back and then looked at Chanelle again. She moved away from the railing, and he did the same. Surely he didn't intend to follow her? She was planning to head over to the Ristorante Mezza Luna for dinner, having made reservations at this specialty restaurant when she had booked her cruise, deciding that she deserved to pamper herself.

And after this double encounter with this playboy, Chanelle was anxious to start relaxing. She nodded dismissively and walked toward the glass doors, deciding to freshen up in her stateroom before heading to the restaurant. She saw his reflection and felt her stomach muscles tighten. Inside, the lights of the chandeliers made her blink.

She headed to the elevator, and when she turned, her heart jolted. Vance was striding toward her, but his phone buzzed again and he slowed down to glance at it. Chanelle hurried into the elevator, but before the door closed, she saw him glance up and across at her, his eyes glittering like the chandelier crystals above his head.

Mariah had texted Vance the first time to say that she was almost ready. He had laughed inwardly. His sister's sense of time was faulty at best. "Almost ready" could mean "I need another half hour." But she had surprised him with her second text that she was in the restaurant and had already ordered them drinks.

Vance had messaged her that he needed a few extra minutes.

He glanced at the closed elevator doors before striding over to a recliner near a lounging nook and thought about what had just happened with Chanelle.

Chanelle… What a soft, feminine name. A name fit for an angel, except that there had been nothing angelic about the look she had flung at him.

Why had she appeared so dejected when he had first spotted her? His heart had begun to thump against his rib cage when he had seen her gripping the railing in that isolated corner of the deck… And at the sight of the tears glistening on her cheeks, the thump had turned into a hammer. He had been ready to leap toward her, and then she had turned to look at him…

Relief had swirled through him like an electric current. He had wanted to wrap his arms around her—an irrational impulse, considering he didn't know her, but he couldn't deny that he had felt a surge of protectiveness that had stunned him.

He had immediately noticed that she wasn't wearing her

ring, which was why he had presumed that she and her fiancé had had some kind of disagreement, or maybe even a fight. No wonder she was sad, especially if she was having problems in her relationship. Had she ended the engagement? Had *he*? Vance's jaw tensed at the thought that Chanelle's ex-fiancé might have cheated on her. Maybe that was why she seemed so irritated with *him*. Maybe she was projecting her anger and hurt on him or any other male who crossed her path or even looked at her the wrong way...

But why was this Chanelle taking up so much space in his thoughts? He squeezed his eyes shut for a moment, then relaxed them. Tensed his shoulders, then let go. He did this a few times, and after a few deep breaths, he opened his eyes.

Vance checked the time and sprang to his feet. He had kept Mariah waiting far too long. At the entrance of the Ristorante Mezza Luna, the maître d' greeted him and led him to a far table, where Mariah was already enjoying a glass of white wine and a plate of cheeses and spiced olives. "Sorry I'm late, sis," he said with a rueful smile. He sat down, and after the waiter had filled his glass, he explained what had happened earlier with Chanelle, reassuring Mariah that Adrien had never been in danger. "How is the little munchkin?"

"Adrien's having room service with Mom, then they're going to watch a movie and go to bed early," Mariah said.

Vance nodded and took a drink of his wine.

"Don't look now, Vance!" Mariah lowered her voice to a whisper. "There's the lady who couldn't mind her own business."

Vance set down his wineglass and tried to ignore the skip of his heart beat. "Mariah, I told you, she was just worried—"

"Okay, okay. I can't fault her for that, *Sir Vancelot*."

She chuckled as he rolled his eyes at her childhood nickname for him.

Vance turned casually. Chanelle hadn't spotted him. She was smiling brightly at the maître d' and nodding. She had changed from casual wear to a long magenta skirt with a shimmer of sequins along its flaring hem and a body-hugging black top that accentuated her slender neck and feminine curves. The maître d' led her directly toward the table next to his and Mariah's.

Mariah's phone rang, and Vance could hear that it was his mother's voice on the other end.

Chanelle suddenly stopped walking. Vance met her incredulous gaze. He held up his glass and nodded with a polite smile. It was obvious from the rosy hue of her cheeks that she was flustered to be seated so close to *him*. And Mariah.

Chanelle gave a brief nod and looked away, focusing on what the maître d' was telling her about the wine selections. She murmured her choice, and he nodded. "Certainly, Miss Robinson."

Vance didn't know if it was the wine or the discovery of Chanelle's last name that ignited a shiver of heat inside him. He said it under his breath. Chanelle Robinson. He liked the way it sounded. Soft. Silky. Just like that mane of hair tumbling over her shoulders.

The next time his glance coincided with Chanelle's, he flashed a smile and nodded. Her eyes fluttered briefly, and she responded with a nod that made him think of a robin giving a tentative peck at the grass. Her cheeks were now almost as red as a robin's breast, and the way her arms lifted and then dropped helplessly made it clear to him that if she could fly away, she would.

"Mom says Adrien feels a little warm. Probably too much excitement today," she murmured, arching her eyebrows in Chanelle's direction. "I'm going to check on him. If he's okay, I'll meet you in the theater."

Vance stood up and met Chanelle's eyes. Even in the dimmed lighting of the restaurant, they were stunning, their green-hazel depths looking like a mystical pool from an enchanted land.

"I hope you're enjoying Mezza Luna's fine offerings, Miss—Chanelle," he said as they approached her table. He gave her a casual smile. "Oh, and please allow me to introduce you. Chanelle Robinson, this is Mariah Kingston... my sister."

CHAPTER THREE

CHANELLE STRUGGLED TO keep her surprise in check. *His sister?* And how did he know her last name? Oh, yes, the maître d' had said it…

Feeling awkward at the realization that she was just blinking back at him, Chanelle turned and offered a tentative smile to his sister.

Mariah held out her elegantly manicured hand. "Nice to meet you. *Again.*" She blew her brother a kiss. "I'm going to go and check on Mom and Adrien and then head to the Milky Way Theater. See you in a bit, *Sir Vancelot.*"

Chanelle watched her leave, a petite swirl of pink silk and ivory linen above shapely legs and stiletto heels that Chanelle wouldn't hazard to wear. When she had walked into the restaurant and had caught sight of Mariah sitting across from Vance, something in Chanelle's chest had deflated, and she had considered making an excuse to the maître d' and filing out of the restaurant. The last thing Chanelle had counted on was bumping into the both of them so soon after the earlier incident…

Discovering that the lady he was with was his sister and not his wife had caused a thumping against her rib cage that almost made her look down at her chest self-consciously.

Vance put his hand on the chair opposite her. "May I?" he said, his blue eyes appearing more like indigo in the muted light of the restaurant.

"Um…" She glanced from him to the waiter. "Okay," she replied slowly, irritated both by his question and by the way her pulse had spiked.

How could she tell him, with the waiter standing right there, that she had been looking forward to a quiet dinner?

Despite feeling flustered, Chanelle couldn't help thinking how drop-dead gorgeous he looked in his gray suit with the salmon-colored shirt making a striking contrast with the extraordinary purple-blue of his eyes. They reminded her of the rich hue of the delphiniums in her summer garden.

"Will you be joining Miss Robinson for a glass of white wine, sir?" the waiter asked Vance, naming the vintage she had selected.

Vance nodded his approval. "I could tell you were a woman of good taste," he said, flashing Chanelle a smile. "May I join you?"

Chanelle hesitated before giving a curt nod.

Vance turned his gaze back to the waiter. "Put it on my tab, Luciano."

Chanelle gazed from one to the other and opened her mouth to protest, but Vance put up his hand firmly. "That wasn't necessary, Mr.…Vance," she said when the waiter had left.

"No it wasn't, Miss *Chanelle*." He leaned forward. "It's just my way of thanking you for looking out for Adrien."

Chanelle frowned. "You weren't too pleased about me getting involved earlier."

He clasped his hands under his chin and gazed at her squarely. "I admit I may have overreacted." His eyes glinted. "I'm sorry. Can you find it in your heart to forgive me?"

Chanelle was at a loss for words. From the slightly amused tone of his voice, she didn't know whether he was being genuine or mocking her. And at the same time, she was trying to process the fact that he wasn't married after all, that Adrien was his nephew, and that his earlier offer of buying her a drink wasn't the act of an unfaithful womanizer.

Which meant that she had overreacted as well.

So maybe you should apologize, too, her inner voice suggested. *And if this hunk wants to treat you, let him! You have a choice—you can tell him to take a flying leap, or let him spend his money on you... Live a little! And if he flirts with you, give it back to him. You've forgotten how to have fun, girl!*

As she framed some words of apology in her mind, the waiter reappeared with the wine. Vance tasted and approved a sample and nodded for the waiter to fill their two glasses. He held his glass up and waited for Chanelle to clink hers with his, but she ignored his cue and went ahead and took a sip.

"Mmm..." Chanelle closed her eyes momentarily, unable to control a little shiver. She was entering into unknown waters, she warned herself. She felt her nerve endings tingle and realized she could either take this opportunity to enjoy the cruise, or leave it...

The excitement stirring in her stomach gave her the answer. She wasn't going to mope around anymore. She was going to loosen up a little. She had always been too serious growing up and had proceeded with caution in every aspect of her life, even when she had left home. Chanelle breathed in deeply, her chest expanding, and she felt like a Sagittarian warrior, ready to rise up to anything or anyone. Especially one like the Dionysus sitting across from her, twirling his wineglass with a gleam in his bewitching blue eyes.

Vance looked at Chanelle as the waiter asked her if she had decided on her entrée. She chose a seafood risotto, and

Vance decided to order the same for himself. "Excellent choice, Chanelle. It's one of my favorites," he said after the waiter had left. Chanelle paused, her eyes widening as if she had just realized that he was not going to be leaving after he finished his wine. And the slight flutter of those long lashes made him wonder how she was feeling about that…

"This is even better than the wine I had in my room." Chanelle's words came out in a rush. "And I thought that one was superb. I must say I'm impressed with the perks on this cruise. The complimentary gift basket was such a lovely surprise, with the scrumptious chocolates and all those other goodies." She flashed him a smile before taking another generous sip of wine, her eyes a combination of amber and emerald as they blinked at him above the rim of her glass.

Vance certainly hadn't expected this…this about-face. But then maybe Chanelle was trying to drown her sorrows, the sorrows of a broken relationship…

"Cheers, *Sir Vancelot*," she said with a tinkling laugh as she raised her glass and cocked her head at him, her hair cascading down like a shimmering curtain. His heart did a flip, and he had to stop himself from extending his hand to let her rest her head against it.

Vance gazed at Chanelle's flushed cheeks and long eyelashes. He had no illusions that they were fluttering for *his* benefit, yet he couldn't help being mesmerized by their languorous movements, allowing him glimpses of the heady hazel depths of her eyes.

He coughed, and feigned a frown. "Now don't *you* go calling me by that silly name, Chanelle. My sister likes to torment me occasionally with it, with maybe just a *little* less frequency than when we were kids and playing with my medieval castle." His eyes narrowed. "I'm neither a sir nor a chivalrous knight."

Chanelle gave him a shy smile that made his stomach muscles contract. "You were ready to rescue me earlier... That proves you're chivalrous." She averted her gaze to help herself to an olive and immediately exclaimed at its spiciness. She ran her tongue over her lips and fanned them with her hand.

As Vance watched her mouth, a spiral of heat flicked throughout his body. The waiter set down their plates, and after thanking him, Chanelle gave a self-conscious shrug and dug into her risotto. Vance suppressed a smile. It was refreshing to see a woman enjoy food, unlike a couple of the willowy high-fashion models he had dated who had pretended to be happy with a few pieces of lettuce and a couple of carrot sticks.

"Are you a pescatarian?" he wondered aloud.

"No. I just stay away from red meat."

"So no bacon for you."

"I'm into *baking*, not bacon." She laughed, lifting her wineglass to her lips.

He grinned. "Since you've ventured into the world of puns, perhaps you should consider a job in comedy..."

The humor suddenly disappeared from Chanelle's face. Her eyelids fluttered briefly, and she stared down at her plate. He saw her jaw muscles flexing. When she looked back up, her eyes were glistening.

Vance set down his glass. "I'm sorry, Chanelle. Did I say something wrong?"

She put her fork down. "No, I'm... I'm..." She shook her head. "I'm just a little down about my job." She cocked her head at him as if she were trying to ascertain whether she could trust him to tell him more.

"It's a tough job," he said gently. "Dealing with vulnerable children and harsh situations day in and day out. I can only imagine—"

"I thought I would last longer than this…"

"You left?"

"I'm on a leave. Burnout." She sighed. "I love kids, I love seeing bad situations turn out for the better, but it hasn't always worked out that way…and it has affected me off the job as well."

"You're only human." He controlled his impulse to reach out and tap her reassuringly on her arm. "It's obvious you care, and with your background, it's no wonder you were alarmed when you saw Adrien on that chair. Your devotion to children is admirable," he added softly.

"I'm too devoted, according to my fiancé." She bit her lower lip and leaned back. "I mean my ex-fiancé. He broke off our engagement."

"I'm sorry to hear that," he murmured. "You've been through a lot."

"I have to take some of the responsibility," she said, her mouth twisting. "I spent too much time working."

And her fiancé hadn't liked it.

Vance watched as Chanelle slumped forward, her chin resting in one hand. Her earlier levity was gone, and he suspected the wine might have had something to do with her shift in emotions. He couldn't imagine her spilling all this personal stuff to him otherwise.

He glanced at his watch and sprang out of his seat. "I'm sorry to cut this short, Chanelle, but I have to be somewhere else. Five minutes ago, actually," he added ruefully. "I'll let you enjoy your dessert in peace. By the way, will you be catching the opening night's performance in the Milky Way Theater?"

"I—I…maybe," she said cautiously before picking up her fork again to dig into her risotto.

"Okay then," he said slowly, nodding. "Maybe I'll see you there. *Arrivederci.*"

Vance glanced at her left hand. He was about to add something and then decided against it. Feeling a strange tug in his stomach muscles, he rose and left.

Vance sprinted toward the theater. He had been totally absorbed—*distracted*—with Chanelle Robinson. Thank goodness he had looked at his watch or he would have been inexcusably late, missing his cue to address the guests on this special cruise.

In five minutes, the cruise director would be welcoming the crowd, then he'd be introducing him, and Vance would share the reason he and his family were on board the *Aquarius*. They had decided to keep it from the media and had simply wanted to have a relatively small celebration of Vance's official position as president. They had decided on a five-day cruise just to relax, mingle with their invited guests—who had promised to keep the event under wraps—and have a gala evening midweek, when Vance's mother would announce her retirement and formally pass over the business to Vance.

The uninvited guests were in for a surprise, for the gala would be open to them also, in appreciation for their patronage and, for some, their loyalty in returning to Zodiac Cruises for a holiday. In fact, what seemed to be trending was for Zodiac faithfuls to book a different Zodiac ship each time they cruised. Vance had already met a group of nine forty-something women who had already cruised on four of the ships in the fleet. They had been friends since high school, and although they didn't all live in the same town, they reunited every year for their one-week cruise.

Vance had smiled at them earlier in the lobby of the art gallery. As he had strolled by, he had heard one of them whisper, "He doesn't have a ring. He must be unattached…" And one of her friends had chortled. "Lucky gal who gets to attach themselves to *that*. I'll be having sweet dreams tonight…and of course, *I'll* be the lucky gal." And at the resounding laughter, he had stifled a chuckle and had gone to chat with the art rep.

Now, entering the slightly dimmed theater, Vance looked around. Spotting Mariah, he made his way to the third row in the orchestra section. Mariah smiled at him and continued checking her messages on her cell phone. Vance sat back and thought about what the ladies had said.

"He must be unattached."

Well, they were right. For the most part. At the moment he was not seeing anyone. His last relationship had fizzled out after his father had died. Brianna was a wealthy socialite his mother had invited over one night, someone she had thought might be a good match for Vance. They had seen each other for several months, but Vance hadn't been ready for a serious commitment, and Brianna *had*.

If she had been the right one, wouldn't he have wanted to settle down?

His mother had hinted more than once—and not too subtly—that perhaps he should start trying to find someone who could become more permanent in his life. He was thirty-four, after all, and didn't he get tired of dating one beautiful woman after another? Vance smirked at the memory of the comment she had made once—that he changed women as often as he changed cars.

"You're not getting any younger, son, and neither am I. I don't expect to have grandchildren when I'm too old to be able to lift them. Or play with them."

Occasionally she had taken a sterner approach, pinning him with her steel-blue eyes.

"You can't be a playboy all your life, Vance. It's time to get serious…serious about settling down."

Vance had instinctively known that his mother had felt responsible for indulging him and his sister in all ways.

They had grown up spoiled and entitled, he had heard her complain to his father, and now they expected that lifestyle to continue.

Especially Vance. At least Mariah had married and blessed her with a grandson. She could be high-maintenance at times, but being a parent had tamed her somewhat. Now Vance, on the other hand…

A week after his mother had voiced her concerns, his father had died. And the lifestyle Vance had known had come abruptly to a halt. There were matters to take care of, both personal and business, and his mother had been too distraught to deal with any of them. It had been left to Vance to make the funeral arrangements and to be the strong shoulder for both his mother and sister.

Brianna had expressed sympathy, but she was used to a certain pace in her life, and she had expected Vance to keep up with her high-profile social events and private parties a few weeks after the funeral.

But the passing of his father had taken the desire for partying right out of Vance. The immensity of his father's responsibilities and the esteem in which his business associates had held him had made Vance acutely aware that *his* involvement in the company had been peripheral at best. And when it had been time for the last goodbyes, and his mother, sister, brother-in-law and nephew had walked away, Vance had stayed behind to quietly reiterate the vow he had failed to make to his father before he died.

Soon after, when he had told Brianna about his intentions and that he couldn't make a firm commitment, Brianna had skipped out of his life.

Vance checked the time on his phone. One minute before the show… He glanced at Mariah and saw that she was texting her husband, who hadn't been able to join them on the cruise, as he was tending to business in Europe.

Vance glanced around and was pleased to see that the theater was filling quickly. His eyes narrowed as he searched the moving groups for a sign of Chanelle. And then he checked himself.

Why did he even care if she attended the opening or not?

The orchestra started up, and a minute later, cruise director Jake Ross walked out on stage. At his cue, Vance strode to the side door that led to the stage and waited for Jake's intro. Jake warmed up the audience with his jokes and stories about funny experiences onboard, and when the laughter had subsided, his tone became more serious.

"Ladies and gentlemen, I have the distinct pleasure of welcoming you to the *Aquarius* and to our opening night show here in the beautiful Milky Way Theater. You are in for a few surprises this week, starting with the man you are going to meet shortly. He is someone who has taken on the monumental task of leadership of Zodiac Cruises these past nine months since the passing of Mr. Bruce Kingston—Zodiac's founder and president—proving with his unreserved determination, razor-sharp focus and relentless efforts and inexhaustible energy that he has everything it takes not only to continue in his father's fine footsteps, but to leap beyond. He will reveal his vision for the company during this cruise, and I am sure that you will be as excited as the staff of the *Aquarius* and of the entire fleet of Zodiac Cruise ships to hear about his initiatives and to celebrate during this special cruise." He turned toward his right and extended a hand. "And now, please join me in welcoming Mr. Vance Kingston, acting president and co-owner of Zodiac Cruises!"

Vance stepped out to a resounding applause. He was moved by Jake's words and the crowd's enthusiasm, and after thanking them for their presence and participation in a Zodiac cruise, he explained why he was there, and what they would be in for.

At the loud cheers of approval and whistles, he gave a bow, and when he raised his head, his gaze landed on a guest who was just sitting down on the far end of a middle row in the right-hand section of the theater.

Chanelle...

Had she arrived in time to hear him from the beginning? He pulled his gaze away from her. Ordinarily, he had no problem addressing a large crowd, but somehow, knowing she was there, he suddenly felt awkward. He hadn't told her anything about himself, and he couldn't help wondering if she'd be feeling awkward as well when she realized who he was.

He finished up his address and thanked the audience again. His gaze swept casually over the crowd, and for a few seconds, Chanelle seemed to be looking straight at him. As the orchestra started up with a musical number that would take the audience through decades of Broadway theater productions, Vance strode off the stage, the cue for the *Aquarius* dancers to appear.

He and Mariah had chosen seats near the front on the left-hand section of the theater. Vance was too far away from where Chanelle was sitting to even get a glimpse of her. As he sat down, he exchanged smiles with Mariah, who squeezed his arm in approval. The chandeliers were dimmed, and the dancers burst onto the stage in a swirl of sequins, lights and music. Vance sat back in the plush seat to take in the spectacular opening, but as the dancers spun past, it was a pair of hazel-green eyes that danced before him...

CHAPTER FOUR

CHANELLE HAD ALMOST made up her mind to call it an early night after her dinner and go back to her stateroom. She knew that she had indulged in more wine than usual, and she had been aware that her responses to Vance had been less careful as a result. It made her cringe to think of how she had giggled and made a ridiculous remark about him being chivalrous. And how she had called him Sir Vancelot. And if that wasn't bad enough, she had nattered on about her job and her past.

By the time she had finished the restaurant's signature tiramisu, Chanelle had felt like she could easily go straight to bed. Her appetite had been quelled in the most decadent way, and the rich food and the wine had made her quite mellow. The restaurant had almost filled to capacity and the alternating levels of voices had started to become overwhelming.

She had been wondering whether she could handle sitting for over an hour in the Milky Way Theater when her eyes had started to droop. It had been an emotional day in more ways than one, and she had debated whether she could even take the sensory stimulation of the opening night performance when all she wanted to do was lie on her bed with the balcony door open and listen to the relaxing sound of the waves...

But Vance Kingston will be there, remember?

Chanelle had smiled and thanked the waiter. As she had walked out, the image of Vance's inky-blue eyes as he had said earlier, "Maybe I'll see you there," had made her stop in her tracks. It might have been a totally casual statement, but the thought of encountering Vance again had made her heartbeat quicken, even if he'd be there with his sister.

Why was he on this cruise with his family? Was it a special birthday for his mother? Chanelle had wondered if she'd get the chance to find out more about Vance on the cruise.

She had kept walking, her steps suddenly lighter, her drowsiness gone. Outside the restaurant, she had checked the time. The show had started at nine, and she had already missed ten minutes. But a glance toward the theater doors had confirmed that people were still filing in. She had heard laughter from the audience, and the thought had occurred to her that it might do her a world of good to laugh, especially after spending the last few months dealing with the reality of job burnout and, a couple of months before that, her broken engagement with Parker.

Chanelle's counselor had encouraged her to find opportunities to lighten up her life with events that would bring her joy and laughter. She needed to balance her life, have more fun…

At the next peal of laughter, Chanelle had ignored the voice in her head that told her it had been a long day and she should just go to bed. She had followed a family into the theater and spotted an empty aisle seat to her right.

Settling in her seat, she had caught the last few minutes of the cruise director's comedy routine before he began his announcement. She had started at the mention of Mr. Bruce Kingston, and a few moments later, felt a greater jolt at hearing the name of Vance Kingston, "acting president and co-owner of Zodiac Cruises." Her gaze had riveted to the man walking across the stage.

Her Vance?

What a ridiculous thought. He was not *her* Vance. But he *was* co-owner of the cruise line. She had felt a flutter in her chest as she recalled his earlier words: *"I can't have anyone on my ship looking so sad..."* So she *had* heard correctly.

Chanelle had joined the rest of the audience in clapping their welcome, and when the noise had subsided, she could hear the thumping of her heart against her ribs. Even from a distance, the way he had looked in his tailored suit had caused her to draw in her breath, and her cheeks had flamed at the tingling that had begun navigating throughout her nerve pathways.

Three women in the row ahead of her had nudged each other and exchanged whispers about the "hunky owner" of the cruise line. Chanelle had difficulty trying to listen to Vance while overhearing descriptions about his sexy attributes.

She had been relieved when they had stopped their chatter and focused on what Vance was saying, allowing her to focus as well. She had listened to his deep voice welcoming the crowd, thanking them for having selected Zodiac Cruises for the very first time or for their loyalty in returning.

He had proceeded to give a summary of his father's vision and accomplishments, and then his voice had wavered for a moment when he declared that his focus was to keep his father's company thriving. As the audience responded with enthusiastic applause, Vance had scanned the theater with an intensity that made Chanelle's insides flip. Could he be searching for *her* in the crowd? she had mused. He *had* said, "Maybe I'll see you there..."

She had shaken her head at her silly presumption. Vance

Kingston was for all intents and purposes *president* of the cruise line. He had obviously just been showing her the courtesy he would have displayed to anyone else on the ship. But after her embarrassing behavior in the restaurant, she'd vowed to make every effort to avoid him.

And then she had frozen. For a moment, it had looked like Vance was staring right at her, and the applause and people around her had became muted as she held her breath at the possibility... And then he had shifted his gaze and continued speaking. He had promised the audience that they were in for some special perks and surprises on this particular cruise, and that the cruise director would keep them informed every day of what was happening, along with the daily bulletin they would be receiving.

Finally, Vance had thanked them again, told them to enjoy the opening show and, flashing the crowd a smile that elicited a couple of whistles, had walked off the stage.

Vance was nowhere to be seen as the crowd exited the theater, and Chanelle had to admit to herself that despite her vow to avoid him, she felt a little disappointed. She returned to her stateroom and had a quick shower, her earlier drowsiness completely gone. While her hair was drying, she searched online to see what she could find out about Vance Kingston. Chanelle discovered that he had been a person of interest in the world of the elite for quite a while, frequenting exotic locales and attending high-profile events— dealing with art, cars and entertainment—that attracted the rich and famous, many of them women.

Some of the headlines had proclaimed him to be one of Canada's most eligible bachelors, not only ruggedly handsome, but easygoing and extravagant, indulging in a variety of interests and activities all over the country. One week he'd be seen skiing in Whistler, British Columbia, among

Hollywood celebrities, and the next he'd be at some posh literary or art event in Toronto or at Montreal's jazz festival. From the look of any one of the women in his company, it was obvious that they were happy to share the spotlight with him.

After checking more recent sites, Chanelle learned that Vance Kingston had been employed as head of acquisitions at an art gallery in Toronto's Distillery District until the death of his father nine months earlier. Recent articles described him as almost reclusive now, totally focused on carrying on the family business.

Chanelle turned off her cell phone and ventured out on the balcony. She stared down at the water, swirling and cresting and catching the light of the moon in shiny arcs and squiggles. She could have stayed there longer, but her common sense reminded her that a good night's rest had been what her doctor and counselor had recommended.

Lying under the bedsheets with her balcony door partially open, Chanelle listened to the slurping water sounds and thought about the opening night show by the *Aquarius* singers and dancers. It had been spectacular and as dazzling as a top-rated Vegas show. But the image that kept returning to her mind was that of Vance Kingston. The way he had sounded, his voice velvet smooth. And the way he had looked, tall and male-model gorgeous, his golden-brown hair glinting under the spotlight. Flashing that killer smile at the audience that had made her stomach flip and scanning the crowd with brilliant blue eyes that she knew could change like the waves.

Seeing Vance up on that stage had been the first shock, and learning that he was soon to be the official president of Zodiac Cruises had been the second. The memory of him in that tailored suit and the sensual thrum of his voice as he had addressed the audience ignited a tingle throughout her body.

Although it was a balmy night, Chanelle shivered and pulled up the covers. She nestled into a side position, sinking into the comfortable pillow with a sigh. There *had* been a lot of pulsating lights and energetic musical numbers, but she had left the theater less affected by the overstimulation than she had expected. *And more affected by Vance Kingston.*

Chanelle had hoped for a relaxing holiday where she could shake off some of the built-up stress of the past and try to come up with a plan for the future. She *had to* make a decision where work was concerned. She couldn't remain on a leave indefinitely. Getting away on a cruise had seemed like the perfect opportunity to resolve the issue of whether to return as a front-line child protection worker or to seek work in an area that wouldn't consume so much of her time and energy.

But how relaxing could this cruise be, knowing that she might cross paths at any time with Vance Kingston? Would he be dining at the same restaurant? Swimming in one of the pools? Catching the nightly shows? And what about the gala? Surely he must have a special somebody in his life who would be here to celebrate his new position with him and his family?

So what? an inner voice interrupted her thoughts. *Why wouldn't you be able to relax? Just because he treated you to some wine doesn't mean he's going to seek you out again.*

And why would he? With his family onboard, and probably a group of close friends and associates, he would hardly be intending to pursue *her*. For conversation or otherwise.

Chanelle felt her eyelids getting heavy. She wondered what it would be like to be pursued by Vance Kingston. And then she immediately chastised herself for having such a hare-brained thought. She had other things to deal with now instead of indulging in a ridiculous fantasy about the president of Zodiac Cruises.

She was not interested in anybody pursuing her.

Not. Interested.

The last thing she wanted was to be embroiled in a relationship.

Chanelle exhaled noisily. What a ridiculous notion she had had earlier, that of encouraging herself to flirt with Vance Kingston. The wine had been to blame for that. It had addled her brain, loosened her tongue, and of all the people who could have witnessed her temporary lapse of sanity, it had to have been the *president* of Zodiac Cruises.

She closed her eyes and scrunched them tight before releasing the tension, willing the image of cobalt-blue eyes to disappear from her mind.

Vance tossed his jacket onto his couch and loosened his tie. He ran his fingers through his hair. He was happy with the success of the opening night show, but he would have been even happier if, after the show, he had been able to speak with—

He stopped himself. What was he thinking? Just because he had spent some time with Chanelle Robinson before the show didn't mean that he needed to connect with her afterwards. He gave a curt laugh and shook his head before heading to the shower. He had other things to think about, like the upcoming gala.

Mariah had brought up the subject as he was walking her to her stateroom after the show. She had glanced at him speculatively and said she was surprised that he hadn't invited "anyone special" to accompany him on the cruise.

"Currently, there are no contenders in that position," he had replied wryly, raising an eyebrow. "Taking over for Dad has been my priority… And even if I wanted to, there's no time."

"Mom said that Brianna phoned the house the other day. She said she hadn't been able to reach you on your cell."

"I don't have time for Brianna," he had replied dismissively. "Or her universe." He had had no problem inhabiting her universe in the past, but somehow, he had no inclination to get caught up in it again.

In the shower, Vance let the streams of water relax his shoulder and back muscles. Thoughts of Brianna dissipated as frames of Chanelle flicked through his mind like a slideshow: Chanelle reaching for Adrien, her brow creased in alarm; the way she had cocked her head and smiled at him when she called him Sir Vancelot; the flicker of genuine concern in her eyes when she talked about her line of work; the look of her walking into the restaurant with that curve-hugging black top and magenta skirt that matched the color of her lips exactly; and—

He groaned. Chanelle was a witch, she had to be, to have put some kind of spell over him that had her appearing in front of his eyes even when she wasn't there. *Damn!* He had vowed that he wouldn't let women distract him from what he needed to accomplish at Zodiac Cruises… There was too much at stake, especially his self-respect. He had made a promise to himself, and he had every intention of keeping it.

And for the past nine months, he had succeeded. After Brianna, there had been no one. Oh, he had been all too aware that there were women who still had hopes when it came to winning his favor, but he had not succumbed to their discreet and not-so-discreet invitations.

Despite the fact that he had sometimes felt tempted…

He knew it was guilt over his lack of involvement in the business before his father had passed away that had something to do with it. *Everything* to do with it. And his failure to make a deathbed promise to his father to take over the business. Yes, guilt had put a giant wedge between him and any thoughts of involvement with another woman.

Vance stepped out of the shower, briskly towel dried his hair and wrapped the towel around his hips. He sauntered over to his minibar and extracted a bottle of ice wine. He poured himself a small glass and walked out to his balcony.

Was Chanelle out on hers? Or sleeping?

An image of her lying on the bed with her lustrous hair spread across the pillow sent a shiver through him. Vance finished the wine and went back inside.

He replaced the towel with a robe and stretched out on his bed, his hands cradling the back of his neck. There was something that made Chanelle Robinson different from the women he had dated in the past.

She's not into herself, he realized with a start. She was *real*. No artifice or pretensions. No glossy manicure or designer clothes. Not that there was anything wrong with a glossy manicure or designer clothes. In his experience, it was the *attitude* that sometimes accompanied them that was pretentious.

And Vance hadn't detected any of that kind of attitude from Chanelle. She seemed down-to-earth, and it was obvious she had been dedicated to her job. He frowned as he pictured her walking into a home and having to remove the children because of neglect or worse. Having to deal with belligerent parents…

Vance breathed in sharply. Had Chanelle ever been in danger? A spiral of anger shot through his veins, quickly followed by that surge of protectiveness again. With a groan, he vaulted off the bed. There was no use even attempting to turn off his thoughts and go to sleep. He glanced at the clock. Not quite eleven o'clock.

He considered running around the track on the upper deck and then changed his mind. He tried reading a book, but his mind kept wandering. Frustrated, he put the book down, flung off his robe and slid between the cool sheets of his bed. With a deep sigh, he allowed thoughts of Chanelle to slip in beside him…

CHAPTER FIVE

WHEN CHANELLE WOKE UP, her eyes followed the light to the balcony. This was their first at-sea day, and all that was visible were water, clouds and sky. The clouds were low and tinged pink and coral. So pretty… The sun was just rising, a hazy golden orb veiled by the shifting clouds. Chanelle slid open the door wider and stepped onto the balcony. She stood by the railing, breathing the fresh air and watching the clouds' transformations.

She went back inside and changed into a mint-green swimsuit, deciding to do a few laps in the pool before breakfast. Now that she couldn't use work as an excuse not to exercise, she could invest some time in the physical fitness department. And she rather relished the thought of having the pool to herself. She didn't imagine too many people would be there this early, including…

Chanelle felt her cheeks prickling with heat at the thought of Vance Kingston doing laps in the pool alongside her, his muscular arms and chest—

Stop! She frowned at herself in the mirror. "You, Chanelle Robinson—" she pointed an accusing finger "—are pathetic, daydreaming about the president of Zodiac Cruises. Pathetic and ridiculous."

She stuck her tongue out at herself and, after tying her hair up in a ponytail, put on a peach-colored cover-up.

Grabbing her beach bag and towel, Chanelle headed to the pool on Deck Twelve.

The view at this height was enchanting, and for a moment, she stood at the railing, absorbed in the gentle collision of pink and saffron clouds as they floated across the horizon. She could do this all day, she mused. *This* was relaxation. And she had had too little of it for ages.

The pool water was balmy, and Chanelle floated for a while, eyes closed, concentrating on the delicious feeling of weightlessness. She would definitely have to make this an early-morning ritual.

Breaking into a front stroke, she swam the length of the pool and back six times. After rinsing off, she briskly dried herself with the oversized towel and stretched out on her chaise lounge. She would read for a bit, and then she'd go and shower and dress before heading to the Galaxy Café for breakfast.

Chanelle felt her eyelids getting heavier as she was reading. Despite the comfort of her king-size bed, she'd had a fitful sleep, waking two or three times during the night. Turning the book over onto her lap, she let herself drift off, lulled by the water gushing out of the nearby fountain—an Aquarius water bearer...

Vance had always enjoyed working out in the gym first thing in the morning. Besides keeping him fit, it helped him work out his feelings. Whatever frustrations he had had about his father, by the time he had bench-pressed two hundred pounds or sweated through countless repetitions of weight-lifting exercises, his pent-up emotions had been released, if not completely resolved.

His father had been a workaholic. He had spent his energy on building his company, and he had made a fortune with twelve ships in the fleet, each one carrying the name of a zodiac sign. Zodiac ships were not the largest of cruise ships, but they had the reputation of being among the most luxurious. The first ship to sail had been this one, the *Aquarius*, named after Vance's sign.

Immersed in the growth of his company, his dad had left the rearing of his children to his wife, who had joined him in running the company only after the kids were in school. Vance had grown up missing a father at school concerts, basketball games and tournaments, and sometimes at family holidays and special occasions. Like his birthday. And graduation.

Vance had vowed that he would never become like him. His disdain had manifested in teenage rebellion whenever his father had shown up, and he and his father had clashed incessantly. The more his dad had gotten on his case, the more Vance had acted in outrageous ways.

Like buying himself a Harley when he was eighteen and literally zooming off into the sunset with a motorcycle gang. Not a nefarious gang, just a bunch of wild and moderately rebellious guys like him. They had raced their way west across the Trans-Canada Highway, enjoying the commotion they caused entering every quiet little town or bar. They had especially liked the attention of groups of women in these locales.

They had happened to end up in Alberta just in time for the Calgary Stampede. They had arrived at the beginning of the annual ten-day festival in July and had enthusiastically joined the cowboy and Western-themed party that attracted over a million visitors every year. They had bought themselves cowboy hats and had whooped it up at the rodeos, parades, concerts and chuck wagon competitions. They had taken their fill of pancake breakfasts, barbecues and gorgeous cowgirls in sexy hats, formfitting jeans and pointy leather boots.

Vance had returned to Toronto with two souvenirs, his cowboy hat and an Aquarius tattoo on his upper back. His father had been none too pleased. He had accused Vance of being a spoiled, ungrateful son, worrying his mother half to death and wasting *his* hard-earned money instead of doing something useful, like working his way up in the company.

He *had been* spoiled. Had spent money without much thought. He had taken luxury for granted, having never known anything but fine food, designer clothes, flashy cars and no shortage of women who appreciated such finery.

Though his adventures with motorcycles had eventually waned, Vance had still wanted to travel. Over the last ten years, he had grown accustomed to visiting exotic locations on a whim and acquiring real estate in Canada—an artist's retreat on Salt Spring Island off the West Coast and a spectacular saltbox house in Newfoundland's Conception Bay. His other home away from home was Coral Haven, the island in the Caribbean that his parents had purchased and where they had built a luxurious villa. The island was uninhabited except for the people employed to travel back and forth from Grand Cayman to keep the villa maintained and prepared for the family's visits.

He was looking forward to spending time at Coral Haven during this cruise. While guests enjoyed the excursion to Grand Cayman, he and his family would spend the day at their villa.

After his strenuous workout, Vance was ready for a refreshing dip in the pool, located on the same deck. As the invigoratingly cool water splashed over his heated face and body in the pre-pool shower, he glimpsed a figure on one of the chaise lounges.

He squinted and diverted his head from the spray of water. He could see the woman better now: her long, curvy legs, a book overturned on her right thigh, her silky mint-green swimsuit with a flounce ruffle top, wet from her recent swim. Her eyes were obscured by ridiculously large sunglasses, but the ribbons of auburn hair flanking the curves of her face gave her identity away.

Vance felt a drumming in his chest. The *Aquarius* was not a small ship, yet it seemed that at every turn, he was practically bumping into Chanelle Robinson. Vance strode to the deep end and dived into the pool. When he surfaced, he shook his head and glanced toward Chanelle, but she hadn't budged. He began his laps and tried to concentrate on his strokes, but every time he approached the end of the pool near the spot where Chanelle was, his heartbeat seemed to accelerate.

When Vance hauled himself out of the pool, he was surprised to see Chanelle was still sleeping. Her oversized sunglasses had slipped crookedly down her nose, and her shifting had caused her book to tumble over the chaise lounge onto the floor. He toweled himself quickly and sauntered over to pick up the book with the intention of placing it on the corner of her chaise, when he noticed her stateroom key card at the foot of her chaise. He couldn't help glancing at the number on it.

Chanelle gave a sudden vigorous stretch, catching him soundly on his backside with the back of her hand. He swiveled and met the startled and blinking green eyes that he was beginning to know so well…

CHAPTER SIX

CHANELLE STARED. WHAT was Vance Kingston doing, standing there wearing nothing but his swim trunks and holding her book in his hand? And standing so close that she had whacked him in the rear? Had he been watching her as she slept?

She was mortified, irritated and embarrassed all at once. The last thing—or person—she had expected to see was *him*. Like *this*. Her eyes swept upward past his trim waist, muscled chest and arms and broad shoulders. And disturbingly amused turquoise eyes.

She straightened in her chaise and pulled off her sunglasses. "Excuse me?" she said pointedly.

"Shouldn't that be a statement instead of a question?" he said with a crooked half smile.

Chanelle gaped at him.

"I mean, I don't know if it was intentional, but your backhand was quite forceful. I'm afraid there might be some bruising..." He patted his backside gingerly and made a grimace.

"It was *not* intentional," she said defensively. "Your rear just happened to be in the way."

She frowned. "Why *were* you in the way?" She stared at the book he still held in his hands. "I can't imagine it was because you wanted to borrow my book."

Vance glanced at the cover of the paperback, and Chanelle wished she hadn't brought attention to it. It featured a blue-eyed frontiersman clasping a brown-eyed heroine with windswept hair by her scarlet-corseted waist. Chanelle felt currents of heat sizzling through her, making her cheeks feel as fiery as the dress on the cover.

"I hadn't intended to." He checked out the back cover and then gazed back at her. "I saw it had fallen, and I was just about to carry out my one good deed of the day and pick it up." Vance's eyes seemed to twinkle at her. "But maybe you can lend it to me once you're finished." He handed it to her. "*If* you think I'll enjoy it."

Chanelle took it and placed it on her chaise. He was teasing her, of course. Or mocking her. She doubted that he was the type to read historical romances. In any case, she was at a loss as to how to answer him.

And at a disadvantage, with him practically standing over her. Chanelle wished she had put on her cover-up. Despite the fact that her swimsuit was a one-piece, she still felt rather exposed, and the tingly sensations within her were causing her to shiver uncontrollably, making her even more self-conscious. She quickly crossed her arms in front of her.

Chanelle heard approaching voices and looked past Vance's shoulder. A family of five was making its way toward the pool attendant. Vance followed her glance. "Time for me to go." He grinned. "Enjoy your book." He turned and strode toward the entrance leading to the elevator foyer. Chanelle's gaze leaped to his broad back, where a tattoo in various blues was splayed on his upper right side. A stylistic double wave design with a realistic-looking splash of water curving below. The same astrological sign as the ship. *Aquarius.* Unable to divert her gaze, she watched the movement of his arm and back muscles until Vance disappeared around a corner.

Chanelle blinked and swallowed and realized she hadn't answered him.

* * *

After her shower, Chanelle changed into a pair of navy capri pants and a sleeveless red-and-white-striped top and sat on the balcony to check her phone messages while her hair dried. Her mother had messaged.

Enjoy, relax and pamper yourself, my darling girl. No one deserves it more than you! Love you!

And her stepdad.

Be well, Chanelle my belle, and contact me day or night if you need to, okay, sweetheart? By the way, I'm bringing back a cuddly friend for you... Love you lots!

And he had attached a photo of himself holding a plush koala bear.

Chanelle smiled and then almost immediately felt a wave of sadness engulf her. It was moments like these when she missed her family terribly and felt so alone... As she stared out at the brightening sky, she felt the prickle at the back of her eyes intensify, and a moment later, tears began to trickle down her cheeks.

She *was* alone. Alone with her fears for the future.

Would she be able to return to her job? The work conditions wouldn't change; *she'd* have to change, or she'd end up in the same boat. Chanelle groaned at the unintentional pun, wiped her eyes and strode to the door. *Stop feeling sorry for yourself,* her inner voice chided. *Get out there and start enjoying this cruise!* Chanelle took a deep breath, tossed her hair back and decided to do just that, starting off with a lovely breakfast in the Galaxy Café.

She opened her door and let out a startled cry at the

man standing directly in front of her, his hand raised in the knocking position.

Chanelle blinked at the same rate as her heartbeat. She willed her eyelids to slow down, but her heart continued racing of its own accord.

Vance Kingston brought his hand down. He lifted his other one and Chanelle recognized what he was holding—her sunglasses. Her gaze flew to his, riveted by piercing eyes that looked more blue-green now, with the teal shirt he had changed into.

"You left these behind," he said drily, "and I convinced myself it wouldn't hurt to carry out a second good deed of the day. I noticed them when I went back to get my towel and gym bag." He chuckled. "I guess forgetfulness is a trait shared by Aquarians and Sagittarians."

Vance gazed into green-hazel eyes that had a luminescence that hadn't been there earlier. She'd been crying...and her cheeks and nose were slightly flushed. He felt the muscles in his stomach tightening. Could it have something to do with her ex-fiancé?

"How did you find out my stateroom number?" Chanelle's eyes bored into his as she took the sunglasses from him.

"Your key card was on your chaise. I couldn't help seeing the number." Something in her expression gave him a jolt. "Good heavens, I hope you don't think my intentions are dishonorable, Chanelle. That would be most unpresidential of me, don't you think?" He waited for her to reply, but she just continued to stare at him.

"Look, I'm sorry if I caused you even momentary worry," he said huskily, raising his right arm to the door-jamb. "I'm not trying to stalk you, Chanelle. I just wanted to get your sunglasses back to you…and now I just want to make sure you're okay."

The way Chanelle was studying his face reminded him of a teacher trying to ascertain if her student was lying. He tried not to make his mouth twitch in amusement and was relieved when her features relaxed slightly.

She cleared her throat. "Okay. *Fine.* I mean, I'm okay and I—I accept your apology." A corner of her mouth lifted briefly. "I'm sorry if I seemed a little testy…"

"Seemed?" he said, raising his eyebrows.

Her eyes widened, as if she didn't know how to take his remark. "Okay, I'm sorry if I *was* a little testy," she said wryly.

"A little?"

She looked at him incredulously. "You make it seem as if I was biting your head off…"

He burst out laughing. "Interesting choice of words." Something flipped inside him when she laughed back, making her eyes take on an emerald hue. "Speaking of biting… would you care to have a bite with me? Breakfast, that is?"

Her eyebrows went up, as if that were the last thing she'd expected to hear from him. She blinked at him as if he had just asked her a complicated algebraic question and she didn't have a clue as to where to start with the answer. "I—I was just about to go to the Galaxy Café," she finally replied.

"I see," he murmured. He looked past her. "I hope you're finding your stateroom to your satisfaction?"

"It's very nice—roomier than I thought it would be." She nodded and shifted awkwardly in the doorway. "Uh… I forgot my sunscreen in the washroom. I plan to enjoy the sunshine after breakfast, but unless I want to end up with a million freckles, I really should—"

"Would you like me to wait here, Chanelle?" He didn't

know what had possessed him to invite her for breakfast, but he had, and there was no way of taking it back.

She hesitated, then shrugged. "You can step inside. I'll just be a minute." She turned and suddenly paused. He followed her gaze to the king-size bed, still unmade, her skimpy teddy tossed on top of the sheets. When his gaze returned to her, her cheeks had already reddened.

He pretended not to notice and immediately sat down on the couch and picked up a magazine. He started leafing through the pages, but out of the corner of his eye, he saw Chanelle walking over and pulling the covers casually over the bed to conceal her teddy. Without glancing his way, she headed to the washroom and closed the door. He heard the water flowing and imagined her splashing cool water over those peachy cheeks.

He was feeling rather heated himself, thinking of Chanelle in that teddy... He tossed the magazine back on the coffee table and leaned back to survey the room. She had some of her toiletries organized neatly on one night table, and there was no sign of her suitcase. He spotted her swimsuit draped over a chair on the balcony and wondered what her reaction would have been if he had been in time to join her in the pool.

The washroom door opened, and Chanelle came out, her hair now held back by a wide navy headband. The casual style emphasized her heart-shaped face and exquisite cheekbones. She had also applied a lustrous red lipstick, and in that snug red-and-white T-shirt and navy capris, she looked like a classic beauty from a bygone era. Innocent and sensual at the same time. Like it or not, that combination sent flickers of desire through him. And the fact that she was unconscious of the effect she had on him made his pulse spike even higher.

She grabbed her tote bag and then suddenly hesitated. "Will you be joining your family?"

He couldn't help chuckling. "Mariah won't be up for a while. And neither will Adrien. As for my mother, she will have already ordered room service at the crack of dawn and is now probably consulting with some of the staff about the gala preparations."

Chanelle nodded, her shoulders relaxing. "I guess we'd better get going, then."

He glanced at the time on his sports watch. "I know the Galaxy Café can get quite busy, especially around this time. How would you feel about trying a spot that's quieter? The Constellation Club, for example."

Her eyebrows shot up. "I… I read that that was for exclusive Zodiac Club members," she said, her cheeks flushing. "I could only afford the basic cruise plan." She gave an embarrassed half smile.

"I can guarantee you won't be turned away," he said solemnly. "If you don't mind going as my guest."

Chanelle blinked. "But…" She looked down at her outfit. "Is there a dress code?"

"Yes," he said with a chuckle. "You have to wear clothes. What you're wearing is absolutely fine, Chanelle. It's not what you think. People aren't parading in black-tie attire and ball gowns." His mouth twitched. "In fact, they're not parading at all. At least not for breakfast."

"I—I don't know. I've budgeted for dining in one specialty restaurant, but this is—"

"On me," he said firmly. "And if you really object, you can offer to do your dishes afterward."

She looked at him hesitantly, then gave a nod, a mix of relief and disbelief in her expression, and Vance felt a warm rush infuse his chest. What he was more accustomed to was seeing a look of smug expectation on a date's face. Not that

Chanelle was exactly a date, but it was refreshing for him to know that a lady wasn't expecting him to pick up her tab.

Vance followed her out of her stateroom, breathing in her perfume—a sweet berry scent—and as they walked side by side in the hallway on their way to the elevator lobby, he greeted the housekeeping staff they encountered with a friendly smile and a few words to thank them for the exceptional job they were doing.

The elevator was empty. As the doors closed, he lifted his hand to press the number to the top deck, and as he did so, it brushed against Chanelle's. Their eyes met, and for an instant, he had this crazy desire to lean down and kiss those fabulous lips. When her mouth opened slightly, it was all he could do to force himself to pull his gaze away from hers and press the button.

Finally, after what seemed like an eternity, the door opened, and he indicated to Chanelle to precede him. Her eyebrows lifted, but she accompanied him down the hall without saying anything. When they came to a door marked Constellation Club, Vance pulled his card out of his pocket and tapped it against the brass plate to the left of the door handle. He opened the door wide and smiled. "Welcome to the club, Chanelle."

CHAPTER SEVEN

CHANELLE GASPED IN AWE, her eyes widening as she entered. She couldn't have imagined anything like the room she had just stepped into. The entire ceiling was a glass dome from which were suspended thousands of stars. Chanelle felt like she was taking in a crystal wonderland.

A waiter in a crisp white shirt, black trousers and aqua-marine cummerbund greeted them and led them to an oval glass table with silver legs. The upholstered chairs were ivory damask, and as Chanelle sank into one, she gave Vance an incredulous look. "This place is out of this world," she said, expelling a deep breath. Her gaze returned to the ceiling. "There must be a thousand stars up there."

"Two thousand, five hundred, to be exact," Vance said. "Each glass star is crafted by hand in Murano, Italy. They sparkle with the natural light of the sun in the day, and the dome has a fiber optic star ceiling. But on starry, starry nights—" he flashed a smile at her "—the dome halves retract and the club members are treated to a night under the real stars. And if they're really lucky, they get to see a meteor shower or a shooting star."

"Stunning," Chanelle breathed. She looked around at the gleaming glass tables, each decorated with a multifaceted crystal vase holding a couple of stargazer lilies. In the center of the room, a life-sized and slowly rotating Aquarius statue poured water into a pool from a gilded urn, its gentle

gurgling sound adding to the relaxing ambience. The sides
of the pool were transparent, and dozens of exotic fish of
all colors flitted past each other. Chanelle was mesmerized
by their flecks of gold and turquoise, crimson and black,
emerald and orange. And their varied shapes and sizes. She
could have stood there for hours, enchanted by this giant
aquarium. And all around it, the marble floor resembled
the ocean, with its varying hues of blue. Sea and sky, she
thought. What a heavenly place…

When her gaze returned to Vance, she didn't know what
to make of the indulgent look on his face. Was that a flicker
of compassion in his eyes? She stiffened. Maybe he was
just feeling sorry for her with her limited budget. Perhaps
he made it a point to be charitable to a guest every time he
went on one of his cruises… She felt a sudden hot prickle
inching up her neck.

What had she gotten herself into? She was way out of
her league. A few female guests had turned to scrutinize
her from head to foot, and from their raised eyebrows and
whispered comments to their partners, Chanelle had begun
to feel self-conscious. For a moment, she considered making an excuse to leave, but then her inner Sagittarian warrior voice reminded her of her vow to enjoy the cruise and
new experiences.

She straightened in her seat and tossed her hair back.
Vance was still looking at her with a bemused expression.
She picked up her menu and, while scanning it, wished she
knew exactly what he was thinking.

She thought she had sensed something more elemental
in the elevator, but it must have been her imagination…

The way he was looking at her now was exactly how
he had looked at the housekeeping employees. No hint of
flirtation in those aqua depths. Yet Chanelle couldn't help
feeling conflicted. She hadn't booked this cruise hoping

to hook up with some guy to make her boo-boos better. In fact, after Parker had left, she had vowed to focus on work even more and not bother with men at all. And she had certainly succeeded. Except that the consequence of her increased devotion to her job had taken its toll physically and emotionally. No wonder it was called *burnout*. She had felt scorched and withered, like a tree caught in a summer fire.

And now her cheeks were burning as Vance's cool blue eyes gazed at her calmly. Nothing in his expression or body language even hinted that he was in playboy mode. And anyway, why would he be wanting to play with someone like *her*? She had seen the photos of some of the women he had dated, with their perfect features and haute couture.

Some of their handbags had cost more than her monthly salary…

No, she was definitely not his type. All Vance was doing was engaging in a kind act for a guest whom he had caught being upset and in tears over something…and he had considered the fact that she wouldn't want to face a lot of people after that.

Nevertheless, she still felt awkward. He wasn't just *anybody*.

"I usually eat breakfast alone," she said, eyes fixed on the menu. Her words came out more gruffly than she had intended. "In fact, I had almost changed my mind about taking this cruise. I just wanted a holiday where I could relax and be pampered and not have to deal with socializing."

She looked up to see Vance gazing at her quizzically. "You can relax and be pampered here. After breakfast, I can introduce you to our spa professionals…"

Chanelle felt the temperature in her cheeks climbing a few notches at the image that flashed in her mind: Vance lying on a spa bed with hot lava stones positioned down his strong, muscled back. And his Aquarius tattoo on the upper right side…

"Um, thanks, but I'll be fine." Besides, her budget had been stretched far enough. She looked around. The view was stupendous. Endless sea and sky. The clouds had shifted, and the sky was a mix of blues with the occasional ribbon of pink.

Vance had been saying something, but *what*? She looked at him blankly. Her stomach did a flip.

"Coffee or tea?" he repeated.

"Sorry…" She held up her hand. "I don't think I should be here." She bit her lip. "I should go." She caught his frown as she began to rise and then promptly sat down again. She owed him an explanation, at the very least. Her heart thumping, she looked at him squarely. Why be anything but honest? "I have to admit I'm feeling a little out of my element," she said. She glanced toward the other guests before turning her gaze back to Vance.

He leaned forward, both elbows on the table and his hands clasped under his chin. "I think you have all the right elements," he said lightly. "And if you're referring to your bank account, it's not an issue, remember? I'm pretty sure I can cover it, unless you're intending to eat me out of house and home. Or should I say ship and stern?" His mouth quirked to reveal a flash of dimple.

"I—I'm…well…*okay*," she relented. Why was she making such a big deal about the whole thing? She needed to take her own earlier advice and lighten up. "I have to warn you, though," she said, managing a tentative smile, "I do have a good appetite."

Vance nodded his approval as he handed her the menu. "Good. Go crazy. I'm ordering my favorite—buttermilk applesauce pancakes with Ontario maple syrup." He grinned. "Something sweet for a sweet Canadian boy."

Chanelle felt laughter bubble up inside her. She sensed that something was shifting between them. Or maybe it was just *her*. Maybe some of her inhibitions were losing their grip on her. Perhaps it was time to let go of her tendency to control the situation and just enjoy the moment...

She had read enough to know that letting go completely could be a challenge for highly sensitive people like herself. Well, she would rise to the challenge, she decided. Why not enjoy this unexpected turn of events instead of being overwhelmed and feeling out of place? How often would she get the chance to be in the company of a gorgeous guy in a fabulous restaurant on the top deck of his cruise ship? A guy with a dimpled smile that made her stomach swirl in a good way...

"I'll try the crepes filled with hazelnut chocolate and ricotta cheese," she said decisively. "For a sweeter Canadian girl."

He burst out laughing, his eyes crinkling at the edges. "So the Sagittarian has a competitive streak, does she?"

For timeless moments, Chanelle felt like she was suspended in a cloud of pure pleasure as they exchanged smiles. Then the waiter appeared with a carafe of coffee, took their order and reassured them it would be ready shortly.

"So where does this sweeter Canadian girl live?" Vance said, pouring her coffee first.

"Sault Ste. Marie, Ontario," she replied, adding cream to her cup.

He nodded. "Ah, the Soo. Been there. Stopped overnight on my way to Lake Superior for a fishing trip with some guys—let me see—three years ago. Nice little town. Big Italian population, right?"

Chanelle nodded, taken aback that he had come through her hometown.

"We stayed at a hotel by Saint Mary's River. Checked out the Station Mall; one of our absentminded buddies had brought all his fishing gear but had forgotten the important stuff, like clothes and underwear." He chuckled. "While he went searching for his designer boxers, the rest of us waited it out at a pizza and gelato place." He sighed. "I ordered a double scoop of hazelnut and pistachio. *Heaven.*"

Her eyes widened. "You've got a great memory."

He looked at her unblinkingly. "I remember anything that looks good and tastes even better," he said, his mouth tilting up at one corner.

Chanelle felt a warm rush swish through her. Flustered, she looked down and took a sip of her coffee. Her mind was zooming to places she didn't want it to go, and she'd be horrified if Vance even suspected what she was conjuring up in her imagination…

"So after Pete was done, we spent a few hours at the casino, then had some amazing Italian food at the Marconi Club." He chuckled. "*Mamma mia*, just the memory of it is making my mouth water. I'd go back to the Soo again just for the food. Although—" he raised an eyebrow conspiratorially "—I suspect the people are just as appealing…"

Chanelle raised her chin. "Yes, we are. And the Soo is a great place to live. Not too big, not too small. I don't know if I could ever live in a huge city like Toronto or Vancouver. Mind you, I visited Toronto a few years ago. I actually went on a weekend bus tour with a couple of my friends to catch a show at the Princess of Wales Theatre. It was a long trip, though. Eight hours or so."

"So you've been to my hometown. We have great Italian food, too." He grinned. "And every other cuisine you can think of."

"Do you love it? Living in a huge city, I mean?"

"I enjoy all the big-city perks, but I do need the occasional getaway."

"Where do you get away to?" Chanelle asked casually. "Other than Lake Superior."

"British Columbia, Newfoundland, California, the Caribbean…usually a place where there's a large body of water," he said with a laugh. "Do you have any special places you like to escape to?"

"I've stayed pretty much close to home," she said sheepishly. "Worked a lot of overtime hours… But I do have some special spots in and around the Soo. A beautiful beach called Pointe des Chenes. And I've camped up north, Lake Superior way. Batchawana Bay, Pancake Bay. I'm a northern Ontario girl. Love my lakes and forests."

Vance was staring at her with an intensity that made her breath catch in her lungs. *He's genuinely interested in what I'm saying*, she thought in wonder.

The waiter returned with their orders. Chanelle took a first bite of her crepe and closed her eyes. "Heaven," she murmured, before realizing she had used the same term Vance had used to describe his gelato.

"Of course it is." He nodded. "It's the *nocciola*."

Hazelnut. Of course. Her workplace was on Queen Street East, within walking distance to the Station Mall, and she often had lunch at one of the eateries there, ending it occasionally with a gelato at the same place he had been to.

"So we share the same taste in Italian ice cream." Vance drizzled syrup over his pancakes and cut a wedge. "Delicious," he said, and slid the plate closer to her. "Want to try?"

The familiarity with which he spoke made Chanelle's pulse skip. "That's okay, thanks. I think I have more than enough on my plate." Her fork paused in midair. "Literally and figuratively."

Vance looked at her thoughtfully. "Are you thinking you might go back to the same job?"

Chanelle swallowed. "I'm not sure. I loved my job." She heard the defensive tone in her voice.

Vance poured more syrup on his second pancake. "What made you decide to get into social work?"

Chanelle looked down at her half-eaten crepe and tapped it mindlessly with her fork. "I spent my childhood without a father," she said, "and I became self-conscious when there were events at school where parents were invited. My mother came when she could, but most times, it was too hard for her. She was working two jobs to pay the bills. My grandfather had health issues, so he and my grandma couldn't always be there, either." She looked up. "I think subconsciously, I internalized the fact that my father had denied my existence. Even before my mother told me that he had taken off before I was born, I intuitively felt my father's abandonment." She paused, expecting to see a skeptical look in Vance's eyes, but what she saw were his furrowed brows and eyes narrowed in concern.

"I know now that having a sharper intuition is characteristic of a highly sensitive person. Which is why, I believe, I knew early in life that I wanted to help others, starting with my mother. I felt her pain, even though she tried to put up a good front. So I helped around the house without being told, was a high achiever at school, did everything possible to avoid making life harder for her." She gazed away from Vance, recalling how happy she had been when her mother eventually married her stepdad. On the other hand, her unresolved feelings about her biological father had continued to intensify over the years, and she had felt lingering hurt and resentment that he hadn't valued her from the moment he'd known she existed, hadn't deemed her worthy to claim her as his daughter.

Parker's breaking off their engagement and leaving had ignited similar feelings…

Stop thinking about Parker, she chided herself. *He's not worth it.* She turned her gaze back to Vance, who was still looking at her with an intensity that made her heart twinge, but not in a hurtful way.

"I'm sorry, I'm sure you don't want to hear me keep chattering incessantly."

"Don't be sorry, Chanelle. It's obvious that your caring personality growing up under challenging circumstances was a good indication that you'd eventually choose a helping profession."

"Some kids had it worse than I did. One of my classmates came to school with bruises on her arms and face one Friday. I felt so bad for her. She had moved to town about a couple of months earlier, and we were getting to be good friends."

Chanelle gave a shiver. "Kayla had parents, but the rumor was that they were drug addicts. She told the teacher that she had fallen down some stairs, and she was quiet all day. She didn't tell me anything. The teacher told the principal, and on Monday, Kayla didn't show up." They had been in grade nine, and the defeated look she had seen in Kayla's eyes had haunted her all weekend.

Chanelle drew in a deep breath. "We found out that Children's Aid had investigated and removed Kayla from her home immediately. Fortunately, she had a caring aunt out of town who took her in." Chanelle couldn't keep her eyes from blurring. She wiped at them hastily with her napkin. "I knew then that I wanted to become a social worker so I could protect children from abusive or neglectful family members." She sniffed. "I never saw Kayla again, but I have something she had given me for Kris Kringle." Chanelle extended her arm to show Vance the bracelet around her left wrist that Kayla had woven with a variety of colorful threads.

"You've kept it all these years?" Vance looked at her incredulously.

Chanelle nodded. "I became a child protection worker because of her." She smiled. "I don't usually wear it around the clock, only when I'm at work. You could say it's my Sagittarian quiver, loaded with arrows. I know it may sound silly, but wearing the bracelet makes me feel strong, makes me believe that I have the protection I need, especially when I have to rescue kids."

"Wow," he said huskily, shaking his head. "Wow." He reached out to take her hand and stroked the bracelet thoughtfully with his thumb. "It's not silly at all, Chanelle." Suddenly his other hand closed over hers as well. Chanelle's heart flipped and started thumping so hard she missed most of what Vance was saying next.

Her stupefied look must have clued him in. "You're stronger than you think," he repeated, his eyes narrowing. He withdrew his hands as the waiter appeared, asking them if he could take any plates away.

They both nodded, and when the waiter was gone, Chanelle gave a big sigh. "I'm hoping that while I'm on the cruise, wearing the bracelet will help me decide where to go from here…" She let her gaze drift beyond Vance to the sky, now a deep azure that seemed to be an extension of his eyes. "But right now, I just can't see myself in another job."

"Give yourself time, Chanelle," he murmured. "You'll know when the time is right… So while you're on this cruise, I want you to give yourself permission to relax and have fun. Live a little. You deserve it." He stood up. "Starting now. Captain's—no, president's orders. Got it?" He looked at her sternly then flashed her another one of his ridiculously gorgeous brighter-than-sunshine smiles.

Chanelle pulled her chair back and rose. "Got it," she said, flinging her hair back. "I'd hate to disobey and end up walking the plank."

He burst out laughing. "Are you implying, fair lass, that I have the black heart of a pirate?"

Chanelle's pulse vaulted, his words and hearty laugh evoking an image of him in full pirate regalia standing on the bow of a treasure ship, one eye covered by a black patch, the other pinning her with the same crystal clarity as the turquoise waters below.

She couldn't stop the corners of her mouth from lifting. "If not a pirate, then perhaps a scallywag," she said, feigning haughtiness. And flipping her hair back, she strode off toward the exit.

After Chanelle disappeared, leaving him dazed with the memory of her flashing eyes and pixy smile, Vance checked in on his mother, Mariah and Adrien, and then returned to his stateroom to try to sort out some issues that were playing around in his mind as well as the jumble of emotions Chanelle had activated in his gut.

Some of the details that Chanelle had shared about her life had disturbed him. His gaze had been riveted to the shifting emotions on her face as she'd told him about her father abandoning her and her mother's challenges raising her, and he had felt his stomach twist at the difficulties she had experienced. And when she had teared up about Kayla, he had felt a strong urge to wrap his arms around her and hold her head against him.

Her impish smile as she strode off after implying he was a scallywag had caused a different feeling in him—a hammering in his chest that had reverberated throughout his body…

Now, stretched out on the recliner on his balcony, Vance thought again of Chanelle's early years growing up without a father. His own father had been present only minimally, so he could just imagine what Chanelle had felt, especially being so sensitive.

Vance's memory shifted to how he had immersed himself in a new and heavily structured routine after his father had passed. This week—with nothing specifically planned except for the midweek gala—was throwing him off. He might have been more laid-back when it came to work in the past, but that had changed dramatically in the last nine months. He had conditioned himself to get up at 5:00 a.m. every morning, work out at the gym in his condo, shower, have breakfast and be at the office before eight. And most nights, he wasn't back at his condo until after nine.

He'd had no time to think about women.

Until yesterday, after seeing an auburn-haired beauty trying to rescue his nephew from danger.

And after spending some time with Chanelle Robinson in the Mezza Luna Ristorante, and foolishly inviting her to have breakfast with him in the Constellation Club this morning, he was now in danger of losing his resolve to focus on work, not women. Or more specifically, *this* woman.

Vance pursed his lips. He would be on this cruise for three more days after today. And when the cruise was over, he'd never see Chanelle Robinson again. He might not even run into her for the remainder of the cruise.

The important thing to remember was not to seek her out. It would only weaken his resolve. So despite the undeniable way his senses were stirred around her, he had to ensure that he did not act on his feelings. How could he take advantage of her in the vulnerable state she was in, having suffered a broken relationship and work stress?

You've changed, big boy, whether you like it or not.

He froze at the words that had shoved their way into his consciousness. They were true. Before his father died, Vance had never suffered pangs of guilt around relationships, familial or otherwise. He had justified his rebelliousness as a teen and young adult as his way of striking out at a father who was never home. A father who seemed to care more about work than his kids...

The feeling of guilt had sprung up when his father died, knowing he had allowed his built-up resentment to stop him from granting his dad's dying request. Since then, he had been trying to make up for it.

Yes, he had changed, all right.

He had made work his priority, just as his father had done, and slowly, Vance had begun to understand how a person could become consumed with work, with passion, to the point of neglecting everything else.

He could congratulate himself for repressing his playboy ways while focusing on carrying out his father's last wish, but he couldn't deny that certain feelings had been reactivated.

By a fascinating woman who probably wanted nothing to do with him or any other man right now...

But it wasn't just her outer beauty that attracted him. He was intrigued by the depth of her character, her small-town charm and honesty. Her devotion to her job, the children she was so passionate about protecting. Her goodness.

And how could he not be affected by those limpid green pools for eyes, those peachy cheekbones and silky lips? How could he ignore the sleek curves of her body...and that riotous head of hair that he envisioned blowing in the wind as she stood on a rocky outcrop looking out at the endless ice-blue waters of Lake Superior? A Sagittarian warrior, softhearted yet strong and determined, ready to fling her Archer's arrow...

A thought entered his consciousness, shocking him like his very first dip in Lake Superior.

He was falling for Chanelle Robinson.

Falling hard and seeing stars...

CHAPTER EIGHT

CHANELLE HAD WATCHED Vance leave in a swirl of emotions. She had felt some undercurrents in Vance's presence... undercurrents that confused her. Like the intensity in his gaze earlier in the elevator. It had only lasted for a couple of seconds, but the expression in his electric-blue eyes as he looked down at her had galvanized her to the core. And then minutes later, in the Constellation Club, his expression had been genuinely reassuring, making her doubt her earlier assessment.

But the way he had been so attentive, fixing her with that enigmatic gaze, was causing uncertainty in the pit of her stomach about his true feelings.

What true feelings? an inner voice scoffed. *You just met the guy. Do you actually think he has feelings for you? And if you're feeling anything for him, it's because he's gorgeous and rich. And what's wrong with that?*

Chanelle scowled. Yes, how could she not find Vance Kingston attractive? Very attractive. The memory of the Aquarius tattoo on his muscled back made her catch her breath. But it hadn't been thoughts of his wealth that had generated flutters in her chest, that had sent tingles to every part of her. It was the way he had given her all his attention, as if her every word mattered to him. It was how he had validated her by listening to her story, acknowledging her strength, showing concern for her work situation and encouraging her to give it time and to have fun on the cruise.

She couldn't dispute the fact that Vance Kingston was gorgeous and rich. He had asked her to join him for breakfast and he had shown himself to be considerate and thoughtful. But it was just plain silly to think that the president of Zodiac Cruises was at all interested in her in any other way.

And even if he *was* taking a break from his playboy lifestyle for the sake of work—if the articles online were true—Chanelle couldn't imagine someone like him changing his ways after his self-imposed period of solitude.

She shook her head impatiently. Vance had taken up enough of her head space. She was here to relax and enjoy the cruise, just as he had suggested, and not to waste time fantasizing about him or any other man.

Chanelle focused her attention on the Star Guide, an interactive screen that displayed a map of the entire ship and the features on every deck. She decided on a visit to the art gallery on Deck Five. The stunning art collection would be a welcome distraction from her thoughts of Vance Kingston.

There were dozens of international artists featured, not only in the gallery itself, but displayed along the walls on each deck. Chanelle spent close to an hour marveling at the diversity of styles, the vibrancy of the colors and the intricacy and detail in each painting. One particularly captivated her, with its depiction of a moonlit and starry sky mirrored in the indigo-blue undulations of the sea. It was called *Enchantment*, and simply signed *SV*.

A glance at the price made Chanelle's eyes widen. A fairy godmother would have to appear and sprinkle some magic fairy dust in Chanelle's wallet for her to be able to afford it.

Chanelle picked up a complimentary booklet showcasing the artists and their works but couldn't find anything about the artist and his or her painting. An elegantly dressed woman sitting at an ornate French Provincial desk walked over with a smile and told Chanelle that the artist wished to remain anonymous. She gave Chanelle a card with information about the champagne art auction that would be taking place during the mid-cruise gala, and explained that there would be many more pieces featured. And complimentary champagne, of course, a door prize, and some special surprises...

Chanelle slipped the invitation into her handbag and smiled her thanks at the woman before moving on. It sounded like fun, but she doubted that there would be a painting that her budget could accommodate.

Chanelle slowed her pace as she entered the Galaxy Shops. She had splurged on booking the cruise itself and had vowed to be strict with herself when it came to shopping, whether on the ship or during her off-ship excursion. But there was no harm in just looking, she told herself, surveying the luxurious brands of purses and luggage. She checked the price of a coral clutch that caught her eye and sighed before moving on to the jewelry displays. One of the sales staff approached her with a welcoming smile, telling her about the day's special of fifty percent off select brands. Chanelle thanked her, flushing, and told her that she'd have a good look. Which wasn't exactly lying. She *would* look through the sparkly selection.

A pair of ruby earrings in a flower design caught her eye. She noticed the price, then began to walk away. How could she justify spending money unnecessarily, especially when she wasn't one hundred percent sure that she would be returning to her job in a month's time? How was she supposed to recover from five years of intensive work stress in one month? And then what? Would she be ready to get right back into it?

She had rent to pay. And now that she was back on her own, she might even have to look for a new place…or move back in with her mom and stepdad.

Not that she didn't love them, but it would be hard after five years of independence in her own space.

"I'll take these amethyst earrings, dear," a woman said close by. "I think they'll match my violet gown perfectly for the gala."

Chanelle turned and saw a sixty-something woman sporting a smart pixie cut with side-swept bangs that suited her silver-gray hair. She was wearing turquoise palazzo pants and a sleeveless ivory chiffon top. She had removed her turquoise earrings to try the amethyst ones against her ears. On the third finger of her left hand, an enormous diamond sparkled under the ceiling lights.

The woman's open handbag slipped off the counter, spilling some of its contents. Chanelle quickly bent down to retrieve what she could and handed the items to the woman, who gazed across at her with a grateful smile. "Thanks for your help."

"My pleasure," she replied, startled by the crystal clarity of the woman's blue eyes.

Chanelle was about to stand up, too, but a flash on the floor under the counter caught her eye. It was a photo of a child, encased in a plastic folder. A boy with the same arresting blue eyes as the woman.

And the president of Zodïac Cruises.

Something fluttered in Chanelle's chest as she stood up and handed the photo of the little boy she had tried to rescue yesterday to his grandmother. *Vance Kingston's mother…*

No wonder Chanelle had sensed something familiar about her.

After the woman left, Chanelle returned to the jewelry display to look at the ruby earrings. A new voice was telling her, *Relax and have fun. Live a little. You deserve it!*

Foolish or not, Chanelle listened to the voice. Which, she realized as she walked away with her little velvet box tucked away in a Zodiac Cruises gift bag, was the voice of Vance Kingston.

Vance looked over the series of sketches he had been working on for the last hour. There were at least a dozen variations of the logo he was designing for the new cruise line in the Zodiac fleet, its first ship scheduled to launch the following year. His father had initiated the project, and now it was in his hands.

He had to come up with a new name as well, and he had jotted down a half dozen possibilities, including Nebula Cruises, What's Your Sign? Cruises and Stellar Cruises. None of them quite clicked for him, though. He pursed his lips. The logos all had one thing in common—undulating waves. Once he decided on a name, he'd connect the letters with the waves in a flowing forward motion. And maybe add the profile of a sea goddess…

Vance turned to a new page and started another sketch. It was neither a logo nor a name. It was a face with sculpted cheekbones and full, curving lips. Eyes framed with long, feathery lashes. And thick waves of hair cascading down to the shoulder lines.

He took a green and a gold pencil and added color to the eyes. He set his pencils down and took a long, hard look at the result.

Chanelle Robinson was staring back at him…

Time to take a break, he told himself, shaking his head in wonder.

* * *

Vance greeted the art representative at her desk and strolled through the gallery, noticing the new paintings that had been added. Vance enjoyed perusing each one, familiar with many of the artists. He was looking forward to the champagne art auction and wondered if Chanelle planned to attend.

He stopped when he came to the *Enchantment* painting and looked at it thoughtfully.

"It's getting some attention," the art rep said as she joined him.

"Oh?" Vance's eyebrows lifted. "Did someone ask about it, Stephanie?"

"A young lady kept going back to it. She must have stared at it for a good ten minutes." Stephanie smiled at Vance. "She was obviously enchanted by it."

Vance's mouth curved. "But not enchanted enough to buy it," he chuckled.

"Well, perhaps she might consider it at the auction on gala night, Vance. I gave her a card."

"Was she one of our regular cruisers?" Stephanie had been with the *Aquarius* since it launched, and she had become familiar with returning customers, especially the art patrons.

"No, this was a first-timer," she told him. A few guests entered the gallery, and she turned toward them.

"Did you happen to catch her name?" Vance said as casually as he could.

Stephanie looked back. "I spotted her first name on her lanyard. It was different; it reminded me of Chantilly lace." She laughed. "Chantelle. No, *Chanelle*." She walked over and welcomed the guests, and Vance turned back to gaze at the painting.

Enchantment. Why had this painting caught Chanelle's attention? he mused. His gaze swooped over the stars and the waves of blue and indigo before landing on the initials in the bottom right-hand corner. *SV.* His mouth lifted at one corner. He had done this painting while he was working on his masters of fine art degree, and not wanting his father to denigrate it on the rare occasions when he came home, Vance had chosen not to sign it with his own name. He had to thank his sister for giving him the nickname Sir Vancelot...

CHAPTER NINE

CHANELLE PUT ON a light robe and drew the tie around her waist. She had returned to her stateroom feeling over-whelmed at bumping into Vance's mother—and overheated after spending time in the shop—and had immediately taken a refreshing shower.

She inhaled and exhaled deeply, feeling much more re-laxed now, and headed to the balcony. She could stare at the water for ages, watching the cerulean waves change to turquoise and turquoise to cobalt blue. The sun was add-ing magic to the scene, making the water's surface shim-mer with glittering diamonds.

In the next few weeks, she hoped it would be clearer to her what direction to take as far as her job was concerned. This cruise would hopefully give both her body and mind a rest, and then she could decide if she could handle con-tinuing in the same line of work, or if she seriously needed to consider a change of some kind.

But now she didn't really want to think about it. She just wanted to enjoy the glorious view of sky and sea.

Chanelle went back inside and stretched out on top of the bed. She checked the time on her phone. Plenty of time to relax before dinner.

She reached for the daily cruise guide, and while she was checking out the featured events of the day, the daily horoscope caught her eye. She couldn't help skimming the page until her gaze landed on her sign.

Sagittarius, you're in for some surprises. With your ruler Jupiter in retrograde, your inner world is transitioning and spinning you to a higher consciousness. Don't fight it; let yourself enjoy your burgeoning awareness. You may have felt the universe is not on your side after some personal and work upsets, but take heart, Sag. If you stay focused on what's in front of you, what's to come won't be problematic. Go with the flow, Archer, and that arrow will land where it needs to…

Chanelle frowned. It was so *eerie* how much the words could be applied to her situation. And then she scoffed at herself. Parts of the description could apply to tons of people, no matter what their sign was.

Despite her skepticism, she couldn't help reading the horoscope for Vance.

The stars will collaborate to help a business matter come to fruition. Complicated family issues will untangle, and with Uranus guiding you, you will be able to see clearer when it comes to matters of the heart. Concessions may need to be made, and your compliance with the forces of the universe will result in a shower of positive changes.

Chanelle set down the guide and let her gaze drift to the ceiling. Could Vance, despite his calm and collected exterior, have some personal issues of his own he was dealing with? A woman who was waiting for him to ease up at work and shower her with more of his attention?

She shook her head. What was she doing conjuring up possibilities around Vance and his relationships?

Time to get back to reality.

She picked up the guide again. A glance at the time confirmed that she had a few free hours before dinner. Did she really want to spend them lying down on her bed? She was on a spectacular cruise ship and before she knew it, it would be over...

She might as well enjoy every delicious bit of it.

Chanelle perused the activities listed for the afternoon: a tour of the ship kitchens, a magic show featuring a Las Vegas regular, an art class with a high-profile artist, a wine-tasting class, Latin dancing or belly-dancing instruction, a rock-climbing wall, a pool volleyball tournament, a '70s disco party and a dozen other choices.

Chanelle began to reread the list, the times and the locations. She didn't really feel up to doing anything that required dressing up; after all, she'd be doing that for Canada Night. But she really should consider doing something a little out of her element. After all, what would be the likelihood of her going on another cruise any time soon? She might as well try something new. *And exciting...*

As she skimmed down the list, her gaze landed on something that she had missed. The Sky Promenade. It was an extensive course of colorful horizontal rope ladders that were suspended a hundred feet above the skating rink on the top deck, connecting to rope bridges, slopes and descents that had to be navigated by walking while wearing a safety harness.

Chanelle flicked on to the TV channel that featured videos of all the day's events. As the Sky Promenade video started, she gave a little shiver. Heights had always made her feel a little queasy, and this activity would require a stomach of steel, looking down between the ropes to the crystal-clear surface of the ice rink.

There was no way she could do that. No. Way.

She'd be terrified, even knowing that she'd be wearing a safety harness. The motion of the ropes along with the bird's-eye view of the sea on the periphery would throw her off balance with her first step. She clicked off the remote. There had to be something else she could try that wasn't so scary.

Chanelle leaped off the bed and changed into a pair of purple leggings and a thigh-length fuchsia T-shirt before tying her hair up in a ponytail. She'd do something outdoors, she decided, but something less extreme. Perhaps she could try the rock-climbing wall...

Vance's cell phone buzzed, making him start. It was Mariah, reminding him that he'd promised to take Adrien swimming. He checked the time. He'd also planned a quick meeting with the director of environmental operations later in the afternoon for an update on her latest initiative. He smirked. He was supposed to be taking a break from work while on the cruise, but he was realizing just how hard it was to break an established habit...

And after the meeting, he would join Mariah, Adrien and his mother for dinner in the Galaxy Café. Tonight was Canada Night on the ship. The theater would be featuring Canadian singers and comedians, and the Galaxy Café would be serving a signature dish and dessert from every province. There would be wine from the vineyards of the Okanagan Valley in British Columbia and Ontario's Niagara region, cheeses from Quebec, seafood from off the Pacific and Atlantic coasts, organic breads from the Prairies, and more. And sweets galore, like Nanaimo bars, butter tarts and *tarte au sucre*, three of his favorites.

Those who wanted to experience a Canadian winter would have the option of skating on an outdoor ice rink located on the top deck on the opposite side of the Constellation Club. It would be lit up after dark, and there would be blowers blowing in soft imitation snowflakes. And there would be hot chocolate stations and beaver tail pastries made and served on the spot. It couldn't get more Canadian than that.

Vance smiled. The deep-fried pastry, shaped like a beaver tail and topped with anything from cinnamon and sugar to whipped cream and hazelnut chocolate spread, was something he always enjoyed after skating on Ottawa's Rideau Canal, one of Canada's iconic landmarks. There were thousands of skaters and always a line for the beaver tails.

As he changed into swim trunks and a white cotton T-shirt, Vance couldn't help wondering what Chanelle was doing now, and where she would be dining this evening.

Playing volleyball with Adrien in the pool gave Vance a feeling of lightness that he hadn't felt in a long time. Along with a twinge of guilt. He had neglected his godfather duties these past months, and he had missed this. Having fun with a kid. A special kid, who had stolen his heart from the moment Vance had seen his pink and puckered little face in the hospital.

Mariah had asked him if he would be the child's godfather.

"Hell, yes," he had blurted, and then, more cautiously, "Does that mean I have to change diapers?"

"That's part of the deal, Sir Vancelot," she had replied with a shake of her head. "Don't worry, we'll have you practicing on a regular basis. You'll be a pro by the time you have one or nine of your own." Vance had feigned looking horrified, and Mariah and her husband, Chris, had burst out laughing.

Mariah had been true to her word. Adrien had gotten used to Vance being around from the very beginning, and whenever Chris was out of town on business—which was often, since he was the head of a mining engineering company that had projects all over the globe—Vance had gladly stepped up his godfather duties.

Enjoying double-scoop ice cream cones after their swim, Vance felt a contentment that had eluded him after his father had died. He realized that a part of him—maybe a big part of him—had shut down. The part that was all about the enjoyment of simple things, like splashing around a pool and having a cone with his nephew.

But he was determined to change his routine of the past nine months. He would spend more time with Adrien.

And maybe it was time to make some other changes, too...

Vance felt a thrumming in his chest as an image of Chanelle broke through his thoughts.

A coil of desire skimmed through his veins at the memory of her lying on the chaise lounge with that mint-green swimsuit clinging to her body like a second skin.

Yes, he needed to make some changes.

Starting with bringing Adrien back and then seeing if he could find Chanelle.

A flash of pink and purple caught his eye as he leaped up the open stairway to the top deck. From this center point, he could see a number of people clambering up the rock-climbing wall, and a line of others waiting for their turn. The pink and purple lady at the end of the line had auburn hair tied up in a ponytail.

Could it be Chanelle?

She turned slightly, and Vance's pulse leaped. It *was* her. He strode toward her, a strange wave of happiness washing over him. He had decided on a whim to start looking for

Chanelle on the top deck and work his way down. Maybe this was a sign…

"Hey, miss," he called, just steps behind her.

She whirled around, her ponytail flicking him sharply across the chin. "Oh, sorry," she said, her eyes widening. "Didn't mean to strike, but you kinda crept up on me."

"There you go, insinuating that I'm a creep again," he said, smiling at her crookedly.

Chanelle's eyelashes fluttered, and her mouth opened defensively. "And there *you* go, putting words in my mouth again."

An electric tingle radiated through Vance at the teasing tone of her words. He gazed at her wordlessly for a few moments, unable to draw his eyes away from the gleaming hazel green of hers.

Finally the line shifted as another rock climber began his ascent. "So is this your first time?" he said, gesturing toward the wall.

"Yes, I've mustered up the courage to try something new on this cruise," she said with a chuckle. "I considered the Sky Promenade, but after watching the video, I decided to leave that to the daredevils."

"Hmm." He surveyed her thoughtfully. "Are you afraid of heights?"

"Well…" She turned to scan the extensive series of ropes positioned above the skating rink at one far end of the ship. "I'm afraid that with *my* luck, *I'll* be the one whose safety harness breaks."

"Not gonna happen," he said, shaking his head. "I think, Miss Robinson, that there are some trust issues here that we have to deal with." The line moved forward again, leaving two more people waiting in front of Chanelle. "Come on, let me show you that you can do this. Conquer your fear, put your trust in the universe…"

"The universe isn't going to catch me if I fall," she retorted.

"But *I* will." He heard the words jump out of his mouth. "Look, Chanelle, you don't even have to worry about me catching you, because you won't fall. Safety is our number-one priority onboard this ship. Trust me."

Vance saw her forehead crease. "Okay, here's the deal. I haven't actually tried the rope walk myself. And to tell you the truth," he murmured, leaning forward as if to share a secret he didn't want anyone to hear, "*I'm* not exactly crazy about heights. I'm a water guy, remember?" He patted himself on the back, where he had the Aquarius symbol tattooed. "So how about we both try something new and scary together?"

Chanelle was gaping at him as if he were delusional. "You've got to be kidding." She was momentarily distracted as the person in front of her went to get fitted with her safety harness. She turned back to Vance. "You're *not* kidding."

Vance grinned. "Come on, Chanelle. It's now or never. If you can do *this*, you can do anything."

Chanelle blinked at him. Then her gaze shifted upward to the Sky Promenade.

She took a deep breath and slowly exhaled, her eyes meeting his again. "Fine," she declared. "Lead the way!"

From her platform, strapped into her safety harness, Chanelle scanned the view around her with a fluttering in her stomach that continued downward into her legs. The sky was a calm blue with the occasional fluffy cloud drifting nonchalantly by. The sea below was a deeper blue and not as calm, the froth of whitecaps disappearing and reappearing with every undulation. Lined against the side of the ship was a series of lifeboats. Chanelle breathed in and out slowly, hoping she wouldn't hyperventilate.

What on earth had made her agree to this?

Her gaze shifted to the colorful system of thick rungs that resembled a giant crocheted doily suspended above the ice rink. Each stretch of ladder led to a post with a circular platform where you stopped and gathered your courage before attempting the next rope ladder. Some ladders were horizontal, some slightly vertical, with vertical ropes suspended on either side.

Chanelle held her breath as Vance took his first step. She watched the rope ladder swing with his every movement, and she gasped when his foot seemed to be slipping. And then Vance gingerly made his way across the next half dozen rungs before stepping onto the circular platform and turning around to give her a thumbs-up sign.

Chanelle looked above to the metal track into which her safety rope was inserted, so she could glide along as she maneuvered the swinging steps. She could either cling to this rope, which was attached to her body harness, or grasp the cord dangling on either side of her to help her keep her balance.

Why am I doing this? she asked herself again. Vance had encouraged her to conquer her fear, put her trust in the universe…to trust him.

Perhaps she *did* have trust issues, as he had suggested. Maybe deep down she was afraid that history would repeat itself when it came to men, and that whoever came into her life would eventually abandon her… Maybe she was afraid of letting go of her job and trying something new. Maybe she was afraid of letting go of the HSP safety net that kept her cautious and protected.

But maybe it also kept her from experiencing life fully. When had she last felt adrenaline pumping in her veins like right now? Yes, she was afraid, about to step out onto the rope ladder, but she felt an exhilaration at the thought of doing it anyway. She looked across at Vance, who nodded at her with a confident smile and gave her another thumbs-up.

With her heart clanging against her ribs, Chanelle clasped the vertical ropes on either side of her and planted her foot on the first rung. The view below her made her knees tremble. She forced herself to focus on the rung, and gripping the ropes even harder, she put her left foot forward.

The sway of the ladder made her give a yelp. There was no way she could continue…

"You can do it, Chanelle."

Vance's calm voice reached her, and her head snapped up to look at him. His expression was just as calm, as if he knew that that was what she needed instead of a loud exhortation or cheer.

She had to believe that the harness wouldn't let go, that she wouldn't plummet to the ice rink. *Trust me*, Vance had said.

With whatever ounce of courage that still remained in her, Chanelle wobbled across the ladder and stepped up on the platform and into Vance's arms.

Vance tightened his arms around her. "I knew you could do it," he murmured close to her ear. Chest to chest, the heightened pumping of his heart—and hers—made him wish they were alone somewhere so he could savor the sensation that was flooding him.

He felt something primal, instinctive…a desire to protect this woman who had been brave enough to go against her own natural instincts and put her trust in the universe. *In him.* And the way she was clinging to him made him wonder if she could sense his feelings.

Out of the corner of his eye, he could see the attendant waiting for him and Chanelle to proceed before allowing the next guest to take a step forward. There were still plenty of ladders and bridges to navigate. They had to move on.

"Okay, Chanelle, one step at a time. Ready?"

She looked up at him, and his heart swelled at the look in the misty green depths of her eyes. This was not going to be easy for him, either. He would rather be in the pool than up in the air. Taking a deep breath, he released his arms around Chanelle and grasped the vertical ropes. "I'll be waiting for you," he told her huskily before stepping forward.

With open arms.

"My legs feel wobbly," Chanelle said as they left the Sky Promenade. "In fact, I feel wobbly all over…"

Vance nodded. "Join the club. It's the adrenaline rush." He put his hand under her elbow. "How about we sit down for a few minutes with a nice refreshing drink?"

"No alcohol for me," Chanelle protested. "That would finish me off. You'd have to carry me the rest of the way."

"I meant something fruity. Like a tall, cool glass of freshly squeezed lemonade. Or a mango-peach power drink. And by the way, Chanelle," he added with a grin, "my knees are wobbly, too, but not too wobbly to carry a Sagittarius warrior." He raised a hand to give her a high five. "You killed it up there."

She lifted her chin. "I did, didn't I?" She gave a little laugh. "So yes, I'll let you buy me a drink. Mango-peach sounds yummy."

"Mmm. I don't recall offering to foot the bill. But since I'm such a chivalrous guy, I'll do the chivalrous thing. *This time.*"

"Thank you, *Sir Vancelot.*" She beamed at him. "And by the way…you killed it up there, too!"

CHAPTER TEN

CHANELLE WANTED SOMETHING a little more dressy for Canada Night. The captain of *Aquarius* and some of the senior officers and staff would be greeting guests on Deck Five from eight to nine, and those who wished could have their professional photo taken with the captain during the last half hour. Not that *she* was interested in a photo…

Stop kidding yourself, an inner voice taunted. *You may not be interested in meeting the captain of Aquarius or getting a photo, but there will most certainly be a certain Vance Kingston there to impress...*

Did she want to impress him?

Maybe, a small voice admitted.

Something had happened between them up on the Sky Promenade. She wasn't sure if it was the moment when she had looked across at him on the circular platform, and he had nodded for her to proceed, his eyes as calm and blue as the sky above them. Or when she had made it across the first ladder and had literally sunk into his arms. All she could hear against his chest was his heartbeat along with hers.

She had accomplished a feat she had never thought herself capable of. And she would have never done it without Vance's encouragement. Every step of the way. His arms around her had given her such a wondrous feeling of support.

Or maybe something more...

She felt excited about the evening ahead. She was here on a cruise, and she intended to enjoy as much of it as she could.

Chanelle sifted through her dresses in the closet for something that might go with the Canada Night theme. She stopped when she came to a white cotton dress with splashes of red poppies. Well, they were as close as she could get to the red maple leaf on the Canadian flag. The dress was sleeveless, with a fitted bodice, snazzy red belt and skirt that flared from the waist, reaching to above her knees. And her new ruby earrings matched perfectly. As Chanelle swirled to look at herself in the mirror, she felt like a different person. A carefree, much younger person, without the preoccupations that had clung to her while at work.

Chanelle took a deep breath. She hadn't made much time to go out in the evenings when she had been working. She had usually come home late, exhausted, with thoughts only of getting into a shower and pajamas. Had Parker ever even seen her dressed up like this?

The thought of Parker vanished as quickly as it had come. All she could picture in her mind was the expression she hoped to see on Vance's face when he caught sight of her in this gorgeous dress... She swirled around, loving how the skirt swirled with her. The words of her horoscope came back to her:

Your inner world is transitioning and spinning you to a higher consciousness.

She smiled at herself in the mirror. She was spinning, all right.

And she liked how it felt.

Chanelle chose a black purse that matched the black

centers of the poppies, slipped on black high-heeled sandals and headed to the Galaxy Café. She looked forward to enjoying some of the featured dishes—like Digby scallops and other maritime delights—and then she'd make her way to Deck Five.

The place was bustling. As Chanelle looked around for an empty table and didn't see one, she regretted not arriving earlier. Pursing her lips, she considered leaving and trying one of the other dining spots but was blocked by a passing group.

"That's the nice young lady who helped me today," a voice came out of nowhere. "Invite her over, Vance. There's an empty spot at our table."

Through the shifting throng, Chanelle turned and caught sight of Mrs. Kingston, who was smiling directly at her while nudging Vance gently on the arm. Vance's sister and nephew were staring at Chanelle openly, and as Chanelle met Vance's enigmatic gaze, she felt a flush travel up her neck to her cheeks, which she was sure were now as red as the poppies.

"That's the lady who tried to rescue me," Adrien cried, pointing directly at Chanelle.

Chanelle wished there was a way of rescuing herself. She hadn't expected to meet Vance's family, let alone dine with them. Now she had no choice but to wait for Vance to approach. A few moments later, the group had moved on and Vance was striding toward her. Before her eyes met his, Chanelle just managed to scan gray straight-leg trousers that fit impeccably and a baby-blue fitted shirt and a Canadian-themed tie with alternating rows of loons and maple leaves. Under other circumstances, she might have joked about it.

"The Archer—slash—good fairy strikes again," he said, a glint in his blue eyes.

"It happens when I least expect it," she replied, unable to keep a note of defensiveness from creeping into her voice.

Her pulse spiked when Vance cupped her elbow to direct her toward his table. "I believe you've met everyone in my family but haven't been properly introduced to my mother. Chanelle Robinson, Elizabeth Kingston."

"Nice to see you again, Mrs. Kingston." Chanelle noticed that they had started on their meal, but Vance's spot was empty. "I'm sorry to disturb your dinner."

"Please call me Betty." The older woman smiled as they shook hands. "And it's not a disturbance. Is this your first cruise, Chanelle?"

Chanelle nodded.

"And you're traveling alone?"

She nodded again, feeling a prickling sensation at the back of her neck. It happened whenever she became anxious, and right now she was very apprehensive about being questioned about her personal life. If there was anything she was highly sensitive about, it was either about work or *that*.

"That's very adventurous of you. Well, since you were so kind to help me today, Chanelle, I'm sure Vance here will be happy to help you in any way during the cruise. Right, son?"

Chanelle groaned inwardly. She was afraid to look at Vance. He must be feeling even more cornered than *her*.

"It would be...my pleasure," he drawled. He grinned as Adrien took a huge bite of a butter tart. "Would you care to join me for dinner, Chanelle? My family started without me, as I was at a meeting. They'll be leaving shortly and I'll be all by myself." His eyes glinted at her expectantly.

Chanelle's heart flipped. "Oh...um...sure," she said and, nodding to the group, she strode toward the nearest buffet, her nerve endings tingling knowing that Vance was right behind her.

When they returned to the table, Vance's family was ready to leave. "Goodbye, Chanelle," Betty said. "We'll be heading to Deck Five for the captain's event. Perhaps we'll see you there?"

"Perhaps." Chanelle didn't want to commit; *this* encounter had already made her feel somewhat overwhelmed. She smiled her goodbyes and tried to focus on enjoying the famous scallops from off the Nova Scotia coast while Vance dug into his *tourtière* and poutine. She glanced at him as he was licking a dribble of the cheesy gravy before it slid down to his chin, and the split second that he caught her gaze, she felt her insides quiver. He ran his tongue over his lips and then flashed her a grin. *"Je m'excuse,"* he apologized. "I adore Quebecois cuisine, and it adores my face." He slid his empty plate away and reached for the dessert plate. "And now for the pièce de résistance…"

Vance bit into his butter tart. It was sweet, but not as sweet as the woman sitting across from him, munching delicately on the lacy cookie she had chosen. Her auburn hair was gleaming in the sun that streamed through the window, and with the stunning dress she had chosen, she could easily be the subject of a painting.

Vance was convinced now that fate was deliberately making them cross paths.

It was impossible not to notice someone as beautiful as Chanelle. But being with her again, something deep inside him was telling him it was more than just her looks that was drawing his attention. It was her actions, whether it was the way she had sprung up for Adrien or how she had readily helped his mother.

He was seeing glimpses of her highly sensitive qualities, he realized. And he liked them just as much as her physical qualities…

They hadn't exchanged much conversation over dinner. She had seemed very pensive, and he hadn't wanted to disrupt her thoughts. As he bit into his second butter tart, a drop of syrup began to slide down one corner of his mouth. He saw Chanelle's mouth twitch and he laughed. "I told you, French Canadian food and I have this mutual attraction…"

Vance wiped his mouth with a napkin. Chanelle was gazing at him enigmatically, and he felt something shift inside his chest. He wanted to reach out and squeeze her hands and impulsively tell her that sharing her company had been another treat for him, and that he had also enjoyed their time together in the Sky Promenade and afterward at the fruit bar.

It was crazy, but despite his intention earlier to not seek her out, Vance suddenly wished he could take hold of Chanelle's hands and get her out of that chair and into his arms. Right or wrong, he wanted to taste her lips, and trail kisses down her neck to that lovely spot at the base of her neck where her pulse was softly beating.

His eyes burned with longing as he held her gaze, and a flicker in Chanelle's green hazel depths made him wonder if *she* could possibly be feeling the same way…

CHAPTER ELEVEN

CHANELLE DIDN'T KNOW if she should feel relieved or upset at the sudden appearance of a waiter with a jug of water to refill their glasses. For a moment there had been something in Vance's expression that had made her want to catch her breath. But when she transferred her gaze from the waiter back to Vance, whatever she had seen—or imagined— was gone.

He rose and asked her if she would be going to the captain's event. Unsure if he was leading up to asking her to accompany him, or if he was just being polite, Chanelle hesitated. Maybe that look in his eyes had just been a figment of her imagination. Like a mirage for a desert traveler seeking water...

So what had she been seeking? An indication that Vance Kingston—a seasoned playboy—had feelings for her? Feelings that went beyond a physical attraction?

You're delusional, her inner voice mocked. *Do you actually think this Zodiac magnate would be interested in you in that way? Wake up and smell the sea air, honey.*

She saw Vance glance at his watch.

He was obviously anxious to get back to his family.

She stood up. "I think I'll just go back to my stateroom," she told him. "I've developed a bit of a headache, and if I rest awhile, it may not develop into a migraine."

Vance frowned. "Do you suffer from migraines often?"

"When I've been under a lot of stress, or if when the barometric pressure changes. Usually before my head starts pounding, I get a warning, an aura."

He raised his eyebrows. "What do you mean?"

"Auras can vary. For me, it's a zigzag that flashes in my eye, making it hard to focus," she said. "So if I'm looking at you, I don't see you the way you are. I see you like a Picasso painting..."

"Wow, I had no idea," he said. He peered at her closely, as he were expecting to see an aura develop right then and there. "Will you be okay to go back to your stateroom alone?"

"My vision is fine at the moment," Chanelle said drily. "Your features are perfectly in place."

And perfect, she added silently.

"If you *do* end up with a migraine, please don't hesitate to dial the medical facility. And if you want to de-stress, you might want to consider a spa treatment while you're here."

"Thanks. I'd better go. I'm keeping you from the captain's event," she said lightly.

"Not at all," he murmured. "Take care of yourself, Chanelle. And if you *do* feel better, I hope you consider coming back to the event."

She nodded and started to walk away. Of course she would take care of herself. But she had no intention of going to the captain's event with Vance. Even though she had seen something in his eyes moments earlier that had ignited a spark of excitement in her veins...

No, she tried to convince herself as she entered her stateroom and plopped down on the edge of her bed, she had only imagined something in Vance's eyes.

Chanelle caught sight of herself in mirrored panels on either side of the television unit. Her cheeks didn't need blush; they never had. They were quite rosy right now, a telltale sign of the anxiety caused by her ambivalent inner voices: *Vance Kingston is interested in you. There is no way Vance Kingston is interested in you.*

Chanelle couldn't imagine finding someone who would understand her sensitivities and the demands of her work. Her previous relationship had crumbled because she had made her work a priority.

Maybe she just didn't know how to be in a balanced relationship.

She had things to work out about herself…her job…her future. So how could she possibly entertain even the remotest idea of being with another man? It hadn't even crossed her mind when she had booked this cruise…

Chanelle shook her head in frustration. Here she was, stuck and feeling restless in her room, while people were enjoying themselves at events all over the ship. She could be at the featured artist event or magic show, or at the '70s disco party, or maybe trying out her luck at the casino…

Who was she kidding?

She probably didn't have the concentration to sit through a gallery presentation, she didn't know if her head could take the blaring disco music and she didn't even gamble. Chanelle sighed and impatiently grabbed the pamphlet showing the evening's events. This was apparently the other side of Sagittarians. The negative side. Restless and impatient. Yup, that was *her* right now.

Chanelle tossed the pamphlet down. Being highly sensitive hadn't always worked in her favor over the years. She had taken herself out of play in many situations—often social ones in high school and university, and later, with work colleagues—because of her HSP sensibilities. Which meant she had missed out on fun opportunities because of her inhibitions and inability to loosen up. She hadn't given herself the chance to explore new friendships, new possibilities.

And in worrying about the negative, she had missed out on the positive.

She was still doing that.

It was time for her to stop second-guessing herself and start taking chances.

Take a leap of faith.

Chanelle stood up and smoothed down her dress. She would not stay cloistered in her stateroom and miss out on the fun on the ship. She freshened up, took a pill for her headache and, after applying a new coat of lip gloss, she grabbed her purse and made her way toward Deck Five.

Her brain might be trying to convince her that Vance Kingston had absolutely nothing to do with her decision, but deep down she knew the opposite was true.

And she was willing to risk everything to discover how he really felt about her by looking into his eyes...

The captain had welcomed everybody on deck, introduced some of his crew, and was now engaged in the photo session with guests. He'd be at it for a while, Vance thought, eyeing the line. In the meantime, the jazz musicians had begun their repertoire, and couples were already moving toward the dance floor. His mother, Mariah and Adrien had said their good-nights. They would be getting up fairly early to board the tender for Coral Haven, and so would he, but he had told them that he wanted to stay behind for a bit to enjoy the music and relaxed atmosphere.

That had been a white lie. He was waiting to see if Chanelle would come back. His anticipation had caused a tensing of his stomach muscles as he directed regular glances toward all the possible entry points she could take to Deck Five. He had almost finished his brandy, and he'd have to make up his mind whether to order another.

Occasionally a couple or small group of women would come up to chat with him. Some of the women glanced at him with undisguised interest, and he satisfied them with a generous smile and a group selfie if they asked.

The dance floor was filling up. The deck had a patio atmosphere, with strings of multicolored suspended lights that provided a soft illumination under the starry night. And sensual music that made you want to slow dance for hours…

If you had the right woman in your arms.

A waiter came by, and Vance ordered another brandy before walking to the railing to look out at the shifting waves. He couldn't help thinking that taking a cruise by oneself could be difficult emotionally, especially when couples were dancing nearby, their arms clasped tightly around each other.

Vance felt a jab in his gut. For the first time in his life, he had a feeling that there was something—no, *someone*—missing in his life. Not that his life had been devoid of women before his father had died. Far from it. But they had all been superficial relationships, with no commitment. He had never *pretended* to be committed. Wasn't that the reason he had earned the title of playboy? And he had enjoyed it for quite a while.

But those relationships were over. He didn't want superficial any longer, he realized. And as Vance stared at the expanse of sea under the stars, he realized something else: he needed to let go of the coping mechanisms he had subconsciously constructed in the past that had affected his relationships.

If he wanted more than just a temporary fling with a woman, he'd have to break down the walls of distrust around his heart and allow himself to be vulnerable. To not withhold his emotions in order to prevent himself from getting abandoned.

And hurt. Like he had done with his father.

His dad was gone.

And after his death, Vance had risked everything for the business. Yes, he had done it initially out of guilt, but as the weeks went by, the sense of guilt had diminished as his interest and passion for the company had grown.

And now his gut was telling him that he needed to take a new risk and allow himself to be open to a serious relationship…

He gulped back the remainder of his brandy. Turning around, his pulse spiked at the sight of Chanelle making her way past a group of couples who were chatting with drinks in hand. Vance saw every movement she made as if his vision had clicked to slow motion mode: the toss of her shiny auburn hair, the tentative smile on her poppy-red lips, the gentle sway of her hips in that fabulous dress and the even more fabulous curves of her legs. And how could he fail to notice the glances directed her way, both male and female?

Chanelle looked more enchanting than ever. And Vance was more than ready to be enchanted. With his heart drumming so loud he couldn't hear the music around him, he headed toward her.

CHAPTER TWELVE

AT CHANELLE'S FIRST SCAN of the guests on deck, she didn't see Vance, and disappointment hit her like a cold wave. And then she spotted him leaving his place at the railing and walking toward her, and that cold wave turned into warm and bubbly surf.

Vance extended his hand and she took it, letting him lead her to a table for two further away from the musicians. He asked how she was feeling, and Chanelle told him that she was feeling better. She accepted his offer of a drink, and a waiter returned with a virgin Caesar for her and a coffee for Vance.

"I had my drinks before you arrived," he told her. "While I was sticking around to see if you'd come back." He looked at her with those intense blue eyes, and the warm feeling inside her climbed up a few notches.

They sat companionably as they listened to the music and watched the guests dancing. When the jazz musicians took a break, two new performers proceeded to the stage with their Latin guitars. And when they began their second song, Vance asked her to dance.

She could hardly believe that here she was on the second night of the cruise, in the arms of Vance Kingston. *Slow dancing...*

Chanelle couldn't blame the drink for feeling as if she were up in the clouds, floating toward heaven. So the only thing she could blame was Vance Kingston, and his touch that was making her pulse throb erratically. And his spicy cologne that was driving her to distraction. She caught her breath as he pressed her closer, and her forehead brushed against his jawline. If she turned to the right, his lips would be close enough to...

This was madness. How had this happened?

Chanelle had not envisioned a man in the picture—*her picture*—for a long time. And a known playboy, who was doing what he did best: flirting and making her fall for him like every other woman he had played with in the past. Only, unlike those women, Chanelle was neither glamorous nor wealthy...

Chanelle stiffened as the stark truth hit her. The stars in her eyes dissipated and left a dark, black void full of doubts.

"Are you okay, Chanelle?" Vance said huskily against her ear, and she realized that she had stopped dancing.

How could she possibly respond?

She didn't want to be rude, but she had to protect herself. These were dangerous waters she had entered. And judging from her body's reaction to the man who had led her there, she had to make her way back to safe shores before something happened that she would regret. In a few days, the cruise would be over. She was delusional if she thought this shipboard flirting could lead to anything else. She had to put a stop to it.

Now. She was way out of her league.

"My headache's back," she lied. "I think I'll just return to my stateroom."

Vance's blue eyes pierced hers. He didn't release her hand, nor his arm around her waist.

"We can go somewhere quieter..."

"I don't think—" Chanelle hesitated as a couple, locked in an embrace, bumped into them.

Chanelle and Vance broke apart, and after the couple apologized and continued dancing, Vance said brusquely, "Okay, let's go."

Chanelle felt his arm around her as he ushered her inside and she was conscious of a few curious gazes following them. Were they thinking that she and Vance…? Her cheeks burned. She hadn't expected Vance to accompany her.

When they got to her stateroom, Chanelle unlocked the door, opened it a crack, then turned to Vance. "Good night," she murmured.

His eyes glittered down at her. "How can it be, when you don't trust me?"

Chanelle's eyes widened. She opened her mouth and then shut it, completely at a loss for words.

"Chanelle, I haven't known you for very long, but from the time I *have* spent with you, I have picked up on a few cues. Like how your lovely cheeks flame up when you're feeling stressed or distressed." He cocked his head at her appraisingly. "Now I could be wrong, but I have a wild hunch that you were worried about my intentions and therefore had to come up with an excuse to leave."

Chanelle's cheeks were burning. She heard voices approaching from the end of the hall and quickly opened the door wider. The last thing she wanted was people seeing who was at her stateroom door at this time of night. "Please come in for a minute," she urged.

A few moments later, she had no choice but to face him. And be truthful.

She sighed. "I'm sorry I had to make up a fib this time. I was telling the truth earlier, though, and I did take a pill before going to Deck Five." She looked up at him warily.

Vance's mouth quirked, and he reached over to take one of her hands. "Chanelle, I'm not your confessor," he said huskily. "But please tell me if I'm right. I can handle it." His eyes met hers without wavering.

Chanelle bit her lip. He had spoken candidly and hadn't sounded as if he were playing games with her or trying to manipulate her in any way. "You're right," she conceded. "I don't know you very well, and I'm not sure I can trust your intentions. And if you want me to be honest—" she eyed him defensively "—your reputation precedes you."

Vance's eyes narrowed. "Ouch. But thanks for being honest." He looked down at her hand in his and was silent for a few moments. When he looked up, there was regret in the depths of his eyes.

Chanelle felt a twinge of guilt. She hadn't intended to hurt his feelings. *So now what?*

"The past is the past," he said quietly. "I can't undo that, Chanelle. But I'm not the same man I was nine months ago, and the years before that." He gently let go of her hand. "The death of a family member changes you…"

Chanelle felt a lump in her throat as Vance's voice wavered. Maybe it had been wrong of her to bring up his reputation, but it had slipped out before she could think clearly.

She realized the stateroom was dark except for the dim light in the entrance. She should turn on the other lights.

"Now that I know how *you* feel, Chanelle, would you want to hear the truth about *my* feelings?"

"You must feel that I'm judging you…"

"No worries. I have a thick skin. Or rather, a layer of chain mail under these clothes." He suddenly grinned at her. "I'm not called Sir Vancelot for nothing."

Chanelle couldn't help smiling, and some of the tension in the air seemed to dissipate.

"So may I have your ear, Lady Chanelle?"

"I suppose I can spare a minute or two," she murmured. "But then you'll have to go. I've booked an early excursion

tomorrow on Grand Cayman." She strode into the room
and turned on a light. She sat on one edge of the couch and
Vance sat down beside her.

"Swimming with the stingrays?"

"*Not!* With my sensitive skin, I'd probably break out in
some kind of a rash."

"Going to Hell?"

"Pardon?"

Vance chuckled. "It's a town named for its unique rock
formations. It's part of the island tour and includes the
turtle center."

Chanelle laughed. "For a moment I was about to tell
you where to go!"

Vance burst out laughing. "And I called you a *lady*?"

Chanelle pretended to look at him with disdain.

"Well, where will you be heading, my lady?"

Chanelle felt something flip in her chest at the smile
in his voice and eyes as he said *my lady.* "I'm heading to
a beach with the name of some kind of alcohol. Whisky
Beach or something to that effect."

He chuckled again. "Rum Point Beach."

"Yes, that's it! Rum, whisky—it's all the same to me,
since I indulge in neither."

"You're a funny lady."

"Why? Because I don't drink much?" Chanelle frowned
at him, confused.

"Because you make me laugh."

"Is that what you wanted to tell me? That you find me
amusing?"

Vance gazed at her without responding for a few moments. And then he placed his hand over hers. An inner
voice told her to move her hand away, but a stronger voice
said the opposite. She couldn't tear her gaze away, either.

"I want to tell you a lot of things, Chanelle. Yes, I

find you amusing. And kind. And dedicated. And—" he squeezed her hand gently "—and beautiful." His eyes seemed to darken as they gazed into hers with such intensity that she caught her breath. And then he was leaning toward her, and the magnetic force that his eyes had ignited seemed to be pulling her toward him as well.

When their lips touched, her eyes closed automatically and she was unable to process anything else but the instinctive need to respond. She felt Vance release her hand, and a moment later both his hands were cupping her face, deepening his kiss until her whole body tingled. Had a kiss ever felt this sweet? This…delicious?

When he finally pulled back gently to look into her eyes again, Chanelle felt like she was swimming in their darkest, deepest, most pleasurable depths.

She traced her fingers against the stubble of his jaw. Vance caught his breath and suddenly brought her hand down. "I need to go now, Chanelle," he said gruffly. "I'm sorry, but I don't want to stay and have you regret it later."

Vance felt like an absolute heel, leaving Chanelle with that look in her eyes. The look of a dejected puppy. But how could he stay without knowing for sure that she wasn't just caught up in the moment and later wouldn't blame him for taking advantage of her?

Kissing her had been his first big mistake. Yes, she had responded, and yes, he had wanted to continue, but something inside him had tugged on the reins of his passion and made him stop. Chanelle Robinson was vulnerable. She had had two big changes in her life in the past year and had booked this cruise to relax and make choices about her future, not get involved with *him*.

Vance returned to his stateroom and walked out to his balcony. He watched the waves rising and cresting, and he felt a similar agitation inside. A swell of happiness that Chanelle was attracted to him, and then a sense of deflation that somehow he had handled it all wrong.

He should have kept it light. They had been laughing, caught up in a play of words, and he had to go and spoil it by letting his testosterone take over.

Vance groaned. He could have even stopped after he had told her that she was beautiful. But he hadn't been content with the sparkle that had lit up her eyes at his words. He had wanted further proof of her feelings…

Well, he had gotten proof, all right. But when Chanelle had demonstrated her desire, his inner voice had abruptly broken through the sweetness of her kiss to tell him to slow things down, that she was vulnerable and that she needed space to work things out in her life.

He started to unbutton his shirt when a tentative knock on his door made him freeze. His heart jangled against his rib cage. He leaped to open it, but it wasn't Chanelle standing there. He tried to control his emotions and smiled at the environmental director he had met with earlier. He and Pauline had become friends since he had started working at Zodiac, and she would be leaving the next morning for her upcoming wedding on Grand Cayman Island at the end of the week.

She handed him a gift box. "Since I won't be at the gala to celebrate your new position, *President Kingston*," she said, hugging him.

"Thanks, Pauline. And I have a surprise for you when we're all back in Toronto."

"Sounds good," she said with a laugh. "I like surprises."

He wished her the best, gave her another hug and watched her leave. Turning to reenter his stateroom, he started at the sight of Chanelle halfway down the opposite hallway, her face as frozen as her body. She had intended to come to his stateroom, he realized, only to find him hugging another woman who was just leaving.

He had to explain…

But before her name had finished leaving his lips, Chanelle had turned around swiftly and disappeared around the corner.

CHAPTER THIRTEEN

AFTER VANCE HAD left her stateroom, Chanelle had remained transfixed on the couch, her face feeling as numb as her brain. What had just happened?

Vance had ignited something within her that she had never experienced in her previous relationship. A combination of feelings that had produced an alchemy that was powerful, magical.

A desire to know Vance to the core.

The magic had been sparked by his touch, his kiss, his words…

And then he had pulled away.

Because he had thought that if he stayed, she might regret it later…

He couldn't have been more wrong.

Chanelle had stared woodenly at the door, considering a swirl of other possible reasons for his decision. Farfetched though it seemed, could it be that deep down, he was worried about her motives?

That she was really after his money and was trying to ensnare him?

Chanelle did not want to accept the excuse Vance had used. He had pinned his decision on *her*, making it look as if he was considering her feelings before his own. Feelings that she *might* have regrets if they had allowed their passion to play out…but then, she *was* terrified of getting hurt again. Did she go into self-protection mode whenever things got serious? Maybe…

But *he* had decided to play it safe and deny them both what they had been close—*so close*—to experiencing.

And he hadn't given her a say about it.

Chanelle had felt shortchanged. With an unexpected surge of warrior determination, she had leaped off the couch and decided to talk to Vance, thinking that at the very least, she could ask him to open up about his true feelings, just as she intended to be about *hers*.

And then, whatever would be, would be…

Minutes later, the elevator had opened to the lobby on Vance's deck. Chanelle's nerve endings were practically crackling, and she had breathed deeply to try to steady her heartbeat. She had turned into the long hallway, only to spot a woman wearing the familiar Zodiac employee blazer hugging Vance. And then he was telling the woman that he had a surprise for her when they were back in Toronto. She had laughed, and then Vance had given her another hug.

At this point Chanelle's feet had felt cemented to the floor. Like in a nightmare, with her vocal cords frozen as well.

Seconds later, Vance had gazed *her* way, and Chanelle had clearly seen the dismay on his face.

She hadn't wanted to stick around. Nothing he attempted to say would have mended the gash in her heart.

Once a playboy, always a playboy, she had thought bitterly as her gaze dropped to his unbuttoned shirt. And she had turned and fled, taking the stairs instead of waiting for the elevator. It was only when she had arrived back in her stateroom, and she had bolted the door, that she had burst into tears.

Damn him, she thought now between sobs. He had played her for a fool. No wonder he hadn't wanted to stay.

He had planned an *encounter* with an employee he was obviously involved with on the ship and back in Toronto.

Well, he could have her. And while he was at it, he could also go to hell.

Vance had considered running after Chanelle but had decided against it. She would not have wanted a scene of any kind in front of other guests. He would wait awhile and then go and knock on her stateroom door. And hope that she would let him in and give him the chance to explain.

Would she hear him out after what she had witnessed? Being highly sensitive, Chanelle would have arrived at the worst possible conclusion about him. And he couldn't blame her.

Putting himself in her shoes, he could understand why she wouldn't want to face him. She had been on her way to see him—that alone made his heart twinge—only to find him hugging another woman. And Chanelle must have heard the exchange between him and Pauline as well. His promise of a surprise when they were back in Toronto...

He had to talk to Chanelle. Make her understand...

Vance had another thought. Chanelle was probably not only thinking the worst about *him*, but also about herself. That hurt even more. He groaned. Chanelle had had a rough year personally and professionally, and the tenuous feelings of trust that she had shown him must have immediately shattered. He had seen it on her face.

She would be blaming herself for having allowed him to get so close...and feeling humiliated...

Vance rose and strode to the door. It was almost midnight, but there would be no rest tonight unless he got through to Chanelle. He did up the buttons on his shirt and headed to her stateroom, his pulse as fast as his footsteps.

CHAPTER FOURTEEN

CHANELLE LOOKED AT herself in the bathroom mirror. Her eye makeup had smeared from all the crying she had done, and her eyelids were puffy. *Absolutely beautiful*, she thought bitterly, using Vance's earlier words.

Chanelle was too upset to even attempt sleeping, so instead of changing into her teddy, she put on a pair of shorts and a T-shirt. Knowing that her thoughts would just continue to torment her, she turned on the TV and started flicking the channels mindlessly. Propped up on pillows against the headboard, she felt a flutter of anxiety at the thought of having to spend three more days on the cruise with the possibility of crossing paths with Vance.

If she did run into him, she would not let him see how shattered she was. She had her pride.

And she had absolutely no intention of seeking him out. *Not a chance in hell.* She had allowed herself to succumb to his charms and had ended up feeling like a complete fool.

As she continued changing the channels, Chanelle realized she was clenching her jaw again. And watching TV wasn't helping. She pressed the off switch and turned off all the lights except the lamp by her bedside. She breathed in deeply and tried to focus on the sound of the waves from the open balcony door.

Her attempt at mindful meditation was interrupted by a soft tap at her door. Chanelle felt her stomach coil instantly into a hard knot. She remained motionless. Had it been her imagination?

The knock came again. "Chanelle? Please give me a chance to explain…"

Chanelle's heart tumbled crazily against her rib cage. She couldn't believe that Vance had the nerve to think that she would give him the time of day. Or night. The last thing she intended on doing was opening the door and letting him in. She had made that mistake once, and she wouldn't be so foolish as to allow him in her space again.

"Chanelle? I know it sounds like a cliché, but it's not what you think. You'll understand if you let me in."

Vance was keeping his voice low, but Chanelle could hear both urgency and frustration in it.

"I don't want to explain out in the hall… Please answer, Chanelle."

Chanelle turned off her lamp and pulled the covers over her head.

There's your answer, Mr. Kingston.

She woke up to a baby-blue sky that was painted with soft brushes of pink. It was such a peaceful sight and a sharp contrast to how she felt inside. She couldn't get the memory of Vance and the woman out of her mind. She had had a troubled sleep, waking up every two to three hours, and at one point, she had almost been tempted to go to an upper deck to walk around and clear her head.

Chanelle was glad she had set her cell phone alarm. She couldn't wait to get off the ship and spend the day by herself on Rum Point Beach. Sure, there would be other guests who would be thinking along the same lines, but she was determined to find a quiet spot and just forget everything that had happened to her so far.

She stepped into the shower and tried to keep thoughts

of Vance from following her in. *Fat chance.* How could she forget the feel of him as they danced? The muscled shoulders, his hand firmly clasping hers…and then later, the heady sensation as his lips took possession of hers…

Stop! He used you!

Chanelle turned off the shower. *That's* what she should be focusing on, not his body or his lips, she thought, scowling. She wrapped herself in the guest bathrobe and a few moments later changed into a navy bikini before slipping on a knee-length yellow cotton dress with eyelet accents and spaghetti straps. The multicolored wrap bracelet Kayla had given her was her only accessory.

Chanelle prepared a large beach bag with the essentials and then checked the time. Room service should be arriving shortly. Another smart decision she had made yesterday. She would have her coffee and toast and then make her way down to the tender station on Deck Two. She would at least enjoy the beach today, Chanelle promised herself. And there would be nothing or nobody to prevent that from happening.

Least of all Vance Kingston.

Chanelle took the elevator down to Deck Two. She had received a call from Guest Services while she was having her coffee, advising her that her time to board the tender had changed. For unspecified reasons, she would be leaving half an hour later than she had planned.

When she arrived, there was a group just about to get onboard. She rushed to join them and presented her identification card to one of the security officials. A whistle sounded, and a few moments later, the group proceeded to board. There was a substantial breeze, so Chanelle opted for the covered lower deck. She made her way carefully down the steps, glad to see there were plenty of good seats.

She made her way toward the back, and a sudden shuffling made her look to her right. Her heart felt like it was about to rocket out of her chest…

Chanelle swayed sharply as the tender started moving, and she plopped down hard on the seat closest to her, just arm's length away from where Vance Kingston was standing. And at the far end of the tender, his family was smiling and waving at her.

Vance wished Chanelle would have heard him out last night. He had stared at the door of her stateroom for a few minutes after his last appeal, hoping that Chanelle would change her mind. He had gotten the message loud and clear when he saw from the space at the bottom of the door that she had turned off the light. Giving up, he had headed back to his own stateroom.

He had felt like a total jerk to have hurt Chanelle, even if it *had* been unintentional. And none of it would have happened if he had just continued kissing her instead of leaving her at such a vulnerable moment.

But where would they be now if he had let himself give in to the passion that had been steadily building inside him?

He had to make amends to Chanelle.

For several hours, Vance had racked his brain as to how he should handle this highly sensitive situation with an even more highly sensitive person. Staring up at the ceiling above his bed, Vance had come up with a few ideas and then scrapped them. And then he remembered that she was heading to Rum Point Beach. And he and his family would be taking one of the tenders to Coral Haven. The passengers would all be getting off at Grand Cayman, and Vance's tender would continue on.

The only thing he had to do was to ensure Chanelle boarded the same tender he would already be on. That could be arranged with a quick call. And then Vance would attempt to make another appeal for Chanelle to hear him out. And if he couldn't convince her, she'd still have the option of getting off at Grand Cayman. If Chanelle continued to Coral Haven, it would have to be entirely of her own free will.

Vance met Chanelle's incredulous stare with a polite nod. He had known that it would be as awkward as hell trying to discuss the matter between them with people all around, but he had no other option. He would give it his best shot, and if Chanelle could be convinced to remain on-board instead of going with her original plan, they would be heading to a place that Vance considered heaven on earth. While Mariah, Adrien and his mother relaxed in one section of the rambling villa his father had had built five years ago, Vance would have a better opportunity to set things right with Chanelle.

And if the stars and planets were all aligned in his favor, he and Chanelle would spend an idyllic day together before the tender arrived to take them back to the *Aquarius*.

Vance closed the distance between them by sitting opposite her. He leaned forward. "Chanelle, I can't say a lot now, but I promise you'll understand if you let me explain."

Chanelle's cheeks were like smoldering coals, but her eyes flashed ice. "Oh, I understand," she said stiffly, keeping her voice low.

She turned her gaze away from him to look out at the scenery. He felt bad that her first excursion off the ship had to be tainted by bad feelings. If only she would gaze into his eyes and see the genuine tenderness he felt for her. But of course she couldn't, with the thorn-covered glasses she was wearing…

Vance gazed at Chanelle's profile and felt his heart expanding. It wasn't just *tenderness* he felt for her, for God's sake, it was more than that. It was a truly happy feeling that had eluded him in the past, even when he had thought he was enjoying himself with other women. It was the feeling that he had found a rare treasure when those green-hazel eyes had sparkled under the patio lights on Deck Five.

It was the way his heart had vaulted when she returned his kiss…

Maybe he wasn't quite ready to put a name to it just yet, but if it was what he thought it was, he'd find the right way to let Chanelle know…

Before time ran out on him.

CHAPTER FIFTEEN

COULD *ANY* MAN be trusted? Chanelle tried to focus on the enchanting views of palm trees and charming villas as the tender sped past, but Vance's proximity made it impossible. The lump of bitterness and disillusionment that had settled in her throat and stomach after last night's discovery hadn't lessened any, and now, facing Vance but unable to express herself with so many people around them, Chanelle felt frustrated. And angry.

Chanelle swayed forward as the tender hit a choppy patch of water, and she caught her breath as Vance's arms shot out to steady her. His face was inches away from hers, and now she could see the faded blue of his eyes and the shadows beneath. His Adam's apple bobbed as he swallowed.

He hadn't slept much, either, she thought. Could it have been the result of a guilty conscience? *Good.*

As Chanelle stared at him defiantly, something in Vance's expression made her falter.

There was something there that was different than the way he had looked at her in the past. A look of…of *sadness* that seemed to reach across and connect with something in her own eyes.

And then he smiled at her as he released his hold, but the sadness remained in his eyes.

Chanelle felt a vague urge to let him explain. Her heart started drumming.

Should she relent and at least hear him out?

A chorus of excited voices distracted her. A group of passengers around her rushed off to get a better view of something in the waters.

"A pod of porpoises," Vance said. "Always a delight for tourists."

Chanelle started to rise, but she hesitated as Vance touched her arm. "Can we talk? At least while this diversion lasts?"

Chanelle looked down at his hand at the same time that he withdrew it. His touch, although gentle, had sent a sizzle along her nerve endings. She felt a flush creep up her neck. Taking a deep breath, she sat back down.

He was leaning forward, his brow creased above blue eyes that startled her with their clarity. "Chanelle, I know you're planning to go to Rum Point Beach. But I don't think you'll be able to enjoy it fully with this misunderstanding between us. If you give me a chance, I will clear everything up."

Chanelle raised her eyebrows. How much could he clear up with her before the passengers returned to their seats? "This—this is awkward," she admitted. "I should never have—"

"No, Chanelle. I take full responsibility. I want to explain—better than I did last night—why I needed to leave. And that the person you saw at my door is not who you think she is."

They both turned at another wave of excited shouts from the passengers.

"Look, Chanelle." His voice had a sudden note of urgency. "In a minute—or less—they'll be back and we won't be able to talk. I need more time. I'm asking you to trust me and to stay on the tender. Come to Coral Haven with me instead of going to Rum Point Beach. There will be time and space to make things right." His eyes bored into her like blue spears. "I want to make things right with you, Chanelle."

The passengers started clapping. "That's the end of the porpoise show," Vance said. "And we're almost at Grand Cayman…"

Chanelle had no time to respond as the passengers made their way noisily back to their seats. Her eyes met Vance's as a couple of teenagers zipped past them. No, there was no time—or space—to hear him out.

Do you want to?

She bit her lip, the thrumming in her chest increasing as the tender neared the shore. Moments later, the passengers started to file up the stairway and out, and Chanelle knew she had less than a minute to make a decision. She glanced at Vance's mother and sister, who were absorbed in something Adrien was saying.

Chanelle glanced quickly at the family now exiting the tender. She stood up, her knees feeling wobbly. If she was going to leave, she'd have to go. Now.

Her gaze flew to Vance. He hadn't moved, but his eyes were fixed on hers like lasers. Her brain willed her body to start walking, but her feet were rooted to the floor of the tender.

Chanelle opened her mouth to say something, but the whistle of the tender operator startled her. She bit her lip and, feeling a tremor of anticipation course through her, she promptly sat down.

Vance's heart had jolted when Chanelle had stood up, but when, timeless seconds later, she sat down, his heart had started pumping so hard that he almost put his hand over it to try to calm it down.

This was big. He had seen the indecision on Chanelle's face, the flicker of a frown as she debated in those few seconds whether she should leave and proceed to her excursion on Rum Point Beach or stay and give him the chance to explain. He was both stunned and elated at Chanelle's decision.

He wanted to say something, but his words were stuck in his throat. Chanelle had turned slightly to look out at the activity on Grand Cayman, and he was relieved to have some time to process the impact of her decision. And his reaction to it.

Vance hadn't taken it for granted that she would choose to continue on to Coral Haven. And he had felt a current of indecision himself before he suggested it to her. Was he doing the right thing? Why was he choosing to make things right with a woman he had known for less than two days? And why was he bringing her to Coral Haven? He hadn't brought Brianna there, despite her not-so-subtle hints that she'd love to see his island.

He knew he was complicating things. He had sacrificed so much of the last nine months to the promise he had made to lead the company. He had made it his top priority. Nothing had competed with his razor-sharp intentions. Nothing and nobody. Especially a woman. He had instinctively known that to succeed, he had to suspend his playboy inclinations. At least until he had proven himself at Zodiac Cruises.

But something had changed since he had stepped onboard the *Aquarius*. In his previous relationships, Vance had played it safe, controlling the extent of his emotions. He hadn't allowed himself to become emotionally entangled with any woman. And they had seemed satisfied—for the most part—with the limited scope of his intentions.

It was different with Chanelle. No other woman in the past had intrigued him the way she had. Instantly. And after two days of spending time with her, something deep inside was telling him he needed to take a risk with this woman. Risk showing her that he genuinely cared about her feelings. About her.

He wanted more with her.

And he had to find out if there was any chance that she wanted more with him. If she would let him teach her how to trust.

He couldn't play it safe anymore, and he couldn't toy with Chanelle's emotions. The only way to discover what she wanted was to act now, before the cruise ended and she went back home.

Which was why he had had to provide an opportunity for them to be together.

He wanted more than just work in his life. He didn't want to end up like his father. And he knew now that he wanted—needed—more than just a physical relationship.

He wanted love.

Vance gazed at Chanelle's profile. He felt an ache in his chest, but it wasn't painful. It was an ache of longing, of anticipation, knowing he had to make a conscious decision to take a risk. A risk at letting love in.

He watched the breeze ruffling the long, thick waves of Chanelle's hair. Her complexion was peach soft, with a rosy glow on her cheekbones. He caught a whiff of her perfume, its sweet peach scent making him feel like he was in an orchard in BC's Okanagan Valley or in Ontario's Niagara-on-the-Lake. He breathed in deeply, and at that moment, she tossed her hair back and met his gaze.

She blinked at him wordlessly, the sweeping motion of her eyelashes over green-hazel eyes mesmerizing him, the

curve and fullness of her lips making his pulse quicken. He
wanted to talk to her, but they were a few minutes away
from Coral Haven, and he didn't want to start something
he couldn't finish.

He would get that chance soon enough…

CHAPTER SIXTEEN

CHANELLE HEARD ADRIEN shout something excitedly. She pulled her gaze away from Vance's and saw that they were approaching an island. Coral Haven. She drew in a breath, already enchanted by what she saw. The surf cresting on the whitest beach she had ever seen, leaving what looked like the scallop-edged lace hem of a wedding gown. Lush vegetation and palm trees swaying in the breeze. And glimpses of a sprawling villa beyond with its coral facade, canopied windows and elegant balconies.

"Pinch me," she murmured, and then realized she had said it aloud.

"I would," Vance replied huskily. "But I'd get into trouble with my mother."

How was she supposed to respond to that?

Fortunately, she didn't have to. Vance answered his cell phone, and Chanelle couldn't help hearing his responses to someone called Valentina, thanking her and Carlos for looking after the villa and preparing it for their visit. He told Valentina the tender was approaching and just minutes away, and her response made him chuckle. "I'm sure 'the little breakfast' you prepared for us is more like a banquet, Valentina." He glanced over at Chanelle. "So it's a good thing I've brought an extra guest."

Another pause followed by a deep laugh. "No, Valentina, the only Mrs. Kingston with me is my mother. My *other* mother besides *you*," he joked.

Moments later, the tender was moored near a large boathouse and Chanelle waited for Vance's mother, sister and nephew to precede her as they stepped onto the long dock. Vance followed behind her, and as the rest of his family strode briskly toward the path that would lead to the villa, Chanelle slowed her pace to gaze around her. The view was stunning, with the clear azure water lapping at the pristine shore, changing to various hues of turquoise in deeper waters.

"Do you still want me to pinch you?" Vance's amused voice behind her made Chanelle realize that she had stopped walking altogether.

"Thanks, but no thanks," she returned with a slight edge. "I can usually bring myself back to reality without having to be pinched." She quickened her pace.

"Chanelle, you know I'd never hurt you." His voice was soft as he stepped up beside her.

"Well, you have," she blurted, forgetting her earlier intention of not letting him see how shattered she was. She felt a prickle behind her eyelids but couldn't bring herself to look at him.

"Uncle Vance!" Adrien left his mother's side to run back toward them. "Can you come and swing with me in the gazebo? Mommy's going inside to help Valentina, and Grandma's going to check on the rose garden…"

Vance bent to catch Adrien as he approached and lifted him high over his head. Adrien squealed, "Let me down, let me down," but as soon as Vance complied, he cried, "Lift me up, lift me up!"

Vance burst out laughing, and Chanelle couldn't help smiling. Their gazes met when Vance, holding a giggling Adrien up in the air, turned to glance at her. Despite her comment moments earlier, Chanelle felt a sizzle run through her at Vance's boyish grin. The rest of him was anything but boyish, she couldn't help thinking as he brought Adrien back down. Her gaze took in his strong shoulders and muscled biceps, enhanced by his tan T-shirt. His well-fitting jeans couldn't disguise his muscular legs, either.

The dock ended and a charming stone walkway began, flanked on both sides by agave and other exotic plant species that made Chanelle catch her breath with their vibrant colors. An artist's paradise, she thought, her gaze flitting from the brilliant multicolored crotons and hibiscus varieties to the giant pink-and-coral peony blooms that perfumed the air as they walked past. She caught her breath at the variety of orchids. She had read up on the flora of the islands and had learned that there were twenty-six varieties of native orchids, and one in particular called the wild banana orchid, which was the Cayman Islands' national flower.

Chanelle gasped when the sprawling two-story villa came into full view, with bougainvillea spilling over balconies and yellow-green canopies adding charm above the windows of the coral stucco walls. Absolutely enchanting.

Her gaze wandered to a courtyard featuring white rattan furniture with red-and-yellow floral cushions and giant glazed pots bursting with flowers of the same color. Four umbrella tables were set with cut flower arrangements in decorative clay vases, and two hammocks swayed slightly in the breeze at one edge of the courtyard, near the rose garden that Vance's mother was now inspecting.

"The pool and gazebo are on the other side of the villa," Vance told her, as Adrien pulled him in that direction. "Why don't you join us, Chanelle?"

They disappeared around a bend before Chanelle could reply. She gazed toward the beautiful rounded door of the villa. It was painted the same green as the window canopies and looked like an illustration from one of Chanelle's childhood fairy-tale collections.

Chanelle strode quickly toward the path Vance and Adrien had taken. Things might be strained between her and Vance, but she didn't really want to put herself in a position where she would be open to questioning by the women in Vance's family.

And at least Adrien would be a buffer. She wasn't ready to be alone with Vance again. *Not just yet...*

The other side of the villa was just as breathtaking, with its wraparound porch and massive sunroom. The pool area, with its outside bar and elegant chaise lounges, was an oasis in itself, with potted palms and water fountains and an outdoor shower at each end. The center tiles at the bottom of the pool featured the Zodiac Cruises name and logo, and the twelve zodiac signs were displayed on the outer tiles.

Chanelle felt like she was in another world. Vance's lifestyle was so far removed from her own. Why, her entire apartment could fit in the sunroom. She sighed. It wasn't that she was begrudging any of the Kingstons their material possessions. Vance's parents had worked hard to achieve their success, making many sacrifices at the beginning, according to the online articles she had read about their rise to success in the cruise business. And now Vance was leading the company, showing initiative and a fierce commitment to its continuing success.

Chanelle watched the soon-to-be official president of Zodiac Cruises swinging away with his nephew in the gazebo, grinning as if he were a kid at the midway. It was a huge white structure on a solid foundation, with an overhanging roof and rolled-up canvas panels between its twelve wooden posts. On the end opposite the swing, there was a hammock big enough for two people, a bistro set and a bar-size refrigerator.

Chanelle couldn't help wondering if Vance had made use of the gazebo with any of his female friends on sultry island nights... All he'd have to do was to roll down the canvas panels and he'd have a summer bedroom...and a bottle of wine in the fridge waiting to be savored...

Vance's gaze met hers as she stood a few feet away from them, and he waved her over, bringing the swing to a stop. "Come and join us," he called. "There's nothing more relaxing than an old-fashioned ride on a swing."

Chanelle eyed the swing. She would sit across from Vance and Adrien. She could handle *that*.

But could she handle having those blue eyes continue to look at her that way?

Vance tried not to make it obvious, but he couldn't help gazing at Chanelle and the striking picture she made. No, *striking* wasn't the perfect word. She was eye candy in her yellow dress with its eyelet sections, revealing glimpses of navy and bare skin underneath. And her bare shoulders—under the thinnest spaghetti straps—and curvy legs elicited thoughts that made his heart drum an erratic beat against his ribs.

He couldn't believe that she was actually here on Coral Haven, especially after he had basically given her the brush-off last night. The excuse he had tried to convince himself with was that Chanelle might have regretted it later if he had stayed. And that had been a valid supposition, but there had also been another reason why he had backed off. *Fear.* Fear that making love to Chanelle would force him into a commitment, and he hadn't been sure that he had it in him to commit to a serious relationship.

He didn't exactly have a good track record when it

came to commitment… But then again, he had never met a woman he had wanted to commit to.

He had screwed up with Chanelle. But now he had the opportunity to make things right. Explain his reasons. *His fears.* Show Chanelle that he wasn't playing with her emotions or with anyone else's.

As soon as he could get her alone…

Valentina had prepared a feast. The gleaming modern sideboard displayed platters of croissants, pastries, steaming omelets and sausages. She had put on the strong coffee that Vance and Mariah preferred and Earl Grey tea for their mother.

Minutes earlier, Valentina had sounded a bell, and after rolling down the canvas panels of the gazebo to keep it cool, he, Chanelle and Adrien had gone inside. Vance had introduced Chanelle, and Valentina had given Vance a wink and an approving nod before leaving for the day.

Breakfast was not as awkward as Vance thought it might be. Mariah was treating Chanelle like a longtime girlfriend. And his mother was chatting easily with Chanelle about her rose garden.

Vance reached for another custard-filled croissant. There was no rush to do anything but enjoy the moment. And he certainly was enjoying how things were playing out with Chanelle and his family.

It shouldn't be too long before he had Chanelle all to himself…

CHAPTER SEVENTEEN

AFTER VANCE'S MOTHER and sister had left to go up to their respective rooms, Vance turned to Chanelle. "Look," he said, "we're here for a good stretch. I *do* want to explain what happened last night...and apologize for any misunderstanding... but could you just indulge me for a few minutes and let me show you around the place?" He tilted his head at her—if she wasn't so upset with him, she'd find his puppy dog look humorous.

Chanelle pursed her lips. Maybe he was trying to ease into it...and maybe she needed a few moments to mentally prepare what to say to *him*. "Fine," she said coolly, wishing those baby-blue eyes weren't so easy to look at. She couldn't let them distract her from the reality of his true nature...even though he had made her feel things she never thought she would feel again...

Despite her intentions to remain indifferent, Chanelle found herself captivated by the beautiful rooms and eclectic furnishings. She found herself listening as Vance explained how his mother's love of antiques was reflected in areas like the main floor living room, with its mahogany Chippendale highboy and gleaming secretary desk, along with more traditional floral upholstery.

His preference for elegant simplicity was the inspiration for the sunroom, he told her, indicating the ivory Italian leather couches and scarlet cushions positioned around a red-lacquered circular coffee table. Chanelle's eyes widened at the massive bay window that overlooked the pool and gazebo area and provided a stunning view of the beach a short distance away.

Vance had selected many of the paintings throughout the villa, and he gave Chanelle a blurb about each artist and the inspiration behind the work.

"Wow," she said. "I didn't expect you—"

"To be so smart?" His mouth twisted wryly, and he gazed down at her with raised eyebrows.

"That's not exactly what I meant," she said, flushing.

"I *did* major in art history and design, and before stepping into my father's shoes, I curated an art gallery. Although I sadly neglected my own art after discovering the art of being a playboy," he added wistfully.

Chanelle's eyes widened. How could he be so...so *casual* about it?

"Forgive me for being blunt, Chanelle, but it is what it is. My parents weren't very happy, as you can imagine. My mother wanted me to use my degree in some capacity in the company—designing and overseeing the art galleries and auctions, for example—but I was caught up in my own self-indulgent world. And I couldn't see myself working for or with my father."

"You didn't get along?" Chanelle ventured.

Vance gave a curt laugh. "Ah...no. He was barely around. He was a workaholic. And when he did come home, he made it clear that he had no use for my art."

Chanelle felt a pang at his words. She understood what being a workaholic was all about. And now she could see how that had affected her relationship.

"Both sides lose out," she murmured. "It must have been hard having a father but hardly ever seeing him. And having him not take your art seriously."

"I had a hard time investing any emotions—positive ones, that is—in an absentee father," he said, his voice steely. "And I swore I'd never turn out like him."

His gaze shifted to a stunning landscape on one of the walls of the sunroom. She had recognized it immediately as a painting by one of the iconic Group of Seven upon entering the room. Now at close range, she saw that it was one of J. E. H. MacDonald's scenic landscapes. Vance turned to Chanelle. "I like to have a bit of Canada with me when I'm away." He smiled. "I also have a Lawren Harris in my bedroom. I was inspired by the Group of Seven. I started sketching and painting in high school and had filled a sketchpad with my drawings to show that I was serious about pursuing art at university." His smile disappeared. "My father got angry. Tossed it aside. For him it was get involved in the company or nothing. And back then, I chose the nothing."

"Our past experiences and choices help make us who we are," Chanelle said. "When we're young, we subconsciously tell ourselves stories in order to cope with our situation. You internalized the fact that your father put his work before you and probably concluded that he didn't love you. But now, as an adult, having stepped into his shoes for the last nine months, your perspective has probably changed a little. Maybe you can see that he was focused on building a future for you, possibly because his father wasn't able to do that for him. And maybe he was worried, knowing how hard it is for artists to make a living…"

Chanelle hesitated. What was she doing? She had no business speculating on his personal situation or feelings toward his father. She was here to listen to what he had to say, not to give him a social worker's take on his relationship with his father.

A muscle flickered along Vance's jawline. His eyes had

narrowed and he was looking at her intently, but Chanelle had a feeling he wasn't really seeing her at that moment. And then he turned abruptly and strode to a curving alabaster staircase that led to the second floor.

Passing the closed doors of the bedrooms where he said Mariah, Adrien and his mother were resting, Chanelle followed Vance through a long hallway to a central foyer with an antique drop-lid desk, built-in bookshelves and two recliners. When he gestured to Chanelle to sit down, she complied, her pulse quickening.

Okay, here it comes, she thought, trying not to look as cynical as she felt. *The excuse for kissing me like the ship was about to go down, then leaving me in the lurch to take up with a Zodiac employee.*

She bit her lip. Despite the rather personal exchange between them a few minutes ago, the fact remained that he had some explaining to do.

Why was he staring at her like that? He wasn't waiting for her to begin, was he? Because if that was the case, she had plenty she could say to him, starting with—

"Chanelle, before I get into what I really want to say, I have to thank you…"

Chanelle couldn't help making a sound that came out as a half laugh, half cough. "You're kidding me. For *what*, exactly? For providing you with some onboard entertainment?" She tossed her hair back and stared at him pointedly.

She was satisfied to see his eyebrows furrow and a hurt expression cross his features.

"Ouch," he said softly. "Chanelle, you've got it wrong. And I promised to explain—"

"I think I can figure it out," she said, raising her eyebrows. "As I might have mentioned before, your reputation precedes you. Leopards can't change their spots."

Vance clutched at his chest. "That's another arrow to the heart, Sagittarius. Didn't you see the sign on the tender? No archery allowed…"

"This is not a joking matter," Chanelle said curtly. She shook her head and stood up, heat sizzling through her veins. She strode to the French doors and stared out. The sun had disappeared, and the swiftly moving clouds were darkening. Just like her mood: She was already upset at *him*, but now she was upset with herself.

Vance sprang up from the recliner and strode over to stand beside her. "Look, Chanelle, please let me explain, okay?"

Chanelle turned to face him as a few drops of rain began to plop against the panes.

"I wanted to thank you for giving me your take on the situation with my father. My perspective has changed," he said huskily. "I gave up the playboy lifestyle after my father died." His gaze shifted to the view. "I was too stubborn to promise my dad on his deathbed that I would carry on the business. And when he died, I was filled with guilt." He gazed back at Chanelle. "I realized I had to let go of some things. First of all, years' worth of resentment for a father who had spent more time at his job than with his kids. And second, life as a playboy." His eyes pierced into hers. "This leopard *has* changed, Chanelle. No spots in the last nine months. And the woman you saw me with is our director of environmental operations. She came by to drop off a gift for me since she wouldn't be at the gala."

Chanelle raised her eyebrows, remembering Vance's unbuttoned shirt and the hug he and the woman had shared.

"I was hugging her because she was leaving this morning to meet her fiancé in George Town," he said, as if he had just read Chanelle's thoughts. "They're getting married at the end of the week and then going on their honeymoon."

He gave Chanelle a few moments to digest this information. "She's not only a great employee, but she's become a good friend. And in case you heard mention of a surprise in Toronto, I was referring to a surprise party from the staff to congratulate them on their wedding."

Chanelle pursed her lips. So if Vance had given up his playboy ways, why had he paid any attention to *her*? Kissed her so...so—

Vance stepped closer to Chanelle. Her pulse rate had increased exponentially as Vance had proceeded with his explanations and now, with him standing so close that she could feel his breath on her forehead, she was overwhelmed by a feeling of light-headedness. She looked up at his firm jawline and curves of his mouth, and when her gaze met his, the intense look in his blue eyes startled her. She inhaled sharply as Vance leaned down to kiss her.

She had wanted to ask him why he had left her stateroom so abruptly, what he had meant when he had said, "I'm sorry, but I don't want to stay and have you regret it later..." but his kiss blocked her words. And now his lips were moving over hers with a gentle pressure that was sending a swirl of desire throughout her. When he suddenly clasped her and deepened his kiss, Chanelle felt her thoughts and unspoken words scatter.

She wanted to believe him.

And she wanted this fantasy to continue...

Chanelle felt her sense of caution dissipating with the intoxicating pressure of his lips on hers. She wrapped her arms around his neck, and with the deliberateness and precision of a skilled Archer, she slid her fingers under his T-shirt to where the Aquarius waves were tattooed on his back. Pressing him closer, she returned his kiss with the passion that he had ignited, confident that her invisible arrow was hitting its mark.

* * *

Vance could feel his heart thumping erratically as Chanelle responded to his kiss, and when they finally broke apart, he realized the extra pounding was coming from the fat drops of rain pelting the French doors. A flash of lightning appeared, followed by a crackle of thunder that made Chanelle jump.

Sudden rain showers were common enough in these parts, and he was sure that this one wouldn't last long. He was disappointed, though. He had hoped to walk along the beach with Chanelle and show her around the island…

He wrapped his arm tighter around her. Her face had paled and her green-hazel eyes were blinking. "My, what big eyes you have." He smiled at her. "Don't worry, Chanelle, the house won't blow down. It's a good thing we're here, though, and not out on the water."

"I'm not worried… I guess. But I think you're referencing two different fairy tales."

He laughed. "But there's a wolf in both, right?"

"Yes, and I'm hoping there are no wolves in sheep's clothing around here."

Vance couldn't resist leaning in to nibble Chanelle's neck, his pulse spiking when she gave a little shiver. "And what would you do if you came across one?" he teased.

"I'd distract him with custard-filled croissants," she shot back with a grin. "I'm sure he'd find them much more tasty…"

"I don't know about that," he murmured, leaning toward her again. Another clap of thunder reverberated around them, and Vance heard the alarmed voices of his mother and sister calling him from down the hall. His mother was probably worried that some windows were open and that the rain was pouring in. "I'd better check the windows," he said, squeezing Chanelle's hand.

"You're not leaving me here," she said. "I'm coming with you, Vance. I don't like big storms." She looked up at the ceiling as if she were afraid that it would cave in from all the rain. "Shouldn't we be hunkering down in the basement?"

Vance couldn't help chuckling. "You're in the Caribbean, Chanelle, not Canada. We don't have basements here."

They met his mother and Mariah in the hallway. Mariah rushed to him, grabbing his arm.

"I can't find Adrien," she cried. "I peeked in on him earlier and he was napping, so I had a snooze, too. When I heard the storm, I went to get him, and he wasn't there." She started shaking, and Vance took hold of her arms.

"Stay calm, Mariah. He must be in one of the rooms. You check the rest of the rooms on this floor, and we'll start on the main floor."

She ran down the hall toward the central foyer and where Vance's bedroom was located, calling Adrien's name. Vance turned to his mother. Her face was pale as well, and he felt his heart, which was already drumming over Adrien, twinge. "Mom, you and Chanelle wait downstairs. Chanelle, maybe put on some herbal tea for my mom, okay? I'll search for Adrien. He's probably doing a puzzle in the family room."

He gave them both an encouraging smile and descended the stairs two at a time. He hadn't wanted to show how worried he was, but as he filed through room after room with no sight of his nephew, a feeling of dread enveloped him.

By the time he returned to the kitchen, Chanelle was pouring the tea, and Mariah was running into the room. She burst into tears when she saw that Adrien wasn't with him.

"He—must be outside," she sobbed, trembling. "I'm going to go find him."

"No!" Vance said brusquely. "I'll go."

CHAPTER EIGHTEEN

CHANELLE POURED CHAMOMILE TEA into a cup as steadily as she could, not wanting to show how distressed she was. A child was in danger. Someone she knew, and someone who was precious to Mariah and her family. To the man she was losing her heart to.

"I'm going out to help Vance," she told them and rushed out of the kitchen as Vance's mother was formulating a protest.

Chanelle couldn't just sit there. She wasn't programmed that way. She had been trained to act with lightning speed when alerted to a dangerous or volatile situation involving a child. And right now, the storm was a danger. An enormous danger, with the intermittent lightning, slashing rain and what seemed like gale-force winds. She forced her mind not to think about any number of frightening possibilities as to where Adrien might be.

Chanelle was relieved to find another raincoat in the foyer armoire. It was oversized, but at least it would keep most of her protected. As she put it on, she decided that since Vance had gone out this way, he'd probably be checking the front of the villa and the covered boathouse. She would check the back.

As soon as Chanelle stepped outside, the wind whipped the hood of her raincoat back, and she knew it would be hopeless to even try to put it back in place. She wished she had at least put her hair up in a ponytail, which would have prevented her from being blinded at every turn by stinging strands of her hair along with the lashing rain. It was just early afternoon, but the sky had darkened ominously, and in the heavy downpour, Chanelle could barely discern what was two feet in front of her. An icy fear gripped her.

She prayed Adrien was safe...

Her sandals were soaked, and since the raincoat just came down to below her knees, her legs were drenched as well. It was hard to keep her eyes open, and she had to concentrate on which direction she was going. At one point she slipped into a flower bed that the deluge had reduced to a muddy soup, and she let out a cry at the stab of pain as her knees crashed into a decorative stone slab.

Her legs coated in mud, Chanelle regained her balance and continued toward the gazebo. She reached the pool area first, and her heart twisted at the thought that Adrien might have ventured into the pool.

But surely he wouldn't have dared without an adult with him...

With the reduced visibility, Chanelle had to skirt around the perimeter of the pool, peering in for any sign of Adrien. He had been wearing a red T-shirt...

Thank God, she murmured under her breath, seeing nothing. She plodded on toward the beach. She thought she heard a voice as the rain continued to pelt down, but the sound was quickly swallowed by the wind.

Chanelle was thoroughly soaked through. The raincoat had not been able to prevent the rain from streaming down her neck and drenching her dress right through to her bikini. She pushed her hair away from her eyes as a streak of lightning lit up the sky and made the area around her seem like something out of a supernatural movie. At the next boom of thunder, she made a dash for the gazebo, her heart responding with its own boom.

As she scanned the darkened interior, she spotted a hump in one corner of the gazebo. It looked red… She yelled out his name, and Adrien ran crying to her and wrapped his arms around her waist.

Vance ran as far as the boathouse, the blood pumping so hard in his veins that he was oblivious to everything but the sound of his own heartbeat. Who could have known that the weather would flip? And that Adrien would impulsively venture out of the villa?

He was five years old. And a boy who loved to explore around the island…

Vance backtracked and sprinted toward the shed near the rose garden. He glanced at the roses his mother had admired earlier, now flattened, with petals scattered all around the lawn.

Would Adrien have gone to seek shelter in the shed if he had been playing in the nearby sandbox when the storm had hit? Vance faltered at a sudden muscle cramp in his leg and came to a stop. He swore under his breath and bent to massage his calf, wincing at the pain. When it eased, he continued toward the shed, walking as quickly as he could instead of running to avoid the risk of cramping up again.

Vance called out Adrien's name and looked inside the shed. Disappointment lumped in his throat. He prayed that Adrien might have made his way to the gazebo, the only other outside structure on that side of the property.

As Vance passed in front of the villa, the front door opened, and his mother called out.

Had she and Mariah found Adrien in some unsuspected place inside?

He stopped, chest heaving, only to hear his mother say worriedly that Chanelle had gone out to look for Adrien as well, and she had seen her heading toward the back of the villa.

The lump in Vance's throat slid and landed in his gut like a boulder.

In heaven's name, why hadn't Chanelle stayed put? Now he had two people to worry about. *Two people he loved.*

Cramp or no cramp, Vance sprinted around to the back, yelling out Chanelle's name. His hood had flown off long before, and he couldn't be bothered to keep it over his head. He clenched his jaw as thunder rumbled around him, and he prayed that Chanelle and Adrien were nowhere near areas vulnerable to lightning strikes.

He reached the pool and scanned the water that was agitated by thousands of needlelike raindrops. Now he knew what *desperate* felt like. With an ache in his heart that made him cry out, he made a run for the gazebo.

Vance knew that he had only been outside for minutes, but somehow it felt like an ordeal of hours. He reached for the canvas flap, and seconds later, he wanted to collapse in relief as his eyes made out the huddled figures of Chanelle and Adrien in the corner near the hammock.

Vance called out Chanelle's name at the same time that she called out to him. He ran to her and Adrien and hugged them tightly. "Thank God you're both safe," he said hoarsely, not having the heart to scold either one of them.

"I just got here," Chanelle told him, her voice trembling. "I couldn't just stay inside—"

"We'll talk later," Vance said brusquely. "Let's get out of here. Wait," he stopped her as lightning illuminated the canvas panels. "Okay, Adrien, come with me," he urged when the flashes stopped. "Chanelle, stay right beside us.

We'll go in the sunroom door." He took off his raincoat and put it around Adrien before lifting him up and carrying him across the property and past the pool, looking over his shoulder at Chanelle every few paces.

Vance set Adrien down once they were in the sunroom. He called out to Mariah, and in moments, she was running toward them, crying in relief.

Adrien hadn't said anything up to this point, his face frozen in shock, but when he saw his mother, he ran into her arms. "Mommy, Mommy. I was so scared."

"I know, baby. Mommy was scared, too."

Vance's mother was close behind, and when she reached them, she hugged Adrien tightly, despite the fact that he was dripping wet, the raincoat dwarfing him. "Run a nice warm bath for him, Mariah, and I'll get him some milk and cookies after I grab some towels for these drenched souls."

Mariah turned to hug Vance and then Chanelle, despite their dripping state. "I can't thank you enough," she said tremulously.

"Chanelle found him in the gazebo," Vance said, keeping his voice steady.

"You're an angel." Mariah hugged her again. "A true guardian angel." She stepped back and then looked down with a frown. "Chanelle, you're bleeding."

Vance turned to look. Below Chanelle's raincoat, her legs were smeared with mud and trickles of blood. "I'll take care of her, Mariah."

When they had gone, Vance helped Chanelle out of her raincoat. Her clothes were just as plastered as his, the only difference being that her knees and legs were bare and his weren't. He frowned upon closer inspection of her scraped knees. He wrapped a towel around Chanelle and brushed the last towel quickly over his hair and body before flinging it onto a wicker chair.

"You leave me no choice, Chanelle," he said firmly, "but to play doctor with you." And before Chanelle could respond, he lifted her up in his arms and made his way through the villa and up the alabaster stairway to his bedroom.

CHAPTER NINETEEN

As CHANELLE FELT herself being whisked up by Vance's strong arms, she had no choice but to clasp her arms around his neck, her heart thudding like a jackhammer. She closed her eyes as he proceeded up the stairway, anticipating a very uncomfortable landing should he lose his balance and fall...

But he didn't miss a step or even falter, as if carrying a woman up the stairs this way was something he was used to doing.

Chanelle opened her eyes and let out her breath. They passed the center foyer where they had been sitting earlier, and after a few moments, Vance paused at a set of double doors and reached for the handle. Chanelle caught her breath at the sight of the four-poster king-size bed and the stunning Lawren Harris painting above, a winter landscape that didn't seem at all out of place in this villa.

Vance's bedroom.

He carried her to a roomy walk-in closet revealing a row of shirts and pants and shelves with at least a dozen pairs of footwear below. "I hope you see something you like in here," he said, setting her down, and although she couldn't see his face just then, she could tell he was smiling. "Because you're going to have to get out of your wet clothes."

Chanelle's mind whirled. "Maybe Mariah has something I could borrow?" She looked down at her yellow dress, its thin cotton material plastered to her body and revealing the navy bikini underneath. Her neck started prickling with discomfort, and she pulled the towel more snugly around her.

"Maybe," he said, his gaze telling her that he had observed the revealing state of her clothes. "But she's busy now, and I'm not going anywhere until we fix up those knees. Before they get infected…"

He motioned for her to proceed into the ensuite bathroom and to sit down on a black leather chair near the marble-sided shower stall. Chanelle was dazzled by the gleaming luxury of the room, with its sleek granite countertop, floor of diagonal white and black marble tiles, and crystal spiral light fixture.

"I can take care of them," she told him. She winced. "I'll just need—"

"Don't move, Chanelle," he said firmly. "I have everything I need in my medicine cabinet. Now just hold tight and it will be over in a few minutes…" His mouth quirked. "You look like a wet little duckling in that yellow dress. And no, not the one in the fairy tale," he added quickly. "Quite the opposite."

She flushed. He was delusional if he thought she looked *pretty*. She had caught a glimpse of herself in the large vanity mirror above the black granite countertop. Her hair framed her face in tangled ropes, and her eye makeup had smeared and run under her eyes in black and navy streaks.

Yeah, real pretty.

Vance strode over to a gleaming white cabinet, withdrew a few items and deposited everything on the side table next to Chanelle. "I'll be back in a second," he told her.

She was tempted to start cleaning up her knees on her own. He had brought over a bottle of antiseptic, some sterile cotton gauze sponges, a couple of wide bandages and some antibacterial ointment. But as she went to grab the bottle, he returned with a chair from his bedroom.

He wagged a finger at her. "Now, now, Miss Robinson…" He deposited the chair opposite her, grabbed a lined waste-paper basket and set it down beside his chair. He washed his hands in the sink, and Chanelle felt like squirming when he glanced in the mirror a couple of times and caught her watching him. After drying his hands, he sat down on the chair.

"Okay, let's do this." He took a deep breath and poured some of the antiseptic on a gauze sponge. He leaned forward and was eye to eye with Chanelle. "I'll need your leg, miss," he murmured.

Chanelle stared at him. He raised his eyebrows. "Oh…" She blinked.

Did he want her to stretch out her leg on his lap?

He held out his hand. "May I?"

"Okay."

What else could she say?

She was already barefoot, having removed her soaked sandals in the sunroom. She extended her leg slowly and tried to keep her breathing steady as Vance put one hand under her calf and the other under her ankle before placing her right leg on his left thigh.

"Okay," he repeated. "Now this might just sting a lit—"

Chanelle let out a cry as the antiseptic soaked into the scraped areas, and her arms flailed, throwing the towel off her shoulders.

"I'm sorry, Chanelle. I know it must sting like hell. But we have to clean it out."

"Just hurry," she replied through gritted teeth and gripped the sides of the chair. Chanelle closed her eyes as he poured and dabbed, using a new gauze pad for each area. She felt like her knee was on fire, and it took all she had not to jerk her leg and accidentally kick him in the face.

"Okay, there, there. Your wound is clean. I'm just going to put some of this antibacterial ointment on the bandage and cover it lightly."

Despite the throbbing in her knee, Vance's soothing voice was helping her to relax a bit. But he still had her other knee to tend to…

He set her leg down gently and lifted her other one onto his thigh. "Okay, here goes. We're almost done."

"You haven't even started the torture," she retorted, her eyes already closed.

"You're being very brave, Chanelle," he said solemnly before applying the antiseptic.

This time she did jerk her leg as she cried out, and when her foot made solid contact, she opened her eyes to see Vance holding his hands over his mouth and jaw.

"Oh, my God," she cried. "I'm so sorry. I didn't mean to kick you."

"I think some teeth are loose and are about to fall out," he said, his voice muffled behind his hands. "Oh, well, it's a good thing I've given up my status as a playboy." He shrugged. "Because I'm pretty sure being toothless is not one of the prerequisites."

Chanelle watched anxiously as he moved his hand away, expecting to see blood and teeth spill out. He gave her a sudden grin, and she saw that his teeth were intact.

Perfectly intact.

She glowered at him. "That was not necessary. You scared me."

"I'm sorry, Chanelle." He gave a soft laugh. "I just couldn't resist…"

She pursed her lips and then smiled. "Apology accepted.

I'll *try* to resist kicking you again." She closed her eyes and then reopened them. "But I can't promise."

"Duly noted. Now let's finish this operation. My other patients are waiting."

Chanelle felt a warm stirring inside at their banter. And then clenched her teeth as Vance proceeded with the next round of dabbing. When the second bandage was in place, Vance looked at her quizzically.

"I've cleaned all around your knees," he said, "but we still have to get some mud off you." He looked pointedly at the streaks on her lower legs.

"I can do that myself," she told him. "I'll sit on the edge of the tub and wash it off." She eyed the streaks her feet and legs had left on his jeans. "And I think you'll need to wash up as well, Dr. Vancelot. And dry."

She felt a warm rush as he smiled at her, his eyes a startling azure. "Um… I'll just need a clean towel," she added.

"Right in the tall cabinet," he murmured. "And I'll use the guest washroom in the room next door." He strode to the door. "You should change into dry clothes right away, Chanelle." His gaze dropped to her legs. "My pants certainly won't fit you, but I do have a pair of light pajamas with a tie belt." His mouth curved. "I'll leave them and some T-shirts on the bed for you…and Mariah can find something for you afterward."

Vance let the warm jets of water pulsate over his body in the guest room shower. He felt some of the tension ease out of his neck and shoulder muscles. For all his levity with Chanelle a few moments ago, he hadn't been as relaxed as she might have thought.

First of all, the fear of what might have happened to Adrien had made every nerve and muscle in his body so tight that he could still feel a residual ache. And then learning that Chanelle had gone out...

Discovering them in the gazebo had made Vance almost collapse with relief. But he had had to be strong for the both of them. Strong physically and emotionally. The physical side had been the easy part. Carrying Adrien inside and then carrying Chanelle upstairs, no sweat. It had been the emotional part that had drained him. Staying calm when he wanted to scream his frustration at every minute of his search that had proven fruitless.

In these past nine months at the helm of Zodiac Cruises, Vance had taken his position seriously, and as he had vowed after his father's death, he had stepped up to the plate and taken control. Out in the storm, he had felt all control slipping away from him. He had not been able to control either Adrien or Chanelle from going out and potentially putting themselves in danger.

He could have lost either one of them.

A lightning strike, a heavy falling tree branch, a misstep causing them to slip into the water or hit their head on something and pass out—any of these situations could have happened.

Vance had experienced the feeling of pure helplessness out in the storm.

And it had shaken him to the core.

But despite this feeling, his instinct to protect his family had kicked in. Every last neuron in his body had been primed to battle the elements and bring his loved ones back home safely.

Home. It wasn't the villa, beautiful though it might be. Home was the people in it, the people you loved.

His home was his family.

And Chanelle.

The storm had shaken up his thinking, too. His thoughts about commitment, about trust.

And if he had hesitated in the past about commitment, it was simply because the right woman hadn't been in his life at the time.

Chanelle was the right woman. He felt it in his gut. And he was ready to shift the scales in his life and find a balance between work and love.

Images of Chanelle flashed in his mind, from the first time he had seen her grab hold of Adrien with her white jeans and fuchsia T-shirt, to her elegant skirt and black top in the Mezza Luna Ristorante, and to that sexy white dress splashed with red poppies… And the yellow dress she was wearing now, wet and clinging to her body, revealing her bikini underneath…

Yes, her physical beauty had aroused his senses, but it had been her inner beauty that had touched his soul. Chanelle was kind, sensitive, courageous, funny, hardworking…and she loved kids.

His pulse quickened at the thought of having children one day…a thought he had never seriously contemplated until now.

But that would mean having a woman—Chanelle—being as committed to him as he was to her.

Aren't you jumping the gun a bit? His inner voice shoved its way into his consciousness. *You haven't even told Chanelle that you want to be in a committed relationship. You just told her you've given up your playboy lifestyle, explained about Pauline, and then you kissed her. Get with the program, buddy. If you want her, you'll have to get more creative. A kiss alone isn't going to do it.*

Vance smiled ruefully. No, he *hadn't* made it clear to Chanelle how he felt. But the storm had made his feelings clearer to *him*. Now he just had to figure out how and when to communicate those feelings to Chanelle.

Vance stepped out of the shower and dried himself brusquely with a large, plush towel before changing into white Bermuda shorts and a turquoise shirt.

In the shower, Vance had come up with a crazy idea that would show Chanelle how committed he was to her… but he needed to sketch out his ideas on paper. And once he was satisfied with his plan, he would present it to her.

When Vance returned to his room, he was disappointed that Chanelle had already gone. He checked the time on his phone. They had about an hour and a half before the tender returned to pick them up to head back to the *Aquarius*. Looking out his balcony doors, he was relieved to see that the storm had diminished significantly to a light sprinkle, and the skies had brightened. There was no danger that they wouldn't be able to return to the ship.

He sat down at his desk. He would work on his idea before going downstairs. And if he didn't get the chance to share it with Chanelle before heading back, he'd save it until later tonight at the gala.

CHAPTER TWENTY

CHANELLE HAD FELT a little strange, sitting on the edge of Vance's bathtub in her bikini, rinsing off her legs. How could she *not* imagine him soaking in it, with the jets sending water swirling all over his body?

It was so unnerving…

He'd laid out three T-shirts and a pair of pajama bottoms with alternating loons and red maple leaves—that reminded her of the tie he'd worn for the Canada evening—and the words *Loony for You* on the rear.

Really? In any other situation, she would have found the Canadian-themed pajamas amusing, but all she could think about was how ridiculous she would look in them. With a sigh, she changed into a black T-shirt and the pajamas and headed downstairs.

At least her face and hair no longer looked like she had come out of some lagoon, she thought. Chanelle found Mariah and Adrien in the kitchen. Mariah laughed when she saw the loony pajamas. "Don't mind me," she said. "I can't help cracking up every time I see those. Can you tell Vance is a proud Canadian? Right down to his pajamas. And boxers. But don't tell him I told you." She laughed again.

"Don't tell me what?" Vance said, entering the room. "That Adrien's eating all my cookies?" He winked, ruffling Adrien's hair.

"Nice pants, Chanelle," Vance continued, chuckling. "You're welcome to keep them as a souvenir."

Chanelle's mouth dropped, and Mariah burst out laughing. "I can see how thrilled you are, Chanelle. Come on, let's go wash and dry your clothes and see what we can find for you in my room."

Chanelle was aware that Vance was watching them as they walked out of the room. Or more specifically, *her*. His gaze had swept over her T-shirt, and she had a feeling that his gaze was now taking in the *Loony for You* on the rear of the pajamas.

Upstairs, Mariah waited for Chanelle to get her wet dress and bikini and then proceeded to the laundry room. "They shouldn't take long," Mariah told her. "I'll put them through the quick cycle."

"There's no point in me borrowing your clothes, then."

"Okay, well, do you want to come back downstairs or wait in the guest room? There's a fabulous window seat with a great view, and a pile of books and magazines."

"I can wait in the guest room, thanks."

"No, thank *you*, Chanelle. Please know that you're welcome to visit us here any time."

The guest room was bright and roomy, with coastal decor. The linens were done in white and sky blue, with big accent pillows in a fresh butter yellow. Chanelle sat down at the window seat and looked out at the brightening sky, trying to figure out why she felt a sudden sense of foreboding.

Soon they would be back on the ship, and Coral Haven would be just a memory. She just wished she had been able to explore the island a little more, walk on the beach, swim in those jeweled waters…

It had been kind of Mariah to invite her to come back

and visit, but what reason would she have to come back to the Kingstons' private island?

Soon the cruise would be over, and she would have to make a decision about her job. That was the reality she faced. And sharing passionate kisses with Vance Kingston wasn't going to change that reality. How could it?

The anxiety she had felt searching for Adrien made her realize that she had also been anxious about returning to the same job. Important though it was, it was also highly stressful, and she had had more of her share of stress these past years.

You're stronger than you think, Vance had told her. *You'll know when the time is right.*

Maybe it was time to look at a career change.

No, there was no maybe about it. It *was* time. Time to find something in a related field that wouldn't take all her energy. That would allow her to lead a more balanced life.

There! She had come to a decision! As soon as she returned home, she would start her search for a new job. And a new life. Chanelle automatically reached for her bracelet and realized with a jolt that it wasn't on her left wrist. And then she remembered…she had left it on one corner of the tub.

She would run in and retrieve it before Vance came back upstairs. And then she'd grab her clothes, dry them, get dressed, return to the ship and enjoy her remaining time on the cruise before getting back to reality.

A reality that didn't include Vance Kingston.

While she was exploring other job options in Sault Ste. Marie, Vance would continue his job as president of Zodiac Cruises in Toronto. He had said that his playboy lifestyle was finished, and maybe it was.

But the way he kissed you…

So Vance had gotten carried away after some emotional

sharing about his father…and so had *she*. But that didn't mean Vance wanted anything more. She had been a temporary diversion. He had encouraged her to have fun on the cruise. Live a little.

She would be crazy to think that Vance Kingston could figure in her life after the cruise.

Chanelle bent forward to pick up her bracelet, trying to ignore the sudden heaviness in her chest.

"Nobody ever showed me they were 'loony for me' quite like that before."

Chanelle froze outwardly, but inside, it felt like a lava flow.

She straightened and turned around, holding out her bracelet. "I came back for this," she said as evenly as she could. The room seemed to be closing in on her. She couldn't breathe. She needed air.

She wanted out. Out of the room, out of the villa, and off the island.

And away from Vance.

Away from the man she knew would only ever be a fantasy…

Chanelle was too hot in Vance's black T-shirt. It was making her suffocate. She wished she could just tear it off. And the stupid pajamas, too. She needed to go and get her clothes.

Now, before she…

Vance leaped to catch Chanelle as she fainted. Her face had been flushed, and he had thought it was embarrassment at his comment—which he had instantly regretted—but he suspected that it was something else. Perhaps something to do with the barometric pressure, since she *was* highly sensitive to changes in temperature.

Vance's heart began to pound.

Was she breathing?

Her body had flopped onto his chest, and her head was drooping to one side. He placed his cheek against Chanelle's neck and felt the fluttering of her pulse. Relieved, he lifted her and carried her to his bed, where he set her down gently.

Vance raised both her feet and stuck a pillow underneath, while watching her mouth and eyes for any sign of movement. Had she been too hot? He couldn't very well remove her shirt, though. He put her feet back down and felt for Chanelle's pulse on the side of her neck.

Thank God, or he would have had to initiate CPR…

Vance leaped to the minibar fridge for a bottle of water. She'd need it when she regained consciousness. He set it down on his night table before leaning forward to feel for her pulse again. Watching her filled him with a sudden feeling of tenderness that made the backs of his eyes sting.

And a feeling of terror.

She needed to come to. Calling for emergency services would take far too long.

"Come on, Chanelle, my love. Wake up. *Please.*" He brushed a kiss on her forehead.

She gave a soft moan, and her eyes fluttered. And opened.

Vance let out a deep breath. *Thank God.*

Chanelle tried to move.

"No, Chanelle. You have to stay still for at least fifteen to twenty minutes."

"Why?" Her eyes widened. "Where am I?"

"Shh. You're on my bed and you've just regained consciousness."

"From what?" Her eyes widened. "We didn't…"

"No, silly. From fainting. And you scared the hell out of me," he said gruffly. "For the second time today."

Her brow wrinkled. "Why?"

"Why are you asking so many questions?" He felt her forehead. "Just relax. You might be dehydrated. Here, have some water."

He put the bottle to her lips while supporting the back of her head with his other hand. She lay back down, and her hazel-green eyes pierced his. "Why?"

"You're a stubborn one, aren't you? Okay, do you really want to know why, Chanelle? It's because I...I—"

"Vance?" Mariah called from the hallway. "The tender is here."

CHAPTER TWENTY-ONE

CHANELLE WATCHED THE island recede until she could no longer make out the coral walls of the villa. In reality she had only been there for hours, but it had seemed so much longer…and now she was leaving with this inexplicable feeling that she had lost something before she had had enough time to figure out what it was.

When Mariah had called out to Vance, his mouth had clamped shut, and whatever he had been about to say was left unsaid. He had left quickly, and a moment later, Mariah had entered his room to keep an eye on Chanelle. Chanelle had closed her eyes, not feeling up to chatting. After ten more minutes of lying still, she had risen slowly to find that Mariah had retrieved her dry clothes. "Come down when you've changed, Chanelle. The tender is waiting for us."

As they all left the villa moments later, Vance tried to catch her eye, but Chanelle deliberately avoided his gaze. He offered a hand as she was about to step into the tender, but she ignored it with the pretense of helping Adrien. Vance frowned and looked sideways at her, but she continued moving on.

Now, heading back to the *Aquarius*, Chanelle focused on the shifting blues of the sea.

Better than focusing on the shifting blues of Vance's eyes, she thought cynically.

It was choppier going back, a residual effect from the

storm. By the time they boarded the ship, Chanelle's stomach was feeling unsettled. She couldn't wait to go back to the privacy of her stateroom. She'd order a soothing pot of herbal tea and maybe a bite to eat later, if she was up to it. As they waited in the lobby for the elevator, she said as much to Mariah, who quickly reminded her about the gala later in the evening and the champagne art auction. "Have your tea, Chanelle, and a rest, too, but please come to the gala. It's the highlight of this cruise! We'll save you a place at our table, okay?"

Chanelle felt a heat searing her nerve endings, knowing that all eyes were on her. Especially Vance's. It was even worse once they filed into the elevator. His breath fanned her neck, and the spicy cedar notes of his cologne tickled her nostrils. When the bell sounded and a couple excused themselves to exit, there was more shifting, and Chanelle felt Vance's hands encircling her waist to gently indicate that they needed to get by. Chanelle started and took a step sideways while her heart did a somersault.

She held her breath as the door closed, expecting Vance to move his hands away, but as the seconds ticked by in her mind, they stayed put. Chanelle felt sure everyone could see her flaming face, and she was just as sure that Vance could feel her erratic breathing reaching the span of his hands.

Another group needed to exit, and this time, Vance complied with Chanelle's silent wish. Hers was the next stop, she thought, breathing out her anxiety. At the ding, she stepped out and turned to wave. "Thanks again." She smiled, focusing her gaze on Mariah and Vance's mother. "Have a good evening." She turned away quickly, letting out a big sigh of relief as she heard the elevator doors close.

Chanelle repositioned her beach bag over her shoulder and started to walk toward her stateroom when she heard footsteps behind her.

"Chanelle…"

Chanelle turned slowly and stared into cobalt depths that made her feel that she had just entered the eye of a storm.

"You're looking at me like I'm a boogeyman, Chanelle." Vance ventured a crooked smile.

"I—I just wasn't expecting you to follow me," she said without smiling back.

Vance was puzzled. Was she upset at him about something? It was obvious that the dynamic between them had changed. Maybe her fainting spell had something to do with it.

"You looked like you wanted to be alone in the tender, so I didn't want to bother you, Chanelle. I figured you had a headache." He took a couple of steps closer to her. "How are you feeling now?"

Vance saw confusion flitting across her face.

"I'm fine," she said curtly.

"Well, I'm glad I was there to catch you before you hit that marble floor," he told her huskily.

"Yes," she said, her voice softening slightly. "I don't think I thanked you for that." She nodded. "Thank you."

"You're very welcome, Chanelle." He paused as the elevator opened and let out a family. When they had filed down the corridor, he closed the gap between himself and Chanelle. "I'll walk you to your stateroom."

Vance was convinced there was something bothering her.

Why else would she be treating him so indifferently?

Her kiss before the storm hit had been anything but indifferent… It made his stomach flip just thinking about it.

What had changed? Certainly not *his* feelings. If anything, they had intensified when he saw her lying on his bed and thought of how devastated he would have been if he hadn't been there and she had fallen to the floor and seriously hurt herself.

Vance realized with a jolt that Chanelle had stopped walking and was at her door, looking at him pointedly, her hand on the doorknob.

"Chanelle, I wanted to talk to you back at the villa before we left…" He looked at her earnestly. "There's something I need to say to you." He watched as her eyebrows furrowed. His gaze lowered to her lips and to that tiny turquoise vein pulsing at the base of her neck. Vance felt his jaw tensing. He wished he could just kiss her now and leave no doubt in her mind as to how much he wanted her…

"I'm sorry, Vance," Chanelle said stiffly, turning the door handle. "I think it's best if you go."

CHAPTER TWENTY-TWO

OUR LIVES ARE galaxies apart and always will be.

Chanelle hadn't had the nerve to tell him that to his face. But since she had woken up from her fainting spell, it was as if the fairy-tale fog she'd been in had lifted from her mind and now she could see the situation for what it was. She had thought about nothing else during the ride back to the *Aquarius*.

Chanelle closed the door firmly and plopped herself down hard on the couch, wincing as the muscles stretched in her knees.

Nice shape you're in, girl. Your knees are scratched up and now your heart is broken.

It served her right. How ridiculous to have fallen for Vance Kingston in the short time she had been on the cruise. What had she expected? That the president of Zodiac Cruises would be captivated by her brooding disposition and declare his undying love and affection for her?

Yes, they had shared a passionate kiss, a kiss that had had her yearning for more. Vance had swept her off her feet—both figuratively, sending her into wispy clouds of fantasy, and literally, carrying her up a grand flight of stairs like in some old-fashioned movies she had enjoyed watching before life had gotten too busy with her work.

But she had to listen to the voice of reason in the back of her mind. The niggling voice that was telling her that this physical attraction between her and Vance wasn't going to end up like a fairy tale. How could it? In a few short days, she'd be stepping off the ship and making her way back home. The idea that Vance Kingston was contemplating anything more than a casual flirtation with her was simply ridiculous. *A fantasy.*

And *she* had to make it clear to him that she wasn't going to encourage any further contact with him. Because although she had every intention of staying rooted in reality, she knew that there was always a chance that being alone with him could weaken her resolve…just like the spicy cedar scent of his cologne weakened her knees and made her want to—

She was obviously more vulnerable than she had thought.

Chanelle let the tears well up, feeling sorry for herself and even more sorry that she couldn't cry on anybody's shoulder. When her tears were spent, she walked out to the balcony to watch the sky and the sea as twilight began to set in. Since she wasn't hungry and had no intention of attending the gala, she would take this time to explore some options about her future.

Chanelle placed a hand over her bracelet. Becoming a social worker hadn't been a bad choice. Working in child protection had just become too much for her. Maybe a highly sensitive person like herself would have a difficult time thriving in such a stressful, emotionally charged job for her entire career…and maybe the five years she had devoted to this area of social work was all she was meant to do. But what other job *could* she do?

Chanelle looked up at the sky, a palette of blue, pink and magenta. Something deep inside told her that she would discover the answer if she kept open to new possibilities.

Send it out to the universe!

How often had she read *that* advice in self-help books?

"Okay, I'm sending it out to you, universe!" she called out to the sky before going back inside.

She couldn't let this thing with Vance destroy her peace of mind. She was stronger than that. She had to accept the fact that they had been physically attracted to each other and that was all. And if she wanted to be open to new possibilities, she needed to get herself out of her stateroom and allow herself to live a little.

Maybe she'd go to the gala after all.

What would there be to lose? She could handle it. She'd enjoy the musical entertainment and the complimentary champagne at the art auction, and then she'd sleep in tomorrow and enjoy one last sea day before they arrived back in Tampa the morning after.

And then she'd be ready to start a new chapter in her life.

Do you really think you can handle going to the gala? You're taking a risk—

Chanelle squeezed her eyes shut, as if the action could put a stop to her HSP voice. It had worked for her in the past, allowing her to be cautious, be safe. Protecting her from frightening possibilities…

Her eyes flew open. What was there to be frightened of? Yes, she was taking a risk. But that wasn't going to stop her. She was a Sagittarian, wasn't she?

They had chosen to have the gala on the top deck. A section of the Constellation Club had been cleared for the ship musicians, and after the official announcements, they would be performing a medley of popular tunes from the last four decades.

Vance clapped along with the guests after his mother thanked them for joining the staff of the *Aquarius* in celebrating her retirement. Her tribute to Vance's father had moved the audience.

After the applause subsided, she called Vance up to join her. She looked at him for a moment, her mouth quivering slightly. "I can only imagine how difficult it has been, son, for you to have accepted the challenge of taking over where your father left off…" She bit her lip, and Vance felt a lump form in his throat.

This was difficult for her, too. It had always been difficult for her, raising him and Mariah single-handedly most of the time. He hadn't been the only one who had suffered… and now he could see that she had also suffered for him, lacking a proper relationship with his father.

"I'm so very proud of your commitment, dedication and hard work, Vance. You've proven yourself—as I knew you would—not only to your family, but to the entire company, and there is no doubt in my mind that your father would have been just as proud." Her voice trembled at her last phrase, and Vance felt his eyes begin to mist along with hers.

"So, with all my love and pride, I congratulate you for your leadership, and I'm absolutely thrilled to officially name you president of Zodiac Cruises."

Vance blinked a couple of times to keep his emotions in check as he and his mother embraced. When his vision cleared, he looked beyond the clapping hands to his sister's table. Mariah was there with Adrien, but she was not looking in his direction. She was waving at someone. He followed her gaze and spotted Chanelle standing near a column.

She stepped forward, and what he saw took his breath away. She was wearing a floor-length deep purple satin gown with a filmy silver shawl over her shoulders. And she had arranged her hair in a side-swept style, held back with something that glittered under the string lights. His pulse hammered against his veins as he watched her walk over to sit next to Mariah. She waved to Adrien and said something to make him laugh.

Vance heard his name again, and he turned and saw that his mother was looking at him with raised eyebrows.

It was his turn to speak.

He hadn't written out a speech; he knew exactly what he had to say. After thanking his mother for trusting him to carry on the business, he announced his new plan: a new cruise line that would cater to social service organizations, offering their employees a special discount for a Zodiac R&R Cruise. Not only would the employees get the rest and relaxation that they so greatly deserved, Zodiac would treat them with special perks and discounts in all areas of the ship. The first ship in the fleet would be in operation by the following year.

"Society doesn't always recognize the tremendous work and sacrifices made by social workers, nurses and teachers, to name a few," he said, scanning the crowd. "Zodiac Cruises wants to support those who support others." He paused as the guests applauded enthusiastically and, glancing in Chanelle's direction, saw that her attention was riveted on him.

Great—if he could figure out a way of speaking to her alone, he could tell her the rest of his plan…

Vance thanked everyone for choosing Zodiac Cruises and for sharing in the celebration. He guided his mother toward their table, relieved that the entertainers would now be in the spotlight before the art auction began.

He had some unfinished business with the beautiful lady in purple…

As they approached the table, he saw a man stooping to talk to Chanelle, and a moment later, he was leading her toward the other dancing couples.

Where had this guy come from?

Vance tried not to make it obvious that he was watching them as he helped himself from the hors d'oeuvres tray that one of the waiters was holding out to him.

Vance had no idea what he had just swallowed. His thoughts had returned to Chanelle's abrupt manner after her fainting spell.

As he had changed into a white shirt and black suit, he had wondered why Chanelle's behavior toward him had shifted from sizzling hot to disturbingly indifferent. Could she be deliberately repressing feelings for him that went deeper than the physical chemistry that they had both felt? She was probably holding back, believing that they would never see each other again after the cruise.

He would find out tonight, he had vowed, adjusting his tie. And if Chanelle decided not to attend the gala, he would find a way to see her and clear things up with her. Make her understand that he wanted *her* in his life after the cruise. And forever. With that resolution, Vance had made his way to his mother and Mariah's stateroom, feeling much lighter than before.

It wasn't going to be easy to approach Chanelle now, though, with a man having suddenly appeared out of no-where to whisk her away to dance. They seemed to be chatting easily, and Vance felt a stab of jealousy. *He* should be the one holding Chanelle. He rose, intending to cut in for the next dance, but a few guests stopped to congratulate him and his mother, and he had no choice but to engage with them for a few minutes.

When they moved on, Vance strode toward a less crowded section of the deck, where the smooth operator had managed to lead Chanelle.

Luck was on his side this time, he thought smugly as the song came to an end. But the fellow did not let go of Chanelle.

And had his hand slipped down to her hip?

"May I have this next dance, Chanelle?" Vance gazed at her first, but before she could answer, he turned to stare pointedly at the guy, his mouth curved slightly but his eyes sending a clear "Back off" message.

The guy released his hold on Chanelle, smiled awkwardly and told Chanelle he'd see her in a bit.

Like hell you will, buddy.

Vance nodded with a congenial smile and took Chanelle's hand.

His other hand settled around her waist. He felt her stiffen, and when his gaze met hers, her eyes seemed to be shooting sparks at him from their hazel-green depths.

And then she pressed closer and went on tiptoe to place her cheek against his. His pulse leaped as her lips brushed his cheek and earlobe.

"I *don't* want to dance with you," she hissed in his ear.

CHAPTER TWENTY-THREE

CHANELLE FELT VANCE's body tense up. She hadn't meant to sound so rude, but the words had escaped before she could think of another way to give him the message.

"Why not, Chanelle?" he said, with genuine curiosity in his voice.

Chanelle was taken aback. She didn't know what she had expected him to say, but she certainly hadn't expected him to ask her to explain. Now she had to answer. And there was no point mincing words. She turned to meet his gaze. "I—I don't want to dance with someone who…who makes me want more…when I can't have more." Chanelle felt her neck prickle with heat at the intensity in his eyes. They had some kind of magnetic pull that kept her from looking away. And to make it worse, the musicians started performing "Stairway to Heaven." The string lights suddenly dimmed, and Vance drew her closer.

"What makes you think you can't have more, Chanelle?" he murmured against her ear as he initiated the slow dance. "You've got your facts wrong."

Chanelle's heart was jumping hurdles. "But the cruise will be ending in two days…" She felt his lips brush against her earlobe and rest there as they danced. The touch made her nerve endings sizzle and her body shiver at the same time.

"Chanelle, let me say what I wanted to tell you at Coral

Haven. You're an enchantress—who looks absolutely stunning in purple, I must say—and someone whom I'd like to continue to see even after the cruise ends."

Chanelle froze and as Vance's words sank in, her feet and arms feeling woozy. The couples dancing around her became blurred, and the music seemed to pulsate right through her body. And then she felt Vance's arms tighten around her, and her arms rose of their own accord and wrapped themselves around his neck. Her cheek grazed his chin, and when their eyes met, it felt like nobody was on deck except them and the music was playing for them alone.

Vance's gaze was intoxicating, and when he pulled her tightly against him, she marveled at how her body fit right into his. They slow danced for what seemed like forever, and when the song finally came to an end, Vance nuzzled her earlobe again and whispered, "Chanelle, do you believe me?"

She opened her eyes with a start, and as some of the couples dispersed, she saw Mariah walking up to them. She broke away awkwardly from Vance.

"Hey, you two," she smiled. "We're heading back to our stateroom. Adrien's starting to nod off. But don't stop dancing on our account. Good night, Chanelle. Good night, *Sir Vancelot*. Don't drink too much champagne…"

As they left, there was an announcement that the art auction would begin after the next mix of songs, and the champagne would start to flow. At the beginning of a classic rock song that everyone started singing to, Vance lifted an eyebrow. "Stay or go?"

"Go," she told him. "I want to end the evening on a quiet note."

"It's quiet in my stateroom."

Chanelle felt a moment of panic. She was at a total loss as to what to do next. Here she was, having just danced as close as two people could possibly get, and she couldn't seem to process Vance's words that she was someone he'd like to see after the cruise, let alone his invitation to go to his room.

He had asked her if she believed him. *Maybe…a little…*

There was no doubt in her mind that there was chemistry between them.

Incredible chemistry.

But he hadn't said *I'm in love with you* or *I want to spend the rest of my life with you*. He had just said she was someone *he'd like to continue to see…*

And there was no guarantee that came with the Vance Kingston package, the guarantee that he wouldn't leave her in the future. Just like her father and Parker had done…

Chanelle's mind filled with doubts.

Maybe they had both been swept away by their physical attraction to each other…and that was the extent of it.

"Chanelle, you're frowning. Are you okay?"

"I—I'm just tired," she said.

She was tired of exhausting herself by trying to analyze Vance's every word or action.

She knew that this was part of her highly sensitive nature, and sometimes—many times—she wished she could just sail along in life without her brain getting twisted up in knots about everything.

What was wrong with her? She was sure most women would jump at the invitation to join Vance in his stateroom.

"Chanelle, if you're too tired, can you just come to my room for a few minutes? There's something I've been designing for Zodiac Cruises, and I'd love to get your input." Vance's eyebrows lifted as she waited for his response.

Chanelle searched his eyes and saw nothing but earnestness in them.

But what if—?

No! She wasn't going to let her doubts control her this time. She was just going to allow herself to sail along for once. Vance's words popped back in her mind: *You're stronger than you think.*

Yes, she was strong enough to handle anything the future had in store for her. But it had taken a little help from Vance to remind her of her inner strength. Her sense of self. She needn't be fearful of anyone abandoning her anymore, least of all herself. She was a Sagittarian, wasn't she? Vance had called her that enough times to make her come to the realization that she had power over her life, her choices, her loves...

And no one could ever take that away from her.

"Sure," she said decisively. "I can spare a few minutes."

Vance led Chanelle toward the sliding doors leading to the elevator lobby. The gala was in full swing. The captain and some of his crew were drawing a lot of attention, so Vance knew his absence wouldn't be obvious. The guests were drinking, dancing and having fun, and they would be happy about another photo opportunity with a handsome man in uniform. Or three. The art auction would begin shortly, then more music, followed by an unexpected surprise: a spectacular display of fireworks. Mariah and his mother would be watching from their balcony, and maybe Adrien would be, too, if he was still awake.

As he and Chanelle approached his stateroom, Vance felt his stomach contract with anticipation. He had thought long and hard about how to tell Chanelle about his feelings. About how he couldn't imagine her stepping off the ship and never seeing her again. About how he couldn't stop thinking about her, and how she had inspired him...

And now, he finally had the opportunity to show her. As he swiped his card against the door plate, he glanced at Chanelle. She was holding her clutch purse and looking down, biting her lip. Was she having second thoughts? His heart hammered softly. She was the kindest, most sensitive woman he had ever met. And the only one who had managed to break through the defenses around his heart. The heart that was finally ready to let someone in.

With any luck, he'd convince her tonight that they belonged together. *For life.*

CHAPTER TWENTY-FOUR

CHANELLE SAT DOWN on the edge of the couch and watched as Vance strode over to his desk. She wondered if what he was designing had something to do with his plans for Zodiac's new cruise line. His announcement that the latter would cater to social service organizations, offering their employees a special discount for a Zodiac R&R Cruise, had jolted her.

In a good way. How could she fault him or his company for being sensitive to people like her?

And when Vance had added that Zodiac Cruises wanted to support those who supported others, Chanelle had felt a stirring in her chest, pretty sure that he had been looking right at her. And then moments later a gentleman had appeared and asked her to dance...

Chanelle hadn't really been in the mood, but her nagging inner voice had reminded her about her intention of enjoying herself tonight.

She sat back on the couch now and tapped her fingers on the cream-colored leather hand rest. The sky's earlier brilliance had faded to dusky blues and pinks, with fading ribbons of gold and magenta. She tried to stifle a yawn.

"Hey, don't fall asleep yet," Vance chuckled, sitting beside her. "First I'd like your two cents about my design."

"Sorry, it's been a day."

"You *are* tired." He gazed at her for a moment and added softly, "This won't take long."

Chanelle looked at the sketch pad in his hands. "Does this design have something to do with your new cruise line?"

Vance's eyes crinkled as he smiled. "It sure does."

"That's a great idea to offer special packages to service organizations." She had to give him that.

"Thanks. I've been working on the idea of a new line for months now," he murmured. "But I was stuck on the purpose behind the line. I wanted to find a new angle, and I did…because of *you*, Chanelle."

Her eyes widened, and her heart started a gentle drumming. "Wh—what do you mean?"

"You made me see what can happen to a dedicated employee in your line of work. How important your job is, and how you give your all to help others. People like you need to be rewarded, not get to the point where they burn out. But sometimes burnout happens, to social workers, teachers, nurses, etcetera." He tapped her gently on the arm. "So *that* became my angle. Supporting those who support others."

Chanelle watched Vance open up his sketchbook and prop it up so she could see what he had done. She gave a soft gasp at the first drawing. *Of her.* Her thoughts swirled, and she couldn't bring herself to look up from the page. As he turned the next few pages slowly, the drumming in her heart became magnified. She saw a series of rough sketches with variations on the new name for the R&R cruise line. And then he turned to the last page with a finished sketch.

Chanelle's heart stopped.

She saw two intertwined Cs in the words *Chanelle Cruises*, with each C extended to represent waves in the sea and an archer's arrow zooming upward. She stared at it for a few moments, and when she looked up, Vance's face was blurred. She wiped her eyes and saw that his eyes had misted also. And then Chanelle remembered what she had thought earlier, that Vance hadn't told her he was in love with her or that he wanted to spend the rest of his life with her. No, he hadn't told her.

But he had just shown her.

Chanelle gazed at him in wonder.

Was she dreaming? She must be dreaming…

Vance closed the sketchbook and placed it on the coffee table. She felt immobilized as he reached over to grab something leaning against his side of the couch. He turned it toward her and she gasped. It was the painting she had admired in the art gallery. *Enchantment.*

She was speechless as Vance stood up and propped it against the back of the couch.

"Is that…" Her gaze dropped to the initials, and her eyes widened. "Did *you*—"

"Yes, it's one of mine." He gave her a sheepish smile. "The art rep mentioned that a guest was admiring it. And she noticed your name on your lanyard." His blue eyes gleamed. "It was going to be in the art auction, but I replaced it with another painting when we returned on the ship. I wanted you to have this one."

She gasped as he suddenly dropped to one knee.

"I have fallen under the spell of your enchantment, my lady," he said huskily, taking her hand and kissing it. "Will you do me the great honor of bestowing me with your hand?"

"You already have it, Sir Vancelot," she murmured with a soft laugh.

"I was speaking of your hand in marriage, my haloed beauty." He grinned, caressing her hair with his other hand. "In anticipation—and hope—of your positive response, I have begun to design your engagement ring…but in the meantime, I hope this humble handmade gift will suffice."

Several loud pops filled the air. "Come with me, Chanelle," he said urgently. He led her to the balcony, and as they stood at the railing, they heard a whizzing sound and more popping as the sky sparkled with the most dazzling fireworks display Chanelle had ever seen.

They watched for a few minutes and then Vance turned her toward him and, wrapping his arms tightly around her, kissed her thoroughly, sending sparks to every last inch of her body. When he released her, his eyes pierced hers, reflecting the flashes in the sky.

"Do you believe me, Chanelle?" he said huskily, repeating the question she hadn't answered earlier. "And will you—"

"I do," she breathed, and reached up to show him with her own kiss.

Vance gave a moan of pleasure. "I almost forgot to add," he said, while brushing soft kisses along her neck, "Zodiac Cruises will be in need of a director of children's activities. Someone who loves kids and can plan year-round events that are fun and safe." He paused to gaze deeply into her eyes. "I must warn you, though. Job hours vary and may require some night shifts…and plenty of cruising."

Chanelle felt a sudden flutter in her gut. Was she actually ready to leave her small-town world and take such a leap? To a new city, new job and, most important of all, a new relationship? Her gaze melded with his. What she saw in the depths of Vance's ocean-blue eyes was a bright promise…

Yes, she was quite ready to take that leap.

"I'll cruise with you anywhere and everywhere," she sighed, slipping her hand underneath his shirt to caress his back. She felt him shiver as her fingers brushed over his Aquarius tattoo.

"I love you, my Sagittarian angel," he murmured against her ear as the boom in the sky intensified. Without waiting for her to answer, he scooped her up in his arms and carried her to his bed, where Chanelle knew the fireworks were only just beginning…

* * * * *

LET'S TALK

Romance

For exclusive extracts, competitions
and special offers, find us online:

[f] facebook.com/millsandboon

[y] @MillsandBoon

[o] @MillsandBoonUK

Get in touch on 01413 063232

For all the latest titles coming soon, visit
millsandboon.co.uk/nextmonth

MILLS & BOON

THE HEART OF ROMANCE

A ROMANCE FOR EVERY READER

MODERN

Prepare to be swept off your feet by sophisticated, sexy and seductive heroes, in some of the world's most glamourous and romantic locations, where power and passion collide.

HISTORICAL

Escape with historical heroes from time gone by. Whether your passion is for wicked Regency Rakes, muscled Vikings or rugged Highlanders, awake the romance of the past.

MEDICAL

Set your pulse racing with dedicated, delectable doctors in the high-pressure world of medicine, where emotions run high and passion, comfort and love are the best medicine.

True Love

Celebrate true love with tender stories of heartfelt romance, from the rush of falling in love to the joy a new baby can bring, and a focus on the emotional heart of a relationship.

Desire

Indulge in secrets and scandal, intense drama and plenty of sizzling hot action with powerful and passionate heroes who have it all: wealth, status, good looks…everything but the right woman.

HEROES

Experience all the excitement of a gripping thriller, with an intense romance at its heart. Resourceful, true-to-life women and strong, fearless men face danger and desire - a killer combination!

To see which titles are coming soon, please visit

millsandboon.co.uk/nextmonth